"Rowland has a painter's eye for the minutiae of court life, as well as a politican's ear for intrigue."   —*The New York Times Book Review*

"*The Fire Kimono* is an exercise in pure entertainment. . . . It takes us to an exotic time and place and overwhelms us with intrigue, romance, adventure, and frequent bloodshed. . . . Rowland writes gracefully, and much of the pleasure of the book lies in her portrait of a society largely unknown to most of us."   —*The Washington Post*

"[*The Fire Kimono*] displays Rowland's gifts for seamlessly incorporating period detail and historical information into the traditional mystery format. Fans of historical mysteries—at least those few who haven't already sampled this series—should be enthusiastically steered in Ichirō's direction."   —*Booklist*

"Sano may carry a sword and wear a kimono, but you'll immediately recognize him as an ancestor of Philip Marlowe or Sam Spade."   —*The Denver Post*

"Blending political intrigue and barbed social commentary, *Red Chrysanthemum* is a crisply lurid *Rashomon* mystery."   —*Entertainment Weekly*

"A compelling and lively series."   —*The Dallas Morning News*

"[Rowland's] Japan is a mix of Kabuki theater–like stylized formality, palace intrigue, and physical action that would do a martial arts movie proud."   —*The New Orleans Times-Picayune*

"Demonstrating an impressive level of sustained excellence, Rowland's mysteries set in seventeenth-century Japan form one of the best recent series in the genre."   —*Publishers Weekly* (starred review) on *The Snow Empress*

Also by Laura Joh Rowland

THE 火 FIRE 火 KIMONO

Laura Joh Rowland

MINOTAUR BOOKS

NEW YORK

THE FIRE KIMONO. Copyright © 2008 by Laura Joh Rowland. All rights reserved. Printed in the United States of America. For information, address St. Martin's Press, 175 Fifth Avenue, New York, N.Y. 10010.

www.minotaurbooks.com

The Library of Congress has catalogued the hardcover edition as follows:

Rowland, Laura Joh.
    The fire kimono / Laura Joh Rowland. — 1st ed.
       p. cm.
    ISBN 978-0-312-37948-3
    1. Sano, Ichirō (Fictitious character)—Fiction. 2. Japan—History—Genroku period, 1688–1704—Fiction. 3. Samurai—Fiction. I. Title.
    PS3568.O934F57 2008
    813'.54—dc22

                               2008025100

ISBN 978-0-312-58886-1 (trade paperback)

First Minotaur Books Paperback Edition: October 2009

10 9 8 7 6 5 4 3 2 1

To all the readers who have supported this series.
You know who you are.

Edo
Genroku Year 13, Month 2
(Tokyo, March 1700)

Prologue

A fierce windstorm swept the hills outside Edo. Lightning seared bright white veins down the gray sky while distant thunder reverberated. A Shinto priest hurried along a path through the forest. He clutched his black cap to his head and staggered as the wind buffeted him. His white robe flapped like a swan in mad flight. Dirt and leaves swirled around him in cyclones that stung his face, blinded him. He stumbled faster uphill toward the shrine, where he could take shelter.

The trees swayed, creaked, and thrashed. The wind's howling force knocked the priest to the ground. As he struggled to regain his feet, he heard an ominous cracking noise, as if the world were splitting. He saw a huge, dead oak tree pitch toward him. Crooked, leafless branches reached down like monstrous hands to grab him as the tree toppled, its massive trunk a black battering ram aimed to kill. The priest flung his arms over his head and screamed.

The tree crashed with a thud that shook the world. Branches scraped the priest, enmeshed him. He was stunned but miraculously alive. The wind's fury ebbed. Untangling himself from the branches, he saw that the heavy tree trunk lay close beside him. The gods had spared his life.

Dazed, the priest climbed the hill, gawking at the fallen corpse of the tree. The roots had torn loose from the dirt. They'd left a yawning hole in the forest beside the path. Something in the lumpy earth just below the surface level at the edge of the hole caught the priest's attention.

The object was brown from the soil, with a rounded top the size of a small melon. The priest squatted for a closer inspection and recoiled in dismay. Empty eye sockets stared and bare teeth grinned up at him. It was a human skull.

1

Lady Reiko rarely left home, and never without an army for protection.

In the past few months, the strife between her husband, Chamberlain Sano, and his rival, Lord Matsudaira, had escalated drastically. Their troops brawled in the streets of Edo, eager for war. No one was safe; anyone could be caught in the violence.

Riding in a palanquin through the city, Reiko peered through the window shutters. Her mounted guards blocked her view of the high walls and roofed gates of the mansions in the official district. All she could see were armored legs astride moving horse flanks. Her bearers marched in time with the steps of the foot soldiers in her entourage, which numbered fifty armed men in all. Reiko leaned back on the cushions and sighed.

Not a glimpse of the city's color and bustle or breath of spring air could reach her. Yet these precautions were vital. Last winter, Lord Matsudaira had served notice that Sano's family wasn't off-limits in the power struggle. He'd had Sano and Reiko's then-eight-year-old son, Masahiro, kidnapped and sent to the far north. Knowing that she might be the next target, Reiko left Sano's estate inside Edo Castle only on the most serious business.

Her aunt had died, and although they hadn't been close, the

woman had been kind to Reiko during her childhood. That fact, plus family duty, had obligated Reiko to brave venturing outside to attend the funeral. Now her procession suddenly slowed. Guards at the front ordered, "Get out of the way!"

She risked opening the shutters a crack and saw two oxen yoked to a cart filled with lumber blocking an intersection. Such carts, owned by the government, were the only wheeled vehicles permitted in Japan. Forcing everyone to travel by horse or by foot prevented troop movements and insurrection—at least in theory. Soldiers behind her called to the others, "Keep going, don't stop!" The front guards yelled, "Move it now, or die!"

A jarring thud hit the top of the palanquin. Reiko gasped as her bearers wobbled under the extra weight. One of them shouted, "There's a man on the roof!"

The man must have jumped off the wall. While her guards shouted and jostled around her palanquin, she felt another thud as another man landed.

"Ambush!" shouted the guards.

The doors of the palanquin burst open. Reiko screamed. Her attackers—two young samurai with knives gripped in their teeth— swung upside down from the roof at her. As she drew the dagger she wore in a sheath strapped to her arm under her sleeve, they flipped into the palanquin, transferring their knives from teeth to hands.

"Help!" Reiko shrank into the corner and lashed her dagger at her attackers.

Her blade cut their arms. They seemed not to care. Blind savagery glazed their eyes as they slashed at her. Their hot breath and pungent sweat filled the palanquin. Reiko saw the crests stamped on their kimonos. They were Lord Matsudaira's men, no surprise. She frantically parried against their blades. One grazed her face. Outside, swords clashed while her guards fought off more Matsudaira troops who'd joined the attack. The combatants' bodies thumped against the palanquin. Horses whinnied as the battle raged.

"Turn around!" her guard captain shouted. "Head back to the castle! Somebody get those bastards off Lady Reiko!"

Reiko heard her chief bodyguard, Lieutenant Asukai, call her name. As her attackers pinned her arms and she kicked at them, he lunged into the palanquin and seized one of the men. The palanquin veered in a jerky about-face. The bearers broke into a run.

Lieutenant Asukai dragged the man outside. They tumbled into the street under the horses' skittering hooves and the feet of the battling soldiers. The attacker still inside threw himself on top of Reiko. He clutched the wrist of her hand that held the dagger. His weight immobilized her. She desperately thrashed and writhed, beating at him with her free left hand. His blade strained toward her throat. Reiko could see her terrified face reflected in the shiny steel.

"Hold on, Lady Reiko, I'm coming!" Lieutenant Asukai shouted.

He grabbed her attacker's legs. Reiko struck at the man's face and sank her fingernails into his eyes. He screamed, let go of her, and reared up. Lieutenant Asukai yanked at his legs until he flew backward out of the palanquin, bleeding from the eyes, knife raised, mouth yowling.

Reiko saw the portals of Edo Castle ahead, promising sanctuary. The castle was neutral territory in the conflict between Sano and Lord Matsudaira, by tacit, mutual agreement. They both lived inside it; neither wanted war on his own doorstep. The sentries stared in amazement at Reiko's palanquin hurtling toward them and the battle that trailed it like unruly streamers.

"Let us in!" Lieutenant Asukai shouted, running beside Reiko.

The sentries swung open the huge, iron-banded gate. Winded and puffing, the bearers staggered carrying the palanquin through it. The gate slammed shut. Reiko sighed in relief.

"That was too close a call," Sano said.

He crouched on the floor beside Reiko, in their private chamber, watching grimly as the doctor dabbed medicinal ointment on the cut on her cheek. First his son kidnapped, now his wife ambushed. Lord Matsudaira had gone too far. Sano tasted fury as raw as blood.

Reiko managed a brave smile. "It's just a scratch. I'm fine, really."

The doctor finished, gathered up his medicine chest, and departed. Reiko spoke to Masahiro, who knelt near her. "I don't look half as bad as you do."

Masahiro, nine years old, had come running when he'd heard about the attack. His white martial arts practice uniform was dirty from wrestling on the ground; he sported cuts and scrapes on his hands, arms, and knees. A fading purple bruise surrounded his left eye. Ever since his abduction, Masahiro had pursued his martial arts studies with punishing vigor, the better to defend himself. This was no longer just a game he was good at, but a matter of life and death.

Now he said, "Don't joke, Mama." His tone was serious, reproving, and adult. "You could have been killed."

Sano hadn't wanted Masahiro to know about the attack, had wanted to shield him from adult problems. But Masahiro had a way of finding out what happened; his sharp ears and his nose for information rivaled those of any spy in the government intelligence service. And he'd matured a lot during his experience in Ezogashima. Having survived it by his own wits and courage, he'd earned himself a new place in their family. Sano beheld his son with a mixture of love, pride, and sorrow.

He could see Reiko in the shape of Masahiro's eyes, and himself in the set of his jaw; but Masahiro was his own, unique person, and he was growing up too fast. There was little room for childhood in their harsh world.

"Masahiro is right," Sano said to Reiko. The boy sat straighter, gladdened by his father's approval. Sano remembered looking up to and aspiring to be like his own father, now dead eleven years. How long before Masahiro became aware of his failings and the hero-worship ended? "You can't go out again."

"Yes," seconded Masahiro. "You have to stay home."

Reiko had opened her mouth to object, then closed it, taken aback by his authority. Sano hid a rueful smile. She would need to get used to having two men telling her what to do. This time she conceded. "For how long?"

She spoke as if she didn't expect Sano to answer, and he didn't.

He only wished he knew how long this feud with Lord Matsudaira would go on.

Unhappiness shadowed her beautiful face. "What are you going to do?"

"I'm going to see Lord Matsudaira," Sano said.

"Are you going to declare war on him?" Reiko asked.

Excitement charged the air as she and Masahiro waited for Sano's reply. They thirsted for a showdown as much as Sano did. But Sano knew the odds better than they, and he said, "No."

Indignation appeared on their faces. Reiko said, "Not even after what Lord Matsudaira did to my son?"

"And to my mother?" Masahiro said.

"It's not the time for me to challenge Lord Matsudaira in battle," Sano said. "His troops outnumber mine by too many."

Sano's army had shrunk drastically since last autumn. He'd come home from Ezogashima to discover that he'd lost entire regiments during his absence. Without Sano here to keep them in line and their morale up, Lord Matsudaira had easily won them over. That was just as Lord Matsudaira had planned when he'd kidnapped Masahiro, and Sano had gone to Ezogashima to rescue his son.

"And I can't afford to run a war for more than a few months." Sano had also lost key allies among the *daimyo,* the feudal lords he'd counted on to fund a military venture.

"It can't be that bad," Reiko said. "You still have many allies." She named some, all wealthy, powerful *daimyo* with large armies. "You can win."

"Let's declare war!" Masahiro's face shone with zeal and confidence in Sano. "You're not afraid of Lord Matsudaira."

Sano dreaded the day when he would see Masahiro begin to doubt him. Now he needed to give Masahiro a lesson as difficult to teach as to learn.

"Of course I'm afraid," Sano said, even though he hated admitting fear. "A samurai who isn't afraid of a dangerous enemy isn't a hero; he's a fool." More and more often, Sano heard his own father's words coming out of his mouth. "A truly courageous samurai masters his fear."

Impatient, hardly listening, Masahiro jumped up and paced back and forth, Reiko's habit when excited. "I'll ride into battle with you. Together we'll defeat Lord Matsudaira."

Sano ached with pride in his son's spirit. Reiko looked aghast. "You can't go to battle. You're not even fifteen yet!"

Fifteen was the age at which samurai boys officially became adults, when the forelock that Masahiro wore tied above his brow would be shaved during his manhood ceremony.

"A war could last six more years until he is," Sano pointed out. "The wars that ended with the Tokugawa on top went on for almost a century."

"I'm almost as tall as a lot of boys who are fifteen," Masahiro said, standing still and drawing himself up to his full height. "And I'm a better fighter."

"You're also too modest," Reiko said, tart in her fear for him. She turned to Sano. "All right, I don't want a war, either." She'd clearly lost her appetite for it now that she saw her son headed for the front lines. "But if you're not declaring war on Lord Matsudaira, why go to see him?"

"To propose a truce. To make peace if I can."

Reiko stared in disbelief. "You mean you're going to let him get away with what he's done?"

"He deserves to be punished!" Masahiro clenched his fists.

"The country doesn't," Sano said. "If we go on like this, there will eventually be war, and Japan will suffer. War involves more than the two top men fighting it. Should it spread beyond Edo, cities and villages everywhere will be destroyed. Thousands of innocent people will die."

"I don't care," Masahiro said stubbornly.

He was too young for the consequences of war to seem real to him, Sano thought. Despite the maturity forced on him, Masahiro was a child, with a child's limited understanding.

"As the shogun's second-in-command, I have to care," Sano said. "It's my duty to protect the country and the people. And when you inherit my position, it will be your duty."

Masahiro nodded, swelling with pride at the thought that he would someday succeed his father. Hoping he could hold his position long enough to pass it on, Sano rose to go.

Sano summoned Hirata—his chief retainer—and Detectives Marume and Fukida, his two top personal bodyguards. Accompanied by a squadron of troops, they went to the special compound inside Edo Castle where the Tokugawa-branch clan members lived. Lord Matsudaira, the shogun's cousin, had the largest estate. Sentries were posted outside its gate, at intervals along the high stone walls, and in the watchtowers. When they saw Sano's party coming, their hands flashed to their swords.

"I want to see Lord Matsudaira," Sano told the four gate sentries.

Their leader said, "With all due respect, Honorable Chamberlain, you have a lot of nerve coming here. After what you've done today."

"After what *he's* done?" Hirata said. "What are you talking about?"

Noting the mystified expressions of Sano and his companions, the man smirked. "Looks like you and your people have lost your memories, Chamberlain Sano. Well, don't worry; Lord Matsudaira will fill in the blank spaces."

He sent a runner to tell Lord Matsudaira that Sano was here. As other guards opened the gate and escorted Sano's party inside, Sano exchanged perturbed glances with Hirata, Marume, and Fukida. This was a strange reception that didn't bode well for their peace mission.

They moved through courtyards and passages lined with armed, hostile soldiers. If not for the prohibition against violence inside Edo Castle, they would have attacked Sano. The air smelled of gunpowder.

Sano found Lord Matsudaira waiting in his reception room. Flanked by bodyguards, with troops stationed along the walls, Lord Matsudaira stood on the dais. His posture was arrogant, his expression murderous. But he was thinner, and visibly older, than when Sano had left for Ezogashima only six months ago. The strain of building his army, juggling allies, and battling treachery had carved new lines in his strong-featured face. The fire in his eyes verged on fever.

"What in hell do you want?" he demanded.

"I have a proposition to make," Sano said, even as his hatred toward his enemy flared. He hadn't started this quarrel; he'd been willing to work with Lord Matsudaira to serve the shogun, their master. It was Lord Matsudaira who wanted to be shogun himself, who saw Sano's power as a threat. "I'll excuse your attack this morning, if you'll agree to a truce."

Astonishment raised Lord Matsudaira's eyebrows. "A truce? Are you insane? And I didn't attack you this morning."

Infuriated by the denial, Sano said, "Your men ambushed my wife and tried to kill her. Or have you forgotten you sent them?"

Lord Matsudaira seemed as much confused as scornful. "I didn't." He pointed a finger at Sano. "It was *you* who just sent *your* men to kill *my* wife."

Sano thought of what the sentries had said. Consternation filled him. "You'd better explain what happened."

"Playing innocent, eh?" Lord Matsudaira's face darkened with anger. "I suppose you came to gloat over what you've done. Well, all right, I'll show you. Come."

Beckoning, he stalked outside. His troops herded Sano's party after him, into the garden. More troops patrolled amid azalea bushes in bright red bloom. Increasingly baffled, Sano followed Lord Matsudaira to the heart of the estate, a group of low buildings connected by covered corridors. One lay half in ruins, walls broken, the tile roof collapsed. The ruins were covered by black soot. Servants labored, cleaning up the mess.

"These are the women's quarters," Lord Matsudaira said, gesturing angrily. "My wife was inside. She has burns all over her. It's a miracle she wasn't killed. One of her attendants was." He glared at Sano. "Don't say it's not your fault."

"It isn't," Sano said, as disturbed as sincere.

"No more lies! Two of your men sneaked into this estate and

threw jars of kerosene plugged with burning rags into the windows. My men caught them running away from the explosion. See for yourself."

Lord Matsudaira led Sano to a blanket spread on the charred grass near the ruins. He flung back the blanket, exposing two young samurai who lay dead and bloody.

"They're not mine. I've never seen them before in my life." Sano turned to Hirata, Marume, and his other men; they shook their heads.

"You have so many retainers that you don't know everyone who works for you," Lord Matsudaira said. "Look at the crests on their clothes." He pointed at Sano's flying-crane insignias. "They're yours, all right."

Sano didn't see any point in arguing; Lord Matsudaira would never believe him. "Well, I have two bodies of men that my troops caught and killed after they tried to stab my wife. They're wearing your crests."

"I had nothing to do with that," Lord Matsudaira protested. "Whatever business I have with you, I would never attack your woman." His tone scorned that as cowardly, dishonorable, beneath him. "This is the first I've heard of it."

His shock and dismay seemed genuine. A familiar uneasy sensation trickled through Sano. He said, "This isn't the first time that people on your side have been attacked and I wasn't responsible, or that people on mine have been and you've claimed you weren't."

During the past six months, Sano's troops had been ambushed, had been the target of firebombs and snipers. So had Lord Matsudaira's. The frequency of the attacks had increased since Sano had returned from Ezogashima. Each rival had blamed the other, with reason based on evidence as well as motive. But Sano knew he wasn't to blame, and he was ready to acknowledge that perhaps neither was Lord Matsudaira.

"Something is going on," Sano said.

He'd had ideas about what it was, yet they remained unproven. Although he'd investigated the attacks, he'd found no substantiating clues as to the person behind them. He'd never mentioned his suspicions to Lord Matsudaira, who would only think Sano was trying to trick him.

"Of course something is going on, and I know what," Lord Matsudaira said. "You've been faking attacks against yourself, to make me look bad and justify attacking me. Now you've violated protocol against attacking inside Edo Castle." Lord Matsudaira bunched his fists and shook with fury. "Merciful gods, you'll stop at nothing to destroy me!"

"The two of us should stop our quarrel," Sano said, although he realized it was futile to hope he could convince Lord Matsudaira. "Agree to a truce. Then we can get to the bottom of these attacks and work out a peace treaty."

"Take your peace treaty and shove it up your behind," Lord Matsudaira said. "Now leave before I throw you out."

As they glared at each other, Sano felt the war he wanted to prevent rushing on them like a tornado. The sensation was as exhilarating as it was dreadful. When he and his men turned to depart, Lord Matsudaira warned, "Remember that your home is a target, too."

A servant came running up to them. "Excuse me, but I have an urgent message."

"What is it?" Lord Matsudaira barked.

"The shogun wants to see you. And Chamberlain Sano. At once."

火

2

火

火

The shogun received Sano and Lord Matsudaira in a courtyard of the castle, inside a gate normally used by servants. Loads of coal, hay, and timber surrounded him and the ten personal guards stationed in a tight cluster. Near them stood Yoritomo, the beautiful young samurai who was his favorite companion and lover. As Sano, Lord Matsudaira, and their entourages bowed to the shogun, he rubbed his frail hands together, and his gentle, refined features shone with excitement.

"Something, ahh, momentous has happened," he announced.

Lord Matsudaira said under his breath, "It must be momentous indeed to lure you outside the comfort of your chambers."

Sano knew that Lord Matsudaira hated being inferior to the shogun, that he envied the shogun his position at the head of the Tokugawa dictatorship. He thought it should belong to him, by right of his superior intelligence and strength. The strain of grasping at it had taxed his patience for dancing attendance on the shogun. These days he barely managed to hide his contempt.

"What's happened, Your Excellency?" Sano asked politely.

"It had better be worth dragging me over here," Lord Matsudaira muttered.

"There was a, ahh, big windstorm near the Inari Shrine in the hills this morning," the shogun said. "It knocked down a big tree."

"Why do we care?" Lord Matsudaira interrupted. "If there's a point to this story, let's get to it."

The shogun narrowed his eyes at his cousin. Sano had noticed that the shogun appeared more nervous lately than usual, as if he sensed something was amiss. He didn't know that Lord Matsudaira virtually controlled Japan, that Sano was contesting Lord Matsudaira, that the two were on the brink of war. No one had told him, and he was astoundingly unobservant. Furthermore, Sano and Lord Matsudaira enforced a nationwide conspiracy of silence because if the shogun did find out, the ramifications could tip the precarious balance of power. But even if he didn't understand what was going on, he must have perceived that his cousin was the source of the trouble.

"When the tree fell, the roots, ahh, came up out of the ground," the shogun continued, speaking slowly, deliberately annoying Lord Matsudaira. "In the hole was a human skeleton. It had been buried beside the tree, in an unmarked grave." He gestured dramatically toward his guards. "And here it is!"

The guards parted to reveal an iron trunk. The shogun stood as far away from it as possible, avoiding the pollution of death. Yoritomo kept quietly to himself, avoiding attention. Sano understood why. Yoritomo was the son of the former, ousted chamberlain Yanagisawa. Although Lord Matsudaira had exiled Yanagisawa and his family, Yoritomo remained in Edo because the shogun had insisted on keeping him. The shogun's fondness protected Yoritomo from Lord Matsudaira, who wanted to eliminate everyone connected to his onetime rival, but Yoritomo wasn't taking any chances.

Sano and Lord Matsudaira gazed at the trunk, nonplussed. "Why are you so concerned about an old skeleton, Honorable Cousin?" Lord Matsudaira forced courtesy into his tone. "It probably belongs to some pilgrim who took ill and died at the shrine ages ago."

"It does not," the shogun said, triumphant. "I know who it is."

"How, if the grave was unmarked?"

The shogun beckoned to a guard, who stepped forward holding a long, narrow, cloth-wrapped bundle. The guard unwrapped the cloth from around two swords. They were blackened by dirt, corroded by rust, and shorter than the weapons samurai carried. Sano estimated them as slightly longer than the ones he'd given Masahiro. They'd belonged to a child.

"The swords were buried near the skeleton," the shogun said. "See the characters on them?"

Sano read the characters that gleamed gold amid the rust: "'Tokugawa Tadatoshi.'" He turned to the shogun in surprise. "He belonged to your clan."

"Yes. Do you know who he was?" the shogun asked, with the air of a child playing a guessing game.

The Tokugawa family tree was huge, many-branched. Before Sano could think through it, Lord Matsudaira said, "He was your second cousin, Your Excellency."

"That's right," the shogun said, clapping his hands.

Lord Matsudaira gave Sano a smile that said he'd scored a point in their competition for the shogun's favor. Whoever lost it could find himself thrown out of court, banished, or executed. The shogun still had that power.

"Tadatoshi disappeared when he was fourteen years old," Lord Matsudaira recalled. "In Meireki Year Three, on the eighteenth day of the first month."

"The day the Great Long-sleeves Kimono Fire started," Sano said.

"Well, well, the honorable chamberlain knows his dates."

Everyone knew that infamous date forty-three years ago. No one could forget that fire, Japan's worst disaster.

The Great Long-sleeves Kimono Fire derived its name from its origin. A girl named Kiku had fallen in love with a pageboy and made herself a long-sleeved kimono, worn by unmarried girls, out of fabric that matched the boy's clothes. Kiku suddenly died, and the kimono was placed over her coffin at her funeral. Afterward, the kimono was passed on to another girl, named Hana. Hana died a year later, and the kimono covered her coffin. The same fate befell another girl, Tatsu. The girls' families decided the kimono was bad luck and should be cremated in a ceremony at Honmyo Temple. When the priest lit the kimono, it went up in flames that set the temple ablaze. The fire spread across town. Eventually, some two-thirds of the city burned to the ground.

"I remember the Great Fire," the shogun said mournfully. "It was terrible, terrible. I was eleven years old. My family took shelter in the, ahh, western part of the castle and watched the rest of it burn. I was so scared."

Sano had been born two years after the Great Fire. His knowledge of it was limited to what he'd read in accounts and heard from other people, although not from his parents. They hadn't liked to talk about those times.

"Tadatoshi was thought to have died in the fire," Lord Matsudaira said.

"Over a hundred thousand people did," Sano recalled. The casualties had exceeded ten percent of Edo's population.

"I always wondered where he went," the shogun said. "Now we know. But how did he, ahh, end up buried by the shrine?"

Sano pondered the remote site, the unmarked grave, the child's disappearance. "It smacks of foul play."

"Really?" The shogun's eyes widened and his mouth opened in awe. "I hadn't thought of that."

"Anybody but you would have," Lord Matsudaira muttered.

The shogun glanced at Lord Matsudaira and frowned. "Well, I would like to know exactly what happened to Tadatoshi. Chamberlain Sano, I order you to find out."

Sano had seen this coming the moment he'd heard about the skeleton's identity. Now he experienced two contradictory reactions. One was eagerness for a new mystery to solve, a chance to seek the truth. Detective work was his vocation, and he missed his old job as the shogun's *sōsakan-sama*—Most Honorable Investigator of Events, Situations, and People. His spirit craved escape from the pressure of running the government while neck-deep in political intrigue. But Sano's other reaction was sheer horror.

He didn't have time for an investigation. Not while he was fighting for survival; not while he had a country to save from civil war. Chasing down the truth about a long-ago death would be suicide.

And Lord Matsudaira knew it. He looked as though he'd just received a miraculous gift. His careworn face relaxed into a smile as ugly as it was delighted. "That's a wonderful idea, Honorable Cousin. We can count on Chamberlain Sano to get the facts."

The shogun beamed at this approval from the cousin who intimidated him. Sano could imagine the blows Lord Matsudaira would deal his side while he was busy with the investigation. His men's faces reflected his dismay. Hirata stepped forward and said, "Your Excellency, the investigation into Tadatoshi's death is within the scope of my duties." He'd advanced to the post of *sōsakan-sama* when Sano became chamberlain. "I'll be glad to handle it for you."

"Ahh?" The shogun squinted at Hirata as if he didn't quite remember who he was. "Hirata-*san?*"

Sano had to admit that Hirata had changed since the shogun had first met him. He'd been away much of the past five years, studying the mystic martial arts. Rigorous practice had whittled the spare flesh off his frame and turned his boyish, innocent face serious and wise. Once crippled by a leg wound in the line of duty, he'd transformed himself into a magnificent fighter. But his reputation at court had suffered.

"I'd almost forgotten you," the shogun said. "You're, ahh, hardly ever around." His voice took on a petulant tone. "You can help Chamberlain Sano investigate this matter. It's too important to leave entirely to someone who might, ahh"—he flapped his hands like birds' wings—"go flitting off again."

The death of a Tokugawa relative was too important, even after forty-three years had passed, for Sano to balk at the investigation, even though the timing couldn't have been worse. "It's my honor to serve Your Excellency," Sano said.

He felt the excitement that he'd once felt at the start of each new case, and a sensation of all the time since his first one, eleven years ago, rushing him to this instant. He remembered the man he'd been then—the lowly *rōnin,* tutor, and martial arts teacher turned reluctant police commander. That man wouldn't have believed he would ever become the shogun's second-in-command, would ever fight for control of the Tokugawa regime. That first case had been a crossroads for Sano. He had a hunch that this case would prove just as decisive, the climax of his journey.

"I want progress reports every day," the shogun said. "What will be your, ahh, first step?"

"I'll determine the cause of Tadatoshi's death," Sano said.

"Just how do you propose to do that, when all that's left of him is a skeleton?" Lord Matsudaira spoke with relish at the difficulty of Sano's task.

"I'll look into his disappearance. Following his trail may lead me to the answer." Sano would do that, but he had another method in mind that he couldn't mention.

"And if it doesn't?" Lord Matsudaira said.

Ignoring him, Sano asked the shogun, "What are you going to do with the skeleton?"

The shogun chewed his lip. "I can't keep it here." He eyed the trunk as though afraid it would contaminate the whole castle.

Hirata said, "I suggest that it be taken to your family mausoleum at Kannei Temple."

"Ahh, what a good idea," the shogun said, relieved.

"I'll do it for you," Hirata said.

Sano knew that Hirata would take the skeleton on a long route to the mausoleum, with a stop on the way. "If you'll excuse me, Your Excellency, I'll begin my inquiries at once." The sooner started, the sooner finished. Would that his world didn't fall apart in the meantime.

As he and his men departed, he caught Yoritomo's eye. Yoritomo gave Sano a strange look of sympathy mixed with apology. Lord Matsudaira called, "Good luck, Honorable Chamberlain," in a voice filled with barely suppressed glee.

3

After Sano left, Reiko tried to rest, but she couldn't because she kept reliving the attack. Her heart raced with panic that roiled through her in waves. The walls of the mansion seemed to press in on her. She felt trapped, like an animal in a cage. Today's trip outside had been her last for the foreseeable future.

She heard children laughing outside and stepped onto the veranda. Her little daughter toddled across the garden and bent over to examine something in the grass. The sun shone on Akiko's glossy cap of black hair. In her pink kimono, she looked like a flower. Reiko smiled. She walked down the steps toward the child.

"What have you found, Akiko?" she called.

Akiko looked up. Her smile faded as she recognized Reiko. She straightened, clasped her hands behind her back, and stood rigid, as if afraid of being hurt. Reiko's heart ached with sadness because while she'd been in Ezogashima rescuing her son, she had lost her daughter.

She'd left for Ezogashima when Akiko was a year old. By the time she'd come home almost three months later, after a long, difficult journey, Akiko had forgotten her. When Reiko had tried to hold Akiko, she'd cried and screamed. Now, after three more months, the little girl was aloof. Sometimes Reiko wondered if Akiko thought her mother had abandoned her and was punishing Reiko.

Whatever the explanation, the bond between mother and child had been disrupted, if not forever broken.

"Come here," Reiko said, holding out her arms.

But Akiko backed away. A little girl and younger boy came running around the house. Behind them strolled Midori, their mother, who was Hirata's wife and Reiko's good friend. Akiko ran to Midori and clutched her knees. The ache in Reiko's heart throbbed more painfully.

Midori had taken care of Akiko while Reiko was gone, and Akiko behaved as if Midori was her mother and Midori's children her sister and brother. Reiko understood why she preferred them to her real family. Midori was cheerful, cozy, and devoted to the children. Her boy and girl had adopted Akiko as a favorite pet. In contrast, Reiko and Sano were absorbed in their troubles. Reiko had chosen rescuing Masahiro over staying with Akiko. Sano left the house early in the morning and came back too late at night to see Akiko before she went to bed. Masahiro was too busy with his martial arts lessons to play with his sister. Akiko had attached herself to the people who made her feel wanted and loved.

"Go to your mama," Midori said with an apologetic look at Reiko.

"No!" Akiko's voice rose to a wail. She hugged Midori tighter.

"Then go play."

Akiko cheered up and ran off with the children. While they amused themselves by throwing pebbles in the pond, Midori said contritely, "I'm sorry, Reiko-*san*. But she'll get over it. Just give her time."

Reiko looked away, blinked, and drew deep breaths.

"I just heard what happened to you," Midori said. "Are you all right?"

"Yes," Reiko said.

But the situation was more serious than the cut on her cheek. All during their troubles with Lord Matsudaira, which had gone on for some five years, Reiko had tried to be strong for Sano and not complain. Now, however, she succumbed to the temptation to unburden herself to Midori.

"I don't know how much more I can bear," Reiko said. Once she'd been an unusually capable woman. Her father, Magistrate Ueda, had brought her up as the son he'd never had, providing her with the classical education and martial arts training usually reserved for males. While watching him conduct trials in his court of justice, she'd developed a fascination with detective work. She had later assisted Sano with his investigations, had bravely confronted murderers and faced danger. But those days were in the past. "I feel so helpless. I can't do anything about my husband's problems. I can't even leave the estate, because it's the only place that's safe."

Then Reiko noticed Midori eyeing her with an expression that portended bad news. "What is it?"

"Haven't you heard?" Midori said. "Lord Matsudaira's estate was bombed this morning. The news is all over the castle." She explained that Lord Matsudaira blamed Sano.

Horror caught Reiko's breath. "Just when I thought things couldn't get worse!" She knew Sano hadn't ordered the bombing, but Lord Matsudaira wouldn't accept the truth. "Lord Matsudaira is sure to retaliate in kind."

She gazed at the bamboo fences surrounding the women's quarters. Beyond them were the stone walls that enclosed the estate, and the guard turrets that rose above the trees into the blue sky. But neither fortifications nor the presence of Sano's army comforted Reiko. The Matsudaira estate had just as much security as this one. The bombing proved that no amount of precaution could guarantee that she and Sano and their children would be unharmed. Reiko could feel the bad wind of Lord Matsudaira's ill intentions seeping through cracks, under gates, threatening her family.

"Don't worry," Midori urged. "The trouble will blow over. Everything will be fine."

Reiko didn't believe it. "No place is safe anymore." Determined to take action against the threat, she called to a passing servant: "Go fetch Lieutenant Asukai."

He soon appeared. "You wanted to speak with me, Lady Reiko?"

His face was bruised and his arm wore a bandage over a sword wound from the ambush.

"Yes. Come with me."

She led Asukai across the garden. On a small rise stood a pavilion with a thatched roof supported by wooden pillars. Reiko and Asukai entered and sat on the bench. From here Reiko could keep an eye on the children, but they wouldn't hear her and her bodyguard speak of troubling matters.

"I must thank you for saving my life," Reiko said.

"No need," Asukai said. "It's my job."

Reiko studied his handsome, earnest face. She was closer to him than any other man except Sano or her father, and she spent more time with him than with them. He'd been her bodyguard for several years, assisting in investigations she'd conducted for Sano and on her own. Under other circumstances, their relationship might have caused gossip. But it was well known that Asukai preferred men to women, and Reiko cared for him as simply a friend. She also trusted him more than she did anyone else except Sano.

"I need your help," Reiko said.

"Of course. I'll do anything for you. Is it a new investigation?" Asukai sounded excited, because her projects often led to adventure.

"In a way," Reiko said. "I need you to find out anything you can about Lord Matsudaira's business, whether he has plans to attack us, and what they entail. Ask everyone you know. Listen for rumors."

Asukai pondered. "Chamberlain Sano has spies in and around Lord Matsudaira's estate. Wouldn't they hear about a plot before I could?"

"I'm afraid they might miss something."

"All right. I know a few men who are retainers to Lord Matsudaira." Asukai came from a big family with many connections; he was also popular and had lots of friends. "He's not an easy man to serve. He's under a lot of strain, and he takes it out on the people around him. They might be willing to inform on him, for the right price."

"Money is no object," Reiko said. Sano let her spend as much as she wanted, and although ladies didn't customarily handle cash, his treasurer had orders to give her some when she had expenses. "I'll give you whatever you need."

Asukai rose and said, "I'll get started. Rest assured that if Lord Matsudaira coughs, you'll know."

As late afternoon waned into evening, three groups of samurai on horseback departed from Edo Castle.

One rode out the front gate. Twenty troops, displaying his flying-crane crest on flags attached to their backs, accompanied Sano. The visor of his horned iron helmet shaded his face. They moved down the wide boulevard into the *daimyo* district.

The second group, identical to the first, left by a side gate. More troops escorted another Sano toward the Nihonbashi merchant quarter.

The third group consisted of three low-rank soldiers dressed in cotton kimonos, leather armor tunics bearing the Tokugawa triple-hollyhock-leaf crest, and plain helmets. They rode out the servants' gate. While the first two groups went their conspicuous ways, the real Sano traveled incognito with Detectives Marume and Fukida. The decoys drew attention away from their secret journey.

Meanwhile, Hirata rode accompanied by his troops toward Kannei Temple. They escorted four bearers carrying a litter. On it sat the trunk in which the skeleton of Tokugawa Tadatoshi had traveled from its grave. At the same time, two porters clad in loincloths and headbands carried a barrel in the opposite direction.

The porters trudged through the Kodemmacho slum. The wind swept debris along the twisting roads and whipped the smoke from outdoor hearths and beggars' bonfires outside miserable hovels. The setting sun reflected pink in open, reeking gutters. The porters skirted garbage dumps and plodded across the ramshackle wooden bridge over a canal that served as a moat for Edo Jail, a dingy fortress whose gabled rooftops lurked behind high, moss-covered walls studded with watch turrets. At the ironclad gates, the porters called to the sentries in the guardhouse: "Delivery for Dr. Ito."

Shortly after the porters entered the jail with the barrel, Sano, Marume, and Fukida arrived, confident that nobody had followed them from Edo Castle. Any spies monitoring Sano's comings and goings must have followed one or the other of his impersonators. When he and his men reached the gate sentries, the brawny, jovial Detective Marume said, "Let us in."

The sentries saw the Tokugawa crests on their garments and obeyed, no questions asked. Sano's group proceeded through the prison compound, unrecognized and unchecked by guards. They dismounted in a courtyard enclosed by a bamboo fence. There stood a low building with flaking plaster walls, barred windows, and a raggedy thatched roof: Edo Morgue, where the victims of floods, fires, earthquakes, and crimes were taken. The porters—men from Hirata's detective corps—sat on the ground near the barrel, which they'd laid at the feet of Dr. Ito.

With his plentiful white hair and tall, upright figure, dressed in the traditional dark blue coat of a physician, Dr. Ito looked no different than when Sano had last seen him almost five years ago, even though he must be over eighty now. When he saw Sano, surprise and pleasure transformed his stern face.

"Sano-*san*! Was it you who sent me this gift?"

They exchanged bows, and Sano said, "Yes. I've come to beg your expert advice."

Once a renowned physician, Dr. Ito had lost his profession, his family, his place in society, and his liberty after he'd been caught smuggling scientific knowledge from Dutch traders and performing medical experiments. The usual punishment for those offenses was exile, but Dr. Ito had received a life sentence as custodian of Edo Morgue.

"In regards to an investigation?" Dr. Ito asked. When Sano assented, he said, "I'm delighted. It's been a long time since the last one." Sano had solved other cases in the past several years, but none requiring Dr. Ito's aid. "It's also been too long since we've met."

"I regret that," Sano said.

Coming to Edo Morgue was a risk Sano couldn't afford except under special circumstances. Associating with a criminal could cost him his good name, his allies, and the shogun's favor. In addition, what happened here during his visits involved foreign science. Should Sano's collaboration in it become public, he would suffer far worse punishment than Dr. Ito had. Sano had much farther to fall.

"You've endangered yourself by coming here today," Dr. Ito said with concern.

"I've taken precautions." Besides employing a disguise and decoys, Sano had covered the trail he'd left in the past. Years ago he'd paid the gate sentries to keep quiet about his and his staff's clandestine visits. Later he'd transferred those men to other, faraway posts. His disguise had fooled their replacements. Now only Dr. Ito and his equally trustworthy assistant would know of Sano's trip here today.

"A man in your position can't be too careful," Dr. Ito warned. "But now that you're here, we may as well get down to business." He gestured to the barrel. "What have we here?"

"The skeleton of Tokugawa Tadatoshi, the shogun's second cousin." Sano described how the boy had disappeared during the Great Fire and today been found buried near the shrine. "I'm hoping you can tell me how he died."

"Fascinating. I'll be glad to try." Dr. Ito called through the open door of the morgue, "Mura-*san!*"

His assistant came out. Mura's gray hair had turned silver, and deep lines etched his square, clever face. He was an *eta*—one of Japan's outcast class that had a hereditary link with death-related occupations such as butchering and leather tanning. Other citizens shunned them as spiritually contaminated. They did dirty work like collecting garbage and nightsoil. They also served in Edo Jail as wardens, corpse handlers, torturers, and executioners. Dr. Ito had befriended Mura across class lines, and they'd worked together for more than twenty years.

On Dr. Ito's orders, Mura lugged the barrel into the morgue, which was lit by lanterns and furnished with cabinets, waist-high tables, and stone troughs for washing the dead. Mura pried up the lid. Everyone peered inside at the jumble of dirty brown bones. The only one Sano could identify was the skull.

"Can you tell anything from that?" Marume said doubtfully.

"Perhaps," Dr. Ito said. "First we must wash the bones."

Mura fetched buckets of water and filled a trough. He gently removed the bones from the barrel, immersed them, and scrubbed them with a brush. He did all the work associated with Dr. Ito's examinations that required handling the dead. The dirt came off the bones, but the brown stain from the earth persisted. When Mura was finished, the skeleton lay on the table like pieces of a puzzle.

"Now we put him together," Dr. Ito said.

He hung a scroll on the wall, an ink drawing of a human skeleton, the bones labeled. Referring to the chart, Dr. Ito picked up the bones with tongs and assembled Tadatoshi's skeleton. Some small bones from the hands and feet were missing; perhaps they'd been lost at the graveside. But when Dr. Ito had finished, the skeleton appeared almost whole. A moment passed in silence as everyone contemplated the structure that had once supported a human body.

"From the size I deduce that this was a child," Dr. Ito said.

"Tadatoshi was fourteen when he disappeared," Sano said.

"He must have died not long afterward. That is to say, he didn't live to grow up before expiring at the shrine." Dr. Ito's gaze moved over the skeleton. "Cause of death can be difficult to determine when the flesh and organs are gone. Let us take a closer look."

Dr. Ito produced a large, round magnifying lens mounted on a wooden handle. He walked around the table, peering at the bones, pausing to study features through the lens. His eyebrows rose, and he pointed at a thighbone. "Observe this marking."

Sano, Marume, and Fukida crowded around the table. The marking was large enough for Sano to see without the lens. It appeared to be a crack in which black dirt remained stuck.

"Here's another," Dr. Ito said, "and another." He indicated similar markings on the ribs, the arm bones.

"They look like the cracks in oracle bones," Fukida said.

The serious, scholarly detective was referring to the animal bones used in magic divination rituals. Fortune-tellers heated pokers in fire and applied them to the bones, causing cracks to form. By interpreting the shapes and patterns of these cracks in the "oracle bones," they read the future.

"Could they be breaks from a fall or other accident?" Marume asked.

"Unfortunately not," Dr. Ito said. "They are cuts. From a sword blade."

Sano hadn't expected the death to have been an accident. If it had, then why bury Tadatoshi in an unmarked grave and let everyone think he'd perished in the Great Fire? The breath gusted from Sano as the idea of murder entered the picture.

"Are you sure?" he asked, wanting to be absolutely certain before he opened a box of troubles.

"Yes. I've seen cuts like these many times."

So had Sano seen many sword wounds, but in flesh, not on bared bones after the body had decomposed. Dr. Ito turned over hand and arm bones with his tongs, displaying more cuts. "He acquired these when he tried to protect himself."

Sano envisioned a boy flinging up his arms as a sword slashed at him, the blade opening bloody gashes. His screams echoed across the years. "Then he was hacked to death."

Dr. Ito nodded. "This is definitely a case of murder. I'm curious about the swords buried with Tadatoshi. Why would the killer leave them as a clue to his identity instead of letting him remain anonymous and forestalling an inquiry into his death?"

"That's a good question." As Sano gazed down at the skeleton, the sword cuts seemed to glow red and give off smoke like cracks burned into oracle bones. He had a disturbing sense that the message they portended for him was pure bad luck.

"My cousin Tadatoshi was murdered?" the shogun said in dismay when Sano delivered the news to him that evening. "How did you find out?"

He lay facedown in bed, covered by a quilt below the waist, while a physician inserted acupuncture needles into his bony, naked back. He suffered from muscle aches, joint pains, heart palpitations, and other ailments real or imagined, and he tried every treatment known to man. The chamber was hot from the many charcoal braziers he needed to keep warm, and smelled of medicines. Sano was thankful that he didn't have to watch the herbal enema.

"I made some inquiries," Sano said, deliberately vague on details. He was glad Lord Matsudaira wasn't present to ask questions. "I've also assured that Tadatoshi's remains have safely reached the mausoleum."

Mura had repacked the skeleton in the barrel, and the porters had carried it to Kannei Temple. There, Hirata had sneaked the skeleton into the trunk. Tomorrow the priests would give Tadatoshi a proper cremation and burial.

"But he cannot rest in peace," the shogun said, wincing as the needles stung him, "not until justice is done. Sano-*san,* find out who killed him."

"Of course, Your Excellency." Sano's code of honor demanded justice for the murdered relative of the master he was duty-bound to serve even while he battled Lord Matsudaira for control of the regime. "Tadatoshi's killer must be punished—if he's still alive."

"If so, I shall help you catch him," the shogun said with uncharacteristic, decisive vigor. Lately he had spells during which he tried to take part in court business. Sano thought he'd become aware that he'd left too many important affairs to his officials and begun to regret how little control he had over the government. "Is there something I can do to, ahh, further your investigation?"

"Perhaps there is," Sano said. "I need to understand Tadatoshi. Can you tell me what kind of person he was?"

The shogun puffed up with pride because Sano was truly consulting him, not just pretending. That didn't happen often. He frowned in an effort to remember. "Well, ahh, it was a long time ago when I knew him. His father used to bring him to play with me. Many children were brought."

Sano figured their parents had wanted to ingratiate them with their future ruler.

"Tadatoshi was rather, ahh, shy and quiet." The shogun flinched as the physician twiddled the needles between his fingers, stimulating the flow of energy through nerves. "He liked to wander off by himself. Once he did it during a visit to me. The servants turned the castle upside down, searching for him. They found him in the forest preserve. But I'm afraid he's, ahh, mostly a blur. I can't recall what he looked like."

At least Sano had the beginning of a portrait of the murder victim. Maybe Tadatoshi had wandered off one time too many, and met his killer. "Do you remember the day he disappeared?"

"I could never forget it," the shogun said with passion. "It was the day the Great Fire started. There had been no rain for almost six months. A strong northern wind was blowing."

He and Sano listened to the wind keening outside, rustling the trees. This winter and spring had also been abnormally dry and windy, and fires had broken out around town.

"Late in the afternoon, we heard that a fire was burning through the city," the shogun continued. "Everyone was afraid the fire would reach the castle. My mother wanted to run for the hills, but we were told that the fire brigades would surely put out the fire before it could reach us."

Edo's fire brigades had consisted in those days of four small regiments levied from the *daimyo*. They'd proved grossly inadequate to combat the Great Fire. Now four squadrons of three hundred men each were managed by Tokugawa bannermen and assisted by the police. The townsfolk had organized their own brigades. Edo had learned its costly lesson.

"A servant from Tadatoshi's house came and asked whether anyone at mine had seen my cousin," the shogun said. "He'd wandered off. But we hadn't seen him. The next day, a second fire started and came toward the castle. There was so much confusion that we forgot about Tadatoshi. It was days later when we heard he'd never been found."

Days later, when the city lay in ruins, the Tokugawa regime had been too busy trying to feed and shelter thousands of homeless people to search for one lost child from a minor branch. Law and order had disintegrated. It had been a good time for somebody to kill Tadatoshi, bury him, and get away with it because he would be presumed a victim of the fire.

"Who might have wanted him dead?" Sano asked.

"I'm afraid I haven't the slightest idea."

"Is there anyone else around who knew Tadatoshi?" Sano asked. "Perhaps his immediate family?"

The shogun's face took on the queasy look that meant he feared being thought stupid. "I don't know. I have so many relatives, it's hard to, ahh, keep track of them all. And I see so few people these days."

Lord Matsudaira controlled access to the shogun in order to cut him off from people who might tell him what Lord Matsudaira was up to and bully him into doing something about it.

"But I'll help you find out about Tadatoshi's family," the shogun said, eager to make up for his ignorance. He called, "Yoritomo-*san*! Come here!"

When he got no response, the shogun sat up, bristling with needles like a porcupine, and clapped his hands. A manservant appeared in the doorway. The shogun said, "Where is Yoritomo?"

"He left the castle a while ago."

Annoyed, the shogun said, "That boy is never here when I need him. Ahh, well, never mind. Fetch Dazai."

The servant hurried off, then soon returned with the shogun's elderly, longtime valet. The shogun said to him, "Chamberlain Sano wants to know if my cousin Tadatoshi has any family still alive and in Edo."

Dazai was a repository of knowledge about his master's clan. "I'm sorry to say that Tadatoshi's father was killed in the Great Fire. Most of the people in that unfortunate household were." The disaster had taken its greatest toll among the commoners but hadn't spared the privileged classes. "But Tadatoshi's mother and older sister survived."

He gave directions to their home, and the shogun dismissed him. Sano said, "Maybe they can shed some light on Tadatoshi's character and his disappearance. I'll speak to them tomorrow."

For now Sano had urgent affairs of state to attend to, which he'd neglected for the sake of this investigation. He would probably be up all night working. And he wanted to see how Reiko was faring after this morning's attack.

As he left the shogun's bedchamber, he heard the shogun call to his servants, "Wherever Yoritomo is, find him. I desire his company tonight."

A small, obscure Buddhist temple stood outside Shinagawa, a village that lay a few hours' journey from Edo along the highway leading west. At past midnight, the temple was deserted, and silent except for the wind that rattled the bamboo canes in the gardens and rang the bells attached to the roof tiers of the pagoda. The worship hall, abbot's residence, and priests' dormitories were dark, but a light burned in the window of a guest cottage. Along the moonlit gravel path to the cottage, a man dressed in a dark, hooded cloak hurried through the shadows cast by pine trees. He carried a walking stick and wore a heavy pack on his back. The cottage door opened, lantern light spilled onto the path, and a voice called softly from inside, "Who goes there?"

The man said, "It is I."

Yoritomo, the shogun's lover, threw back his hood and stepped into the light. Framed by the door stood Yanagisawa Yoshiyasu, once the shogun's chamberlain and second-in-command, now a fugitive in hiding. His head was shaved bald; he wore the saffron robe and brocade stole of a priest. His handsome face shone with pleasure at seeing his son. He quickly let Yoritomo into the cottage and shut the door tight.

"Did anyone follow you here?" Yanagisawa asked.

"No, Father, I was careful," Yoritomo said. "I disguised myself as a religious pilgrim." He dropped his pack and stick. "I used a false name at the highway checkpoints. Nobody gave me a second look."

"Excellent." Yanagisawa didn't want the powers that were to notice Yoritomo's frequent visits to the temple; he didn't want them to know he was here. Better for them to think he was still out of the picture.

After defeating his army and ousting him from the regime almost six years ago, Lord Matsudaira had banished Yanagisawa to Hachijo Island. Yanagisawa had immediately begun plotting his return to the political career he'd built on his intimate relationship with the shogun.

As a young man of great beauty and allure, Yanagisawa had seduced the shogun and become his closest companion and principal adviser. Yanagisawa had thus gained huge authority over the government. For years he'd gotten away with corruption and murder while the shogun remained oblivious. Many people had hated him, but no one had been able to take him down . . . except Lord Matsudaira.

Lord Matsudaira also had great influence over the shogun. Furthermore, he had the advantage of Tokugawa blood, which lent him a stature that Yanagisawa could never achieve. When Lord Matsudaira had defeated Yanagisawa, the only thing that had saved Yanagisawa was his emotional hold over the shogun. The shogun had knuckled under to Lord Matsudaira's wish to get rid of Yanagisawa, but he'd refused to let Lord Matsudaira execute Yanagisawa and had insisted on exile instead. He still cared about Yanagisawa; he'd obviously hoped his dearest friend would someday return.

Heaven forbid the shogun should be disappointed.

After four years on Hachijo Island, Yanagisawa had stolen a ship and escaped. He'd found refuge at various temples, where he had friends. Yanagisawa had lived to fight another day, and now he was back with a vengeance.

"You've learned subterfuge well," Yanagisawa told Yoritomo.

The young man blushed with happiness at the praise. "I've had a good teacher."

Yanagisawa hid the tenderness he felt toward Yoritomo. He had four sons and a daughter, all by different mothers, but Yoritomo was his favorite. Yoritomo represented his second chance at gaining permanent power over Japan. He was the illegitimate product of an affair between Yanagisawa and a lady related to the shogun. His Tokugawa blood made him eligible for the succession—although he was low on the list of contenders—and Yanagisawa meant for his son to inherit the dictatorship and to rule Japan through him someday. For now, Yoritomo was his foothold in the regime, his best spy at court, his secret weapon. But Yanagisawa's attachment to Yoritomo went deeper than politics. Yoritomo was the youthful image of himself, the only person in the world to whom he felt a blood connection.

He and Yoritomo sat in the small room, which was simply furnished with a *tatami* floor, a wooden pallet for his bed, a cabinet for his few possessions, and the writing desk where he formulated his schemes. "What brings you here tonight?" Yanagisawa asked as he warmed sake on a charcoal brazier. "We weren't due to meet for another three days."

"I have news for you," Yoritomo answered.

"Good news, I hope?"

A shadow crossed Yoritomo's face, but it might have been due to the light shifting as a draft flickered the lantern. "I think you'll be pleased."

"Well, don't keep me in suspense any longer."

"Lords Gamo and Kuroda have pledged their support to you," Yoritomo said.

"Excellent." Those lords ruled large provinces, commanded thousands of troops, and possessed much wealth. They were great assets to the force that Yanagisawa needed to regain his position when the time came. He was pleased with Yoritomo, who'd proved skillful at detecting which people were disgruntled with the current regime, ready to cast their lot with an underground renegade. Yoritomo had established himself as the secret rallying point for them. He'd already recruited many powerful men to Yanagisawa's camp. Yet it wasn't just Yoritomo's charm, his closeness to the shogun, or his place in the succession that had won Yanagisawa new followers.

"Lord Gamo defected from Lord Matsudaira," said Yoritomo. "He's tired of Lord Matsudaira bleeding money and troops from him to fight your underground partisans. He thinks Lord Matsudaira has become mentally unstable and can't hold on much longer.

"Lord Kuroda defected from Chamberlain Sano. He wants a showdown between Sano and Lord Matsudaira, and he sees Sano dragging his feet. He'd rather belong to a side that dares to take a chance."

Yanagisawa dared. He had nothing to lose. And even though many people remembered him as a cruel, corrupt, self-aggrandizing official, they were falling in with him. He offered the malcontents an alternative to the status quo.

"Neither Lord Matsudaira nor Chamberlain Sano know they've lost those allies to you," Yoritomo said. "Lords Gamo and Kuroda are putting on as strong a show of loyalty toward them as ever. They won't know until they ride into battle and find that not as many soldiers are following them as they anticipated. And it hasn't gotten out that you escaped from Hachijo Island. The officials there haven't breathed a word in the reports they've sent to Edo. They're afraid of being punished for letting their most important exile get away. Only your top few people know you're back."

"Good." Yanagisawa poured sake into cups. "I propose a toast to new alliances."

They drank, and Yoritomo said, "Speaking of Lord Matsudaira and Chamberlain Sano, they're blaming each other for the attacks on their wives."

"That's just as I planned," Yanagisawa said.

He'd sent his troops, disguised with their crests, to ambush Lady Reiko and bomb Lord Matsudaira's estate. He was also responsible for other attacks that his rivals had attributed to each other. They didn't know the attacks were part of his plot to aggravate their strife into a blowup. They didn't suspect that the attacks had anything to do with him. They didn't think his partisans were capable of such devious, focused strategy, and they were right. Until Yanagisawa had returned, his partisans had been a bunch of badly organized hoodlums who'd struck randomly, hit or miss.

Yoritomo looked disturbed. "I wish we didn't have to attack Chamberlain Sano. He's been a good friend to me."

Yanagisawa had gathered that during his absence Sano had taken Yoritomo under his wing. Even though Yanagisawa hated Sano for winning over his son, he knew that had their positions been reversed, he'd have done the same. It was a smart tactic. But he couldn't afford for Yoritomo to have divided loyalties.

"I know you like Chamberlain Sano," Yanagisawa said. "However, he's not your friend."

"But he's kept your enemies away from me. And what about all the time we've spent together talking and practicing martial arts?" Yoritomo said, distressed. "He's the only person at the castle who really cares about me."

"He cares because you're in a position to help him. He protects you and flatters you; you influence the shogun in his favor. He's using you." The hurt he saw in Yoritomo's eyes pained Yanagisawa. His son was too good and innocent. "I'm sorry, but that's the way of the world."

"Yes." Downcast, Yoritomo murmured, "I see. But it's hard to believe that Chamberlain Sano could be so mercenary."

"Well, he is. I know him better than you do. Should it suit him to betray you, he will." Anxious to comfort Yoritomo without softening the harsh lesson, Yanagisawa said, "Now that I'm back, you don't need Sano anymore."

"Yes." Yoritomo brightened. He looked up at Yanagisawa with a gaze full of faith and hero-worship. "Thank you for dispelling my illusions about Chamberlain Sano."

"Don't let him know your feelings toward him have changed," Yanagisawa warned.

"I won't," Yoritomo said. "I can keep a secret."

Yanagisawa knew he could. After all, he'd kept Yanagisawa's return a secret from everyone except their most trusted confederates. And he would keep it until Yanagisawa had weakened his enemies and built up his own power base enough to launch his comeback.

"I have more news," Yoritomo said. "A skeleton was discovered buried near the Inari Shrine in the hills. It was identified as Tokugawa Tadatoshi, the shogun's cousin. The shogun has ordered Chamberlain Sano to investigate Tadatoshi's death."

"That's interesting," Yanagisawa said, leaning forward, stroking his chin. "Maybe the investigation will prove to be my blessing and Sano's downfall."

Sano was the underdog in the conflict between him and Lord Matsudaira, whom Yanagisawa most needed to defeat if he wanted to climb back on top of the regime. But Sano was still a major obstacle, and he had Yanagisawa's old post. Furthermore, Yanagisawa and Sano had a bad history.

The moment Yanagisawa had laid eyes on Sano eleven years ago, he'd known that Sano would be trouble for him. Sano had immediately become his rival for the shogun's favor. Sano hadn't needed to seduce the shogun with sex; he'd won the shogun with his cleverness and unstinting service. Sano's first investigation for the shogun had resulted in one of Yanagisawa's most humiliating experiences. Since then, Yanagisawa's fortunes had tended to rise or fall in opposition to

Sano's, as if they were counterweights attached to a pulley. Yanagi-sawa had become Sano's biggest detractor and caused Sano as much grief as possible, until a later investigation, in Miyako nine years ago, had led to a truce between them. The truce had been convenient for Yanagisawa as his struggle against Lord Matsudaira began to demand all his attention. But now Yanagisawa hated himself for not crushing Sano when he'd had a chance, for letting Sano live to occupy a critical place on the chessboard that Yanagisawa wanted to dominate.

The truce was off, even though Sano didn't know it yet.

"What has Sano discovered so far?" Yanagisawa asked.

"I don't know. I left Edo before he reported to the shogun," Yorit-omo replied. "But he said Tadatoshi's death smacked of foul play."

Glad anticipation filled Yanagisawa. "If this is indeed a case of murder, then so much the better for us."

"His murder investigations always land Sano in trouble," Yorit-omo said.

The suspects Sano identified were often powerful people. His efforts always put him at odds with them while making him a target of the killer.

"And he always faces the prospect of failure and losing the shogun's esteem. But he has such a foolhardy dedication to pursuing truth and justice." Yanagisawa couldn't understand Sano's readiness to endan-ger himself in the name of honor. "He never backs off, even when he's threatened with demotion, exile, or death for him and his entire family, as he inevitably is. Not that I'm complaining."

Sano's sense of honor had always been Yanagisawa's best weapon against Sano.

"What should we do?" Yoritomo said.

"For now, we wait and watch. Chances are, Sano will dig his own grave."

"But if he doesn't?"

Yanagisawa smiled. "I'll think of something."

"You always do, Father," Yoritomo said with admiration.

Outside, the temple bell tolled the hour of the ox. Yoritomo rose. "I'd better go. The shogun will be wanting me."

"You must keep him happy," Yanagisawa cautioned. He hated pandering his beloved son to the shogun, but he had no choice. Neither had he had a choice when, many years ago, he'd seduced the shogun himself. His intimate relationship with the shogun had been a crucial defense against his enemies. Yoritomo's would protect him until the day when he and Yanagisawa ruled Japan together. "We can't afford to have him wonder where you are and put you under surveillance."

As he let Yoritomo out the door, Yanagisawa said, "Keep me informed about Sano's investigation."

The flame of the lamp blazed its image into Reiko's eyes as she stared at it. She knelt in her chamber, hands folded in her lap, the mauve and green patterned silk skirt of her robe fanned out around her like flower petals. Her beautiful face wore a still, intense expression. The cut on her cheek shone black in the dim light. The house was quiet, everyone else in it asleep. But Reiko had suffered from insomnia ever since Masahiro's abduction, and having him back at home hadn't ceased her late-night vigils.

She was keeping watch over the children, asleep in the adjacent chamber, in case an attack should come. She couldn't bring herself to rely on the guards. She must be alert. As she devised strategies for protecting the children, she looked up to see Sano standing in the doorway.

"Did you just get home?" she asked with a forced smile.

"Yes. I had work to do. More emergencies, as usual." Sano entered the room, knelt opposite her, and studied her with concern. "Are you feeling better?"

His gaze probed at the calm facade Reiko had donned for him. "I'm fine," she said. But after almost ten years of marriage, they'd grown so close that they could often read each other's minds, and she knew that he could see on her face the ill effects of living under strain.

"Are the children all right?" Sano asked.

"They're in bed, fast asleep."

He eyed her, unconvinced that all was well. "I suppose you heard about the bombing at Lord Matsudaira's estate." When she nodded, Sano said, "Don't worry. I've put extra troops at the gates, in the guard turrets, and on the roofs." Reiko had seen them. "Nobody who doesn't belong here can get in."

Lord Matsudaira had thought his estate was secure, too, Reiko thought but didn't say. Sano was doing all he could to protect her and the children. "Has anything interesting happened?" she said, directing the conversation away from the topic that could only make her and Sano feel more ill at ease if pursued.

"As a matter of fact, yes." Sano told her about Tokugawa Tadatoshi's skeleton and the examination at the morgue.

"How fascinating!" Reiko felt a spark of interest brighten her mood.

"The shogun wants me to find out who killed him," Sano said. "This is a first for me—a new investigation of a very old murder."

Reiko thought of the days when she and Sano had worked together to solve murders, which seemed so carefree in retrospect. "Won't a murder case be difficult while you're battling Lord Matsudaira?"

"The timing couldn't be worse," Sano agreed, "but I'm curious about what happened to Tadatoshi. It'll be a challenge to see if I can discover any clues from so long ago."

"Have you any suspects?" Reiko asked eagerly.

Sano smiled, pleased by the revival of her spirits. Suddenly the old days didn't seem so far gone. "Not yet, but maybe I soon will. Tadatoshi's mother and sister are still alive. I'm going to pay them a visit tomorrow."

"That's a good idea," Reiko said. "Even if they had nothing to do with his death, maybe they can point you toward the culprit."

But she couldn't keep up her spirits, for this was one murder case in which she could take no part, no matter how much she wanted to.

The concern in Sano's expression deepened, and he said, "I know that talking to the women is something you would ordinarily do." Reiko often dealt with female suspects and witnesses, who tended to be more forthcoming with her than with a male interrogator. One of her strengths as a detective was her ability to go places and get close to people that Sano couldn't. "But it's too dangerous for you to leave the house. I'm sorry."

Ordinarily Reiko would have tried to change his mind, but not this time. For once, her place was at home with their children, whom she was determined to protect. Reiko would have willingly ventured outside to help Sano investigate the murder despite any risk to herself, but not at their expense.

"That's all right," she said, hiding her disappointment. "I understand."

Sano took her hands in his. "Next time you can work with me. If there is a next time," he added in a joking tone.

His humor and his touch comforted Reiko. "I want to hear all about the investigation. If we talk it over, that might help you solve it."

"All right." Sano was obviously relieved that she didn't argue and glad to have her assistance, no matter how limited.

"And maybe something about the murder will come up that I can work on at home," Reiko said.

"Maybe," Sano said.

But they both knew it was unlikely.

5

At dawn, the wind blew smoke from thousands of hearths across Edo through air tinged with winter, into a clear, pale sky. The sun rising above the hills outside town flashed brilliant rays. The city stirred to life.

Sleepy watchmen opened a gate to a neighborhood on the edge of the Nihonbashi merchant district. A squadron of mounted troops galloped through the gate and over a bridge that spanned a canal lined with willow trees. In the street on the opposite bank, proprietors opening the doors of their shops watched the squadron thunder past them, raising clouds of dust. The troops rode down a narrow side lane and stopped outside fences that enclosed yards behind rows of houses. As they leaped from their mounts, an elderly woman inside a house lay asleep, dreaming.

The dream was always the same, its time the sixteenth year of her life. She ran through the streets of Edo. Her hair was magically no longer gray but black and glossy, her body slim and strong and quick. Around her, people hurried screaming in all directions. Flames leaped and roared from burning houses. Roofs caved in with mighty crashes. Cinders stung her eyes and burned holes in her leather cape and hood. The smoke was so thick she could barely breathe or see.

He pulled her along, his hand tight around hers. He was invisible in the smoke, but she heard him call, "Hurry!"

They veered around a corner and joined a stampede of people fleeing with children in arms, possessions loaded on bent backs. She stumbled and gasped, trying to keep up with him as the smoke thickened. Ahead, buildings were curtains of flame that snapped in the wind. Bodies jostled her as he tugged her through the crowds. They reached a canal and found hundreds more people massed at the bridge. They would never get across to safety.

Before they could turn in another direction, more people jammed against them, trapping them in the mob. Shrieks and wails deafened her. She sobbed in terror. As the crowd battered her, his hand ripped loose from hers. She frantically shouted his name, but he was lost in the crush. She was alone.

Now, forty-three years later, the nightmare imprisoned her, but consciousness penetrated. As terrible as that moment during the fire had been, she knew that what had followed was even worse.

The fire caught her and ignited her clothes. They went up in flames. She wore a kimono made of fire. She screamed.

Shouts and crashes jolted her awake. She sat up in bed, panting and drenched with sweat, her heart thudding. The noises weren't just echoes from her dream. They were in her house.

Alarmed, she called to her maid. "Hana?"

She heard Hana shriek as heavy footsteps marched through the kitchen and dishes shattered. Her room filled with soldiers who surrounded her bed. She pulled the quilt up to her chin and stared in fright at them through eyes clouded by old age.

Hana, as old as she but far braver, fluttered around the soldiers like a hen trying to protect a chick. "How dare you break into this house?" she shrilled. "What are you doing?"

The soldiers ignored her. The leader stepped close to the bed and demanded, "Are you Etsuko?"

Unable to speak, she nodded.

"What do you want with my mistress?" Hana said.

"You're under arrest," he said. "Get up. You're coming with us."

44

"Under arrest for what?" Hana cried in outrage.

"For murder."

Even though flabbergasted, Etsuko felt a sense of resignation, of a prophecy come true. For forty-three years she'd dreaded this day. Her past had caught up with her at last.

The sword came swishing through the air toward Sano. He dodged, whirled, and counterattacked. Masahiro lunged and struck at him again. Sano parried. Their wooden blades clacked as they hit, cleaved empty space while they performed a dance of simulated battle.

No matter how busy he was, Sano tried to make time for early-morning combat practice with Masahiro. It was their special time together, a peaceful oasis in his often tumultuous days. The sun climbed above the wall of the compound where they fought, splaying their shadows across the gravel-strewn ground. Son charged at father, blade swinging, as the gate opened and Detective Marume appeared. Sano's concentration on the battle was disrupted. He turned, a fatal mistake. Masahiro's sword whacked him hard across his rear end.

"Ow!" Sano yelled.

Masahiro's hand flew to his mouth. "I'm sorry, Father! I didn't mean to hit you!"

"No, don't apologize," Sano said, rubbing his buttocks. "I deserved it. Let that be a lesson to you: When you're fighting, never take your attention off your opponent."

He faced Detective Marume, who hid a smile. "What?"

"There's an old woman here to see you. She turned up at the castle gate, demanded to be taken to you, and refused to leave," Marume said apologetically. "She pestered the guards until they gave in. She says her name is Hana."

"Hana!" Now Sano was concerned. Hana was his mother's long-time servant. He'd known her all his life; she'd helped raise him. She accompanied his mother on extremely rare visits to his estate. That she would come now, alone, could only mean something bad.

Sano tossed his sword to Masahiro, said, "Keep practicing," and headed indoors. He found Hana standing in the reception room, guarded by two soldiers, wringing her hands in the apron she wore over her indigo-and-gray-striped kimono.

"Sano-*san*!" She was a tiny, wiry woman with gray hair so thin that her scalp showed through it. She had pouchy cheeks, bags under her eyes, and skin mottled with brown spots, but she'd lost none of her energy to old age. She ran to Sano and exclaimed, "Praise the gods, I was afraid I'd never reach you!"

Sano dismissed the guards. "It's all right, I'm here now," he told Hana. "What's wrong? Is it my mother?"

His mother had seemed in good health the last time he'd visited her—when? Almost three months ago? But she was nearly sixty years old. Sano feared the worst.

"She's been arrested!" Hana cried.

"Arrested!" Shock hit Sano. "By whom?"

"Tokugawa soldiers. They walked into the house this morning and dragged her out of bed."

Sano's widowed mother lived in the humble house where he'd grown up. When he'd begun working for the shogun and moved into Edo Castle, he'd brought her with him, but she'd been so homesick, and so intimidated by her new surroundings, that she'd been unable to eat or sleep. Hana, who'd come with her, had told Sano, "If she stays here, she'll die. You must send her home." Sano had, and she'd lived there contentedly all these years. But now he regretted leaving her on her own. He felt bad because he saw her so seldom and hadn't kept her safe.

"I had to beg them to let her dress," Hana said. "I tried to stop them, to tell them she hadn't done anything wrong, but they wouldn't listen."

"There must be some mistake," Sano said. "Did they say why they were arresting her?"

"For murder!"

Incredulity resounded through Sano. His mother was a good woman, incapable of hurting anyone. She was always calm, gentle; he'd never seen her lose her temper.

"This is insane," Sano said. "Who did they say she murdered?"

"Someone named Tokugawa Tadatoshi."

Enlightenment struck. Sano realized what had happened. He felt even worse. His mother had been swept into the whirlwind of political intrigue that surrounded him and his investigation.

"You have to help her," Hana pleaded. She grabbed Sano by the front of his white martial arts practice jacket and shook him, the way she had during his childhood when he'd misbehaved. "Do something!"

"I will," Sano said, "but first I need to know where my mother is. Where did the soldiers take her?"

"To the palace. They said they had orders to bring her before the shogun."

Sano was already halfway out of the room. "You wait here," he called over his shoulder to Hana. "Don't worry."

Striding down the corridor, he ordered the servants, "Bring my guest some food and drink and make her comfortable." He told his troops, "Go tell Hirata-*san* to meet me at the palace."

Detectives Marume and Fukida fell into step behind Sano as he hurried toward his room to change into the clothes required for a meeting with the shogun. He tore off his martial arts jacket with an angry gesture and spoke between clenched teeth: "Lord Matsudaira is not getting away with this."

"Where are you going?" Midori asked.

"To meet Chamberlain Sano at the palace," Hirata said as he donned his shoes in the entryway of their house.

"Why? What's going on?"

Hirata took down his swords from the rack on the wall. "Something to do with the murder investigation."

"And after that?" Suspicion inflected Midori's voice. "Where are you going next?"

The atmosphere between them had been tense since he'd returned home from Ezogashima three months ago. Before that, he'd been gone much of five years while studying martial arts and roaming the country. The long periods apart had changed her as much as him. She was no longer the sweet, docile girl he'd left. While raising their children by herself, she'd grown a strong will of her own. She'd missed him, but she'd come to resent his absences, his abandonment of her.

"I don't know." Hirata hung his swords at his waist, deliberately uncooperative. He understood Midori's need to keep track of him and her fear that he would leave again, but he chafed at her questions. It was his right to come and go as he pleased. A wife shouldn't infringe on her husband's freedom.

"When will you be back?" Midori said, but she didn't wait for Hirata to brush her off again. "Well, I guess I'll just have to wait and see, won't I?"

They regarded each other with mutual antagonism. Hirata felt a pang of sorrow for the young couple in love they'd once been. Now they were almost strangers, always at odds. They'd not even had marital relations since Hirata had returned. He'd been busy, his strenuous martial arts practice diminished his sexual desire, and Midori was too angry.

From the corridor came the sound of children's quarreling voices and running footsteps. Their little boy, Tatsuo, grabbed Midori's skirts and cried, "Mama, she touched me!"

"I didn't," said Taeko. She tapped her finger on his head and giggled.

"See? She did it again," Tatsuo whined.

Midori said, "Taeko, behave yourself, or I'll lock you in your room. Tatsuo, if you don't stop complaining, *I'll* touch you, and I can promise you won't like it."

She raised her hand at the boy. Hirata was dismayed because Midori had vented her anger at him on their children. They didn't deserve to suffer for what he'd done, and he felt guilty because he'd abandoned them as well as his wife. He and they were strangers, too. He tried to smile at them, but they retreated behind Midori. Tatsuo sucked his thumb; Taeko eyed Hirata warily.

"Your father is leaving," Midori said. "Say good-bye, in case you never see him again."

"Good-bye, Father," mumbled the boy and girl.

"You'll see me tonight," Hirata said, vexed by Midori's sniping. "I'll be back then."

"Go play." Midori turned Tatsuo and Taeko around, swatted their behinds, and sent them running. She focused on Hirata a gaze filled with bitterness. "Don't make promises to them that you can't keep."

Hirata knew how unreliable his promises were. His duty to Sano and his commitment to the martial arts must always come first. He felt torn because he missed his family and wanted a happy life with them. He wanted Midori to give him a chance to start anew. But his own anger and stubbornness prevented him from asking.

"I'm going," he said, and walked out of the house.

Spring graced the palace with blooming azaleas, trees resplendent in new green leaf, and dewy grass. The sun shone on its gabled roofs and half-timbered walls. But scenic beauty was lost on Sano as he and his entourage joined Hirata at the entrance. They barreled past the doors, through chambers filled with officials, and down the passages, and burst into the cavernous main reception room. There Sano found his mother kneeling before the dais, her gray head bowed, her hands tied behind her back with coarse rope. Her frail, bent body, clad in an old brown kimono, trembled. The shogun stood over her.

"Did you kill my cousin?" he demanded. When she didn't reply, he smacked her face. She cringed. He looked excited and proud of himself, a weak person tormenting a weaker one. "Answer me!"

Lord Matsudaira sat nearby on the dais, brimming with evil enjoyment. A few allies knelt behind him, come to watch the fun. Sano noticed a new face among them: Lord Arima, *daimyo* of Kurume Province. Lord Arima's topknot was gray, but his face was ageless, as if his skin were preserved in oil. His expressions were so fleeting that they never left a wrinkle. The Matsudaira troops, positioned with the shogun's along the walls, watched impassively. The scene so enraged Sano that he forswore the required courtesies. He strode up to the shogun and pushed him away from his mother.

"Leave her alone!"

The shogun reeled backward. Everyone else stared, shocked that Sano would lay a hand on their lord. Even Lord Matsudaira appeared flummoxed by Sano's nerve.

"This woman has been accused of killing Tadatoshi," the shogun huffed. "I'm, ahh, interrogating her."

"She's my mother," Sano said, furious.

Hands on his hips, the shogun said, "I don't care if she's the Buddha's mother. If she killed my cousin, I'm going to make her confess."

"Mother, are you all right?" Sano asked.

She gazed up at him. Her gentle, drooping features were blank with terror. She didn't seem to recognize Sano. He untied the rope and held her hands. They were cold and blue from lack of blood circulation. He felt her shivering, heard her soft whimpers.

"She had nothing to do with Tadatoshi's murder," Sano told the shogun. "She's innocent."

"Of course you would say that." The shogun swelled up with obstinacy. "You're her son. But I know better."

"How?" Sano demanded. "What proof do you have?"

"Why, ahh—" The shogun floundered, subsiding into his usual cowed witlessness. "They said so."

" 'They' meaning 'you.' " Sano turned on Lord Matsudaira. "This is your doing. You're attacking me by accusing my mother."

Lord Matsudaira gave Sano a look that warned him not to bring their rivalry into the open. "Consider it retribution if you like. But I'm not the one who accused her."

"Oh?" Sano said in scornful disbelief. "Then who did?"

A samurai stepped forward from the ranks along the wall. "I did."

"Who are you?" Sano asked.

"Colonel Doi Naokatsu."

He was in his sixties, but only his gray hair and the roughness of his voice betrayed his age. His tall physique appeared as strong and trim as that of a man decades younger. The skin on his face stretched as smoothly over its high cheekbones, prominent nose, and square jaw, as if he rarely smiled. An elaborate armor breastplate made of red and black leather marked him as a warrior of high rank.

Suspicion filled Sano. "What's that symbol on your breastplate?"

Doi looked down at it, the Matsudaira clan crest. Now Sano recalled hearing Doi's name before. He'd fought for Lord Matsudaira in the battle against the former chamberlain Yanagisawa. Sano said to Lord Matsudaira, "You put him up to this."

"Why would he do that?" the shogun said, perplexed.

Lord Matsudaira's face was a slick mask of innocence. "Honorable Cousin, Chamberlain Sano, I can assure you that I did not."

"When I heard that Tadatoshi's remains had been discovered, I came forward voluntarily," Colonel Doi said to Sano. "I have information pertaining to the murder. Before you rush to believe that your mother has been framed, you'd better hear it."

6

"Nothing you say can change the fact that my mother didn't kill Tadatoshi," Sano said, offended by Colonel Doi's patently false claim.

"How can you be so, ahh, certain, when you haven't even heard his story?" the shogun said. "I order you to listen." He waved an imperious hand at Doi. "Proceed."

Sano had no choice but to shut up and seethe. The evil smile on Lord Matsudaira's face widened. Doi said, "I was Tadatoshi's personal bodyguard. I lived in his estate."

Here was an ideal witness from those days, but not, unfortunately, with the testimony that Sano had hoped for.

"So did a young woman named Etsuko. She was sixteen years old at the time," Doi said, and pointed at Sano's mother.

"That's impossible," Sano interrupted although the shogun glared at him. "What on earth could she have been doing there?"

Even as he spoke, doubt crept into his mind. He didn't know where his mother had lived before she'd married his father. He didn't actually know anything about her youth, which she never mentioned.

"She was a lady-in-waiting to the women in Tadatoshi's household," Doi said.

"She couldn't have been." About that, Sano was certain. "She comes from a humble family." Which he'd never met; they'd all died during the Great Fire, before his birth. "Only girls of high rank are allowed to serve a Tokugawa-branch clan."

Doi permitted himself a smile that twitched one corner of his mouth. "You have a reputation as a great detective, Honorable Chamberlain, but perhaps you should have used your skills on your own kin. I knew your mother in those days. She belonged to the Kumazawa family. Her father was a respected hereditary Tokugawa vassal. Look in the court records. You'll find her listed."

Too shocked to hide his amazement, Sano turned to his mother. "Is this true?"

She didn't answer. Her gaze evaded his. She tugged the sleeves of her robe down over her hands and pulled the collar tight around her throat. Sano's mind teemed with questions.

His father had been a *rōnin*—a masterless samurai—who'd scratched out a living by operating a martial arts academy. His clan hadn't regained true samurai standing until Sano had been taken into the shogun's service. If Sano's mother was really from a Tokugawa vassal clan, then why had she married so far beneath her? Was her family really dead?

Colonel Doi advanced on Sano's mother. "You know me, don't you, Etsuko-*san*?" He stopped in front of her. His gaze was hard, threatening. "Even though it's been forty-three years since we last met."

As she squinted up at him, her cloudy eyes filled with wonder and fright. Her face blanched; she swayed. Sano put his hands on her shoulders to steady her.

"She recognizes me," Doi said. The shogun nodded; Lord Matsudaira looked satisfied, as did his friend Lord Arima. "She knows the truth."

Sano had always taken his mother for granted, at face value. He was ashamed to realize that even though he loved her, he'd never been interested enough in her to think she'd had a life apart from him. Now she seemed a woman of mystery. The only fact that Sano could be absolutely certain of was that his parents had wed six months after the Great Fire. He'd seen the date written in their family record. What had happened to his mother between then and her stint as a lady-in-waiting in Tadatoshi's household?

"She knew Tadatoshi," Doi said. "She saw him every day while she served his mother and sisters."

Sano couldn't ask his questions even though Doi might very well have the answers. He couldn't afford to expose more ignorance and put himself at a worse disadvantage with his enemies. And he had business more urgent than dredging up his mother's hidden past. He had to defend her against Doi's accusation.

"Suppose she did know Tadatoshi," Sano said. "That doesn't mean she killed him."

"That's not all there is to my story," Colonel Doi said. "Your mother plotted to kidnap Tadatoshi."

More outraged than ever, Sano exclaimed, "That's ridiculous! She would never have done such a thing."

"Perhaps not on her own," Doi said, "but she didn't act alone. She had an accomplice. He was Tadatoshi's tutor, a young Buddhist monk named Egen. They wanted to extort ransom money from Tadatoshi's father."

"How do you know?" Sano said.

Maybe it's true, the detective part of his mind whispered. *You can't decide that a suspect is innocent just because you want her to be. And how well do you really know your mother?*

"I overheard Egen and your mother talking," Doi said. "They said they needed money and Tadatoshi's father was rich. Your mother said, 'He'd do anything to save Tadatoshi.' Egen said, 'We'll watch Tadatoshi and wait for the right moment.'"

The dubiousness of this evidence didn't ease Sano's fears for or about his mother. "This conversation took place when?"

"About a month before Tadatoshi disappeared."

"That would be forty-three years ago," Sano said. "What a memory you have, if you can remember an entire conversation after that long."

"My memory is good," Doi said, refusing to be shaken.

"Then let's test your memory a little further. Did you actually hear my mother and this tutor say they were going to kidnap Tadatoshi and collect ransom?"

"Well, no," Doi admitted reluctantly. "But that's what they meant to do."

"If so, then why didn't you stop them?" Sano said. "You were Tadatoshi's bodyguard. Why did you just twiddle your thumbs and let him be kidnapped?"

"I didn't realize what their conversation meant," Doi said, defensive now. "Not until yesterday, after the skeleton was found. Before then I'd always thought Tadatoshi died in the Great Fire. So did everyone else. But now I know better."

"Was there any ransom demand ever made?" Sano said.

"Well, no, but—"

"You didn't hear my mother and the tutor admit they killed Tadatoshi, did you? Because if you did, you'd have taken action against them then."

Doi's testy expression was his answer. "When they kidnapped him, something must have gone wrong and they killed him instead of ransoming him. He was murdered, and she did it."

He pointed at Sano's mother. Lord Matsudaira and Lord Arima nodded judiciously. The shogun followed their example.

"Those are some pretty big leaps from a vague conversation you heard forty-three years ago to kidnapping to murder," Sano said disdainfully. The shogun frowned as if vacillating, and Lord Matsudaira started to look wary. "Have you any proof that things happened as you expect us to believe?"

"I don't need any." Doi's posture stiffened with anger. "I know what I know."

"That's not good enough." Sano said, "Your Excellency, this man has made up his whole story."

"That's a lie," Doi declared. "Why would I?"

Sano couldn't say, *Because you're Lord Matsudaira's lackey and it would benefit him if my mother was condemned.* For the shogun to learn about their fight for control of the regime would be worse for Sano than for Lord Matsudaira, whose blood ties to the shogun might shield him from execution for treason. He could live to fight another day, but Sano, an outsider, would be put to death.

Instead Sano said, "Maybe you feel guilty because Tadatoshi died on your watch and you need someone to blame. But I bet you have an even more personal reason for accusing my mother. *You* killed him, and you're trying to protect yourself."

"I didn't!" Offense darkened Doi's face. "I was loyal to Tadatoshi. I would never have touched him!"

"My findings indicated that Tadatoshi was hacked to death with a sword. Does my mother look capable of that? It sounds more in your line."

Doi tightened his features, masking alarm. The shogun said timidly, "Sano-*san* has a good point."

"Sano-*san* is just trying to save his mother," Lord Matsudaira said. "Don't listen to him. She killed Tadatoshi. She deserves to be condemned."

"Not on such flimsy evidence from a man who looks to be an even better suspect," Sano said.

"I'll vouch for Colonel Doi's truthfulness, Honorable Cousin," Lord Matsudaira said with a narrow-eyed glare at Sano. "I advise you to execute this woman at once. Furthermore, the murder of your relative constitutes treason. By law, her whole family should share her punishment. That includes her son—Chamberlain Sano."

Sano's men, who'd been listening in appalled silence, stepped forward to protect him. Lord Matsudaira's men surged at them. Sano was sick and tired of being threatened with death during investigations. He swore a private oath that this was the last time Lord Matsudaira would ever put him in that position. But first he had to get out of this mess.

"Don't let your cousin or his flunky manipulate you, Your Excellency," Sano said. "Don't let me, either. Use your own judgment. Look at my mother. Does she seem guilty to you?"

"Well, ahh—" The shogun walked around her, inspecting her

from all angles. She huddled, forlorn and passive. "I must say she looks like a nice, harmless old lady."

Lord Matsudaira started to speak, but Sano said, "Would you want your mother condemned to death based on forty-three-year-old hearsay?"

Everyone knew the shogun was devoted to his own mother. Stricken, he said, "Certainly not. Perhaps I've made a mistake."

He spoke as if that were something new. Sano dared to think his mother was safe. So did Lord Matsudaira and Colonel Doi, judging by their sour expressions. But the shogun said, "Sano-*san*, forgive me if I mistreated your mother, but I'm taking very seriously the, ahh, charges against her. You may continue your investigation, but if you don't exonerate her, I will be forced to execute you both."

"Don't forget his wife, his children, and all his close associates," Lord Matsudaira said, brightening. "In the meantime, I'll take his mother to await her fate in Edo Jail."

Sano was alarmed at the thought of her in that hellhole. "She belongs to a samurai clan. That entitles her to house arrest instead of jail. With your permission, Your Excellency, I'll take her to my estate."

"Granted," the shogun said.

Sano gently raised his mother. "It's all right, Mother, you're coming home with me."

She leaned against him as he walked her toward the door. Colonel Doi watched, his eyes calculating losses and strategies, like a commander on a battlefield. She didn't look at him or anyone else. Sano couldn't begin to think how to exonerate her. His first concern was her health.

"Don't let her get too comfortable at your estate," Lord Matsudaira said, confident that although he'd lost this battle with Sano, he would win their war. "She won't be staying there long. And neither will you."

"Excuse me, Lady Reiko?" said Lieutenant Asukai. He hovered in the door of her chamber.

"Yes?" Reiko knelt at her dressing table, where she'd just finished applying her makeup. "What is it?"

Asukai's expression was somber. "Bad news, I'm afraid."

Reiko glanced at the open wall partitions. In adjacent rooms, Masahiro recited a lesson to his tutor, and Akiko teased the maids while they swept the floor. Reiko pointed to the children and put her finger to her lips as she beckoned Asukai to enter.

"One of my informants has told me that Lord Matsudaira has a spy planted in this house," he whispered.

The news didn't exactly surprise Reiko. She knew that Sano had spies in the Matsudaira house, people who worked there but were also secretly in Sano's pay. Why shouldn't Lord Matsudaira have done the same? But Reiko was dismayed nonetheless.

"Who is it?" she asked.

"I'm sorry to say I have no idea. My informant doesn't know." Asukai added, "But it's someone who has free run of Chamberlain Sano's domain."

Matters were worse than Reiko had initially thought. She didn't like the idea of anyone snooping and eavesdropping in her house, but this spy was apparently someone she and Sano trusted, who had easy access to them, their business, and their family. And Lord Matsudaira might turn his spy to other, more dangerous purposes.

"Try to find out who it is," Reiko said. "In the meantime, I'd better tell my husband what you've learned."

No sooner had Asukai left than Reiko heard a commotion of quick footsteps and loud voices from the women's quarters. Fearing that something else was wrong, she hurried to see what was happening.

火
火
火

7

Reiko entered the women's quarters to find Sano carrying an old woman down the hall. "What's going on?" she asked. "Who—?"

The woman lay limp in Sano's arms, her complexion sickly pale. Her eyes were closed, and she seemed oblivious to the world. Then Reiko recognized her. "Honorable Mother-in-law," Reiko said in surprise, then turned to Sano. "What is she doing here? Is something wrong?"

Her relationship with Sano's mother was cordial but not close. As a new bride Reiko had tried to befriend her mother-in-law, who always seemed nervous around her. The old woman had endured rather than warmed under Reiko's attentions, and they didn't have much to say to each other. Sano's mother had never spent a night in this house during his marriage, and she seldom visited.

"My mother has been accused of the murder of Tokugawa Tadatoshi and placed under house arrest," Sano said. He looked more stunned than Reiko had ever seen him.

"What?" Reiko said. "How can that be?"

She gazed in bewilderment at her mother-in-law, the most harmless person she knew. She felt as if the world had turned upside down.

Sano called to the servants who loitered in doorways: "My mother will be staying here. Prepare a bed for her. And fetch her maid."

He carried her into a guest chamber. Reiko followed. The servants hurried to obey his orders. He gently laid her on the futon that they spread on the floor. Hana rushed in and took charge. Sano and Reiko stepped out to the corridor while Hana got the old woman settled. There Sano described how his mother had been dragged out of her house and brought before the shogun, how Colonel Doi had told his incriminating story about her. Reiko listened in shock.

"Who is this Colonel Doi, and why is everybody taking his accusation seriously?" she asked.

"He's a big man in Lord Matsudaira's army," Sano replied.

"I should have guessed," Reiko said. "Lord Matsudaira is behind everything bad that happens." She remembered the matter that had been foremost in her mind just moments ago. "I know you don't need more problems, but there's something I must tell you that can't wait. My bodyguard has discovered that Lord Matsudaira has a spy in our house."

Sano lifted his eyes skyward, simultaneously alarmed, vexed, and overwhelmed. "You're right, I didn't need that now. But thank you for alerting me. I'll mount a search for the spy as soon as I have a free moment."

Reiko said, "Planting a spy in our midst is bad enough, but now Lord Matsudaira has attacked your poor, helpless mother. This is preposterous! Of course she didn't kill that boy."

"Of course." But Sano's expression was grave, conflicted.

"You can't think there's any chance she did it?" Amazement filled Reiko.

Sano's frown deepened. "I really don't know what to think." He expelled a deep breath. "It seems I don't really know my mother. She led me to believe she was a peasant, but I just now learned that she's from a Tokugawa vassal clan."

As Sano related how this fact had come out, Reiko shook her head. That her meek, shy mother-in-law had a secret past!

But as Reiko recovered from her initial shock, she wasn't really surprised. She remembered things about Sano's mother that had never fit her persona. Her manners had the effortless grace of a lady. Her speech was more refined than a typical commoner's. Although she dressed plainly, her clothes had an elegance that had less to do with expensive fabric and the latest fashion than with the wearer's style. Sano wouldn't have noticed such things; men seldom did. Reiko hadn't told Sano because she hadn't thought it important enough and he would have scoffed at the idea that his mother was someone other than she seemed. But the revelation about his mother explained a lot.

"How did her life turn out the way it did?" Reiko asked.

"I don't know. That's one question I mean to ask her." Sano's expression was stony with hurt because his mother had deceived him, and grim because he now must contend with her troubles as well as his own. "And believe me, I have plenty of others. I have to determine who really killed Tadatoshi, and at the moment she's my only source of clues."

He turned toward the guest room. "She should be settled by now."

"Shall I come with you?" Reiko asked, filled with curiosity.

"No," Sano said. "I'd rather talk to her alone. Whatever she says, I'll tell you later."

Reiko resisted the temptation to eavesdrop. As Sano entered the guest room, she drifted down the corridor, marveling at the turn of events. Last night she'd offered to help him with his investigation if something arose that she could work on at home. Now it had. The investigation had come to her, in the form of the one and only suspect.

Sano's mother lay in bed, propped on cushions, guarded by Hana. Her expression was desolate. She gazed into space, her hands limp on the quilt that covered her. She hadn't touched the tea set on the table. But at least she was calm.

"Mother?" Sano knelt at her feet.

She blinked, and her eyes focused on him. In them appeared the same expression with which she'd beheld him since his childhood—a mixture of love, pride, and maternal anxiety. But there was something new.

It was fear.

Of him.

Sano didn't want to think what her fear might signify. "Are you all right?"

She nodded, murmuring, "I'm sorry to make so much trouble for you."

"Don't worry about me," Sano said with affection. She'd always put him first. "I want to help you. I need to ask you some questions about what's happened. Do you feel up to that?"

"I suppose so." But she looked ill and exhausted.

Sano wouldn't have forced her, except that they had no time to lose. Lord Matsudaira was probably working to ruin them already. "Hana-*san*, will you leave us for a few moments?"

Reluctance compressed Hana's mouth, but she started to rise. Sano's mother said, "Please, I want Hana to stay."

For moral support or protection against him? Sano had never thought to find himself interrogating his own mother who was accused of the crime he was investigating. He could see in her face that her feelings toward him had changed: He was no longer the same son she'd borne. He was the authority, a danger.

"Please don't be upset," Sano said, "but I have to ask you: Did you kill Tadatoshi?"

"No!" Hurt encroached on the fear in her eyes. "I'm innocent. You don't believe him, do you?"

Sano supposed that any woman arrested, dragged out of her house, accused before the shogun, and threatened with death would be afraid, even if not guilty. "Believe Colonel Doi? Of course not. But why would he make up that story?"

". . . I don't know."

Sano noticed the hesitation before she answered, the glance she and Hana exchanged. "Do you know Colonel Doi?"

Although she wouldn't meet his eyes, she nodded.

"How well?"

Hana said, "Tell him."

"Tell me what?" Sano said, mystified.

His mother sighed. "Colonel Doi and I were once engaged to be married."

Sano's body didn't register the shock. His breath didn't catch; no blow landed in the pit of his stomach. It was as if her words had fallen on a cushion whose stuffing had already been punched out by earlier revelations about her. But he felt a sensation like a knife piercing the core of his spirit. That his mother had been engaged to Colonel Doi, and he hadn't known, put to question everything he'd believed about their family.

"When was this?" he asked.

Sadness and shame clouded her face. "Before I met your father."

He'd thought his father had been the only man in her life. He knew it was stupid to be jealous on his father's behalf, or his own. His father had been dead eleven years; nothing could hurt him. And Sano had no claim on his mother before his birth. But emotions were often neither rational nor controllable.

"Did my father know?" Sano asked.

"Yes."

"And neither of you ever told me." Anger gathered heat in Sano. The engagement didn't mean his mother and Doi had been involved in any unseemly way, because most marriages were arranged, and betrothed couples were barely acquainted until their wedding day. But Sano felt as if her prior engagement was a violation of her marriage to his father and their family.

"We didn't think it mattered," she said weakly.

"What happened with the engagement?"

"It was broken."

"Obviously." Had it not been broken, she couldn't have married Sano's father. "Who broke it? Your parents or Doi's?"

Her gaze turned vague. "It was a long time ago. I don't remember."

"Do you remember why it was broken?"

". . . No."

Sano beheld her with disbelief. The breaking of an engagement was a serious matter. In this instance it had resulted in his mother marrying a poor *rōnin* and losing her place in high society. Sano doubted that even after more than forty years she'd forgotten.

"What did Colonel Doi think about the broken engagement?" Sano asked.

"Must we talk about this?" Her voice was querulous, her face wan.

"If you expect me to save you, I have to figure out what's going on," Sano said. "You have to work with me."

She closed her eyes briefly, as if wanting to hide from him. "I'm sorry."

"All right, let's forget Colonel Doi for now," Sano said. She'd already given him a possible clue in that direction. If Doi had been upset about the broken engagement and nursed a grudge all this time, maybe that was why he'd incriminated her. He certainly merited investigation. "Let's talk about Tadatoshi. Do you remember him?"

"He was just a boy. I barely knew him."

Her hand crawled across the quilt toward Hana. The maid held and patted it reassuringly. Her stern gaze disapproved of Sano's treatment of his mother even if it was for her own good.

"Could he really have been kidnapped?"

"I don't know."

Sano remembered the shogun saying Tadatoshi had been prone to wander off. That was a preferable explanation for his disappearance that Doi's story had unfortunately eclipsed. "What can you tell me about the day he disappeared?"

A shadow of memory darkened her eyes. "It was the day the Great Long-sleeves Kimono Fire started. Everyone in the house was supposed to travel across the river, to get away from it. But when we were ready to leave, Tadatoshi was missing. We looked all over the estate, but he wasn't there. His father sent us all out to look for him in the city. But nobody ever found him." Her voice broke. "I was caught in the fire. So were other people from the house. Only a few of us survived."

"Did anyone think at the time that Tadatoshi had been kidnapped?"

"I don't know. There was so much confusion."

"If you didn't kidnap him, maybe someone else did." Sano knew it was dangerous to assume she was innocent, but he couldn't believe she would kidnap a child any more than kill it. "What about this tutor, this monk named Egen, that Colonel Doi mentioned? Could he have done it?"

"No! I mean, I don't know, I can barely remember him." She squirmed in bed, her face averted from Sano. "Please, no more questions. That was such a terrible time. I can't stand talking about it."

Hana said, "Leave your mother alone, young master. Let her rest." She used the same no-nonsense tone as when scolding him during his childhood. "Pestering her isn't going to make her memory come back."

"Very well," Sano said, and watched his mother sag with relief. "But we're going to have to discuss it, the sooner the better. The more information you can give me, the more chance I'll find out who really killed Tadatoshi."

As he left the room, he didn't wonder if she was hiding something. He wondered how much it was, and how bad.

"I didn't want to say this when the young master was here," Hana said, "but maybe you should tell him the whole story."

Etsuko stared at her maid in horror. "I can't."

"But he's said that if he's to help you, you have to help him." Hana was sympathetic but firm. No matter that they were servant and mistress; her long years of devotion gave Hana the privilege of speaking her mind. "I think he's right."

"I've told him plenty." That had been hard enough. Etsuko pulled the quilt up to her chin. She wished she could crawl under the quilt and hide from her troubles, just as she'd hidden for forty-three years. "He doesn't need to know the rest."

"What would it hurt for him to know?" Hana persisted. "After all this time?"

"You saw his face when I told him about my engagement to Colonel Doi. It did hurt him. And it hurt me to see him angry because I hid my past from him." As heartache and shame filled her, Etsuko rushed to justify her decision. "But I hid it to protect our family's honor. For his sake as well as mine."

They shared an understanding glance. Hana knew most of what had happened. She'd stood by Etsuko and faithfully kept her silence. But now she said, "Have you stopped to think that your secrets may come out no matter what you do? There are other people alive who know. Better that your son should hear the truth from you first."

But the truth was even worse than Hana thought. Etsuko hadn't shared the whole story with her longtime confidante. She prayed that those who knew would keep the silence they'd maintained all these years. They had as much reason as she, but could she count on their discretion?

"If you don't tell him, maybe I should," Hana said.

"No!"

Etsuko grabbed Hana's arm and clutched it so tightly that Hana gasped in pain. In her eyes shone the fear that her mistress would harm her to keep her quiet. Etsuko experienced her own sudden trepidations that Hana might know more about her and Colonel Doi, Tadatoshi and his tutor, than she'd thought.

"I'm sorry," Etsuko said, releasing her hold on Hana. "You're right. I should tell him. And I will." She had no intention, but she must prevent Hana from talking. "But not yet." She lay back on the bed, feeling exhausted and ill. "This has been too much for me. I can't bear any more right now."

Relenting, Hana tucked the quilt around her. "All right. Rest awhile. I'll be here if you need anything. We'll get through this together."

Etsuko closed her eyes, but knew she would have no rest. The discovery of Tadatoshi's murder had opened a door to the past, and out of it came the winds of memory, rushing upon her like a storm.

A fierce northern wind buffeted Edo. It shook the houses, penetrated chinks in the walls, rattled bare tree branches, and swept whirlwinds of dust through the streets. After months without rain, the city was as dry as tinder. Every day, sparks from charcoal braziers ignited fires all over town. Buildings burned to the ground in an instant. Fire alarm bells rang continuously. The blue sky was obscured by swirling clouds of black smoke.

Inside the walled estate of Lord Tokugawa Naganori, cousin to the shogun, the gusts jangled wind-chimes that hung from the eaves. Etsuko and a party of other girls were gathered on the veranda, bundled in padded silk cloaks, hoods, and mittens. She was sixteen, the youngest lady-in-waiting to Lord Naganori's wife. They cheered at the antics of Lord Naganori's soldiers, who cavorted in the garden, showing off.

A soldier turned somersaults across the dry brown grass and hit a tree. Etsuko and her friends giggled. His comrades jeered. One said, "My turn!"

Tall and lithe, he balanced himself on his hands and effortlessly walked on them up to the veranda. He flipped backward and landed on his feet. As he bowed, the ladies clapped, fluttery with admiration.

"You're so lucky," one of the women whispered to Etsuko.

Etsuko was the most beautiful lady-in-waiting, envied by her friends, admired by the men. And she was engaged to be married to Doi Naokatsu, the samurai athlete, whose proud, smiling gaze focused on her.

"He's so handsome," sighed another woman.

Even better, he was a favorite of Lord Naganori's. He currently served as chief bodyguard to the lord's son Tadatoshi, but he was slated for a much higher position in the future. When Etsuko married him, her future as the wife of a rich, important man would be secure. Her parents were happy about the match they'd arranged for her, and so had Etsuko been, at first. She'd known Doi forever; his family and hers were old friends. She liked him, and she'd welcomed the prospect of having him for a husband.

Until she'd lost her heart to someone else.

Doi and his friends began a mock sword battle, vying for the ladies' attention. Etsuko slipped into the house. Drafts rattled the lattice-and-paper walls as she tiptoed through the corridors. From a room drifted Tadatoshi's voice. Etsuko peeked through the door.

Tadatoshi knelt at a table furnished with books, paper, and writing supplies. He recited a lesson from the history of Japan. He was such an odd boy that the sight of him gave Etsuko a creepy, uncomfortable feeling. He seldom spoke voluntarily, his eyes never looked straight at anyone, and he had a peculiar smile. Etsuko's gaze fixed on the man who sat beside Tadatoshi. Her breath caught.

His shaved head was turned toward his pupil. A hemp monk's robe clothed his slim body. His long, finely modeled hands toyed with his beaded wooden rosary while he listened. As if Etsuko's yearning gaze had touched him, Egen turned and saw her. His beautiful, sensitive features made Etsuko tremble inside. Her eyes met his deep, somber ones. She almost fainted.

Until Egen had come to the estate last spring, Etsuko had never been in love. The moment she'd laid eyes on him, she'd felt the sweet, exhilarating rapture. And she could tell by his expression that he'd felt it, too. The stories she'd heard, the plays she'd seen, had told the truth: Souls could meet and know in an instant that they were meant for one another.

Now Tadatoshi finished his recitation. Egen corrected his mistakes, then said, "It's time for your sword-fighting lesson. You may go."

Tadatoshi stood, bowed, and exited the room. He had a furtive, scrambling gait. He passed Etsuko without seeming to see her. She hardly noticed him. She floated toward Egen, who rose.

"Hello," he said in his quiet, gentle voice.

"Hello," she murmured.

Love imbued their slightest conversations with profound meaning. Every word spoken between them breathed passion—and despair. They both knew their love couldn't last.

"I had to see you," she said.

68

"I'm glad you came." He moved closer, and Etsuko quaked with the desire for his touch. His smile faded; worry darkened his eyes.

"What's wrong?" she asked.

"You know what."

Her engagement to Doi made a life together as impossible as did his vow of celibacy. The unfairness of their situation was something they often discussed and mourned. But Etsuko sensed more on Egen's mind. "What else?"

"I'm worried about Tadatoshi."

Jealousy stabbed Etsuko. She wanted his concern all for herself. "How can you think of him, when—"

"He's my pupil," Egen hastened to explain. "I'm responsible for him."

"Oh," Etsuko said, trying to be generous and understanding. "Why are you worried?"

"He doesn't have any playmates or seem to want any. He'd rather brood by himself. And sometimes, I swear, he's like a ghost. He disappears, and I can't find him anyplace. Then he reappears as if out of thin air. Where does he go? What's he doing? He's not normal."

Etsuko agreed, but she said, "I don't think there's much you can do."

"I suppose you're right," he said, clearly not convinced. Etsuko smiled up at him and grazed her fingers against his wrist. The worry in his eyes gave way to desire. He closed his hand around hers. "Will I see you tonight?" he asked urgently.

Etsuko nodded, breathless with anticipation.

"In our usual place?"

Footsteps coming down the passage startled them. Egen let go of Etsuko's hand. They sprang apart just as Doi appeared.

"Oh, there you are," Doi said to Etsuko. "The girls sent me to look for you."

Etsuko blushed; her heart pounded wildly. He'd almost caught them!

"Your mistress is going to the theater. You're all to accompany her, and so are some of us men." Doi beamed, glad for a party, for a chance to sit beside her during the play. Etsuko pitied him because he didn't know that her feelings toward him had changed. Doi turned to Egen. "You can come, too."

Shame filled Etsuko. He was a kind, generous man. He'd be-friended Egen, who was an outsider in this house, a gentle scholar and poet among rowdy samurai. And she and Egen were betraying him.

"Thank you," Egen said, and Etsuko could see that he felt as guilty as she did. "But I have lessons to prepare."

"Oh. Well, maybe next time." Doi said to Etsuko, "Come on, let's go."

But he hesitated, looking curiously at her, then at Egen. Etsuko winced inwardly. Did he suspect?

火

8

火

火

"Did your mother tell you anything?" Hirata asked.

"Not enough, but it was a lot more than I'd bargained for," Sano said.

He and Hirata sat in his office, eating a belated breakfast of rice gruel, fish, and pickled vegetables. Sano reluctantly described what his mother had said, ashamed to expose his ignorance about his family even to his closest friend.

Hirata, always considerate, didn't react except to nod. When Sano finished, he said, "She's given us some leads."

Thank the gods for that much, Sano thought. "The broken engagement gives Colonel Doi a possible motive for incriminating her. He's the prime suspect as far as I'm concerned. I'll call in my informants and find out what they can tell me about his doings around the time when Tadatoshi disappeared. But there's another potential witness—and maybe a suspect."

"The tutor?"

Sano nodded, spooned up the last of his gruel, and washed it down with tea. "Not only was Egen a member of Tadatoshi's household, he must have been close to the boy. Maybe he saw something or knows something about his disappearance."

"Maybe he was responsible for it," Hirata said.

"That could be," Sano said. "Tadatoshi would have trusted Egen. It would have been easy for him to kidnap the boy."

"Easier than for a lady-in-waiting," Hirata said.

Sano thought of his mother vehemently denying that the tutor was the killer, then claiming she'd barely known him. Questions interlaced with suspicions in Sano's mind. He must have another talk with her, whether she liked it or not. In the meantime, the tutor offered them a chance at salvation even if he wasn't guilty.

"Maybe Egen could refute Doi's story," Sano said.

"He should, if only to protect himself," Hirata said. "Doi accused him in addition to your mother."

"Supposing he does, it would be his word and my mother's against Doi's," Sano said, although he wondered if that would carry enough weight. Doi was a high-ranking soldier, backed by Lord Matsudaira. Sano's mother was a mere woman, vulnerable to attack by Sano's enemies. The tutor was a nobody. "But we're getting ahead of ourselves. First we have to find Egen. I want you to start looking."

"If he's still alive," Hirata said, "I'll find him."

He and Sano rose. Sano noted the quizzical expression in Hirata's eyes. Not once had Hirata asked whether Sano's mother might be guilty; he was too loyal. But he obviously wondered. So did Sano.

"In the meantime, I'm going to visit Tadatoshi's mother and sister," Sano said. "Maybe they can shed some light on the crime."

As much as he hoped that whatever they said would exonerate his mother, he feared it would dig her grave deeper.

Reiko spoke with Lieutenant Asukai in the garden, where she was watching Akiko play with the children's old nurse. "My husband has enough to do without having to search for the spy," she said, and explained how Sano's mother had been charged with murder. "I think we should handle the problem ourselves." She longed to help Sano, and there wasn't much else she could contribute.

"I'm ready and willing," Asukai said. "But how should we go about it? Have you ever unmasked a spy before?"

"No," Reiko admitted, "but let's try a little common sense. We can't watch all the people in the estate. There are too many." Sano's retainers, officials, clerks, and servants numbered in the hundreds. "And this spy will be careful not to attract attention."

"We might never catch him doing anything to betray himself," Asukai agreed.

"So we must draw him out," Reiko said.

"Good idea." Asukai regarded her with admiration, then puzzlement. "How?"

"We'll set a trap, using something that Lord Matsudaira would want as bait." Inspiration lit Reiko's brain. "I know! How about the secret diary in which my husband has listed the names and locations of all his spies?"

Asukai looked surprised. "Is there such a diary?"

"There will be."

Reiko hurried into the house to her chamber. Asukai followed. She knelt at her writing desk, lifted the lid, and pulled out a book covered in black silk. The pages were blank. She prepared ink, dipped her brush, and wrote a long list of male names as fast as she could invent them. She wrote, after each, "spy," the place where he was stationed, choosing random locales within Edo Castle, around town, inside *daimyo* estates, and among Lord Matsudaira's numerous properties; she threw in cities all over Japan.

"There," she said, closing the book.

Asukai laughed. "It would have fooled me. I'll spread the word that it exists. Where are we going to hide it?"

"We have plenty of choices," Reiko said. "This estate is riddled with secret compartments." They'd been installed by the former tenant—the onetime chamberlain Yanagisawa. So had other unusual architectural features. Masahiro had found most of them. "I know just the place." Reiko described the location, adding, "Make sure you spread that around, too."

"And then we watch to see who goes for the bait?"

"That won't be necessary," Reiko said.

Asukai nodded as he caught her meaning, then said, "Here I go, to lay down the scent for our spy."

Masahiro came in through the door as Asukai exited. "I heard that Grandma is here," he said. "Where is she?"

"In the guest room," Reiko said.

"Can I go see her?"

Both children were fond of their grandmother, Reiko knew. When Sano took them to visit her, she gave them little treats, told them stories, and never scolded them. "You can see her later," Reiko said. "She's resting now."

"Why did she come?" Masahiro said. "She hardly ever does."

Reiko didn't want to frighten him with the details, so she said, "Grandma and your father have some business to take care of together."

"Did she do it?" Masahiro asked.

"Do what?"

"The murder."

"How did you know about that?" Reiko said in dismay.

"I heard the servants talking."

Reiko sighed. There was no hiding anything from Masahiro. Even if she ordered the servants not to gossip in front of him—which she often did—he would absorb information from the air.

"Did she kill the shogun's cousin?" Masahiro persisted.

He spoke of killing in such a nonchalant manner. Reiko worried that he'd become hardened to death and violence far too young. She regretted that he'd already killed, albeit in defense of her and their family, while they'd been in Ezogashima. But she couldn't reprimand him for circumstances that weren't his fault.

"Grandma hasn't killed anyone," Reiko said. "It's all a mistake."

But for the first time she wondered if it really was.

Of course she'd always believed her mother-in-law to be a good, harmless person. Of course she was obligated to share Sano's faith that his mother was innocent. And Reiko knew too little about the crime to judge it based on facts. There was no denying, however, that the woman had lied, at least about her past. Why?

74

Reiko considered the strain that had always existed between her and her mother-in-law, which she'd previously attributed to their different social backgrounds. But now Reiko knew that wasn't the whole story. Perhaps she reminded the old woman of the young lady she herself had once been and the privileged life she'd lost. But it seemed just as likely that she'd been afraid Reiko would notice the discrepancies between her real and her supposed background and mention them to Sano.

Why conceal her background unless there was something in it that she wanted to hide?

"What's going to happen to Grandma?" Masahiro asked.

"Nothing," Reiko said. She was ashamed of her speculations about her mother-in-law. "Your father will prove she's innocent. She'll be all right."

Reiko resolved to withhold judgment at least until she'd talked to the woman herself.

The search for the tutor took Hirata to the Ueno temple district. The buildings of the minor temple to which Egen had belonged forty-three years ago had burned down during the Great Fire. The government had relocated it, and scores of other religious orders, to Ueno, on the city's outskirts. There, the fires in the temples' crematoriums couldn't threaten the town, and the smoke wouldn't offend the citizens.

Hirata rode with a few detectives up Ueno's Broad Little Road, one of many firebreaks created after the disaster. He recalled that their original purpose had been to provide bare space that would relieve overcrowding, prevent fires from spreading, and limit casualties. But land within such a big attraction as a temple district was valuable, and little empty space remained today.

Pilgrims and tourists flocked to the stalls of the marketplace that lined the road. Vendors did a thriving business in Buddhist rosaries and prayer scrolls, vegetables and fish grilled on skewers, china dolls and straw hats, sake and plum wine. Itinerant priests marched, beat drums, and juggled. Acrobats capered on a tightrope. Customers flowed to and from teahouses and brothels in the back streets.

Hirata found Egen's temple inside a small compound enclosed by a bamboo fence. A few worshippers lit incense sticks and knelt before the altar decorated with gold lotus flowers and burning candles in the main hall where Hirata approached an old priest.

"I'm looking for a monk named Egen who belonged to your order before the Great Fire," Hirata said. "He worked as a tutor to Tokugawa Tadatoshi, cousin of the shogun."

"I haven't been here that long," the priest said, "and unfortunately, the fire destroyed all our records."

"Is there anyone here who might remember Egen?"

The priest took Hirata to an elderly monk who was meditating in the sunny garden outside the dormitory. The monk was as lean and tough as a rope. He had no teeth, and his ears and nostrils were filled with tufts of gray hair, but he wore a serene, content expression. When Hirata asked him if he'd known Egen, he smiled and said, "Ah, yes. We were friends. We entered the monastery and took our vows at the same time."

Hirata thought it too good to be true that the old man had remembered so promptly. "Are you sure?"

The monk smiled. "At my age it's easier to remember what happened fifty years ago than what I had for breakfast this morning. When you get old, you'll see."

"My apologies for doubting you," Hirata said. "Can you tell me where Egen is now?"

"I'm afraid not. He left the order."

"Oh. When was that?"

"The same year as the Great Fire."

Hirata felt his hopes deflate, but he said, "When was the last time you saw him?"

"It was some twenty days after the fire." The monk's eyes chased recollections through the past. "The temple had burned down. My brothers and I had run for our lives. We tried to stay together, but we got separated. When the fire finally went out, I walked through the ruins, looking for the others. That was the only way to find anyone."

Hirata remembered his parents talking about the fire's aftermath and the thousands of people roaming the city in search of lost loved ones. Many of his family's relatives had died.

"I managed to find eight of my comrades. We were all that was left of the fifty monks and priests from our temple," the monk said sadly. "By that time, the *bakufu* had begun putting up tents for everyone who'd lost their homes."

A city of tents had grown up in the ashes of the great capital. They'd been hurriedly stitched together from any fabric available—quilts, kimonos, canopies. Hirata saw it in his imagination, a sea of patchwork.

"People rigged up poles beside their tents and flew banners with their family names or crests," the monk continued. "We put up the name of our temple, hoping our brothers would come. The only one who did was Egen. We were overjoyed to see him. We wanted him to stay with us and help us rebuild the temple. But he wouldn't. He said he was leaving the order, leaving Edo."

"Did he give a reason?" Hirata asked.

"He would only say that something had happened," the monk said. "We asked him what, but he wouldn't tell us."

Hirata wondered if his reason had anything to do with Tadatoshi's disappearance and murder. "Where did he go?"

"I don't know. I don't think he had a definite place in mind."

Hirata envisioned the highways, the cities along them, and the villages off branch roads winding through mountains and forests. Even in this rigidly governed land, a man could get lost.

"Did you ever see Egen again?" Hirata said.

"No."

"Have you heard from him since?"

"Not a word."

Discouragement filled Hirata, but he couldn't give up. "Do you know of anyone who might have information about Egen?"

"I'm sorry, I don't."

"How old would he be now?"

"About the same age as me. I am sixty-four."

Hirata thanked the monk, who wished him good luck on his search. When he joined his men outside the temple, he said, "We've got a big manhunt on our hands. Arai-*san*, organize troops to ride along the highways and post notices asking for information about Egen."

Arai looked doubtful. "There's a lot of area to cover."

"We'll cover it as best we can," Hirata said. "If we're lucky, Egen is still alive and he'll turn up."

If not, Sano and his mother might be doomed.

"And we can always hope that Egen has returned to Edo," Hirata said. The city was a magnet for all sorts of people, even those with reason to stay away. Maybe Egen had decided that after all this time, it was safe to come back even if he was responsible for Tadatoshi's murder. "Inoue-*san*, you'll help me mount a search in the city. We'll start by checking the temples in case Egen has joined another order."

As Hirata rode back toward town, he recalled his conversation with Midori. Working day and night for the foreseeable future wasn't the best way to fix their marriage. And the odds were his search for Egen would fail. The tutor was one grain of rice among millions.

9

As Sano rode through the city with his entourage, he felt as if he were traveling into the past. He was about to meet people his mother had known before his birth, who knew things about her that he didn't. He had an uncomfortable sense that he was digging up his own history as well as investigating a crime. He wasn't the same man he'd been yesterday, oblivious to the trouble sleeping under the earth with Tadatoshi's skeleton. And the city around him wasn't the same city as before the Great Fire.

Gray and brown ceramic tiles covered the roofs of the buildings in the Nihonbashi merchant district. Thatch had been outlawed since the fire; it was too combustible. Sano passed through a gate and the square, open space around it, created to prevent people from being trapped while escaping fires. But these changes were superficial compared to the city's wide-scale, profound transformation.

After the Great Fire, a legion of surveyors, engineers, and builders had swarmed over the ruins. They'd resurrected a new, improved Edo. Rearrangement had eased overcrowding and prevented fires from spreading. Tokugawa branch families had moved their estates outside Edo Castle; *daimyo* clans relocated farther from it. The lesser warrior class had moved into the western and southern suburbs. Peasants had gone farther west and colonized new villages; merchants and artisans had been dispersed to Shiba and Asakusa districts. The metropolis grew to more than double its previous size. Many of the new quarters were marshy, at inconvenient distances from the city center, and unpopular, but relocation was mandatory. The alternative for people who resisted was being convicted of arson and burned to death—punishment for fires that would result if they didn't go.

Sano and his men traversed the Ryōgoku Bridge, built to encourage settlement on the east bank of the Sumida River. Tadatoshi's mother and sister lived in Fukagawa, in one of many villas built after the Great Fire. Noble families now usually had three different residences—an "Upper House" near Edo Castle, for the lord, his family, and his retainers; a "Middle House," farther away from the castle, for an heir or retired lord; and a "Lower House," a villa in the suburbs, for evacuation during emergencies or for clan members not needed in town. The villa at which Sano and his men stopped was located in a quiet enclave of samurai residences amid the townspeople's houses and markets. Guards greeted Sano and his men, took charge of their horses. Ushered inside, Sano found himself in a reception room quaintly decorated with a mural of dragonflies and frogs on a lily pond. Servants bustled off to fetch the women.

They returned carrying Lady Ateki, a minute woman more than eighty years old, her bones as fragile as a bird's under her gray kimono. Her nose was shaped like a beak, her sparse gray hair tied in a feathery knot. When the servants gently settled her on cushions, she resembled a dove on a nest. Her daughter sat protectively beside her. Oigimi wore a dark brown kimono, and a black scarf shrouded her head. She kept her face turned to her left, toward her mother, away from Sano.

Tea was offered, politely refused then accepted, and served. Lady Ateki addressed Sano: "Did His Excellency the shogun Tokugawa Ietsuna send you?" Her quiet voice sounded like paper crumpling. The wrinkles in her face drooped downward, giving her a permanently mournful expression.

"No," Sano said. "Unfortunately, he's been dead twenty years. Tokugawa Tsunayoshi is shogun now."

"Dear me, how time rushes by." Lady Ateki sighed. "Who did they say you were, young man? Chamberlain Yanagisawa?"

"No, Mother." Impatience tinged Oigimi's voice. She was in her fifties. Thick white rice powder covered gaunt, plain features on the side of her face that Sano could see. "His name is Sano. You're thinking of his predecessor."

At least Yanagisawa had held office more recently than the past shogun, Sano thought. But if Lady Ateki was this confused, the interview was off to a bad start.

"Oh. Very well," Lady Ateki said. "What brings you here, Chamberlain Sano?"

Sano now faced a task more difficult than coping with an old woman's foggy memory. He had to break disturbing news. "It's about your son Tadatoshi."

Alert and trembling, she leaned toward Sano, one hand on her heart, the other outstretched to him. "Has he been found?"

She had clearly never given up hope that Tadatoshi was alive. Sano hated to disappoint her. He glanced at her daughter, to see how she'd reacted to the mention of Tadatoshi, and did a double take.

Oigimi had turned slightly in his direction. The left side of her face was twisted, seamed, and paralyzed with scar tissue under her makeup. Her lips formed a half grimace. Her left eye was a dead gray orb. Sano realized that she was a living casualty of the Great Fire.

Consternation showed on the intact right side of her face. Whether it was in response to news about her brother or because she'd seen Sano's instinctive revulsion to the ravages of the fire, Sano couldn't tell. She quickly turned away, pulling the scarf over the wreckage.

"I'm sorry to say it was Tadatoshi's remains that were found," Sano said. "He died not long after he disappeared."

"Oh." Lady Ateki's animation faded. "I suppose it was foolish to believe Tadatoshi could still be alive. I suppose I've known all along that he was dead."

"Of course he's dead, Mother." Oigimi's voice sounded unnecessarily harsh. "If he weren't, he'd have come back by now."

"Yes, you're right," Lady Ateki said, and Sano didn't miss the frostiness of her tone. Oigimi might be her loyal protector, but their relationship wasn't all peace and harmony. She turned to Sano. "How was Tadatoshi found?"

Sano explained about the storm near the shrine, the fallen tree, the grave exposed.

"How on earth did he get there?" she said, bewildered.

"Not by himself, obviously," Oigimi said. "What Chamberlain Sano is trying to say is that Tadatoshi was murdered."

"Murdered?" Lady Ateki gaped at Sano. Her hands flew to her face. Her fingers trailed down her cheeks, pulling them farther downward. "But who would kill my son?"

"I was hoping you could tell me. I'm investigating his murder, on behalf of the shogun."

Oigimi said, "Forgive my presumption, but I'd have thought the shogun had more important things to do than bother about Tadatoshi." She had the traditional outspokenness of older women, despite her disfigurement. "Whatever happened to him happened long ago." She eyed Sano suspiciously. "Have you a personal interest in this, may I ask?"

Sano felt he owed these women honesty. "Yes. My mother has been accused of kidnapping and killing Tadatoshi."

Lady Ateki looked too dazed to speak. Oigimi threw Sano a sidelong, puzzled glance and said, "Who is your mother?"

"Her name is Etsuko," Sano said. "She was a lady-in-waiting to your mother. Do you remember her?"

Recognition dawned on Lady Ateki's face. "Oh! That pretty young girl." She smiled. "I was very fond of her."

"You're Etsuko's son?" Oigimi said in surprise.

"I always wondered what became of Etsuko," Lady Ateki said. "She left us very suddenly."

Sano saw a chance to fill in some of the gaps in his mother's story. "When did she leave?"

"It was soon after the Great Fire," Lady Ateki said.

"What was the reason?" Sano asked.

Lady Ateki squinted in an effort to bring the past into focus. "All I remember is that she went home to live with her parents."

Her parents—the grandparents Sano had never met. She'd told him they'd died in the fire.

"I was sad but willing to let her go," Lady Ateki said. "My husband was dead, his estate had burned down. Some relatives took me in. We lived in their summer villa in the hills, very crowded. There wouldn't have been room for Etsuko."

"I never knew why she went," Oigimi said, "but I had other things to worry about at the time." Sano interpreted the bitterness in her voice to mean she'd been suffering from the burns, which must have been painful.

Yet another mystery had arisen for Sano to solve. "Did you ever hear from Etsuko again?" he asked Lady Ateki.

"No, I didn't."

"It was as if she'd vanished off the earth," Oigimi said.

Was it a coincidence that she'd vanished from their lives shortly after Tadatoshi had? Uneasiness crept through Sano. How had his mother spent the months after she'd left them and before she'd married his father? He wondered whether she would tell him if he asked. "Did you have any suspicion that she was involved in Tadatoshi's disappearance?"

"None at all." Oigimi sounded incredulous at the idea. "I thought he'd died in the fire."

"Dear me, of course not," Lady Ateki said. "Etsuko was a good girl. She could never have hurt anyone."

"I agree." Oigimi thought a moment, then said, "May I ask who accused Etsuko?"

"It was Doi Naokatsu," Sano said.

"This is certainly a day for names from the past," Lady Ateki said. "I remember Doi. He was my son's bodyguard."

"He was also Etsuko's fiancé," said Oigimi. "I always wondered why they never married."

Ignoring her hint for information he didn't have, Sano said, "Have you any idea why he would accuse her?"

"None."

"I remember how upset Doi was after Tadatoshi disappeared," Lady Ateki said. "He fell on his knees and apologized to me for not being able to find him. He cried and begged my forgiveness. He was ready to commit seppuku."

Too bad he hadn't, Sano thought. Doi's ritual suicide would have saved a lot of trouble.

"But I was sure Tadatoshi was alive," Lady Ateki said. "I told Doi that he must be ready to serve him when he came back."

Sano wondered if Doi's behavior meant he'd felt guilty about more than failing in his duty. "Do you think Doi could have killed Tadatoshi?"

Lady Ateki exclaimed, "Oh, no. He was devoted to my son."

"The idea of him kidnapping my brother is ridiculous," Oigimi said. "But so is the idea that Etsuko did, and not just because she was too good. Tadatoshi wasn't a baby who could have been easily carried off and killed. He was strong enough to put up a fight. How does Doi say that Etsuko managed to kidnap him?"

"He says she had help," Sano said, "from Tadatoshi's tutor."

The women sat motionless, stunned by this news on top of the rest. At last Lady Ateki said, "I suppose Tadatoshi did have a tutor. Who was he?"

"That monk," Oigimi said impatiently. "His name was Egen."

"Oh. Oh, yes, I remember now."

"I didn't know him at all, but he must have been a decent person or my father wouldn't have hired him," Oigimi told Sano. "Have you asked him if he did it?"

"Not yet," Sano said. "I'm looking for him. Do you know where he is?"

Lady Ateki shook her head. Oigimi said, "We haven't seen him in all these years. He left after the fire."

Perhaps not just because he'd lost his pupil, Sano thought. Maybe Egen had been involved in a kidnapping gone bad. Sano hoped Hirata was making progress toward finding him. For now, Sano needed suspects closer at hand. "Do you know of anyone who would have wanted Tadatoshi dead?"

Mother turned to daughter. Sano saw astonishment in both their profiles. Lady Ateki said, "Could it be?" Oigimi said, "Of course. We should have suspected him ages ago."

"Who?" Sano said.

"Tokugawa Nobunaga." Lady Ateki explained, "He was my husband's brother."

"Why might he have killed Tadatoshi?" Sano said.

"He wanted his son to be shogun," Oigimi said. "Tadatoshi was ahead of his son in the line of succession. With Tadatoshi gone, his son moved up a step."

Political ambition had led to many murders, but Sano saw cause for doubt in this case. "Tadatoshi was far down the line. Getting rid of him wouldn't have moved his cousin much closer to the front."

"My husband and his brother had been rivals since childhood," Lady Ateki said. "His brother was very jealous. He couldn't bear to have my husband ahead of him in anything."

"And we once saw him almost kill Tadatoshi," Oigimi said.

"When was this?" Sano said, intrigued.

"Tadatoshi must have been about twelve years old," Lady Ateki said. "It happened at our archery range. My brother-in-law shot an arrow. It hit the wall right beside Tadatoshi. And he wasn't standing anywhere near the targets."

"My uncle said it was an accident," Oigimi said scornfully.

"After that, my husband kept our son away from his brother," Lady Ateki said, "but he couldn't watch Tadatoshi all the time."

Especially when Tadatoshi wandered off, Sano thought. Maybe, on the day of his death, he'd had the bad luck to meet up with his jealous, homicidal uncle. "Where was your brother-in-law when Tadatoshi disappeared?"

"I don't know," Lady Ateki said. "I suppose I was too upset to care. My husband and so many other people had died in the fire. My son was missing, and I had to take care of my daughter."

"Later, I heard Uncle talk about what he did during the fire," Oigimi said. "He and his retainers and servants put wet quilts on the roof of his house, to protect it from the fire. It burned down anyway. They barely managed to get to the hills before the fire blocked the roads."

He could have happened onto Tadatoshi near the shrine and seen an opportunity sent from heaven. "Where is he now?" Sano asked.

"He's been dead more than ten years," Oigimi said.

"And his son?"

"He died last year."

"Can you think of anyone else who might have killed Tadatoshi?" Sano asked.

Neither woman could. Sano thanked them for their cooperation and rose. Lady Ateki said, "Many thanks for telling me about my son, Honorable Chamberlain. At least I can stop wondering what happened to him. I hope you find his murderer."

"I'll do my best," Sano promised.

He joined Marume, Fukida, and his entourage outside the mansion. "Anything good?" Marume asked.

As they mounted their horses and rode away, Sano related what the women had told him. "Two witnesses to my mother's good character and a new suspect. Not bad for one interview."

"It would be better if Tadatoshi's uncle were still alive," Fukida said, "but his death doesn't let him off the hook."

"We can't have everything," Sano said. His mood had brightened; for the first time since his mother's arrest, things were looking up. "And my favorite suspect is still alive."

"Shall we pay Colonel Doi a visit?" Fukida said.

"There's not much point," Sano said. "What would he say except to deny he's guilty and heap more slander on my mother? I have a better source of information about him. And I've just had an idea that I want to follow up, at home."

10

Reiko sat in the room across the hall from the guest chamber. She waited until she saw Hana come out of the chamber and scurry down the passage, leaving Sano's mother alone. Then Reiko picked up a tray that held a dish of pink cakes filled with sweet chestnut paste, her own favorite treat. She crossed the hall, quietly opened the door to the chamber, and entered.

Her mother-in-law was lying in bed, but when she noticed Reiko, she sat up. She awkwardly smoothed her rumpled gray hair and cotton robe. Her face showed alarm.

"Excuse me for disturbing you, Honorable Mother-in-law." Reiko knelt and bowed. "I wanted to see how you are."

"Much better, thank you," the old woman murmured, her eyes downcast, avoiding Reiko's gaze.

"I'm relieved to hear that."

Reiko covertly studied her mother-in-law. In the light of what Sano had told her, she'd expected Etsuko to look different, to have gained stature befitting her samurai heritage. But Etsuko looked as ordinary as ever, although far from well. The only change was Etsuko's manner toward Reiko. Usually timid, it now resonated with fright.

Wondering why, seeking to put Etsuko at ease, Reiko said, "I brought you some cakes," and set the tray beside the bed.

"Thank you. You're very kind. I'm sorry to impose on you." Meek and contrite, Etsuko didn't touch the food. She waited a moment, as if for Reiko to leave. When Reiko stayed put, she said, "You needn't bother yourself with me. I'm sure you have more important things to do . . . ?"

Reiko understood that her mother-in-law wanted to get rid of her, but she didn't take the hint. "It's no bother. I'm glad to have you with us."

"I apologize for causing you so such trouble, Honorable Daughter-in-law," Etsuko said humbly. "I beg your forgiveness."

"There's no need to apologize, nothing to forgive." Yet Reiko experienced a stab of ill feeling toward Etsuko. The woman was, however inadvertently, the source of a serious threat to their whole family. Reiko thought of other wives she knew, whose mothers-in-law hated and insulted them, beat them and threw things at them. Those problems seemed trivial compared to Reiko's, a mother-in-law who was accused of murdering a Tokugawa clan member, who could bring destruction upon all her kin.

Then Reiko felt ashamed of resenting Etsuko. The woman had always treated Reiko with respect, if not affection. She'd never done any ill as far as Reiko had firsthand knowledge to believe. Furthermore, she'd not deliberately endangered Reiko's family. Lord Matsudaira was using Etsuko against Sano. If he didn't have her, he would find some other weapon. Reiko pitied Etsuko, and she owed Etsuko all the aid she could give. That was her duty as a daughter-in-law, and in her own best interest.

She also owed Etsuko the benefit of doubt regarding the murder.

"Since you're here, I welcome the opportunity to visit with you," Reiko said, "even though it's under difficult circumstances."

". . . Yes."

This one word conveyed how averse Etsuko was to Reiko's company and her acceptance of the fact that a guest must bow to her hostess's wishes.

"My husband told me what happened," Reiko began cautiously.

She saw Etsuko fold her arms, shrink in bed. "I understand why you might not want to talk about it, but maybe I can help."

Etsuko said nothing; she fidgeted with her bedcovers. Reiko wondered whether her mother-in-law knew that she helped Sano with his investigations. She'd never thought to ask. Reiko also wondered if Etsuko was aware of her suspicions, for she sensed that the woman was more intelligent than she'd previously thought.

"Have you remembered anything else since you talked to my husband?" Reiko asked. Sano hadn't told her what he'd learned from his mother, but she would find out later, and she mustn't waste time going over ground he'd already covered.

"No," Etsuko murmured.

"Some things may be easier discussed between women, and between us rather than a mother and a son," Reiko encouraged.

She'd hoped that Etsuko would talk about her family background, but Etsuko didn't answer. And Reiko didn't want to force the issue, lest she further strain their relations.

Changing tack, Reiko said, "What would help my husband clear your name is proof that you weren't at the shrine near the time when Tadatoshi died. Can you think of anyone who can testify that you were someplace else?"

"There's no one," Etsuko said in a barely audible voice.

Did that mean she'd been alone someplace else, without witnesses to observe her, or that she had indeed been at the shrine? Reiko couldn't help wondering. But the lack of an alibi didn't necessarily mean Etsuko was guilty.

"Is there anything at all you can remember that might help my husband prove you're innocent?"

"No," Etsuko whispered.

"I see." Reiko swallowed frustration. Her children's fate depended on her mother-in-law's; the least Etsuko could do was try harder to cooperate. "Is there anything that might get you in more trouble if it became known, that my husband should be prepared to counteract?"

". . . No."

Etsuko's speech was often hesitant, but this time Reiko noticed that she'd delayed answering for a beat longer than normal. It could mean that Etsuko had paused to think, in the hope of recalling a forgotten fact, but it might mean that she was very well aware of some damning evidence that could resurface. But whatever the truth, Reiko realized that her mother-in-law was a tougher nut to crack than other suspects she'd met. Etsuko had shown her samurai blood, a hard core of resolve wrapped in her humble guise.

Yet Reiko still pitied Etsuko and still hoped desperately to exonerate her. This was no ordinary investigation. There would be no rewards for unmasking this suspect as a criminal.

Now Etsuko looked fatigued and weak. Reiko said, "Well, then, perhaps you'd better rest. We can talk some more later." She counseled herself to postpone judgment about Etsuko, at least until more facts came to light.

Sano, Marume, and Fukida ducked under the blue curtain that hung across the entrance of a dingy public bathhouse. They paid coins to the attendant, accepted towels and bags of rice bran soap, and strode into a room enclosed by mildewed walls, where naked people scrubbed and poured buckets of water over themselves or lounged in the sunken tub amid clouds of steam. Edo bathhouses came in various types. Some were for families who didn't have space for tubs at home. In others, illegal prostitutes of either sex serviced male customers. This one, Sano noted, appeared to be a haunt of disreputable men.

As he and his comrades walked among the bathers, he saw *rōnin* with black stubble on their faces and shaved crowns; he passed gangsters covered with tattoos. Sano took care not to look too closely at anyone while he sought the man he'd come to find. A bathhouse like this was ostensibly neutral territory in which the patrons had a tacit agreement to do one another no harm, but they didn't always stick to the agreement. Surly gazes flicked over Sano. He heard his name spoken quietly and saw Toda Ikkyu, master spy for the *metsuke*—the Tokugawa intelligence service—sitting in the tub. At least Sano thought it was Toda; the spy had such a nondescript face, perfectly suited to his work. Although they'd known each other more than ten years, Sano never recognized Toda at first glance.

"Looking for me?" Toda said.

The world-weary voice and expression were familiar. Sano crouched and said, "Your people told me I could find you here. I don't suppose you came for the pleasure of it?"

Toda smiled blandly. "Professional pleasure, one might say. Thank you for not storming in with your whole entourage. That would have foiled my operation."

Sano and his men had come in garments without identifying crests, and they'd left his entourage down the street. While Marume and Fukida kept a covert watch on the other bathers, Sano said to Toda, "Who are you after?"

"Rebels, as usual," Toda said. "In particular, the gang that attacked a squadron of Lord Matsudaira's troops on the highway last month."

Lord Matsudaira employed the *metsuke* to hunt down his enemies. So did Sano. The *metsuke* played both sides of their rivalry, ensuring its own survival no matter which ultimately won. Toda had weathered many political storms, and Sano would bet on him to emerge unscathed from this latest.

"We know who they are," Toda said, "and we got a tip that they like to meet here. We're waiting for them to show."

"We?" Sano said.

"My colleagues are here with me. Don't bother looking around—you won't spot them. Neither will our targets." Toda asked, "What are you after?"

"Information."

Sano had no qualms about seeking it from this spy who helped maintain his enemy in power. Both Sano and Lord Matsudaira trusted Toda because he favored neither. Toda did his best for them both, for his own good.

"About Colonel Doi?" Toda said.

"How did you know?"

"If I were in your position, I'd go after Doi, too. He's the one who's got you and your mother in jeopardy. Take him down, and there's a big problem solved."

"So what can you tell me?" Sano said.

"Doi Naokatsu, member of a minor hereditary Tokugawa vassal clan. His father was an accountant to Tokugawa Naganori, father of Tadatoshi. The young Doi was a cut above average from the start, excelled at the martial arts, clever, too. He was appointed chief bodyguard to Tadatoshi at age fifteen, when ordinary samurai are just foot soldiers at the bottom of the ranks. After the Great Fire, with Tadatoshi's father dead and Tadatoshi presumed to be, most of their retainers became *rōnin*."

They would have numbered among hordes of other new masterless samurai. The fire had ravaged military-class residences inside the Tokiwabashi and Kajibashi gates. Many Tokugawa vassals who'd had their own retainers had died or lost everything, leaving the retainers homeless and impoverished.

"All those new *rōnin* caused trouble," Sano remembered. "They banded together in gangs that marauded through the areas that hadn't burned. They looted shops and squatted in abandoned houses."

Many other survivors had done the same. The fire had virtually wiped out Edo's food supply as well as its housing and created a mass famine. Thousands of people who hadn't been killed by the fire had died of starvation.

"Doi made the best of a bad deal," said Toda. "He volunteered his services to the shogun's army, which was struggling to mount a relief effort. He led a brigade that took food to the people. He ferried rice bales across the river, cooked stew with his own hands, and fought off gangs that tried to steal the food. He became a sort of hero."

The fire had created many heroes who'd risen to the challenge of helping their fellow man. That was the bright side of a disaster. But although Sano could admire Doi, he wondered if the man's efforts had been motivated by something besides valor, and there was a gap in the story.

"Do you have any information about what Doi did during the fire?" Sano asked. "Or about his relationship with Tadatoshi?"

"No." Toda watched the door while people came and went. "During the fire and for quite a while afterward, the *metsuke* wasn't functioning as usual. Neither was the rest of the government. There was utter chaos. And before the fire, we didn't bother watching Doi."

"He was pretty much a nobody," Sano supposed.

Toda nodded. "But after the fire, his accomplishments caught the eye of Lord Matsudaira's father, who took him in. Doi went to work at the Matsudaira provincial estate, as a guard captain. Before he was thirty, he was manager of the estate. Later he came back to Edo and joined the current Lord Matsudaira's inner circle of command."

"Did he ever marry?" Sano asked, thinking of his mother's broken engagement with Doi.

"Yes. His wife is a cousin of Lord Matsudaira's."

She'd been a much better match than Sano's mother. Her connection with Lord Matsudaira had helped Doi further his ambitions. It looked as though Doi had broken the engagement because he'd wanted a more socially advantageous marriage.

"Any children?" Sano asked.

"Two sons and a daughter. The sons are both high-ranking officers in Lord Matsudaira's army. The daughter married into the rich and powerful Niu *daimyo* clan. Doi has twelve grandchildren, all slated for great things."

Doi couldn't complain about how his life had turned out. Sano's theory that Doi had accused his mother because he had a grudge against her was losing ground fast.

"Doi had his latest triumph in the war against the former chamberlain, Yanagisawa," Toda said. "His regiment led the Matsudaira army in number of enemy troops killed."

His career seemed one of the most laudable that Sano had ever heard of, his reputation spotless. "Hasn't Doi ever been in trouble?"

"Not to our knowledge. He doesn't gamble, whore, or drink too much. We've never smelled a whiff of corruption." Toda smiled, rueful yet amused by Sano's disappointment. "I'm sorry. It seems I've put you right back where you started."

With only one visible reason for Doi's accusation—the man's

allegiance to Lord Matsudaira. "Well, I don't intend to stay there," Sano said. "I'm going to do my own checking into Doi."

The *metsuke* didn't know everything, and Toda had admitted that the Great Fire had temporarily put them out of business. Their lapse had created a chance for people to do as they pleased, unobserved. Sano meant to shine a light into that dark havoc in which Tadatoshi had met his death. Sano was certain he would see Doi there with a hand in the murder.

"Good luck," Toda said.

Suddenly he tensed. Sano looked at four men who'd just walked in the door. They were *rōnin,* their faces and clothes worn rough by hardship. Toda put his fingers to his lips and whistled. The loud, shrill noise vibrated the steamy air, echoed off the walls. The *rōnin* froze. Nine bathers erupted from the tub. In a tumult of dripping, naked bodies, they assaulted the *rōnin,* who didn't even have time to draw their swords. Sano, his comrades, and the other bathers watched in amazement as fists flew, limbs thrashed, and bodies thudded. In a mere instant the four rebels were wrestled into submission.

"Good work," Sano said.

Toda smiled, watching his colleagues march the rebels out the door. "Is there anything else I can do for you?"

A thought nudged Sano. "Have you heard any news about Yanagisawa?"

"He's still wasting away on Hachijo Island, according to reports from the officials." Interest animated the smooth, opaque surface of Toda's eyes. "Why do you ask?"

Sano felt his suspicions dwindle. If there was any cause for them, Toda of all people should know. "Just curious."

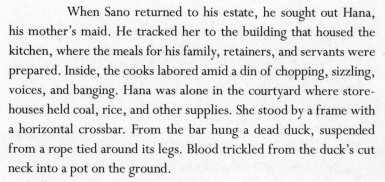

11

When Sano returned to his estate, he sought out Hana, his mother's maid. He tracked her to the building that housed the kitchen, where the meals for his family, retainers, and servants were prepared. Inside, the cooks labored amid a din of chopping, sizzling, voices, and banging. Hana was alone in the courtyard where storehouses held coal, rice, and other supplies. She stood by a frame with a horizontal crossbar. From the bar hung a dead duck, suspended from a rope tied around its legs. Blood trickled from the duck's cut neck into a pot on the ground.

"What are you doing?" Sano asked.

"Making duck stew," Hana said, "for your mother. To restore her strength."

The Buddhist religion outlawed killing animals and eating meat, but made an exception for medical reasons. Hana must have sent for the duck from Edo's wild-game market.

"How is my mother?" Sano asked.

"She's asleep," Hana said. "I hope you aren't going to bother her with more questions. She needs rest."

"I won't bother her," Sano said. At least not yet. "It's you I want to talk to."

"All right." Hana spoke in the same irritated but indulgent manner as when Sano had pestered her during his childhood. The last drips of blood fell from the duck. She untied it. Holding it by the legs, she plunged it into a pot of water that boiled on a hearth.

"How long have you been my mother's maid?" Sano asked.

"I was with her when you were little." Hana swirled the duck in the boiling water. "Don't you remember?"

"Of course." Sano waved away the steam, which smelled of wet feathers. But he knew as little about Hana's past as his mother's. Hana had always been there, taken for granted; he'd never imagined her as a person with a life apart from his. "Were you with her before she married my father?"

"Yes." Hana's resigned, glum air said she'd expected an interrogation along these lines. She pulled the duck out of the pot. It was naked, the feathers scalded off, bits of down clinging to its dimpled pink skin. "Since she was a child."

Sano asked the questions that had been foremost in his mind all day: "Why did she marry my father? Why didn't she marry Colonel Doi?"

Hana rinsed the duck in cold water. She shook her head.

"Do you mean you don't know? Or you just won't tell me?"

"It's not my place," Hana said, thumping the duck onto a chopping board.

Sano was hurt and frustrated by her and his mother's insistence on keeping him in the dark. "Not even to save her life? Any information about that time could help me prove that she didn't kill Tadatoshi and find out who did."

"Her broken engagement had nothing to do with the murder," Hana said stubbornly as she took up a sharp knife. "Neither did her marriage to your father."

"Let me be the judge of that."

Hana clamped her mouth so tightly shut that it looked like a walnut, wrinkled around the slit, tough to crack.

"Maybe you don't understand how much trouble my mother is in," Sano said. "If I can't prove she's innocent, she'll be executed."

"I do understand." The fear in Hana's eyes said she did.

"She needs your help."

Hana expertly slit the duck's belly. "Has she ever told you how we met?" Sano shook his head. "My parents were servants to a family in town. They died when I was ten. I became a beggar. One day I was outside a food-stall in town, eating scraps that people had dropped on the dirt. Along came some rich samurai girls in palanquins. They laughed at me." Hana plunged her hands into the duck and tore out glistening, pungent red entrails.

"One of the girls got out of her palanquin. It was your mother. She ordered her attendants to buy me a bowl of noodles. She kept me company while I ate, and she asked me about myself. When she found out I was an orphan, she took me home with her. Her parents said I was dirty and disgusting, but she insisted on keeping me. They finally gave in. She saved my life."

Sano was surprised as well as moved by this tale, more astonished by his mother's backbone than by her compassion. He'd never known her to stand up for anything. He began to realize where he'd gotten his own tendency to champion the underdog. But what had changed her? Was it only her marriage to his father, who'd been a strict, traditional, authoritative husband?

"Now I'll do anything to save her life," Hana said with passionate conviction.

"Anything but tell the whole truth," Sano observed.

"Anything that will help her. Not telling old tales that won't do her any good."

"Let's try another question," Sano said. "Were you with my mother when she was a lady-in-waiting at Tadatoshi's house?"

"Yes." Hana flung intestines into a bucket, saved the deep red liver and heart.

"Then you knew the people there."

"I was just a maid."

Servants knew their superiors better than most other folks did, and Hana was a shrewd observer. As a child Sano had been amazed at how she'd always known everything that went on in their neighborhood. "Who could have kidnapped Tadatoshi and killed him?"

"Not your mother. I swear."

"I agree, but our opinion isn't good enough. Can you remember what happened in that estate the day Tadatoshi disappeared?"

"The last time I saw him was the day the Great Fire started. We'd all heard about the fire, and his father decided we should go across the river. Everyone was rushing to get ready. But not Tadatoshi. He just hung around.

"Your mother and I packed some things to take with us. We didn't know how long we would be gone. It was hard to decide what to bring and squeeze it into small bundles that we could carry." As she washed the gutted duck, Hana seemed to get lost in the past. "That was when we heard that Tadatoshi was missing. His sister told us." Hana's memory drifted forward. "Oigimi was burned very badly in the fire. She almost died."

"I gathered that when I met her today," Sano said. "She still has scars."

"I heard she never married," Hana said. "She's had a hard, lonely life. But when she was young, she was a very pretty girl. Still, she's lucky to be alive at all. Anyway, her father said everyone had to look for Tadatoshi. Your mother and I helped search the estate. When nobody found him there, his father sent us all outside to look. If we had to scour the whole city, then so be it—we weren't leaving without his son." Hana's expression turned grim. "We never left. Everyone from his estate was trapped by the fire, inside the city. Almost everyone died, all for the sake of one boy."

His household might have escaped the fire had Tadatoshi not disappeared. If he'd been kidnapped, not gone off voluntarily, those deaths weren't his fault. But Sano wondered if they were the motive for Tadatoshi's murder.

"There were crowds in the streets, running from the fire," Hana said. "Your mother and I got separated from the other people from the estate, but we managed to stay together. After the fire, we went back to the estate. It had burned down. But we found your mother's parents and moved in with them. Their house was all right. They lived in Asakusa, which was countryside far away from town back then."

Here was another fact about the grandparents Sano had never known. "When I was young, were they still alive?"

"Your grandfather died when you were nine. Your grandmother a few years later."

Sano suddenly remembered two occasions somewhere around those times, when he'd found his mother weeping. She'd refused to say why. Now he realized that she must have heard about her parents' deaths. "Why didn't I ever meet them? Why did she pretend they'd died before I was born?"

"That's not for me to say. It has nothing to do with the murder. Forget it." Impatient, Hana flung the duck on the chopping board. "What I'm trying to tell you is that your mother didn't have the chance to kidnap or kill that boy." She grasped Sano's hand. He had another sudden memory from his childhood, of teasing a horse and Hana snatching his hand away before he could be bitten. "I was with her the whole time."

Her gaze held Sano's, bright and fierce and unblinking. Sano didn't have to wonder if Hana had told the whole truth; he knew she hadn't. He knew she was doing it for the noblest motive, to protect his mother . . . or was she?

Sano looked down at her hand, locked around his. There was blood from the duck under her fingernails. Maybe she knew, for the best reason of all, that his mother hadn't killed Tadatoshi. The idea seemed ludicrous, yet not beyond possibility.

For now Sano said, "How well did you know Colonel Doi?"

Hana paused before replying. Her eyes gleamed and she smiled, as if at a sudden recollection, or inspiration. "Well enough to know he didn't get along with his master."

It must have been obvious to her that Sano was fishing for that answer, and he couldn't complain because she'd taken the bait suspiciously fast. "What gave you that idea?"

"I overheard Doi and Tadatoshi arguing," Hana said.

"When was this?"

"A few days before the fire." Hana picked up a cleaver.

"About what?" Sano asked.

"I don't know," Hana said. "I came in at the end. But I heard Doi say, 'If you ever do that again, I'll kill you.'"

Here at last was evidence against Doi. Not that Sano wasn't pleased, but he said, "Are you sure that's what you heard?"

Hana began to chop. Whack followed expert whack. Apart came the duck's carcass. "I'm sure."

Sano eyed Hana quizzically. "You remember a snatch of conversation from forty-three years ago."

"A samurai threatening to kill his master isn't something you see every day," Hana said. "It stuck in my mind."

"How convenient that it should pop up now."

"Well, it did," Hana insisted. "That's what Doi said. And I'll swear to it in front of the shogun." She laid down her cleaver beside the neatly dismembered duck.

Hirata entered the kitchen compound and called, "Sano-*san*, the shogun is here to see you."

"The shogun?" Sano was surprised, not just because Hana's mention of the shogun had coincided with his arrival. "Here?" The shogun rarely came to visit. Sano couldn't remember the last time. "What for?"

"He didn't say, but we'd better not keep him waiting."

The shogun sat on the dais in the reception room, with Yoritomo. Servants fanned up fires in charcoal braziers and positioned lacquer screens to shield him from cold drafts. Sano knelt on the floor and bowed, relegated to the subordinate position in his own house. Hirata followed suit. "Welcome, Your Excellency," Sano said.

"Greetings," the shogun said, as casually as if he visited every day.

Yoritomo, a frequent visitor, looked uncomfortable, his handsome face tense. He murmured a greeting.

"May I offer you some refreshments?" Sano said.

Refreshments were politely refused, offered again, and accepted. Servants laid out enough food for a banquet. As everyone sipped tea and the shogun and Yoritomo picked at sashimi, cakes, and dumplings, Sano said, "May I ask what brings you here, Your Excellency?"

"I wanted to talk to you. Away from my cousin." The shogun glanced around nervously, as if Lord Matsudaira might be lurking nearby.

Sano was glad not to have Lord Matsudaira present, but also curious. "May I ask why?"

The shogun knitted his brow. "I know my cousin wants what's best for me. But whenever he's around, things become difficult and troublesome. Have you noticed?"

"I may have," Sano said, trying not to look at Hirata.

"He has the greatest, ahh, respect and affection for me, but sometimes I feel as if he's—" The shogun's tongue worked inside his mouth, as if tasting unpleasant words. "As if he's mocking me. Do you think so, too?"

Here was Sano's chance to repay Lord Matsudaira for all the times Lord Matsudaira had maligned Sano to the shogun. Sano felt sorely tempted, but prudence forestalled him. If the shogun found out that Lord Matsudaira wanted to take over the regime, Sano's own role in the power struggle might become exposed. And the shogun might forgive Lord Matsudaira, his blood kin, but never Sano the outsider, the upstart.

"Perhaps Lord Matsudaira has so much on his mind that he's not aware of what impression he's creating," Sano said.

This evasion quelled the shogun's fears. "Perhaps you're right. Perhaps I'm, ahh, too sensitive."

Sano heard Yoritomo let out his breath. Hirata sat silent, stoic and watchful.

"But at any rate, I came to ask you what, ahh, progress you've made in your investigation," the shogun said. "And I'd just as soon my cousin didn't join us."

So would Sano. "I've interviewed Tadatoshi's mother and sister. They don't believe my mother killed him. In fact, they gave her a good character reference." The shogun wouldn't notice that the word of two women was weak compared to Colonel Doi's without

Lord Matsudaira to point it out. "They also identified someone who wanted Tadatoshi dead." As he related their story about their relative wanting to advance his son up the line in the succession, Sano was glad that Lord Matsudaira wasn't there to harp on the fact that the man was conveniently dead for Sano to frame.

"Ahh, a new suspect," the shogun said, impressed.

But Yoritomo looked unhappy instead of pleased that Sano had made headway toward clearing his mother. Sano wondered why.

"And I've discovered that my mother has an alibi for the murder," Sano continued. "Her maid was with her before Tadatoshi disappeared and during the whole time after."

"So she couldn't have, ahh, kidnapped and killed him," the shogun deduced.

Lord Matsudaira would surely have denounced the alibi as fake, created by a loyal servant in debt to her mistress. But the shogun hadn't the wits to think of that himself. Sano said, "Hana also identified another suspect. She heard him threaten Tadatoshi soon before he disappeared. It's Colonel Doi."

"Doi?" The shogun's mouth fell open. "To think he accused your mother of the crime that he could be guilty of committing!" Enlightenment came over the shogun's face. "Maybe he's trying to protect himself." His ability to draw mental lines between evidence and conclusions improved without Lord Matsudaira around to muddy the waters. "Well, Sano-*san,* I must say that I am, ahh, leaning toward believing your mother is innocent."

Sano and Hirata exchanged a glance of cautious triumph.

Yoritomo cleared his throat and said, "Your Excellency, it's not enough that Chamberlain Sano has produced other suspects besides his mother." He gave Sano a look that was apologetic yet defiant. "We still don't know who's guilty."

Sano regarded Yoritomo with surprise. They'd been friends for years, and Yoritomo had often professed himself willing to do anything for Sano. Why had he now taken on the role of detractor? Sano experienced a moment of déjà vu. Once Yanagisawa had sat beside the shogun and belittled Sano. Now Yanagisawa's son, his very image, was in the same place.

"Yes, that's right. I still want to know who killed my cousin," the shogun said, visibly cooling toward Sano. "What else are you doing to find out?"

Hirata spoke up. "I'm looking for an important witness, the tutor that Colonel Doi says was involved in the kidnapping and murder." He described how he'd gone to the temple that Egen had once belonged to and learned that Egen had left town after the Great Fire. "I've begun a nationwide search for him."

It sounded futile, but Sano was glad Hirata was making such a heroic effort. The shogun said peevishly, "Well, ahh, I guess that will have to do for now." He held out his hand to Yoritomo, who helped him rise. "We must be going. It's time for my medicine."

As they walked toward the door, Yoritomo sidled past Sano, face averted. Sano signaled Hirata, who accompanied the shogun down the corridor, distracting him with conversation. Sano stood in front of Yoritomo so he couldn't follow.

"What's going on?" Sano asked.

Yoritomo looked at the floor. "I don't know what you mean."

"Yes, you do," Sano said. "You deliberately turned the shogun against me."

"I only pointed out a fact that seemed worth mentioning." Yoritomo's voice quavered.

"I thought we were friends. What's the matter?"

The shogun called, "Yoritomo-*san*! Come along!"

"I have to go." Yoritomo ducked around Sano and scuttled down the corridor.

Sano was left with growing suspicions.

12

It was evening by the time Sano rejoined his family.

Reiko and the children sat in the guest chamber with his mother. Etsuko lay propped up on cushions in bed, with Hana at her side. Masahiro arranged his toy soldiers in ranks on the floor while his grandmother smiled fondly at him and cuddled Akiko in her arms. The children chattered. Reiko had been waiting anxiously for Sano, and when he appeared in the doorway, she leaped to her feet. The children ran to him, and Akiko hugged his leg while he greeted his mother. "Are you all right?" he asked.

The smile faded from the old woman's face. She murmured, "Yes." She'd clearly seen from his expression that their problems were far from solved.

So had Reiko. "What happened?" she asked.

"Let's go somewhere else, and I'll explain," Sano said. He tousled the children's hair. "Masahiro, Akiko, keep Grandma company. Mother, I'll talk to you later."

In the privacy of their room, Reiko said, "First, tell me what your mother said this morning."

Sano rubbed his forehead, weary and upset. "She said she didn't kill Tadatoshi. But she does know Colonel Doi, the man who accused her. They were once engaged to be married."

Astounded, Reiko shook her head. There seemed no end to her mother-in-law's secrets. They further undermined Reiko's good opinion of Etsuko.

"But I turned up some witnesses who can help her," Sano said, brightening. "Tadatoshi's mother and sister will vouch for her character. And Hana has said that she and my mother were together before, during, and after the Great Fire. My mother couldn't have gone to the shrine and killed Tadatoshi."

This last news dismayed rather than gladdened Reiko. It contradicted what Etsuko had told her. She could tell by the expression on Sano's face that he'd noticed the worry in hers.

"Has something happened?" he asked.

"Lieutenant Asukai and I have set a trap for the spy," Reiko said, delaying the bad news. She related the details.

"That's good, I hope it works." Sano studied her curiously, then said, "What else?"

Cautious because she knew he wouldn't welcome any statements that put his mother in the wrong light, Reiko said, "I talked to your mother, while you were gone."

"And?"

"I was trying to help her, and you. I asked her if there was anyone who could give her an alibi, and she said no," Reiko said reluctantly. "But if she and Hana had really been together, wouldn't she have told me so?"

Sano frowned, disturbed because Reiko had put the alibi in question. "Maybe she forgot that Hana was with her."

"Maybe." But Reiko doubted that her mother-in-law would have forgotten such a crucial fact. To her, Etsuko had appeared less impaired of memory than deliberately evasive. It seemed more plausible that Hana had lied, Etsuko hadn't known that Hana was going to cover for her, and they hadn't gotten their stories straight.

A moment passed, during which neither Reiko nor Sano spoke. Then Sano said, "Do you think my mother is guilty?" His tone was partly accusatory, partly defensive.

"No," Reiko said, so fast that Sano eyed her with surprise. "But I think she's withholding information—" Reiko faltered under his look, which anticipated betrayal and hurt. An uncomfortable, familiar tension vibrated between them. Reiko had felt it before, on occasions when their opinions of a suspect's guilt or innocence had differed. But this time they couldn't afford to be at odds. "Information that could help her," Reiko hastily amended. "Sometimes people charged with crimes just don't want their private business aired, even if it has nothing to do with the crimes."

She didn't want Sano to think she was digging for proof that Etsuko was guilty and taking the accusers' side against his mother. If their positions were reversed and her father had been accused, she would want nothing less than Sano's complete faith that her father was innocent. Now she saw relief in Sano's expression.

"I could talk to your mother again, if you like," Reiko suggested. "Maybe she'll open up and tell me more."

Sano considered a moment. Reiko could feel him weighing possible benefits and dangers. Then he let out his breath. "All right. I haven't gotten much out of her myself. You might as well go ahead, as long as you're gentle with her. What could it hurt?"

At the temple in Shinagawa, the priests knelt in the main worship hall for evening prayers. Light from a thousand candles shimmered on their saffron robes and their shaved heads, on the golden Buddha statue surrounded by gold lotus flowers upon the altar. Sweet, pungent incense smoke and the rhythmic drone of the priests' chanting rose heavenward.

Yanagisawa knelt in his usual position at the back of the hall. Chanting along with the other men, he didn't look up when Yoritomo, dressed in a hooded cloak, tiptoed into the room and knelt beside him. Nor did Yoritomo appear to notice Yanagisawa. Eyes downcast, they carried on a conversation below the sound of the praying.

"This must be urgent, if you couldn't wait until we're finished," Yanagisawa whispered.

"It is," Yoritomo whispered back. "And I can only stay a little while. The shogun is keeping me on a tight rein." He told Yanagisawa about the good character reference that Sano's mother had received from Tadatoshi's mother and sister, the new suspect they'd named, the evidence against Colonel Doi, and Hirata's search for the missing tutor.

Yanagisawa frowned. "Our friend Sano is doing too well with his investigation."

"I'm sorry to disappoint you." Yoritomo sounded as distressed as if Sano's progress were his own fault.

"But we shouldn't be surprised," Yanagisawa said. "Sano has a talent for fighting his way out of a thornbush. I've been watching him do it for ten years. I swear, he must have a guardian deity."

But not even divine protection could save Sano much longer.

Yoritomo didn't answer. A sidelong glance at him showed Yanagisawa that his son was more distressed than ever. Fearing that Yoritomo had saved worse news for last, Yanagisawa asked, "What else?"

"I criticized Sano in front of the shogun. I turned the shogun against him a little."

"That's excellent," Yanagisawa said. "Why so glum?"

"You should have seen the look in Sano's eyes. He was hurt because I betrayed him."

Yanagisawa refrained from pointing out that Yoritomo could hardly have expected Sano to be delighted. Yoritomo was easily wounded by sarcasm. "Sano is used to treachery. He shouldn't be so sensitive."

"But I feel awful!"

"Don't," Yanagisawa said. "Just remember, taking Sano down is necessary. If he falls out of favor with the shogun, that's good. This is war. It's either him or us."

A mournful sigh issued from Yoritomo. "I know."

"It's done," Yanagisawa said. "Just forget it."

"It wasn't all that happened. Afterward, Sano cornered me. He wanted to know why I did it." Anxiety filled Yoritomo's whisper. "He asked what was going on."

The priests chanted louder, faster. Hands rubbed rosaries between palms. The incense smoke thickened, bittersweet and poisonous. Yanagisawa experienced a pang of fear. "Did you tell him that I'm back and we're in contact?"

He risked a direct look at Yoritomo, who said, "No!" The young man's expression begged Yanagisawa to give him some credit. "I made an excuse, then got away as fast as I could. But I'm sorry, Father—I'm not good at these political games. I think he suspects."

"There's no reason he should," Yanagisawa assured his son. His cover was good; not a single rumor about his return from exile had leaked. But he'd underestimated Sano in the past, to his own detriment. He wouldn't repeat the same mistake. "But we'll play it safe. Don't speak against Sano anymore."

"I won't." Yoritomo spoke with obvious relief, even though he still reeked of unhappiness. After a pause he said, "There's more bad news."

"What?" Yanagisawa braced himself.

"Shigeta, Tamura, Mimaki, and Ota were captured today."

Those men had numbered among Yanagisawa's key underground soldiers. "How? Where?"

"Toda Ikkyu trapped them at a bathhouse."

Yanagisawa stifled a curse. "What's happened to them?"

"They're being interrogated. That was all I could find out without asking too many questions and making people wonder why I'm curious."

Yanagisawa wasn't upset only because he'd lost some important men. "They know I'm here. If they should talk—"

"They won't. They're tough, loyal samurai." Yoritomo sounded as if he were trying to ease his own mind as well as Yanagisawa's. "They'll die first."

"Maybe," Yanagisawa said, "but things are getting too hot. Sooner or later someone will be captured who will talk. We have to act fast."

The chanting rose to a crescendo. The priests' faces wore rapt, urgent expressions. "We can't just stand by and hope Sano's luck will turn bad," Yanagisawa said. "It's time for us to take a more active, personal role against him."

"How?" With one word Yoritomo conveyed that he was unwilling yet committed to helping his father engineer his friend's demise.

A priest near the altar beat a gong, its sound a quickening metal pulse. Yanagisawa thought about the events Yoritomo had reported. He mulled over different aspects of Sano's murder investigation, spied one he could turn to his advantage, and smiled. "I have an idea. Listen."

13

The next morning, while Hirata ate breakfast, Midori entered his chamber, holding a child by each hand. She said, "Good morning, Honorable Husband."

Her manner was polite, aloof. The children gazed curiously at his bowl of fish topped with sliced ginseng root to stimulate mental and physical energy, fleece flower to strengthen the blood, and lycii berries to improve eyesight. They were somber in the presence of this strange father who ate weird food, said little, and did puzzling things.

"Good morning." Hirata hadn't seen Midori since yesterday. She hadn't slept in their room with him last night. Since he'd returned home they'd shared a bed, but they'd not touched except by accident. Now she'd cut off even this physical contact. The distance between them had widened into an unbridgeable gulf.

"Excuse me for interrupting you," Midori said.

Overnight something had changed in her. She was behaving as traditional wives did toward their husbands, with restrained civility. This disturbed Hirata more than her fits of temper. Was it a new tactic in this war of theirs? He studied Midori as he would an opponent on a battlefield. His trained perception sensed no aggression in her, no trick to goad him into another argument. Rather, her emotional energy had contracted within her, giving off neither heat nor light for him to read. Baffled, he settled on caution as his best course.

"That's all right, you're not interrupting anything," he said. "Come in. Sit with me."

"I will if you insist, Husband." Midori was uncharacteristically meek, subservient. "But I have to feed the children." They clung to her hands, regarding both parents in obvious fear of another quarrel.

Hirata was tempted to ask what she was up to, but his instincts warned him off. Revealing confusion to his opponent put a warrior at a disadvantage. He felt vexed because he could figure out any man during a sword fight but not his wife in his own home.

"Very well," he said, matching her formal manner. If this was a game, two could play. "Was there something you wanted to say to me?"

"Yes," Midori said. "Detective Arai is waiting for you in the reception room. I came to fetch you."

Hirata welcomed the prospect of starting the day's work, which was something he could master. He felt a pang of fear stronger than any he'd experienced in battle. It stemmed from his sense that Midori could hurt him worse than could any foe.

"What does Arai want?" Hirata asked.

"He's found someone you've been looking for. A tutor."

"One of my search parties came across a lead a few hours ago," Hirata told Sano as they rode their horses down the boulevard outside Edo Castle. Sano's entourage rode at their front, flanks, and rear, ever vigilant. "They met a fellow who said he knows a man named Egen who used to be a monk."

"Can it really be the tutor?" Sano was hopeful yet not quite ready to believe.

"He's in his sixties, which would put him at the right age," Hirata said. "And he once belonged to Egen's temple."

"And he's right here in Edo." That they'd found the tutor after only a day's search seemed too good to be true. "Maybe this is the break we need to clear my mother, if not solve the crime," Sano said. "Where is Egen?"

"Living in the Kodemmacho district."

This was the same neighborhood through which Sano had passed on his way to Edo Jail two days ago. Now there was no need for a disguise. As they rode down the main street that crossed the slum, his party turned heads among the residents. Women lugging babies on their backs and pails of water in their hands stopped and stared. Not many samurai officials came this way. Laborers on their way to work bowed to Sano. Children and beggars trailed his retinue in hope of alms.

Today Sano saw beyond the poverty and the dirt. This investigation had put the Great Fire on his mind. He noted the smoke from many braziers and hearths, so dense that the atmosphere was gray even on a clear, sunny morning like this. The wind whipped the smoke around dilapidated houses set too close together. A fire that started in one would burn many others before it could be extinguished. Wells were few, water scarce. The narrow streets would impede escape. In any natural disaster, the poor always suffered worst.

"According to directions from the man who gave the tip, this is where Egen lives," Hirata said, leading the way down an alley barely wide enough for the group to pass through single-file. Laundry on clotheslines stretched across the alley brushed their heads. The stench of humans crowded together in unsanitary conditions was overpowering. Hirata stopped his horse at a gate made of dingy boards. "Here."

Sano, Hirata, Marume, and Fukida dismounted. Hirata pushed open the gate. Leaving the troops in the alley, Sano and the detectives followed Hirata down the muddy passage between the blank, windowless walls of two tenements, past reeking garbage containers. They entered a yard enclosed by buildings. Doors on the lower stories opened directly onto the yard. Balconies cluttered with junk fronted second-story dwellings. Sano heard voices arguing and children shrieking, but the yard was empty except for two unshaven, surly men.

One crouched naked on the ground, pouring water over himself, taking an open-air bath. He carried on a muttered conversation with the other man, who squatted inside a privy shed with the door left open. They both looked up at Sano's party, but neither ceased his labors.

"We're looking for Egen," Hirata said. "Where is he?"

The men pointed at a door on the ground floor. Hirata walked over to it and knocked.

"Who's there?" a gruff male voice called from inside.

"The shogun's investigator," Hirata said. "Open up!"

Sano heard shuffling inside. The door slid open a crack. Out peered a watery, red-rimmed eye. "What do you want?"

"Are you Egen?" Sano asked.

"Yes. Who are you?"

Sano introduced himself and said, "I want to talk to you."

"About what?"

"Let us in, and I'll tell you," Sano said.

Egen heaved a sigh of irritation, opened the door, and stepped backward. Entering the room with his party, Sano found a squat old man with frizzled gray hair. His short brown kimono was open to reveal his flabby torso, bare legs, and loincloth. He yawned, evidently having just awakened. His room was a small, dim cave filled with heaps of unidentifiable articles. It smelled powerfully of liquor, sleep, and stale body odor.

"Whew!" Marume said.

He flung open the window. Fresher air poured into the room. Daylight revealed Egen. His face and whole body were covered with pocked, bumpy, discolored skin.

"Whoa!" Fukida said.

"What's the matter?" Egen said, unflinching under the revolted gazes that Sano and the other men couldn't tear away from him. "Haven't you ever seen somebody who's had smallpox?"

"I'm sorry," Sano said politely.

"Don't be," Egen said. "Just tell me what you want."

"I need to ask you some questions."

"What kind of questions?"

"Were you once a monk at Bairin Temple?" Sano said.

"Yes," Egen said crossly. "Who told you?"

"Never mind," Hirata said. "Just answer his questions."

"Forty-three years ago, did you work as a tutor to Tokugawa Tadatoshi?" Sano asked.

"Yes. In another lifetime." Egen recalled his manners and said, "Can I offer you some tea?"

He gestured toward a corner that served as a kitchen. Around the ceramic hearth sat a few pots, pans, and bowls, all coated with scum.

"No, thank you," Sano said.

Fukida examined the heaps, which consisted of old clothes and shoes, broken furniture, chipped dishware and statues, torn paper lanterns, and other damaged items. "What are you doing with all this stuff?"

"I collect it," Egen said, "to sell. I'm a junk peddler."

Marume picked up a small, headless Buddha figure. Egen snatched it away and exclaimed, "Hey, that's valuable merchandise. Do you mind?"

"You've come a long way from tutor in the house of a Tokugawa vassal to peddler of junk," Sano said. "What happened?"

"Bad luck. Is that all you wanted to know?"

"Not quite." Sano couldn't help liking Egen, who seemed to accept his lot in life without complaining and was brave enough to stand up to authority. Despite the man's ugliness, he had a certain charm. "Tadatoshi went missing during the Great Fire. Do you remember?"

Egen nodded. "Oh, yes. I was sent out to look for the brat. Everybody in the house was." Scratching his chest, he yawned again. "I could use a drink." He picked up a grimy wine jar and waved it around. "Join me?"

Sano and his men politely declined. Egen drank straight from the jar, coughed and licked his lips, then said, "While I was looking for Tadatoshi, I almost got killed in the fire, like he did."

"He didn't," Sano said.

"What? But he must have died in the fire, because he never came back."

"Tadatoshi was murdered not long after the fire. His body turned up two days ago." Sano explained about the unmarked grave near the shrine.

"Well, I never would have thought." Egen shook his head. "What happened to him? Who did it?"

"That's what I'm trying to find out," Sano said.

"Pardon me, but why bother? It was a long time ago."

"My mother has been accused of the crime."

"Oh?" Surprised, Egen asked, "Who is your mother?"

"Her name is Etsuko, from the Kumazawa clan," Sano said. It still felt strange to realize that the clan was part of his own family tree and he was a born Tokugawa vassal, not just one who'd earned his way into the regime. "She was a lady-in-waiting to Tadatoshi's mother. Do you remember her?"

"Etsuko, Etsuko," the tutor mulled. "Oh, yes. Pretty girl." He swigged more wine. "Did she kill Tadatoshi?"

"No," Sano said. "I'm trying to prove she's innocent."

"Well, good luck," Egen said, "but what does that have to do with me?"

"My mother's not the only person who's been accused," Sano said. "So have you."

"Me?" Egen pointed to his own chest, taken aback. He thumped the wine jar down on a dingy table. "I didn't kill anyone. Who says I did?"

"A man who was Tadatoshi's bodyguard at the time the boy disappeared. His name is Doi."

"Doi . . ." Recollection showed on Egen's pockmarked face. "So he's still around. What's he doing now?"

"He's a colonel in Lord Matsudaira's army," Sano said.

"Well, well." Egen apparently knew who Lord Matsudaira was. "But I'm not surprised. Doi was headed for big things. So now he's attacked you through your mother." He also knew about the conflict between Sano and Lord Matsudaira and suspected that it was behind Doi's accusation. "What does Doi say I did?"

"That you and my mother conspired to kidnap Tadatoshi for ransom, then something went wrong and you killed him."

"That's horse dung," Egen scoffed.

"Here's your chance to contradict Doi," Sano said. "When was the last time you saw Tadatoshi?"

"The morning the Great Fire started. In the house. After breakfast. I gave him his history lesson," Egen said promptly.

"It was a lifetime ago, and you remember such small details?" Hirata interjected.

"Because of the fire," Egen said. "When something as big as that happens, you do tend to remember things you'd have forgotten otherwise."

"All right," Sano said, willing to accept Egen's story for now. The man was well spoken and confident. "What did you do after you saw Tadatoshi?"

"Helped fireproof the house. A lot of good that did—it burned down anyway. Then I went looking for Tadatoshi. Nine days after the fire was over, I met up with what was left of the household and found out he still hadn't turned up."

"You didn't happen to run into him?"

"No. I already told you. Not after his lesson."

"Was there anybody around to vouch for what you say you did during the fire?" Sano asked.

"The retainers and servants, while I was working on the house. Afterward, when we were all sent out to look for him, I got separated from the others. So, no, I guess not." Egen's expression turned wary. "Hey, what are you trying to do? Save your mother by pinning the murder on me?"

"No," Sano hastened to assure him. "I just need a witness to show that Colonel Doi lied."

Egen grinned. "You found one. I didn't kidnap Tadatoshi or kill him, and your mother and I didn't conspire to do anything at all."

"Good." Relieved that the investigation was nearing a satisfactory end, Sano said, "I need you to tell that to Lord Matsudaira and the shogun."

"Come on, let's go," Hirata said.

"Lord Matsudaira and the shogun?" Egen held up his hands and waggled them. "Hey, wait, no. I can't do that."

"Why not?" Sano said, impatient.

"I don't want to get caught in the middle of any trouble." Consternation clouded Egen's face as he backed away from Sano.

"You won't."

"I sure will if Lord Matsudaira doesn't like what I say."

"If you testify, I'll protect you," Sano said.

"Hah!"

Fukida said to Sano, "Do you want me to tie him up?"

"Not yet." If that proved to be necessary, Sano wouldn't balk, but Egen would make a more credible witness if he testified willingly. Sano tried to reason with him. "You'll get in trouble if you don't testify."

"Oh?" Egen said, suspicious. "How's that?"

"Colonel Doi accused you as well as my mother," Sano said. "If the shogun decides she's guilty of kidnapping and killing his cousin, he won't stop at punishing her. He'll come after you next."

"You'll be executed," Fukida said.

"Your ugly head will be stuck on a post by the Nihonbashi Bridge," Marume said.

Egen staggered with fear. "What am I going to do?" he beseeched Sano.

"If you want to stay alive, then testify," Sano said. "Your story and my mother's will refute Colonel Doi's. It'll be two against one."

"I don't know," Egen stalled.

"It's your best chance," Sano said.

Egen thought for a long moment while Fukida and Marume stood ready to seize him. Then he said with a grudging sigh, "Oh, all right."

火
山
火

14

Reiko was surprised to see that her mother-in-law had made a miraculous recovery.

Etsuko had felt well enough to rise from her bed this morning, wash and dress herself, and eat breakfast. Now she strolled with Reiko and Akiko through the garden. The air was cool and humid. Clouds had blown down from the hills, threatening rain. Akiko toddled beside Etsuko and clung to her hand. Reiko walked on Etsuko's other side. She was hurt because Akiko had refused to hold hands with her and wanted Grandma between them. That did not improve Reiko's feelings toward her mother-in-law, an interloper as well as a suspect in a murder case that threatened her family.

Akiko paused to examine a rock. Etsuko smiled as she chatted with the little girl. Reiko could guess the reason for her restored health.

"I suppose my husband told you what he learned yesterday?" Reiko said.

"Yes." Etsuko's face had relaxed into her usual serene contentment. "He said that Lady Ateki and Oigimi spoke well of me. Things are not as bad as before."

"But not as good as we might wish." Reiko tasted the acid in her own voice. She knew that her jealousy was irrational and unbecoming, but she had better reason to be displeased with her mother-in-law. The trouble wasn't over, Etsuko had done little to abate it, and Reiko was having a hard time treating Etsuko gently, as Sano wanted her to do. "Did my husband also tell you that Hana has given you an alibi?"

"I believe he said something to that effect."

This was an example of the formal speech that sometimes slipped into Etsuko's conversation, that Reiko had thought didn't jibe with her humble background. "But when I talked to you yesterday, you said there wasn't anyone who could vouch that you were someplace other than near the shrine when Tadatoshi was murdered. Then Hana said she could; she was with you. Which is the truth?"

Akiko broke away from them, ran to the flower bed, and bent to sniff the blossoms. A shadow of anxiety dimmed Etsuko's expression. "I wasn't in my right mind yesterday. I was confused. If Hana says we were together, then we were."

How glibly she'd explained the discrepancies between their stories, Reiko thought; and how shrewd of Etsuko to pick the one that served her better. Sano would probably excuse his mother and believe the alibi. He couldn't see her intelligence through her humble guise.

"Very well," Reiko said, "but there's a problem with that alibi, even if it's real."

"Oh?"

"Devoted servants will lie for their employers," Reiko said. "Lord Matsudaira knows that, and he'll be sure to point it out to the shogun."

"We'll just have to pray they believe Hana," Etsuko said, clearly less assured than her words.

"We need to do more than pray," Reiko said. "What would really help is someone else to vouch for your whereabouts during the murder. Can you think of anyone?"

"There's no one. I told you yesterday." A tinge of sharpness crept into Etsuko's voice.

"What about your relatives?" Reiko said, introducing this topic that Etsuko had seemed unwilling to discuss.

Etsuko hunched her shoulders; she took on a tense, cornered air. She looked across the garden at Akiko smelling flowers, as if she wished she could escape Reiko and join the child. "They weren't with me during the Great Fire."

"Maybe they can still help," Reiko said. "The Kumazawa are high-ranking Tokugawa vassals. They might have some influence with the shogun." Etsuko and Sano needed all the powerful allies they could get. "Shall I ask my husband to contact them?"

Reiko was avidly curious about the Kumazawa, her husband and children's new blood kin. She wanted to meet them. But Etsuko cried in panic, "No! Please!"

"Why not?"

". . . I— I don't want to see them. And they . . . they won't want anything to do with me."

"When did you last see your relatives?" Reiko asked.

Etsuko shook her head. She inched away from Reiko, who followed. "A few months after the Great Fire."

Tadatoshi had died during or shortly after the fire; Etsuko and her family had become estranged at around the same time. Did the estrangement have bearing upon the murder? Reiko began to believe so. Something bad had happened back then, and it wasn't just the Great Fire. "Why did you lose contact with your family?"

"I don't remember . . . it was so long ago . . . the people closest to me are all dead now . . . it doesn't matter . . ." Etsuko's evasions trailed off in a shaky sigh.

Reiko felt her patience dwindling fast. "I think it does matter," she said, for a new idea had occurred to her. "I think they know something about you that you don't want anyone else to know. Am I right?"

"No. With all due respect, Honorable Daughter-in-law, you're talking nonsense." The fear that shone in her eyes belied Etsuko's words.

"Is it something about the murder?" Reiko persisted.

Etsuko turned her back on Reiko. "I won't put up with this," she said, her voice tight.

"You'll have to put up with much worse if my husband can't clear your name." Reiko kept her own voice low so Akiko wouldn't hear her, but her own temper snapped. "You'll be executed. Or maybe you don't care. But what about your son? What about your grandchildren?"

She gestured angrily toward Akiko, who picked a flower, oblivious to her elders. Reiko realized that this was her first quarrel with Etsuko, and that Sano wouldn't approve, but ten years of peaceful if strained relations between her and her mother-in-law had just ended. "Do you want them to die? Don't you owe it to them to be honest, to cooperate?"

Etsuko whirled. She faced Reiko, her hands curled into claws, her usually mild face suffused with rage. "Of course I care! I protected my son before you were even born. I would do anything in my power to protect him and his children now. And I'm cooperating as best I can. What else do you want me to do? Confess to the murder?"

She laughed, a harsh, mournful sound. "I would confess if it would save them. But it would only condemn them to die alongside me. If you believe otherwise, then you're not as smart as you think you are, Honorable Daughter-in-law!"

As Etsuko glared at her, Reiko stood openmouthed with shock. It was as if a domestic cat had suddenly turned into a lion, roared, and charged. Reiko saw a different, stronger, ruthless person in Etsuko, a person that she knew Sano had never seen.

She saw a woman capable of murder.

Every instinct told her that her mother-in-law was guilty.

A fretful wind swirled around them. Raindrops dashed the garden. Above them, black clouds encroached on the blue sky. Then Reiko heard Sano's voice from a distance, calling, "Mother! Reiko-san! I have good news!"

Sano hurried across the garden toward his mother, wife, and daughter. He'd ridden ahead to Edo Castle with Marume,

Fukida, and some of his troops while Hirata and the others followed with the tutor. He'd arranged an audience with the shogun, then stopped at home. Now he was glad to see that his mother had recovered from her ordeal, and he anticipated that what he had to say would make her feel even better.

She was standing with her back to him, so he couldn't immediately see her face. He did see Reiko's. Its expression told him that his wife and mother had been quarreling. Then his mother turned, Akiko ran to him, and Sano forgot to wonder why.

"What is it?" his mother said, hopeful yet not daring to believe.

"I've found Egen the tutor," Sano said.

"How wonderful!" Reiko said. The anger on her face changed to a smile of admiration and eagerness for details.

His mother's eyes went so wide that Sano could see the yellowed whites encircling the brown irises. The pupils dilated; the blood drained from her face. She swayed.

"Mother!" Sano caught her before she could topple. "What's wrong?"

She gasped. "Nothing. I— I just felt a little dizzy."

Akiko wailed in alarm. Sano said, "It's all right, Akiko. Grandma's just having a spell. You go and play now."

The little girl ran off with a nervous, uncomprehending look backward. Sano saw the color return to his mother's cheeks. She shook him off, and her eyes shone with an ardor he'd never observed in her before. She clasped her hands, which trembled.

"Where is Egen?" she cried.

Her reaction was extreme, considering the fact that she'd claimed she hardly remembered the tutor. Sano saw Reiko eyeing her with puzzlement. He said, "We found him in Kodemmacho. He's on his way to the castle."

"I want to see him!"

"Why are you so eager to renew an acquaintance with the man after forty-three years?"

Her gaze skittered. "I'm just curious."

That answer didn't satisfy Sano, but he didn't have time to press his mother for an explanation. Neither did Reiko ask; she kept silent. "I'm taking Egen to the shogun," Sano said. "He's agreed to testify that you and he didn't kidnap or kill Tadatoshi. He's going to exonerate you."

"He's coming to save me." As his mother murmured the words, she pressed her hands over her heart. A radiant glow suffused her. The years seemed to fall away from her like a dropped robe.

Sano was disconcerted to see in her the beautiful, passionate young woman she'd once been, whom he'd never known. "After Egen finishes testifying, I'll bring him here."

"No! I can't wait. Take me to the palace with you!"

"That's not a good idea," Sano said. "Lord Matsudaira and Colonel Doi will surely come to hear him testify. You'd have to face them again."

"I don't care!" She grabbed Sano's sleeve. "I must go. Please!"

Sano had never seen her so excited about anything, and he hated to deny her what she wanted so badly. She might as well hear Egen testify on her behalf and the shogun pronounce her innocent.

"All right," Sano said. "Let's go."

As they hurried through the garden together, she smoothed her robes and hair. Sano felt a twinge of a new suspicion that he couldn't, or perhaps didn't want to, define.

He glanced over his shoulder and saw Reiko watching his mother. His wife's face was an exact mirror of his misgivings.

At the palace, Sano and his mother knelt on the lower level of the floor in front of the dais, Detectives Marume and Fukida behind him. The shogun occupied the dais, Yoritomo at his left, Lord Matsudaira at his right. Colonel Doi knelt on the upper level, near Lord Matsudaira. Along the walls Lord Matsudaira's troops, Sano's, and the shogun's guards stood in tense proximity.

"Well, ahh, Chamberlain Sano, who is this witness that you've gathered us all to hear?" the shogun asked.

"It's Egen," Sano said, "your cousin Tadatoshi's former tutor."

Yoritomo didn't look happy. Neither did Lord Matsudaira and Colonel Doi.

"So you've found him," Lord Matsudaira said in a flat tone.

"I suppose you didn't think I would." Sano turned to Colonel Doi. "You must have been counting on Egen never showing up and contradicting your lies."

The shogun frowned as if noticing and trying to understand the hostility between the three men. "Don't, ahh, keep us in suspense any longer, Chamberlain Sano. Where is the witness?"

The door at the back of the room opened. In walked Hirata, escorting Egen. The man had closed his kimono, tied a sash around his waist, and donned a pair of leggings; but the clothes were worn and stained, his frizzy gray hair a mess. The sight of his pockmarked face sent a stir through the assembly.

"Smallpox!" the shogun cried, holding his sleeve over his nose and mouth to prevent the evil spirit of the disease from entering. "Is he contagious?"

"I doubt it, Your Excellency." Sano looked at his mother.

Her eager smile had melted into stunned astonishment. Egen gazed around the room, remarkably nonchalant in the face of the repugnance he'd aroused. He grinned as he knelt and bowed to everyone.

"Egen?" she blurted.

The old man glanced in her direction, then said to Sano, "Is that your mother?"

"Yes," Sano said.

She and Egen regarded each other. Her expression showed her disappointment. "You're so changed," she whispered.

"Forty-three years will do that to a person." His expression showed only mild curiosity. "Did I know you very well when we were living at Tadatoshi's house?"

Sano saw woe and disbelief in his mother's eyes. She said, "Don't you remember?" Sano wondered why she was so upset, but now wasn't the time to ask.

Egen turned away from her to face Colonel Doi, who glared at him. "Is that you, Doi-*san*? You're certainly well preserved."

"Let's stop the chatter and get down to business," Lord Matsu-daira interrupted.

The shogun hesitated as if seeking an excuse to contradict his cousin; not finding one, he nodded. Yoritomo looked anxious. Sano said, "Egen, tell them that Colonel Doi lied about you and my mother."

Egen sat straighter, unfazed by all the attention on him. Breath swelled his chest. He spoke in a deep, resonant voice: "He didn't lie. Not exactly."

15

"What?" Sano couldn't believe he'd heard right.

The shogun wrinkled his forehead, puzzled because Egen had said something other than what he'd been led to expect. Lord Matsudaira and Colonel Doi leaned forward, their displeasure giving way to alert anticipation.

"Doi lied about me," Egen said. "I had nothing to do with what happened to Tadatoshi." His voice was clear, loud enough to fill the room, and adamant. "I didn't kidnap him. I didn't kill him. But *she* did."

He pointed dramatically at Sano's mother. She gaped at him, as horror-stricken as Sano was. For an instant everyone sat in speechless silence. Lord Matsudaira and Colonel Doi traded smug glances: The game had just changed in their favor.

"Hey, that's not what you told us earlier," Marume said to Egen.

"You said neither you nor Chamberlain Sano's mother did it," Fukida said.

The tutor grinned sheepishly.

Aghast and furious, Sano said, "You changed your story!"

"What a shame," Lord Matsudaira said with satisfaction.

"What's happening?" the shogun cried.

"Chamberlain Sano's witness has turned traitor on him," Yoritomo said.

Sano noticed that the young man seemed at once distraught and glad. He grabbed Egen by the front of his robe and said, "Why did you tell me you were going to testify on my mother's behalf, and then incriminate her?"

"I said what you wanted to hear." Fright and cunning glinted in Egen's eyes. "You and your men burst into my house and threatened me. I was afraid you'd kill me if I said anything else."

"He wants to make sure he doesn't get blamed for Tadatoshi's death," Hirata said. "He's throwing her to the wolves to save himself."

"No!" Egen said, clawing at Sano's hands.

Marume grabbed Egen's hair in his fist. "Why did you let us bring you here? How dare you?"

As the man struggled to break free of Sano and Marume, he appealed to the shogun: "Your Excellency, I came because I wanted to tell the true story to you. It's my duty."

"Your duty, my rear end!" Marume shouted. "Take back your lie, or I'll kill you!"

"I say let the man tell his story," Lord Matsudaira said.

The shogun wavered, but Lord Matsudaira's aggressive stare cowed him. "Very well. Let him go."

Sano and Marume reluctantly did, although Marume smacked the tutor's ear. Egen drew himself up with haughty dignity and said, "The day the Great Fire started, Tadatoshi went missing. His father sent everybody in the house out to find him. I tried, but when I went into town, the fire was already raging. I decided to save myself. I ran for the hills.

"I wasn't the only one who had that idea." His voice took on the same dramatic resonance as when he'd flung down his accusation against Sano's mother. The shogun hung on his words. Sano saw with disgust that Egen liked an audience; he positively swelled. "Thousands of people were swarming up the hills. And who did I see among them but Tadatoshi and Etsuko?"

He gestured toward Sano's mother. She stared at him, her mouth open, her hands gripping her middle, as if he'd punched her. "They were with a soldier from the house, a man named Otani. He and Etsuko were lovers. They were holding Tadatoshi by his hands, dragging him along the road."

"How can you say that?" Sano's mother cried. "You know it's not true!"

"Quiet!" ordered the shogun.

"Tadatoshi was crying and lagging behind Etsuko and Otani. I heard him say, 'I want to go home!'" Egen's voice imitated a boy's with startling accuracy. "At the time I thought he was upset and didn't understand that he couldn't go home because of the fire. I thought Etsuko and Otani had found him and rescued him. When they disappeared into the crowd, I didn't run after them because I thought he was safe with them. But later, when the fire was over—"

"You're making it all up!" wailed Sano's mother.

"—Etsuko and Otani came back. Without Tadatoshi." The tutor spoke with emphasis, paused for a theatrical moment.

A glance around the room showed Sano that Yoritomo was listening with horror and awe, Lord Matsudaira and Colonel Doi with cautious satisfaction.

"He never showed up," Egen went on. "They said they hadn't found him, hadn't even seen him. And I realized that they hadn't saved him after all. They'd killed him."

"Did you see them do it?" Sano demanded.

"No, but they must have," Egen said. "I figured they'd cooked up a plan to hold him for ransom. They probably wanted money to elope. Maybe he fought back. Maybe they killed him by accident. But it must have happened. Otherwise, why would they have lied?"

"Why are *you* lying?" Sano's mother began to sob.

"Shut her up, Honorable Chamberlain," Lord Matsudaira said.

"Mother, let me handle this," Sano cautioned her, then asked Egen, "If you thought my mother and this man murdered Tadatoshi, why didn't you say something then? Why did you leave town and wait forty-three years?"

"Because it would have been my word against theirs," Egen said in a tone that proclaimed himself the most reasonable person in the world and Sano an idiot. "They were of the samurai class. Nobody would have believed me, a poor monk and tutor. I'd have gotten in trouble."

"I'll show you trouble." Marume bunched his fists.

Cringing from him, Egen said, "I was ashamed of not speaking up. That's why I left Edo, broke my religious vows, and became an itinerant peddler." Now he sounded pious; he bowed his head. "To punish myself."

Fukida rolled his eyes. Hirata said, "Your Excellency, it's still Egen's word against that of the Honorable Chamberlain's mother. It's also his word against Colonel Doi's. Colonel Doi has said she and Egen are guilty. Egen says he's innocent and puts the blame on her and this soldier—who, by the way, isn't here to defend himself. The stories contradict each other. They can't both be true."

"They have one thing in common." Lord Matsudaira pointed at Sano's mother. "She's a party to the kidnapping and murder in both."

"Maybe I was wrong about her accomplice," Colonel Doi said, "but I'm not wrong about her."

Infuriated, Sano said, "You are wrong. And so is Egen. Neither of you can prove anything you said. You're both lying."

His mother wept. "Egen, how can you do this? How can you betray me?"

He regarded her as if her suffering meant nothing to him. Lord Matsudaira said, "Your Excellency, it's up to you to decide. Is she guilty or not?"

The shogun vacillated, looking to Yoritomo for help. In the past the young man had put in many a good word for Sano; now he sat quiet, eyes downcast. The shogun raised his hand for silence while he thought. At last he said, "I'm afraid that I, ahh, tend to believe that she is, ahh, guilty."

Horror struck Sano. A high, keening moan issued from his mother. No one else made a sound, but Lord Matsudaira and Colonel Doi shone with such victorious elation that Sano imagined he heard them cheering.

"Take her to Edo Jail," the shogun told his guards. "Have her executed at sunrise tomorrow."

The guards descended on Sano's mother. Sano shouted, "No!"

He and Hirata, Marume, and Fukida leaped to her defense. Lord Matsudaira signaled his troops, who seized and restrained them. As they tussled, Sano's troops joined the fray. But the shogun's guards dragged Sano's mother toward the door. She didn't resist, but her sobs rose to a wild, crazed pitch. Between them she screamed Sano's name.

"Mother!" Sano struggled to run after her and rescue her, but Lord Matsudaira's troops held him immobile. He ordered several of his own troops, "Go with her. Guard her with your lives."

They obeyed. Her screams faded down the corridor. The shogun said "Well!" as if proud that he'd dispensed with an irksome job.

Egen cleared his throat and said, "Pardon me, Your Excellency, do you mind if I leave now?"

"Go," the shogun said, waving his hand.

The tutor stood, performed an exaggerated bow to the assembly, then scuttled out the door.

"Hey!" Marume yelled, straining against the Matsudaira troops. "Come back here, you rat!"

But Egen was gone. Sano felt more than rage because the man had stabbed him in the back and gotten away with it. Panic filled him because he knew that worse was yet to happen.

"So much for that." The shogun's smile begged for approval. He flapped a hand at Lord Matsudaira's troops. "You can let Chamberlain Sano and his men go now."

The soldiers did, but Lord Matsudaira said, "Not so fast, Cousin." He reeked of the humor of a man who's had a contest turn in his favor through a heaven-sent piece of good luck. Colonel Doi maintained a somber expression, but he relaxed. "This isn't over yet. Chamberlain Sano's mother is guilty of murder and treason, and so is he, by association. You must condemn him to death, too."

Sano and his men stood speechless with shock even though they'd all seen this coming.

"Oh." The shogun's smile faded. He obviously hadn't foreseen that consequence of his action, and he was alarmed to discover that he'd stepped in deeper water than he liked.

"And not just Sano, but his family and his close associates." Lord Matsudaira eyed Hirata, Marume, and Fukida.

"Well, then," the shogun said faintly; he didn't want to back down and seem weak. "Chamberlain Sano, I am, ahh, afraid I must have you and your people executed . . ."

Neither Sano nor his men spoke, for the shogun had the right to do with them whatever he wished. But the shogun quailed under their outraged stares. ". . . unless you can give me a good reason not to."

Sano pounced on the chance for a reprieve. "I can, Your Excellency." He felt his men waiting in suspense, their lives riding on his wits. Intuition more than conscious thought guided him. "If you kill me, you'll be alone with nobody to advise you—except your honorable cousin." He flung out his hand at Lord Matsudaira. "Do you really want that?"

He willed the shogun to remember the talk they'd had last night. The alarm on the shogun's face said he did.

" 'Things become difficult and troublesome'?" Sano hinted.

Lord Matsudaira's expression went as dark as a storm cloud. "What are you up to?"

"What should I do?" the shogun anxiously asked Sano. "I don't want to kill you, but I can't just excuse you, either. My law says that a criminal's family must be punished."

"How dare he imply that I'm not fit to advise you?" Lord Matsudaira spoke to the shogun, glared at Sano. "This is a trick, Cousin. He's insulting your kin to save his own head. Don't let him manipulate you."

Suddenly furious, the shogun turned on Lord Matsudaira. "Don't tell me what to do! I'm getting sick of your interfering. I'm beginning to think that you think I can't make decisions." Spittle flew out of his mouth at Lord Matsudaira, who flinched. "Stay out of this. I'll handle it myself!" He turned to Sano. "What do you suggest?"

Lord Matsudaira sat dumbfounded and crimson with rage. The spectators' faces were made of stone. Sano said, "Give me another chance to prove that my mother is innocent. Postpone her execution. Let me continue my investigation and find the real killer."

"Well, ahh, that sounds reasonable," the shogun said.

Sano spoke quickly, lest the wind stop blowing in his direction. "In the meantime, have my mother taken to my house instead of jail."

"Oh." The shogun tapped his finger on his cheek. "But she's, ahh, already on her way. It would be too much trouble to change my order." He sounded as if he would have to run after the troops and tell them himself. He probably neither knew nor cared how bad the conditions were in Edo Jail. "I'll tell you what: I'll give you three more days to, ahh, exonerate your mother. If you succeed, she won't have to stay in jail very long, will she?"

He was delighted by his clever compromise. *Three days.* The words felt like a delayed death sentence to Sano. The time seemed cruelly short, his prospect of solving the forty-three-year-old murder case impossible. But Sano didn't argue and risk changing the shogun's mind. Lord Matsudaira's temper visibly brightened.

"If you don't succeed, she must die. As for you and your family and your associates . . ." The shogun creased his brow. The threat of execution, banishment, or being stripped of his rank and samurai status and cast out on the street in disgrace hung in the air over Sano. "I must say I am reluctant to put you to death, because I've always been fond of you. You've always served me well." He cast a dubious look at Lord Matsudaira. "I'll think of something before the time comes."

Sano met Lord Matsudaira's gaze. Lord Matsudaira smiled and mouthed words at Sano. Sano read his lips: *So will I.*

After leaving the palace, Sano returned home with Hirata and Detectives Marume and Fukida. He told his staff not to disturb him for anything less than a second Great Fire. He and his men sat down for an emergency conclave.

"Lord Matsudaira wins this round," Marume said.

"What's our next move?" Fukida asked.

Sano was still reeling from the horror of seeing his mother hauled off to jail and his own fate—and that of everyone who mattered to him—dependent on what he accomplished in three days. He drew on samurai discipline to calm his mind and help him think up a strategy.

"We need to undo the damage that Egen did," he said.

"I say we make him undo it himself," Marume said. "How about I pay him a visit and convince him to eat his words?"

"Good idea," Fukida said. "I'll help you teach him a lesson."

Hirata said, "I'm all in favor of one bad turn deserving another, but coercing Egen won't solve the problem."

"Why not?" Marume said.

"The most that Egen can do for us is admit he lied," Hirata said. "That won't prove Sano-*san*'s mother is innocent."

"He's right," Sano said, and the other men nodded reluctantly. "It also won't help us identify the real killer. What we need is evidence."

"What kind of evidence can we hope to find after forty-three years?" Fukida said.

Marume punched Fukida's arm. "Hey, don't sound so discouraged."

Sano hid his own discouragement. He must bolster his men's morale, keep them and himself moving.

"All right," Fukida said with forced cheer. "Where do we start looking for witnesses and evidence?"

"How about the soldier that Egen said was your mother's partner in crime?" Marume suggested to Sano.

"Chances are he's either dead, lost, or Egen made him up. Let's not waste our time on him." Sano thought about his visit to Tadatoshi's family. "I'd like to talk to Lady Ateki and her daughter again. I'll ask them to testify on my mother's behalf. At least they can give her a good character reference. That would help counteract what Egen said. And maybe they can direct us to other witnesses."

"Maybe those witnesses will lead us to some evidence," Hirata said.

"I had a feeling that Lady Ateki and Oigimi know more than they told me," Sano said. "I'd like to find out what it is."

On his way out of the house, Sano met Reiko in the corridor. She said, "I heard you were home. I need to talk to you." Looking around, she said, "Where's your mother?"

When Sano told her, Reiko's face showed dismay, but none of the shock he'd expected. "What is it?" He recalled how he'd come upon her and his mother arguing in the garden, but he didn't have time for her now. He explained where he was going and why. "Can we talk later?"

Reiko hesitated, then said, "Yes. It can wait."

16

A brief rain spattered Sano and his men during their second trip to Fukagawa. When they arrived at the estate where Tadatoshi's family lived, the wet street was deserted. With its shutters closed against the rain and its eaves dripping water, the house had an inhospitable air. And the moment Sano walked into the reception room, he noticed a change in the atmosphere.

Lady Ateki and Oigimi greeted him with the stiff courtesy due a stranger visiting for the first time. It was as if they'd forgotten the conversation they'd had with him yesterday. Lady Ateki made the usual offer of refreshments. The tiny, birdlike old woman was pensive, her gentle face troubled. She sat in silence while food and drink were brought. Oigimi brooded under the black head drape that hid the scars from her burns. She exuded coldness.

"How may we serve you?" Lady Ateki said politely.

Sano knew something had happened. "I'm still investigating your son's murder, and I'm looking for more witnesses. Do you know the whereabouts of anyone who belonged to your household when Tadatoshi disappeared?"

The women didn't answer.

"Any family members, retainers, or servants?" Sano prompted.

"We have already informed you that most of the people from

my father's estate were killed by the fire," Oigimi said in a distant tone.

"More have died in the years since," Lady Ateki said, equally distant. "Others have scattered. We don't know where or if they're still alive."

"Are any living in this house?" Sano asked.

"No," Oigimi said.

"I'm sorry we can't help you." Lady Ateki's air of finality hinted that Sano should leave. When he didn't, she said, "Was there something else?"

"Yes," Sano said. "I want you both to tell the shogun what you said about my mother yesterday."

"Why?"

"To attest to her good character and help me prove that she's innocent."

Lady Ateki and Oigimi exchanged glances that united them in opposition. "I don't believe we can do that," Lady Ateki said.

Sano began to have an idea why he'd lost their cooperation. "Have you recently had news about Tadatoshi's murder?"

"As a matter of fact, we have," Lady Ateki said.

"We've learned that you've found Egen the tutor," Oigimi said, "and that he says your mother and a soldier from the estate kidnapped and killed my brother."

Bad news traveled fast. Sano was dismayed to have one of his suspicions proved correct. "How did you learn that?"

"Lord Matsudaira was good enough to send an envoy to tell us," Lady Ateki said.

Sano's other suspicion had hit the mark. Lord Matsudaira had wasted no time capitalizing on Egen's treachery. He'd quickly moved to influence these witnesses. They now believed Sano's mother was guilty and so was Sano, by association.

"Egen lied," Sano said, hiding his rage lest it offend the women and increase their antipathy toward him. "He and my mother were both accused of the crime. He told me they were both innocent, but when he testified in front of the shogun, he changed his story. He put the blame on my mother to protect himself. Did Lord Matsudaira's envoy tell you that?"

Sano could tell from Lady Ateki's and Oigimi's blank expressions that they hadn't been told. "Egen can't be trusted. Don't believe anything he said."

"We don't believe everything we hear." Oigimi's tart voice rebuked Sano for implying that she and her mother were so gullible or should take his word as the truth. "But the news about Egen made us think."

"About Etsuko," said Lady Ateki.

"We decided that maybe we didn't know her so well after all," Oigimi said.

"She seemed like a good, harmless girl," Lady Ateki said, "but that could have been just the face she showed us."

"She might have been hiding her true nature," Oigimi said. "She was beautiful. She could have made that soldier fall in love with her. Maybe she talked him into kidnapping my brother to get the money they needed to run away together and elope."

Bitterness edged her voice. Her head turned slightly toward Sano, who glimpsed the twisted, grotesque features on the left side of her face. He wondered if Oigimi wasn't just angry at his mother because she believed his mother had killed Tadatoshi but because her beauty hadn't been ruined by the fire. Probably no man had ever fallen in love with the scarred, mutilated Oigimi. Sano pitied her, but he was also infuriated by her baseless conjecture.

"That's ridiculous," he said. "You've swallowed hearsay from a man you never knew well and haven't seen in forty-three years. You've let it change your mind about my mother."

"With all due respect, Honorable Chamberlain, but it wasn't just Egen's story that changed our minds," Oigimi said haughtily. "While Mother and I were talking, we remembered things about Etsuko that we'd forgotten until now."

"Such as?" A bad feeling slithered, like a poisonous serpent, through Sano.

"Etsuko used to sneak off while she was supposed to be doing errands for me," Lady Ateki said.

"I often saw her roaming around the estate, following my brother," Oigimi said. "I watched her hide so he wouldn't notice her. She was spying on him."

"And why would she, unless she had evil designs on him?" Lady Ateki said.

"So now you must understand why we cannot speak on her behalf," Oigimi concluded.

Things were even worse than Sano had thought. The women had offered more evidence against his mother, and instead of being certain that it was false, he felt his misgivings about her increase. She'd hidden something from him. Could it be the fact that she and an illicit lover had plotted to extort money from Tadatoshi's father, spied on the boy, taken advantage of the chaos during the Great Fire to kidnap him, then murdered him because he'd resisted?

But Sano perceived another reason why the women had changed their tune. "Did Lord Matsudaira's envoy tell you anything besides the tutor's story?"

Another glance passed between mother and daughter. Oigimi said, "He warned us that you were looking for someone else to blame for the murder."

"That I am." And here were two new suspects, Sano thought. They'd taken the envoy's hint; they weren't stupid. They'd chosen to help Lord Matsudaira build up the case against Sano's mother for fear that if she didn't take the fall, they would.

Sano felt the atmosphere change as he shed the role of a son fending off an attack on his mother and reinhabited his position as chamberlain and investigator. Lady Ateki shrank with fear. Oigimi was still hostile, but on her guard.

"Where were you when Tadatoshi disappeared?" Sano asked.

"We were in the house, getting ready to travel across the river," said Lady Ateki.

"My mother and I were together the whole time," Oigimi said.

They were each other's alibis for the kidnapping, if indeed there had been one. Sano said, "What did you do when your father gave orders to look for Tadatoshi?"

"We obeyed," Oigimi said. "When nobody could find him in the estate, we went outside to the city."

"Our attendants went with us," Lady Ateki said.

Which meant they couldn't have done any evil without witnesses. Sano asked, "What happened there?"

"We called Tadatoshi's name up and down the streets. We could see smoke coming toward us." Lady Ateki's eyes searched the distance for her lost son. "The buildings up ahead were in flames. A mob of people came running away from them. We got caught in them, caught in the fire."

Caught up in the memory, she shuddered. "We couldn't get away. We were trapped in a narrow road. The houses around us went up in flames. The wind blew them at us. I heard my daughter scream. Her hair and clothes were burning."

Oigimi sat as motionless as a corpse propped on a funeral pyre. Sano imagined fire engulfing her, blackening her clothes. She stiffened her posture against the recollection.

"The guards beat their capes on her and rolled her on the ground until the flames were out," Lady Ateki said. "She was unconscious. I thought she was dead. The guards picked her up. They carried her as we ran."

Sano pictured the burned, limp girl in the soldiers' arms, the hysterical mother, the crying ladies, their frantic flight through the inferno.

"My ladies-in-waiting fell behind. They were lost in the crowds. I never saw them again. All the guards except the two carrying Oigimi were killed when a balcony collapsed on them. It was only by the grace of the gods that we reached the hills. I held my daughter while we watched the city burn."

Rarely had Sano ever felt such distaste for interrogating suspects. If it was for anyone else besides his mother, he would leave them alone. "You never saw Tadatoshi?"

"No." Oigimi's voice was sharp with impatience. "We thought he'd died in the fire—until you told us otherwise. He never came back."

But Sano speculated that perhaps Tadatoshi *had* come back after the fire, to what was left of his family. "Suppose he had. Would you have been glad to see him?"

"Of course!" Lady Ateki exclaimed. "All I wanted was to have my son again."

"Even though he was the reason you were caught in the fire?" Sano said. "At the time nobody thought he'd been kidnapped; you must have thought he'd wandered off, as he was in the habit of doing."

"He was just a child! He didn't know any better!"

"Fourteen is almost a man," Sano pointed out. "Tadatoshi was old enough to know that when there's a fire and one's family is about to run for safety, one shouldn't go wandering. Because you had to look for him, you never got across the river. Didn't you think to blame Tadatoshi?"

"No!" Lady Ateki cried.

"*I* blamed him," Oigimi said. A strange note pealed in her voice, a chord of anger and hatred muted by time. "But if you're suggesting that he came back and I killed him . . . Well, I couldn't have. I was an invalid for years after the fire. I hadn't the strength."

"Maybe you didn't," Sano said, and turned to Lady Ateki.

She gaped, shook her head, and said, "I never would have hurt my own boy."

"Your husband was killed, and so were most of the people from your estate," Sano reminded her. "Your daughter was burned. Didn't he deserve to be punished?"

"No!" Lady Ateki raised herself up like a wounded bird trying to fly. "I loved him. No matter what!"

Oigimi said, "My mother is innocent. Leave her alone."

"Daughter, mind your manners. You'll offend the honorable chamberlain," Lady Ateki pleaded.

"I don't care. I'm not afraid of him," Oigimi said. "There's nothing he can do to me that's worse than what's already happened."

She flung off her drape. Her neck was corrugated with scars, her scalp crusty and bald on the burned side. Her dead eye stared blankly. She pushed up her left sleeve to reveal the mottled red stump of her arm. Sano's repugnance vied with pity. Oigimi had nothing to lose except her life, which must be a terrible burden.

"You'll never be able to prove we're guilty," she said. Her good eye sparked with fury and triumph. "If you bring us before the shogun and accuse us, we'll testify against your mother. The shogun and Lord Matsudaira can decide who's telling the truth. We're willing to take a chance. Are you?"

At Sano's estate, Reiko and Akiko played ball with Midori, her children, and Lieutenant Asukai in the garden outside the private chambers. Reiko threw the soft cloth ball to little Tatsuo. She noticed that Lieutenant Asukai was good with the children; he gently tossed them the ball, and when they threw it with all their might only to have it land near their feet, he gallantly dashed forward, retrieved it, and backed up for another throw. Although Reiko smiled and cheered with everyone else, her mind dwelled in dark realms.

She was glad she hadn't told Sano about her conversation with his mother. He had enough to worry about already. For him to know that Reiko believed his mother to be guilty would do him no good. And Reiko had no basis for her judgment except her intuition, no proof that Sano would accept. Although Reiko was upset that her mother-in-law was in jail, she couldn't help feeling relieved to have Etsuko out of the house. She thought jail was exactly where Etsuko belonged. Yet Reiko felt no true satisfaction. Etsuko's imprisonment was another step toward disaster for the whole family and a sign that Sano couldn't save them. The fearful tension that had plagued Reiko during the past few days mounted higher.

Sudden loud, agonized screams shattered the peace. Reiko froze. The ball she'd just caught fell from her hands. Her heart stopped in terror, then began to race.

"What was that?" Midori said, looking toward the house, from which the noise had come.

An explanation occurred to Reiko. She rushed into the house, followed by Lieutenant Asukai and the others. They ran down the corridor to her chamber. Inside, the cabinet built into the wall was open. An armor-clad samurai stood in front of the cabinet, one arm thrust into it, the other beating wildly at the air while he screamed and his body jerked. He turned, his face ferocious with pain.

"Captain Ogyu!" Reiko said as she recognized him. He was the commanding officer of the squadron that protected her family's quarters.

"You're the spy!" Lieutenant Asukai exclaimed in disbelief and shock.

"No!" Ogyu roared.

But the truth was obvious. Ogyu had opened the secret compartment in which Reiko had hidden the book that named Sano's "spies." When Sano and his family had first moved into the estate, Masahiro had found the compartment, filled with a stash of gold coins that Yanagisawa had left behind when he'd been exiled. Now the book lay inside the compartment. Captain Ogyu's fingers were touching the black silk cover. His hand was immobilized by a dagger stuck through its back, into the compartment's wooden base. When he'd opened the compartment he'd triggered the trap, a hidden spring that had driven the dagger into his hand.

Reiko was so astounded by how well her plan had worked that all she could do was stand silent, her hand over her mouth. Midori took one look at the captive, whose blood welled around the dagger and spilled on the floor, and hustled the children away. "Wait!" Masahiro cried. "I want to see!"

Captain Ogyu stammered, "I was just— I thought—"

"You thought the book was a list of spies," Lieutenant Asukai said. "You just wanted to steal it for Lord Matsudaira. Well, the book is a fake, this is a trap, and you fell for it." He seized Ogyu by his topknot and banged his head against the cabinet for good measure. "Now we've caught you dead to rights."

Captain Ogyu shouted curses. With his free hand he wrenched at the dagger's handle. He begged, "Get it out of me! Let me loose!"

"Oh, we will," Asukai said. "But don't be in such a hurry. What's going to happen to you next will hurt a lot worse."

17

When Sano and his entourage arrived back at Edo Castle, a sentry at the main gate said, "General Isogai wants to see you."

General Isogai was the supreme commander of the Tokugawa army. He owned the loyalty of thousands of troops, and he'd pledged their military support to Sano. No matter that Sano had important things to do, he couldn't brush off his chief ally.

He found General Isogai at the Tokugawa army's central headquarters, located in a turret that rose up from a wall within Edo Castle, high on its hill. The turret, a square structure faced with white plaster, was crowned with tile roofs that protruded above each of its three stories. General Isogai had an office at the top. Inside, swords, spears, and guns hung in racks on the walls, alongside maps of Japan on which army garrisons and main roads were marked. General Isogai paced the floor like a soldier in a drill. He had a squat, heavily muscled figure and the appearance of no neck between his thick shoulders and his ovoid head.

"Greetings, Sano-*san*," he said in a voice loud enough to carry across a battlefield.

Sano returned the greeting; they exchanged bows. He noted that General Isogai didn't invite him to sit or offer him a drink. "Why did you want to see me?"

General Isogai's thick lips smiled; his eyes glinted with wits and good cheer. "Always ready to get right down to business, aren't you? No wasting time. That's what I always liked about you."

Sano noticed that General Isogai had spoken in the past tense. "I suppose you've heard that my mother is in Edo Jail for murder and I'm three days away from execution for treason."

"Everyone's heard." General Isogai's expression sobered. "The news is halfway across the country by now."

"Somehow I don't think you called me here to sympathize with me," Sano said in a tone that prompted the other man to state his business.

"I do offer my sympathy," General Isogai said, feigning hurt. "Rotten luck for you and your mother. Wouldn't wish that on my own mother, may she rest in peace. I'm not totally without a heart."

"But?"

"But there's something I have to tell you." General Isogai spoke with the air of a judge delivering a death sentence: "I can't support you any longer."

Although Sano had expected as much, he felt as if the loss of General Isogai and the Tokugawa army had knocked his legs out from under him. He couldn't hide his bitterness as he said, "You were among the men who pushed me to challenge Lord Matsudaira. You led me to believe you'd stand by me. And now you back out at the first sign of trouble."

General Isogai bristled at Sano's hint that he was a quitter and a coward. "So I encouraged you. It was your decision, and you were aware of the risks. You know that the wind can change at any moment; alliances aren't necessarily forever. Any man who doesn't is a fool."

"Better a fool than a rat," Sano said evenly.

General Isogai grinned and spread his hands to show that the offense intended hadn't been taken. "Rats are smart. They know to leave a sinking ship. If I'm a rat, I'm not the only one. Uemori Yoichi and Ohgami Kaoru asked me to convey a message to you." Those men were Sano's allies on the Council of Elders, Japan's chief governing body. "They can no longer afford to be associated with you, either."

This was how it felt to be caught in a tornado, fighting to stand upright while one's house and belongings were sucked away by the wind. But Sano didn't protest or beg; that would display weakness, and it was no use.

"Then there's nothing more to say." Sano leveled a cold gaze on General Isogai and started toward the door.

"Nothing except good-bye," General Isogai said, regretful yet pragmatic. "And good luck."

When Sano came out of army headquarters, Hirata and the detectives were waiting for him. "What did General Isogai want?" Hirata asked.

Sano told them. Marume said, "That bastard!"

"It's a good thing you found out before he and his fellow traitors could desert you on the battlefield," Hirata said.

"You're better off without them," Fukida agreed.

But they knew, as did Sano, that he'd just lost more than half his faction. And Sano had even more pressing concerns. "Three days is long enough to lose the rest of my allies, but I don't have time to worry about that now. Three days in Edo Jail could be the death of my mother even if I exonerate her. I'd better go there and make sure she's all right."

As he and his men mounted their horses on the path that ran along the top of the castle wall below the covered corridors, a patrol guard strolled toward them. The guard saw Sano, paused, and said, "Excuse me, Honorable Chamberlain. I've just heard there's trouble at your estate."

Sano, Hirata, and the detectives rushed home. Leaping off his mount at the gate, Sano called to the sentries, "What happened?"

"Lord Matsudaira's spy has been caught," said one of the men.

Marume and Fukida exclaimed in surprise. The sentries opened the gate, and as Sano rushed in it, he asked, "Was anyone hurt?" His heart filled with anxiety about Reiko and the children.

The guard captain on duty met Sano in the courtyard. "Your family is safe," he said, running alongside Sano, Hirata, and the detectives. "The situation's under control."

He led them inside the mansion, to the private quarters. They arrived to see a group of soldiers leading out a man Sano recognized as Captain Ogyu. Ogyu's right hand was wrapped in a bloodstained bandage. When the soldiers stopped him in front of Sano, he hung his head rather than meet Sano's eyes. Huddled against a wall nearby were Lieutenant Asukai and Reiko. They looked relieved and triumphant.

Sano hastened to his wife. "What's going on here?"

While Reiko explained, Sano shook his head in astonishment. "Well," he said, "it was clever of you to put that trap to such good use." He turned to Captain Ogyu and demanded, "What have you to say for yourself?"

Ogyu remained sullenly quiet.

"Are you all right?" Sano asked Reiko.

She seemed to wilt. "Yes," she said with a smile as fleeting as bright. Her body trembled, as if she'd only now just realized that the enemy in their midst could have done worse than try to steal information. Sano saw that the exposure of the spy, so soon after the ambush, had profoundly upset her. Her valiant courage was eroding. Her eyes shone with belated terror as well as relief that the enemy was captured, the danger averted.

"I'd better see to the children." As she hurried away, she swiped her hand across her eyes.

Sano glanced at Captain Ogyu, then said to his troops, "Get this piece of filth out of here and put him to death." He didn't like to use capital punishment, but he would make an exception in this case. Beckoning Hirata and the detectives, he strode out of the courtyard. "Too bad for Lord Matsudaira that his spy is finished. He's lost this round."

As Sano, Hirata, and the detectives mounted their horses outside the gate, Hana came running from the estate. "What's happened to your mother?" she cried.

Sano had forgotten about Hana. He owed her an explanation that he couldn't just yell over his shoulder as he rode off. "Wait," he told his men.

He jumped off his horse and led Hana into the estate, to the grounds that fronted the mansion. These were empty except for a few gardeners working. Sano told Hana how the tutor had incriminated his mother in front of the shogun.

"So Egen turned on her." Distraught but not surprised, Hana said to herself, "I knew nothing good would come of that."

"Come of what?" Sano said.

"Nothing," Hana said quickly. "Did the shogun believe Egen?"

"Unfortunately, yes. He pronounced my mother guilty."

"He did?" Hana stamped her feet. "That stupid idiot!"

Sano blinked. This was the first time he'd ever heard anyone say aloud what many thought of their lord. Hana was angry enough to insult the shogun even though it was punishable by death if anyone reported her.

"Where is your mother?" Hana demanded.

"She's been taken to Edo Jail," Sano said.

As he explained that she'd been imprisoned to await execution, the terrible reality of it sank in. A lump filled his throat.

"No!" Hana was equally devastated. "You've got to get her out!"

"I'm trying." Now Sano saw a chance to break through the barrier of Hana's evasions. "But I need your help."

"I can't bear to think of her in that place," Hana fretted, pacing in a circle like a trapped mouse. "She must be so frightened. I'll do anything. Just tell me what!"

"Tell me what happened during the Great Fire."

Hana faltered to a stop. "I did."

"We both know better. And we can't waste any more time on games. My mother's in jail, I have three days to prove she's innocent, and if I don't, she'll die." Vexed that Hana kept putting him off, Sano said, "Now talk!"

"It won't help your mother."

"Maybe you're wrong. And my inquiries have come to a dead end. You, and she, are all I have."

"All right." Defeated, Hana took a deep breath, then said, "The day the Great Fire started, your mother and I packed our things to go across the river. Then we learned that Tadatoshi was missing. We went out to look for him."

"I've already heard that," Sano said, warning Hana not to repeat her lies.

"I'm getting to the part you haven't heard," she snapped. "I turned my back on your mother—just for an instant. And she was gone." Hana's pupils dilated with the panic she must have felt. "I forgot Tadatoshi. It was Etsuko that I cared about, who was out in the city while the fire was burning, that I had to find. I ran through the streets, calling her name—until I saw the fire coming."

Her eyes shone as if with the reflections of the flames in her memory. "People came running away from it toward me. I was carried along with them. We tumbled down the bank of a canal and into the water. I was pushed under it. All around me people were kicking and screaming, trying to swim." Hana flailed her arms. "I almost drowned. But the water saved my life. The fire leaped across the canal. It passed right over my head to the other side, but I wasn't hurt at all."

Even now, forty-three years later, Hana was clearly awed by the miracle. "It was dark when I climbed out of the canal. It was so cold I almost froze." She bent a vindictive yet sad gaze on Sano. "I didn't find Etsuko until eight days later."

Sano's heart plummeted because Hana had retracted his mother's alibi for the time of the Great Fire, when Tadatoshi had probably met his death.

"I wandered the city, looking for her," Hana continued. "I asked everyone I met whether they'd seen her. By the time the *bakufu* put up the tents, I was so exhausted that I couldn't go on. I gave Etsuko up for dead. I lay down in a tent with strangers and I grieved . . . until the morning I awakened to hear her calling my name. At first I thought I was dreaming. Then I looked outside the tent, and I saw

Etsuko running toward me." Hana's face wore the expression of a person beholding a divine vision. "She was alive!"

Even though Sano was upset to learn that his mother had a period of time unaccounted for, he recognized his good luck. How close he'd come to never being born! He owed his existence to whatever miracle had saved his mother from becoming one of the fire's hundred thousand victims.

"People I'd asked about her had directed her to me." Pantomiming an embrace, Hana said, "I hugged her. We both cried. We were so glad to see each other! But then I noticed the blood."

Sano's sense of good fortune evaporated. "What blood?"

"The blood all over her clothes." Hana stroked her own sleeves, as if touching phantom stains. "I thought Etsuko was hurt. I pulled her into the tent and undressed her so I could find the wound and try to help her. I washed her from head to toe. She was hysterical. But there wasn't any wound on her." Hana's voice rose in surprise. "Not a scratch."

Horror trickled like ice water through Sano, but he felt less surprise than a sense of inevitability. "Then it wasn't her blood."

"No." Hana's relief for his mother's sake mingled with anger at Sano because he'd forced this compromising truth out of her. "When I asked Etsuko where the blood came from and what had happened, she refused to say. She wouldn't tell me where she'd been. I can guess what you're thinking—that the blood was Tadatoshi's."

"It could have come from someone else who was hurt while trying to escape the fire," Sano said, grasping for an excuse.

Hana said bitterly, "Your mother is innocent. I know. But now you know that what I didn't want to tell you isn't going to save her. Don't say I didn't warn you."

18

Sano and his troops thundered on horseback over the bridge across the canal that fronted Edo Jail. Smoke from a nearby fire veiled the roofs. Guards in the towers at the corners of the stone walls kept watch in case the wind should shift and the fire threaten the jail. Sano dismounted, stalked up to the gate sentries, and ordered, "Show me where my mother is."

The guards had clearly been expecting him. Everyone in the jail must have been talking about the incarceration of the mother of the shogun's second-in-command. They opened the gate, and one guard said, "Right this way, Honorable Chamberlain."

Sano followed with a few troops. He'd sent Detectives Marume and Fukida to hunt for people who'd lived at Tadatoshi's estate before the Great Fire, and Hirata to investigate Colonel Doi, still his favorite suspect. Now Sano had plans besides seeing to his mother's health and comfort. The false testimony from his enemies and hers was one matter; the evidence from her own loyal servant, another entirely. Sano had to know the truth, come what might.

The guard led Sano and his men to the dungeon, whose grimy plaster walls rose from a high stone foundation. Sano braced himself for the sight of his mother locked in a filthy cell with thieves and prostitutes, abused by cruel wardens. But the guard took Sano's party through a side door and down a passage where the wails and groans of the prisoners were but faintly audible. They arrived at a chamber that contained only two people.

Sano's mother lay on a bed of clean straw on a wooden pallet. A ragged but clean blanket covered her. Her eyes were closed, her face slack. Kneeling beside her was Dr. Ito.

"Greetings," Dr. Ito said.

Near him sat his medicine chest of herbs and potions in jars, and a tray that held cups, a teapot, and spoons. He gave no sign that he recognized Sano. Neither did Sano address Dr. Ito as his friend: They weren't supposed to know each other. After dismissing the guard, Sano stationed his troops outside the door to keep everyone away.

"I heard they'd brought your mother to the jail," Dr. Ito said when he was alone with Sano. "This is the sickroom, where I treat prisoners who have contagious diseases. I persuaded the chief warden to put her here instead of in a cell."

"A thousand thanks," Sano said. The stench of urine, excrement, and rot in the dungeon was faint here. He knelt and studied his mother. She didn't react to his presence. "Is she asleep?"

"Yes. I gave her a sedative. She was very upset when she arrived. I thought it best to calm her and relieve her suffering."

"I must speak with her," Sano said. "Can you wake her up?"

"She may become agitated again."

"It's urgent."

"Very well, then." Dr. Ito opened a jar from his medicine chest, poured a dose into a cup, and diluted it with water from the teapot. "This is a stimulant." He spooned the potion into her mouth. She grimaced at the taste as she swallowed. After some moments passed, her eyes opened, the pupils hugely dilated.

"Mother?" Sano said, bending over her. "Can you hear me?"

Her gaze fixed blearily on him. Her lips formed his name.

"Yes, it's me," Sano said. "We have to talk, about the murder of Tadatoshi."

She mewled in protest. Even though Sano hated pressuring her in her condition, he said, "I can't let you put me off any longer. Things have gone from bad to worse. Lady Ateki and Oigimi say you were involved with Tadatoshi's kidnapping and murder. They said they saw you spying on him before he disappeared."

Fear welled in her black, drugged gaze.

"That's not all." Sano couldn't keep the anger out of his voice. "Hana told me she lost you during the Great Fire. She told me that when she found you afterward, you had blood all over your clothes. Was it Tadatoshi's?"

". . . Hana wouldn't," she whispered.

Sano pitied his mother, betrayed by her lifelong companion. He loved her as much as ever, but at that moment he hated her more than any criminal who'd ever deceived him. Her actions had put not only her own life at risk, but his family's, his friends'. "Did you kill Tadatoshi?" he demanded.

"No!"

Her voice was weak yet vehement. Sano couldn't tell whether she was denying the accusation or expressing her horror that Sano had found her out. "If you weren't involved in kidnapping him, why did you spy on him? If you didn't kill him, why have you lied to me?"

Impatient, he prodded her shoulder. She convulsed; her breath rasped. Dr. Ito said, "Be careful."

Forcing himself to speak gently, Sano said, "Mother, you have to tell me the truth. No matter how bad it is, at least I'll know what I have to do to save us."

An internal struggle waged within her, twitching her muscles. Then she went limp and closed her eyes. Sano thought she'd fallen asleep, but she murmured, "All right."

Sano was amazed that she'd finally capitulated. Dr. Ito said, "The sedative has the effect of breaking down resistance."

That it could achieve what talk, pleading, and threats hadn't! Sano listened as his mother began to speak.

A sharp-edged silver moon illuminated the garden of the estate. As Etsuko crept through the shadows, her heart raced. All day she'd waited impatiently for her tryst with Egen. She reached the tea ceremony cottage, a small wooden house secluded in a grove of pine trees, unused in the winter. Egen was already there.

He caught her in his embrace. Their desire was so great that they couldn't wait to get inside the cottage. She pressed her body against his and felt the hardness at his loins. He fumbled the door open. They fell into the cottage, onto the mattress they'd sneaked inside. Egen kicked the door shut. Etsuko flung the quilt over them. In the warm, musty darkness under it, legs intertwined with legs. Hands tore open clothes. Flesh met hot, ardent flesh.

The feel of Egen's strong, muscled young body thrilled Etsuko. She climbed atop him and sighed as he caressed her breasts, her hips. Together, in this private place, they could forget the world. They didn't care that it was wrong for them to make love, that she was violating social custom and he his oath of celibacy. Nor did Etsuko care about Doi, her fiancé. Nothing mattered except satisfying this need.

Egen rolled, throwing Etsuko onto the mattress. She pulled him down on her. When he entered her, they moaned at the sensation. The first time, three months ago, had hurt so much that Etsuko had screamed; afterward, she'd bled. But now, as Egen moved inside her, it was pure, astounding pleasure. She arched her back to meet his thrusts. As he shuddered and groaned out his release, she rode waves of ecstasy.

Later, they lay side by side, holding hands, in the moonlight that seeped through the window shutters. Unhappiness filled Etsuko as cold, harsh reality intruded.

"I wish we could run away together and marry," she said.

"So do I." Egen exhaled. The chains of society's rules and their prior commitments shackled them. "But even if we did, what would we live on?"

"You could sell your poetry."

He laughed, a gloomy chuckle. "Who would buy it?"

"Everybody," Etsuko said, wanting to cheer him up, fervent in her belief in his talent. "We'll be rich." She turned over, hugged him. "And happy together forever!"

They embraced in desperate, doomed love. Suddenly Egen raised his head and sniffed the air. "I smell smoke."

Now Etsuko smelled it, too. "Look—it's coming in the windows."

She and Egen threw back the quilt. This fire season was a dangerous one, and as much as they hated to cut short their time together, they couldn't lie abed while a fire burned in the estate. Straightening their clothes, they hurried outside. The smoke billowed from a far corner of the garden, behind trees that raised bare, skeletal branches against the fire's crackling orange light.

"Come on," Egen said, running toward the fire. "We have to put it out."

Etsuko ran after him. The smoke stung her eyes and made her cough. She and Egen halted near the fire—a bush piled with dead leaves, burning like a giant torch. Tadatoshi stood close by it. His face wore an intense, gloating expression; his eyes were huge and round and bright with the flames. Under his kimono, his hands worked at his loins.

"Tadatoshi! What are you doing?" Egen said.

The boy took no notice of Egen or Etsuko. His hands worked faster. He seemed in a trance.

Egen raced to the well. He filled a bucket, ran with it, and threw water on the bush. Etsuko filled the spare buckets for Egen, who lugged water and dowsed the fire until it was out. Egen and Etsuko stood, panting and relieved, by the smoking ruins of the bush. Tadatoshi blinked as if he'd just awakened. His hands dangled. His eyes glowed with reflections of the cold moonlight.

"Why didn't you put it out?" Egen said.

"Why did you?" Tadatoshi sounded oddly disappointed.

Egen looked as puzzled as Etsuko felt. "How did it start?"

A sly expression came over Tadatoshi's face. Etsuko noticed a kerosene jar and a lamp on the ground near the boy. Egen said to him, "*You* started it?"

As Etsuko and Egen gazed at him in shock, Tadatoshi smiled, a private, satisfied smile.

"Why would you do such a thing?" Egen said. "If we hadn't come along, you might have burned down the estate!"

Tadatoshi shrugged. Etsuko felt a ripple of revulsion tinged with fear. He was as strange as Egen had said, but she'd thought him harmless—until now.

"I'm going to tell your father," Egen said.

The boy kept smiling, but his gaze turned hostile. "You'd better not."

"It's my duty," Egen said. "Your father will want to know. He'll teach you not to set fires. You deserve to be punished."

"If you tell anyone, I'll tell everybody what you do in the tea cottage with *her*." Tadatoshi pointed at Etsuko.

Etsuko gasped. Egen demanded, "Have you been spying on us?"

Tadatoshi giggled.

A guard burst upon the scene. "I smelled smoke. Is there a fire?" He looked at Etsuko, Egen, Tadatoshi, and the burned bush. "What happened?"

Etsuko held her breath. Tadatoshi's gaze threatened Egen, who paused before he said, "There was a fire. We put it out. That's all."

The next day, Etsuko waylaid Egen in the corridor. "What are we going to do about Tadatoshi?" she whispered.

Egen was somber, worried. "We can't just do nothing. He might set more fires."

"But if we report him, and he tells everyone about us, his father will dismiss you. Lady Ateki will dismiss me. You'll have to go back to the temple. I'll go back to my parents, who'll never let me out of the house until I'm married." Panic seized Etsuko. "We'll never see each other again!"

"I know, but we have to stop him before he hurts somebody."

Although her relationship with Egen had been her first priority, Etsuko felt the stirrings of conscience. That strange, evil boy could kill innocent people. A sense of responsibility sprang from some hitherto unknown place inside Etsuko. With it came inspiration.

"I have an idea," she said. "We'll keep a watch on Tadatoshi. If he tries to start another fire, we'll stop him. He can't hurt anybody as long as we're on guard."

This was the first original, unselfish idea she'd had in her life. Etsuko was proud of herself, and Egen looked at her with new respect.

So began their spying on Tadatoshi. Daytime was easy. Egen supervised the boy during his lessons. Etsuko helped keep an eye on him during meals and recreation. The nights proved more difficult. While the rest of the household slept, Egen and Etsuko took turns sitting in the hall by Tadatoshi's door. But after six nights with little sleep, Etsuko awakened one morning to realize that she'd missed her shift.

"Why didn't you come?" Egen demanded later.

"I didn't wake up," Etsuko said. "I was so tired."

Egen's eyes were red, with dark circles underneath. "So was I. I fell asleep. But it's all right—Tadatoshi was in his bed when I woke up and looked in on him."

That afternoon, Egen brought Tadatoshi to visit his mother. While she fussed over the boy, and Etsuko and Egen stole glances at each other, one of the maids said, "I heard there was a fire in town last night."

Tadatoshi smirked at Etsuko and Egen. Horror filled Etsuko. Not only had he escaped them; he'd set a fire.

"We can't go on like this," Egen said later, while he and Etsuko watched Tadatoshi practice sword fighting with his bodyguards. "We'll slip up again."

"You're right," Etsuko said. "It's impossible for the two of us to watch him all the time. We need help."

They gazed at Doi, demonstrating sword techniques. He was the only person they could trust. When he stopped for a drink of water, they approached him. Etsuko said, "Doi-*san*, may we speak with you a moment?"

"About what?"

Etsuko explained that Tadatoshi had set a fire last night.

"I don't believe it," Doi said in astonishment.

"It's true," Egen said. "We caught him once before."

"Why didn't you tell anyone?"

"We're telling you," Etsuko said, then fibbed: "We were afraid no one else would believe us. We've been watching him, trying to keep him from setting another fire. But last night he got away from us. He set the fire in town. We can't control him by ourselves. Will you help us?"

His expression said Doi thought they'd gone mad. Suspicion crept into his eyes. "What were you two doing outside in the middle of the night?"

"We couldn't sleep. We went out for a walk, and we happened to meet," Egen said quickly. "That's when we saw the bush on fire."

Etsuko flushed under Doi's dubious gaze; Egen fidgeted with his rosary. Doi said, "This is nonsense," and stalked off.

"I guess we'll just have to carry on alone," Egen said.

"Tonight we'll sit watch on Tadatoshi together," Etsuko decided. "We'll keep each other awake."

By the time night came, they were so exhausted that they both fell asleep by Tadatoshi's door. They were jarred awake at dawn, by shouts. They rushed outside and saw Doi dragging Tadatoshi across the courtyard.

"Let go of me!" Tadatoshi yelled, kicking and struggling.

"Not until I'm ready." Doi was panting with exertion, angrier than Etsuko had ever seen him.

Servants came running to see what the fuss was all about, Hana among them. Doi grabbed Tadatoshi by the front of his robe and shouted, "If you ever do that again, I'll kill you!"

He shoved Tadatoshi. "Go to your room." The boy ran off. Doi turned on the servants. "What are you gawking at? Get out of here."

They fled. Etsuko asked Doi, "What happened?"

The anger drained from him; he looked miserable. "I didn't believe what you said about Tadatoshi, but last night I thought I'd better check on him. I went to his room. You were both asleep outside it. I stood outside the building, and pretty soon he came out. He was carrying a pack on his back. I went after him. He had a ladder hidden in the bushes along the back wall. We climbed over. He sneaked into town, I trailed him. He stopped at a market in Nihonbashi. And then——"

Doi exhaled mournfully. "He took a jar of kerosene from his pack and splashed it on a stall. He lit it before I could stop him. The stall went up in flames. He set a fire. I saw him with my own eyes."

Etsuko was horrified yet glad. She and Egen were no longer alone in the secret.

"What happened?" Egen asked.

"A bell started ringing. I heard the firemen coming. Tadatoshi ran. I caught him and brought him home." Doi cursed, as woeful and ashamed as angry. "My master is an arsonist!"

"What are you going to do?" Etsuko said.

"I'm going to tell his father," Doi said.

Etsuko exchanged a relieved glance with Egen. Now they needn't report Tadatoshi and face the consequences. Later that morning, they eavesdropped outside the door of the office while Doi told Lord Tokugawa Naganori what he'd seen Tadatoshi do.

Lord Naganori said, "I was afraid of this. When my son was younger, I caught him setting fires on several occasions. I thought he was just playing and didn't know any better. I thought he would grow out of the habit, but it's clear he has not. Thank you for telling me. I'll take care of the problem."

For the next eight days Lord Naganori assigned guards to keep a constant watch on his son. Etsuko and Egen didn't have to stay up at night. But Doi began watching them. Once he caught Etsuko sneaking away from a rendezvous in the tea cottage with Egen. She put Doi off by saying she'd gone for a walk, but she feared he wouldn't believe her excuses next time. And Tadatoshi grew restless. Egen said he couldn't sit still during his lessons. His need to start fires seemed to be a compulsion that gave him no peace until it was satisfied.

Something had to happen.

On the eighth day Lord Naganori gathered Etsuko, Doi, Egen, and Tadatoshi in his office. He said, "I've brought you here to announce a decision I've made." He nodded at Etsuko and Egen. "Since you were the ones who first called attention to my son's problem with fires, you deserve to know."

Doi smiled; he thought Etsuko and Egen should be pleased because he'd shared the credit. They couldn't hide their horror. Tadatoshi turned a murderous gaze on them. Lord Naganori didn't notice. He continued. "My son is obviously possessed by an evil spirit that drives him to set fires. Therefore, I'm sending him to Miyako, to a sorcerer who performs exorcisms. He leaves tomorrow."

Relief flooded Etsuko; she saw Egen let out his breath. Tadatoshi was going away. They wouldn't have to worry about him anymore. Doi nodded in satisfaction.

"Doi-*san,* you'll go with him," Lord Naganori said.

The young samurai's expression turned to dismay. Etsuko saw Doi thinking that their wedding would have to be postponed. She rejoiced because she and Egen would have more time together.

"We can't neglect Tadatoshi's education," Lord Naganori said. "You'll go, too, Egen-*san.*"

It was Egen's and Etsuko's turn to be horrified. Who knew when they would see each other again?

No one dared oppose Lord Naganori. When he dismissed them, Etsuko fled, hiding tears. Doi and Egen hurried after her. Tadatoshi followed them outside.

"You told on me!" he shouted at Etsuko and Egen. "Now you'll be sorry!"

Etsuko turned on him, furious and aghast. This was all his fault. "Shut up, you awful little boy!"

"Now I'm going to tell on you." Tics wrenched Tadatoshi's face; his body jittered.

"Tell what?" Doi demanded.

Tadatoshi pointed at Etsuko and Egen. "They've been meeting in the tea cottage at night and mating like dogs, behind your back."

Their secret was out. Shamed to the core, Etsuko looked at the ground. She wished a hole would open and swallow her.

"So it's true," Doi said flatly. "Just as I suspected."

"We didn't mean for it to happen," Egen said.

"Spare me the excuses." Doi sounded even more hurt than furious. "I thought you were both my friends. Well, not anymore!"

The next day, the Great Fire started.

Shocked by what his mother had said, Sano watched her eyes close. "Mother! Tell me what happened next!"

She didn't respond. Her breath sighed quietly in and out of her as she slept on her bed in Edo Jail's sickroom. Sano said to Dr. Ito, "Can you wake her up again?"

"That's not advisable. Giving her more stimulant could have dangerous effects." Dr. Ito paused, then said, "Are you sure you want to hear more?"

Although Sano had come to discover the truth about his mother and the murder of Tadatoshi, he saw Dr. Ito's point: He'd already heard far too much.

19

The wind tore clouds into streamers in the night sky. Fires burned like flares across the city and lit the figures of men who sat in fire-watch towers, peering through spyglasses. Within Edo Castle, gusts blew torches carried by patrol guards into twisting tongues of flame. Servants snuffed the fires in the stone lanterns with sand and placed buckets filled with water at every gate. Inside the parlor of Sano's mansion, drafts fanned smoke from the charcoal brazier on which Reiko heated sake.

Sano, Hirata, and the detectives sat waiting for their drinks. Masahiro played with his toy soldiers while Sano summarized the story his mother had told him at Edo Jail.

"So little Tadatoshi was an arsonist," Marume said.

So my mother had a secret lover, Sano thought. That part of the story had shocked him as much as the part about Tadatoshi setting fires. He wouldn't have believed his mother had been so unchaste, so wanton, had he not heard it from her own lips. But that wasn't the only disturbing thing.

"Why do people set fires?" Masahiro asked, lining up wooden horsemen.

"Maybe because they're possessed by evil spirits, as Tadatoshi's father thought," Sano said. "We may never know."

Something else troubled Sano. It had to do with his mother taking the initiative to spy on Tadatoshi, her enlisting the tutor and Doi in her scheme to prevent him from endangering innocent people. Her actions not only contradicted Sano's whole image of his docile, quiet mother, but they also flouted propriety and tradition.

"Is Lord Matsudaira possessed by an evil spirit?" Masahiro asked.

The detectives laughed. "That would be a good excuse for what he's doing," Fukida said.

Sano was impressed that his son had drawn a parallel between the arsonist in the murder case and the man who'd given him his first personal taste of evil. Masahiro was more astute than most nine-year-olds. But Sano regretted that his insight had come with a price—the loss of innocence.

"Lord Matsudaira is mad for power," Sano said. "Power is a kind of evil spirit. So you could be right."

"An exorcism might cure what ails him," Marume said. "Too bad he's not about to get one."

Reiko poured sake into cups and distributed them. Sano and his men drank while Masahiro marched his toy armies.

"It sounds as if Tadatoshi got his comeuppance," Fukida said. "Whoever killed him did everyone a favor."

Sano noticed that Reiko was very quiet, waiting on the men, effacing herself as conventional wives did. It seemed strangely out of character.

"Your mother's story explains why she was spying on Tadatoshi," Hirata said.

While relating her story, Sano had paused to tell his companions what Lady Ateki and Oigimi had said about her today.

"It also explains why Doi threatened him," Fukida said, alluding to Hana's statement, which Sano had related earlier.

"But it won't help her," Sano said unhappily.

If the story was true, his mother was slated for execution because of a boy who'd deserved to die. Arson was a capital crime, punishable by burning to death, but even if Tadatoshi had been guilty of it, that made no difference.

"Lord Tokugawa Naganori is dead, and Colonel Doi and Egen have taken sides against your mother. Even if they knew Tadatoshi was an arsonist, they're not going to admit it and help her out," Hirata concurred.

"It'll be her word against theirs," Masahiro piped up.

"Good observation, young master," Fukida said. "Chamberlain Sano, we've got a future detective here."

The gods forbid Masahiro to follow in his father's tracks, Sano thought. He looked to Reiko for her reaction. She appeared to be listening hard, yet she had a preoccupied air.

"Who wants to be the one to accuse the shogun's cousin of arson?" Marume said.

No one volunteered. Maligning the murder victim's character wouldn't serve the defendant's interests in this case. To speak ill of a Tokugawa clan member was treason. Should Sano report this story to the shogun, his mother could be put to death for it even if she hadn't killed Tadatoshi.

If she hadn't.

"That's one reason we can't make this story public," Sano said.

"Nobody will hear it from me," Hirata said.

"Nor I," chorused Masahiro and the detectives. Reiko only nodded.

"Here's another reason," Sano said. "Suppose Tadatoshi really was an arsonist. My mother admitted that she was part of a conspiracy to keep him from setting fires. We don't know the rest of the story—she fell asleep before she could finish. What if she was determined enough to stop him that she did more than spy on him?"

"Arson doesn't give his murderer an excuse for killing him," Hirata said. "It gives your mother a motive."

"Lord Matsudaira would certainly use that to his advantage," Marume said.

An idea occurred to Sano. "Tadatoshi never went to Miyako. Because of the Great Fire, Lord Naganori's plan fell through. We still don't know where Tadatoshi was or what he—and my mother—did during the fire."

Hirata frowned as he caught Sano's drift. "The fire started by accident at Honmyo Temple, before Tadatoshi disappeared," he reminded Sano. "He couldn't have set it."

"The city was burning," Sano said. "Everyone was terrified. My mother could have decided Tadatoshi was too dangerous to live. Maybe, when she went searching for him, she found him—and saw a chance to put him out of action for good."

"That would be Lord Matsudaira's interpretation," Fukida said. "He'd rush to foist it onto the shogun."

"So we keep the story quiet," Marume said. "What else do we do?"

"Tomorrow I'll go back to Edo Jail and try to get the rest of the story from my mother. Maybe it will help us." Sano was already dreading that it would do the opposite. "In the meantime, what have you learned?"

"I'm sorry to say we haven't located any of the people who lived at Tadatoshi's estate before the Great Fire," Marume said.

"They're all dead or scattered," Fukida explained.

"I haven't found anything against Colonel Doi," Hirata said. "So far he's got the cleanest record I've ever seen."

"I think that's suspicious," Masahiro said.

Sano nodded, proud yet not exactly pleased that his son had absorbed some basics of detective work. That road led to peril as well as the post of second-in-command to the shogun. "Nobody climbs as high as he's done without getting dirt on his hands. But too clean a record isn't evidence that Doi has a murder in his past."

"So we've come up empty," Fukida said with regret.

"Worse than empty." Sano related what Lady Ateki, Oigimi, and Hana had told him about his mother.

"Tadatoshi's mother and sister not only recant their statements but throw dirt at her, and so does her own maid. That is worse," Marume said. "But we're not giving up, are we?"

"Not while we still have another witness whose story I'm not ready to let stand," Sano said.

"The tutor?" Masahiro guessed.

"Right," Sano said.

"Look out, Marume-*san,* the boy's wits are quicker than yours," Fukida joked.

"I want a little talk with Egen," Sano said.

"Good idea," Marume said. "Make the bastard eat his words."

"I feel responsible for what he did, because I found him," Hirata said. "May I go with you?"

"All right," Sano said. "We'll leave at daybreak. Marume-*san* and Fukida-*san,* you keep searching for other witnesses and for evidence against Colonel Doi."

"Will do," Marume said.

The men bowed and rose to depart. Reiko gathered empty wine cups. Sano thought it odd that she'd participated in the discussion not at all.

"Aren't you interested in the investigation?" he asked her later as they prepared for bed.

Seated at her dressing table, Reiko brushed her hair. She looked in the mirror instead of at him. "Of course I am."

"You could have fooled me." Sano tied the sash of his night robe. "While we were talking, you didn't offer a single opinion or suggestion. That's not like you. What's wrong?"

Outside, the wind scraped tree branches against the roof and tossed dry leaves against the walls of the mansion. It sounded to Sano as if malevolent external forces were trying to breach their safe, cozy chamber.

When Reiko didn't answer his question at once, he knelt behind her. Their worried faces reflected in the mirror together. Their eyes met, and Sano belatedly recalled that Reiko had wanted to speak with him and he'd put her off. He had an idea as to why.

"What happened between you and my mother today?" he asked.

Reiko lowered her eyes and concentrated on brushing a tangle out of her hair. "I talked to her about the murder, as you said I should."

"And?" Sano braced himself. This was a day for news he didn't want to hear.

"I asked her about the alibi that Hana gave her. She changed her mind and said Hana was with her, and she couldn't have killed Tadatoshi."

Sano rubbed his temples, wondering if the flow of bad news would ever stop. "As I said earlier, Hana has changed her mind, too. She admitted she'd lost track of my mother for eight days during and after the fire." And he was more inclined to believe Hana's new story than his mother's. But he didn't like Reiko's expression, which made it clear that she, too, thought his mother was the liar yet again.

"What else?" Sano said.

"I asked her a few questions about her family." Reiko spoke with slow, tentative effort, as if prying pearls from a sharp-edged oyster.

Sano's muscles tightened. This was a sensitive topic, which he'd been loath to raise with his mother. "What questions?"

"When she became estranged from them. And why."

"What did she say?" Although Sano craved the answers, he felt a dread of the unknown.

"They broke off contact a few months after the Great Fire. As to why . . ." Reiko brushed her hair a few more strokes, obviously aware that discussing his mother's family was hard for Sano; she didn't want to be the bearer of bad, secondhand news. "She offered me several answers to choose from: It's not important, she doesn't remember, or her relatives are dead." Reiko's reflection in the mirror lifted her painted eyebrows, then let them drop.

"You think they're all lies?" Sano said, automatically rising to his mother's defense, even though he felt a spark of anger at her for withholding facts that concerned him. His anger extended to Reiko, who was here while his mother wasn't.

A sigh of sympathy, edged with frustration, issued from Reiko. "I don't know."

But Sano thought she did. He also thought she knew more than she'd told him. "What else did you learn?"

"This has been a difficult day. Maybe we should finish our conversation tomorrow."

166

The spark of Sano's ire heated into a flame. "I'm tired of people hedging with me. First my mother, now you. Can't women ever just speak the straight truth?"

"All right," Reiko said sharply, then drew a deep breath. "I think your mother was involved in something bad that happened during the Great Fire, that her family knows about, that she wants to keep a secret. I'm sure it has to do with her and the murder."

"What gave you those ideas?" Sano said, his temper growing hotter. The same ideas had occurred to him, but he'd tried to ignore them, and didn't like hearing them voiced by his wife.

"When I suggested contacting her family, she was horrified."

"Is that your only justification for this theory?"

"No," Reiko said. "There was the way she acted."

Sano saw Reiko's argument taking on a familiar shape that had vexed him in the past and incensed him now. "You mean your theory is based on your intuition."

She looked sad rather than offended by his derogatory tone. "My intuition has been right in the past."

"Not this time," Sano said, wishing he felt as certain as he sounded. "You don't even know my mother. You'd barely exchanged ten words with her before this. Don't make snap judgments."

"Maybe you don't know her any better," Reiko said gently.

That Sano couldn't deny. "Certainly her background was news to me. But I know her as a person." He was less and less sure that he did.

Reiko turned away from the mirror and faced him. With an air of a gambler spreading her cards before her opponents, she said, "Your mother got angry and blew up at me, for the first time ever." A shadow of the awe, fright, and shock Reiko had felt crossed her face. "There's another person inside her that she's kept hidden."

Not just from you, but from me, Sano thought. His anger at the deception goaded him to say the thing that he and Reiko had been avoiding. "You think my mother is guilty."

It was a statement, not a question. Reiko shook her head, not in denial but apology. Sano was horrified because her judgment added weight to his own burden of suspicion. His temper flared.

"There's not a crumb of solid evidence against my mother, and you decide she's a murderess. And you dare to think of yourself as a detective!"

Reiko set down her hairbrush with exaggerated care. "I tried to warn you. I tried to say this was a bad time to talk."

"You've never liked my mother, have you?" Sano demanded.

"Let's stop before we say things we'll both regret."

Sano couldn't stop. "You looked down on her because she was a peasant." He leaped to his feet as his self-restraint broke under the pressure that had been building since his mother's arrest. "And you don't like that she's turned out to be as highborn as you."

"I did like her," Reiko said, goaded to defend herself.

"Did, but don't anymore?" Sano laughed bitterly. "She fooled you. And you hate it." *As much as I do.*

Reiko rose, her hair falling around her shoulders in a black cape. It sparked in the dry air. "You've got to admit that her deception doesn't make her look good."

Sano was forced to admit it to himself, but he wouldn't give Reiko the satisfaction of hearing him say so. "Doesn't make her look good, but doesn't mean she's guilty. Which you should know if you were a real detective!"

He saw Reiko flinch, watched the spasm of pain twitch her mouth. He'd hurt her, and he was glad and ashamed. Now anger lit her eyes, which were liquid with tears. "I know I'm not a real detective, and I never will be. But I know better than to take the part of a suspect who's lied again and again. *I* haven't made the mistake of losing *my* objectivity!"

They glared at each other, but their fury soon turned to mutual distress. Sano realized that on top of all their other troubles, now they were at odds. Their current situation seemed even worse than last winter in Ezogashima.

In Ezogashima, they'd been together in adversity.

Now they were each alone.

* * *

Hirata lay alone in his bed, gazing at the crescent moon through his open window. He heard the estate settling down for the night, the patrol guards' footsteps, the servants' voices growing fewer and quieter as time passed. But Midori didn't come. Hirata sensed her presence with the children in their room down the hall. She was sleeping with them, as she must have last night. Hirata felt baffled, angered, and hurt by her desertion.

What was she doing? How dare she treat her husband like this?

He could order her to sleep with him, but he didn't want to give Midori the satisfaction of knowing he wanted her. And he was too proud to beg.

How long did she intend to keep it up?

As Hirata imagined more solitary nights, loneliness washed through him. He recalled his years of wandering, when he'd gone months without thinking about Midori and then suddenly missed her so much he'd thought he would die. Now that he'd come home, they were even more estranged. His ire surged to the defense of his wounded heart.

If Midori wanted to play games, so would he. He would fight fire with fire in this battle of theirs. Hirata folded his arms. When he won, she would revert to her old self and love him again. That decided, he closed his eyes and fell asleep.

20

At the temple in Shinagawa, sunrise colored the sky pink and the trees came alive with birdsong. Fifty priests in saffron robes, who filed toward the worship hall for their morning prayers, turned at the noise of pounding hooves. A squadron of mounted troops galloped across the temple grounds. The riders wore the Matsudaira crest on their armor. They clattered to a halt before the priests. The elderly abbot detached himself from his flock and approached the invaders.

"Greetings," he said, bowing. "How may we serve you?"

The captain leaped down from his horse. "We've heard reports that there are rebels operating out of this temple. We're here to investigate."

Yanagisawa froze in his position at the back of the line. He'd known that Lord Matsudaira had troops scouring the country for underground rebels. It had been only a matter of time until they arrived here, but he'd hoped to launch his comeback before that day came.

"There must be a mistake," the abbot said. "We're a peaceful, law-abiding sect."

Currents of fear raced through Yanagisawa. He fought the urge to run and mark himself as a criminal.

"Then you won't mind if we have a look around and interrogate your people," the captain said.

Yanagisawa saw his face and panicked. The captain was Nagasaka, once a commander in his army, who'd defected to Lord Matsudaira. What Yanagisawa had feared had finally happened: Someone who would recognize him had come hunting rebels. He ducked behind a tree, barely avoiding Nagasaka's gaze.

"This is highly irregular." The abbot remained calm, but Yanagisawa knew he was terrified because he was harboring a fugitive. Now he tried to stall and give Yanagisawa a chance to escape. "His Excellency the shogun won't approve."

"I have Lord Matsudaira's orders," Nagasaka said. "If you have nothing to hide, you have nothing to lose by cooperating."

He beckoned the priests, said, "Line up over here," then told his men, "Search the whole place. Guard the gates. No one leaves until we're done."

As the priests obeyed, Yanagisawa slipped away through the garden. Troops moved to secure the premises. He had to reach his cottage before they did.

He ran toward the wooded area at the back of the temple that sheltered the cottage. As he veered around the pagoda, he heard troops coming. He raced a zigzag course, ducking behind the giant temple bell, the sutra hall. He almost bumped smack into a soldier, then another, then another. The sun brightened the sky and dissolved the shadows that protected him. At last he plunged into the woods, down the gravel path. Relief filled him as the cottage appeared in view.

The door was open. The sound of voices inside halted Yanagisawa in his tracks. He dove into the bushes outside the cottage and listened, breathless with exertion, his relief turning to terror.

"Someone's been living in here," a man said.

"Probably a guest," said another man. "So where is he?"

Yanagisawa heard thumps, scuffling, and dragging noises. A third man said, "Hey, look at this big hole in the floor."

They'd found his escape hatch that led to a tunnel under the temple wall. Yanagisawa's heart sank.

"He must be a rebel. Why else would he need a secret passage?"

"If he went down there, maybe we can still catch him."

"If he hasn't, we should seal up the other end. We'll go down. You tell Captain Nagasaka."

Yanagisawa cursed under his breath as he heard two men climbing down the hole. The third soldier exited the cottage and walked past him. More troops crashed through the woods. Yanagisawa ran in desperate panic.

The troops multiplied into a horde around him. They swarmed the temple precinct; they occupied buildings. As he swerved to avoid them, he glimpsed Captain Nagasaka and a few troops with the priests outside the worship hall. The soldier from the cottage panted up to Nagasaka and spoke. Nagasaka rapped out orders to the troops. They hurried to join the search for the rebel turned fugitive.

Yanagisawa's strength was failing. His legs buckled; he couldn't breathe enough air. He collapsed behind the kitchen building. His heart felt ready to explode. He couldn't run anymore. Then he saw the well. He crawled to it, lifted the lid off the square wooden base, and climbed inside, bracing his back and feet against the sides of the rock-lined shaft. He reached up and pulled the lid closed.

He heard the troops stampede into the kitchen grounds, heard their shouts.

His exhausted muscles quaked. He slid down the shaft. The rocks scraped his back raw. He plunged into water up to his neck before he managed to fix himself in place. He held his breath and listened.

Troops strode past the well, their footsteps echoing down it. The water was freezing cold. Yanagisawa began to shiver. His teeth chattered; he clenched his jaws. Eons passed before he heard someone say, "There's nobody here."

"He must have gotten away," said Captain Nagasaka. "The abbot claims he's just an itinerant priest, but I don't think so. We'll keep looking."

The herd moved off. Chilled to the bone, Yanagisawa felt only a fleeting relief. Lord Matsudaira's men would come back in case their quarry should return. The temple was no longer safe for him. And the next close call could be even closer.

Sano rose hours before dawn. Disturbed by his quarrel with Reiko, he'd lain awake beside her for hours, knowing that she was awake, too. Neither of them had spoken, lest they quarrel some more and say worse, unforgivable things, and they weren't ready to make peace. Sano kept replaying their argument and thinking of things he should have said, as he supposed Reiko was also doing. Finally, he gave up pretending to sleep and went to his office, where he worked through the mountain of correspondence and reports on his desk in an attempt to keep control over the administration of the country. When his staff arrived, he conducted brief meetings into which he crammed as much business as possible. Then he, Hirata, and his troops headed to Kodemmacho.

The wind had quieted, and the morning was hazy, thick with the city's smoke, dust, and breath. As the slum awakened, people emerged from the shacks, lined up at the well, and built fires from scavenged coal and trash. Sano and his men rode down the foul-smelling alley, under the clotheslines, and dismounted outside the gate to the tenement where Egen lived.

When Sano and Hirata arrived on foot, they found the yard and balconies deserted, although cooking odors and a babble of voices emanated from the buildings. Hirata pounded on Egen's door, called his name, and said, "Open up!"

When he received no answer, he pounded louder. A woman with a crying child slung over her shoulder appeared on the balcony and said, "He's not there."

"Then where is he?" Sano wouldn't have been surprised if Egen had skipped. He must have known to expect consequences for incriminating Sano's mother.

"He moved out," the woman said.

Hirata opened the door and looked into the room. It was full of Egen's junk, but Egen himself was indeed gone. "He left all his wares."

"He said he didn't need them anymore. He was going on to

bigger and better things." The woman sneered, half skeptical, half envious.

Sano didn't intend for Egen to escape without answering for what he'd done. "Where did he move?"

"This is quite a step up from Egen's last place," Sano said an hour later as he and Hirata and their entourage arrived at the tutor's new residence.

The neighbor woman at Egen's tenement had directed them to this expensive inn located near the main boulevard that crossed Edo. "He bragged that he was going where the rich folks stay," she'd said. A bamboo fence around a garden containing cherry and willow trees screened the inn from other, more modest lodgings, the shops and food stalls, and the bustle of the streets. Sano and Hirata entered with a few troops. They followed the path between stone lanterns. The proprietor greeted them in the entranceway to the building.

"Would you like rooms?" His dour face brightened at the prospect of wealthy samurai customers.

"No, thank you," Sano said. "We're looking for one of your guests. His name is Egen."

The proprietor's expression grew hopeful. "Have you come to take him away?"

"Maybe." That depended on what he had to say for himself. Maybe Sano would just kill him. "Why, do you want us to?"

Leading them down a passage to an inner garden surrounded by guest quarters, the proprietor murmured, "The fellow is not the kind of guest I like."

In the garden lay the remains of what must have been a lavish, wild party. Servants picked up strings of red lanterns that dangled from the trees onto the ground, swept up food crumbs, and gathered wine bottles and broken cups. Sano smelled liquor, urine, and vomit. The doors to the rooms that opened onto the verandas were shut, the inhabitants presumably sleeping off their revels.

"Over there." The proprietor pointed at a door.

Sano and Hirata strode up to it. Hirata pushed the door open. A powerful stench of feces hit Sano. He and Hirata recoiled, hands over their noses. Behind them, the proprietor made a sound of disgust.

"What a filthy animal!"

Sano entered the room; Hirata followed. It was dim, the bamboo blinds drawn. Heaps of articles that Sano couldn't immediately identify gave it a resemblance to the room Egen had vacated. Egen lay on his back on the bed. When Sano spoke his name, he didn't answer or move. Sano stepped closer. His heart drummed a cadence of foreboding.

Egen's limbs were splayed, tangled in his garish cotton robe and the quilt. He reeked of liquor and the excrement that soiled the mattress beneath him. His eyes were wide, his mouth parted as if gasping for air. But he neither inhaled nor exhaled any breath.

"Is he dead?" the proprietor said fearfully.

Sano touched Egen's neck. The flesh was cold; there was no pulse. "Yes, he is." Dismay filled Sano.

"He must have drunk too much. He must have choked and died in his sleep." The proprietor sounded eager to believe the death was an ordinary accident.

The witness Sano had come to interrogate had taken whatever he knew about the murder to the grave. There went Sano's hope of learning anything from Egen that would help his mother.

Hirata yanked the cord on the blinds. Daylight brightened the room. He crouched, picked up a cushion from the floor, and examined the silk cover. "This wasn't an accident," he said, handing the cushion to Sano.

Sano saw a wet, bloody spot on the silk. He looked at Egen. There was blood on the tutor's lips and a reddish-purple bruise on his chest. Sano pictured the room in the dark of night, a figure pressing the cushion against Egen's face, a knee planted on the struggling man to hold him down. Sano imagined Egen's muffled cries and waving limbs, his bowels voiding while he died.

"Egen didn't die of drinking too much," Sano said. "He was smothered."

21

After long hours of unhappy wakefulness, after Sano had risen and left their bed, Reiko finally drifted off to sleep near dawn. She slept late into the morning and was awakened by an argument on the veranda outside her bedchamber.

"But I have to go practice martial arts," said Masahiro's strident voice.

"You're not going anywhere, young master," answered the patrol guard on duty. "You know that you and your sister are confined to the private quarters and garden."

After Lord Matsudaira's spy had been unmasked in the estate yesterday, Sano had laid down new rules to protect his family, had assigned extra guards to the innermost part of the estate. But Masahiro didn't like confinement any more than Reiko did.

"That's all right for Akiko, but I'm not a baby," he protested. "Let me out."

"Sorry. If you don't like the rules, take it up with your father."

Masahiro uttered a cry of frustration. Reiko heard a door flung open, his footsteps stomping down the corridor, and Akiko beginning to cry. Akiko was too young to understand what had happened and that the family was in danger, but she was very sensitive to other people's emotions, and she'd caught her brother's bad mood. Shushing sounds came from her nurse, trying to soothe her. Reiko climbed out of bed and went to Akiko, in the next room. But when Akiko saw her mother, she turned and ran. Reiko was left to muster the courage to face the day.

The quarrel with Sano still weighed heavily on her spirits. His mother was in jail, Sano's time for exonerating her was growing shorter by the moment, and what new evil did Lord Matsudaira have in store for them? Reiko's mind swirled with images from the capture of the spy and the ambush in the city. Another day seemed like more than she could endure, but she washed, dressed, put on her makeup, then called a maid to bring her breakfast. She ate mechanically, fueling her strength. She must put on a brave guise for the sake of her family.

Sano looked around the room where Egen lay dead. Among the things piled against the walls were lacquer chests, folded clothes in bright printed cotton fabric, pairs of new sandals, and wooden boxes open to reveal gold statuettes, porcelain vases, and musical instruments.

"He went on a shopping spree after he betrayed my mother," Sano said.

"This collection is a big step up from the trash at his old place," Hirata said. "It would be hard to tell if anything was taken, but note this box full of coins. This wasn't a robbery."

"I don't see any signs of a fight." Sano detected surprise on Egen's face. "The killer must have attacked him while he was asleep." Sano addressed the proprietor, who stood on the veranda outside. "Did you see anyone come in here last night?"

"No," the proprietor said, wringing his hands, upset because a murder had occurred on his premises. A young peasant appeared beside him. "This is the night watchman. Ask him."

When Sano repeated the question, the watchman scratched his chest, yawned, and shook his head. He had a bloated, red-eyed face. The proprietor said, "You've been drinking! Did you fall asleep on duty? You useless oaf!"

"I'm sorry," the watchman said sheepishly. "He had a party. He invited me, and all the guests." He pointed into the room and saw Egen. His bloodshot eyes goggled; his complexion turned green. "Is he dead?"

"He is, no thanks to you," the proprietor said. "You're supposed to protect our guests. But that sounds just like him." His glare turned on the dead man. "He acted as if this were a teahouse in the pleasure quarter. Singing and playing the samisen, hiring girls to dance——"

"And pouring the sake," the watchman said.

"I would have thrown him out today even though he paid for ten days in advance," the proprietor said.

Sano said to Hirata, "A junk peddler moves into an expensive inn and buys all new things. He has money left to squander on parties. How did he come by his newfound wealth?"

"That's a good question," Hirata said.

"But not the only one," Sano said.

"Here are two more: Who killed him, and why?"

Sano thought about the events of the last day in the tutor's life. "I'm beginning to have some ideas."

The inn's guests had heard the commotion and they straggled out of their rooms, curious to see what it was about. Some twenty men gathered below the veranda where Sano and Hirata stood outside the dead man's room. Sano noted their bloodshot eyes and hungover expressions. Four were accompanied by sluttish women with smeared makeup.

"What happened?" asked one fellow with a bald head and his kimono open to display his potbelly and loincloth.

"The host of your party has been murdered," Sano said. Mutters of dismay and ghoulish interest came from the crowd. "How well did you know Egen?"

"I just met him yesterday, when he showed up here," the bald man said.

The other men made sounds of agreement. One of the women spoke up: "He said he was new in town. He'd only arrived a few days ago."

Sano supposed that Egen hadn't wanted his new friends to know he was a lowly Edo junk peddler. But Sano had a hunch that something wasn't right. "Arrived from where?"

"He didn't say."

"What else do you know about him?" Sano asked the crowd.

Heads shook. A man said, "He told a lot of stories and jokes, but he didn't talk about himself."

"He did mention that he'd had a lucky break," said the bald man. "That's why he threw the party."

Sano had a hunch about Egen's sudden wealth and extravagance. He said to Hirata, "Someone paid him for incriminating my mother."

"It's not hard to guess who," Hirata said.

"Lord Matsudaira does come to mind," Sano agreed.

"But I just found Egen yesterday, and I took him straight to the castle. How did Lord Matsudaira get to him?"

Before Sano could hazard a guess, a new crowd poured into the scene. Five samurai clad in leggings and short kimonos carried *jitte*—steel wands with two curved prongs above the hilt for catching the blade of an attacker's sword. The weapons were standard equipment for the *doshin,* police patrol officers. Their leader was a tall, haughty man armed with a lance. He swished toward Sano in flowing silk trousers and a wide-shouldered surcoat made of gaudy silk fabric in the latest style.

"Just when we thought things couldn't get worse," Sano said under his breath to Hirata. "Greetings, *Yoriki* Yamaga-*san.*"

Edo contained more than a million people, but those Sano least wanted to see kept cropping up like bad coins. He and the police commander had been colleagues on the police force some eleven years ago. Yamaga had never forgiven Sano for being promoted out of their ranks. He never missed an opportunity to do Sano a bad turn.

"Greetings, Honorable Chamberlain." His thin lips twisted in a familiar, sarcastic smile. "Perhaps you should enjoy your title while it lasts."

When the conflict between Sano and Lord Matsudaira had started, Yamaga had hurried to jump aboard Lord Matsudaira's ship. The five *doshin* smirked. Sano refused to dignify the barb with a response in kind. "What brings you here?"

"I heard there's been a murder," Yamaga said. "I came to investigate."

Sano exchanged glances with Hirata. Here was another instance of events moving faster than made logical sense. "How did you find out?" Sano asked.

"I received a tip from an informer."

"Who might that be?"

"His identity is confidential," Yamaga said pompously. Beckoning the *doshin,* he strode up the steps and past Sano, who caught his familiar odor of wintergreen oil. Many samurai used the oil on their hair, but Yamaga's valet must apply it with a trowel. Yamaga bumped shoulders with Sano on his way into Egen's room. He and his men grouped around the corpse.

"So this is the witness who changed his story about your mother." Yamaga had obviously heard about the fiasco and had just as obviously enjoyed it. He prodded Egen with his lance, as if to make sure the man was really dead. "Ugly fellow, wasn't he? Look at those pockmarks all over him. But he got you good."

He turned a suspicious gaze on Sano. "How did *you* find out about the murder?"

The commander wasn't so busy gloating that he'd forgotten to ask the important question. Things had changed for the better in the police force since Sano's day. "I discovered the body," Sano said.

"Ah." Interest flared in Yamaga's not-too-intelligent eyes as he recalled that the first person at a crime scene is the first suspect.

The *doshin* began carrying out statues, lacquer chests, and dishware, helping themselves to the victim's possessions. Things hadn't changed so much in the police force after all.

"How did you happen to find the body?" Yamaga asked.

Sano had had enough questions from the gadfly. He had questions of his own. "That's none of your business," Sano said. "You're dismissed. Get out."

His tone reminded Yamaga that however shaky his political position, he was still the shogun's second-in-command and Yamaga's superior. After an insolent pause, Yamaga swept out of the room with his men, who snatched up a few last items. They all knew Sano still had an army strong enough to avenge insults against him—if Hirata didn't break their necks first.

Yamaga faced Sano on the veranda. "Yesterday the victim turns evidence against your mother. Today he turns up dead. And here you are, when the body's barely cold. That doesn't smell like a coincidence."

"It smells like a setup," Sano said evenly. And part of the setup was informing the police about the murder so that Sano couldn't hide the crime.

"I suppose you're going to blame Lord Matsudaira." Yamaga sneered. "But that theory is full of holes. The victim did Lord Matsudaira a favor. Lord Matsudaira had more reason to pay him his weight in gold than to kill him."

Much as Sano hated to admit it, Yamaga was right. Yet every instinct told him that the murder was a strike at him, and if not Lord Matsudaira, who was responsible?

"Lord Matsudaira doesn't benefit from this crime. But you? The chief witness against your mother is gone. Very convenient, I'd say." Yamaga gleamed with vicious satisfaction. "Wait until Lord Matsudaira hears about this."

"Whoever murdered Egen didn't do it for my convenience." Sano saw a flood of new troubles cascading toward him from the crime. "But why don't you go and be the one to tell Lord Matsudaira right now?" Anything to get rid of Yamaga before Sano lost his temper and did something regrettable.

"You can't stop me from investigating the murder. That's my duty," Yamaga said, as if he cared about duty or anything else besides serving his own interests and putting on airs. "I'm going to prove that your people killed that man. And wouldn't that be something? The honorable Chamberlain Sano and his mother both convicted of murders within days of each other."

Yamaga laughed. "And you won't get away with yours even if your victim was a peasant. You'll die as an accessory to the murder of the shogun's cousin, even though it happened before you were born. The executioner can cut off both your mother's head and yours with the same swing."

22

Police Commander Yamaga and the *doshin* surrounded the guests at the inn and started badgering them with questions. Sano said to Hirata, "Let's go."

As he and Hirata and his troops strode out the gate to the street and mounted their horses, he added, "I doubt the killer is among the guests. He's probably long gone by now, and people who've been drinking all night don't make good witnesses. We'll leave them to Yamaga and look for better ones elsewhere."

Along the street, travelers accompanied by porters carrying baggage trickled out from the other inns. At either end of the street was a gate. Choosing at random, Sano led his entourage to the one on his right.

"Were you on duty last night?" Sano asked the watchman.

"No, master, my shift just started."

"Where can I find the man who was?"

The night watchman, a teenaged peasant boy, was fetched. Sano asked him, "Did anyone come through here last night?"

"Yes, master."

When Sano asked who, the watchman said, "Do you mean before or after closing?"

Neighborhood gates in Edo closed two hours before midnight,

before the party at the inn had ended and Egen had died. The closing enforced a curfew that kept troublemakers confined and crime down. Tokugawa law forbade anyone to break curfew and pass through the gates—with certain exceptions. "After," Sano said.

"Two samurai on horseback," said the watchman. The police, the army, and government officials were authorized to bypass the gates after closing. "I let them in, and a little while later, I let them out."

Sano revised his mental picture of the crime to include two men, one kneeling on Egen's chest and holding him down, the other suffocating him with the pillow.

"What did they look like?" Sano asked.

"I couldn't see them very well." The watchman eyed the small lantern hanging from the roof of the gate. "It was dark."

"Did they wear any crests?"

The watchman nodded and pointed at the gold flying-crane crests on Sano's sleeves. "Ones like yours."

Sano was disconcerted until he realized what had happened. "They impersonated my men," he said to Hirata.

"Following Lord Matsudaira's orders, no doubt," Hirata said.

"Where did they go?" Sano asked.

The watchman pointed left down the cross-street. Sano, his troops, and Hirata rode along the suspects' trail from gate to gate, rounding up and questioning watchmen. Some provided more details besides the crests. "They were excited," said the man who guarded a street of shops that led to the Nihonbashi Bridge. "They were laughing and punching each other and saying, 'We got away with it!' "

"They deliberately called attention to themselves," Sano remarked to Hirata as they and their troops rode to their next stop. "They made sure nobody missed them."

"Lord Matsudaira got double the use out of the tutor," Hirata said. "The first time to implicate your mother in a murder, the second time, you. Clever."

Near the border between the merchant district and the official quarter, a watchman said, "One of the soldiers had teeth like this."

He thrust forward his jaw to feign an overbite. "And the other walked like this." He slouched his shoulders and loped.

Sano experienced a twinge of unease. He frowned because the suspects' descriptions hit a chord in his memory.

"What?" Hirata asked.

"I've seen those soldiers before," Sano said, "but I can't place them."

"But it's obvious where they were going," Hirata said.

Sano's unease only grew as he and Hirata rode to the castle and up to the head of a line of people waiting to enter the main gate. They dismounted, and Sano said to the guards, "Show me the record of who came through last night."

The guards fetched the ledger. Sano scanned the list of names and stopped at two. The written characters seemed to fly off the page at him. He felt a thump in his chest as if he'd been punched.

" 'Ishikawa' and 'Ejima,' " Hirata read over his shoulder. "What's wrong?"

The names joined the descriptions with an audible collision in Sano's mind. "I know those soldiers."

He could picture them now, guards on the night shift in his compound. They patrolled together. He had so many retainers that he didn't know all their names and recognized few as his unless they wore his crest, but these men's distinctive appearance as a team had registered in his memory.

"They really are mine."

The revels in the Ginza theater district were in full swing. Playgoers ignored the danger of fire and crowded into buildings whose fronts displayed colorful posters that advertised the dramas and actors. Singing, shouts, laughter, and applause emanated from the buildings. Drums pulsed and music drifted toward the outskirts of the district, where Yoritomo galloped on horseback down a quiet side street. He wore a cloak that concealed his face. He reined his mount to a stop outside a teahouse with red lanterns hanging from its eaves and hurried inside.

A few customers played cards and drank wine. They had blue tattoos that covered their arms, legs, and necks like a second skin, mark of the gangsters. The maid eyed Yoritomo and pointed toward a door at the back.

In the living quarters behind the teahouse, Yanagisawa paced the floor and smoked his tobacco pipe. He recognized his son's footsteps coming down the passage and muttered, "At last!" He flung open the door and pulled Yoritomo into the room. "What took you so long?"

"I'm sorry to make you wait, Father," Yoritomo said, abashed.

"What's the matter—did you have something more important to do than answer my call of distress?"

"I had a hard time getting away from the shogun. He's nervous lately, with all the trouble going on. He clings to me like a barnacle." Yoritomo hung his head. "I'm sorry."

Yanagisawa regretted losing his temper. "No, I'm the one who should apologize." His son was the only person who could make him regret bad behavior. "Forgive me. I'm a bit on edge after what I went through today. It's not your fault."

"What happened?" Yoritomo asked worriedly.

Yanagisawa explained about his close call at the temple. "After Captain Nagasaka and his troops left, the priests pulled me out of the well and smuggled me into Edo inside a trunk. They bribed the checkpoint guards not to search it." Yanagisawa flexed his muscles, which were stiff from the uncomfortable ride. "I disguised myself as a beggar and I walked here."

"I'm glad you're safe," Yoritomo said with relief.

"My accommodations are a far cry from the guest cottage at the temple." Yanagisawa's gaze scorned the cramped room with its bare walls, the worn straw mattress on the dirty floor.

"Couldn't you use one of your other hiding places?"

Yanagisawa had them all over town—in mansions, hillside villas, and *daimyo* estates that belonged to his allies. "I couldn't get to them. Lord Matsudaira has doubled his efforts to capture rebels. The city is full of troops stopping and questioning people. I couldn't take the chance of running into someone else who would recognize me. I had to go to ground as quickly as possible."

"Are they taking good care of you here?" Yoritomo asked.

"Good enough." Yanagisawa's hosts had brought him food, drink, new clothes, and weapons. "One thing I have to say for gangsters: They can get you whatever you need, as long as you have the money to pay." Which Yanagisawa did, because he'd escaped the temple with his emergency stash of gold. "But I'm stuck in this pit."

"I'm sorry. Is there anything I can do for you?"

"Tell me the news," Yanagisawa said.

"I'm happy to report that maybe you won't have to hide much longer." Yoritomo described how the tutor had incriminated Sano's mother, the shogun had sent her to Edo Jail, and Sano had a mere two more days to exonerate her before she and he were both put to death. He said with a mixture of triumph and regret, "Chamberlain Sano is on his way down."

"That's not good enough. Even if Sano fails, I may not survive very long."

The sound of horses' hooves pounding up the street outside froze Yanagisawa and Yoritomo. They waited in fear that troops had come to conduct a door-to-door search for rebels. The noise passed and faded. They let out their breath.

"Sano isn't my biggest problem," Yanagisawa said.

"Lord Matsudaira has gained allies at Sano's expense," Yoritomo agreed.

"Destroying Sano is necessary, but it won't put me back on top," Yanagisawa said. "It's Lord Matsudaira's turn for a little trouble."

"Those soldiers must have been recruited to work for Lord Matsudaira," Sano said as he and Hirata rode through the passages inside Edo Castle. "I suppose I shouldn't be surprised. If my allies are defecting, why not my troops?"

Still, he was shocked and saddened. Lord Matsudaira had gained ground even within his personal army, within his household. How many more men had his rival suborned?

"They should commit seppuku," Hirata said. That was the usual punishment for a samurai who betrayed his master.

Sano nodded. "First I'll hear what Ishikawa and Ejima have to say for themselves."

When he arrived at his compound, he was disconcerted to find a crowd gathered outside the gate, some thirty Tokugawa soldiers. "What's going on?" he asked.

They met his angry bewilderment with stolid gazes: Their superior had deserted his camp and they no longer need answer to Sano. The gate opened, and out marched General Isogai. "Greetings, Honorable Chamberlain," he said with insolent courtesy.

"What is this?" Jumping off his horse, Sano demanded, "Why were you trespassing on my property?"

"Not trespassing." General Isogai's smile reminded Sano that he, as the supreme commander of the Tokugawa army, had free run anywhere in Japan, and his fealty to Sano had ended. "But since you ask, I came to make an arrest."

Behind him emerged more troops, leading Ishikawa and Ejima. The two men looked terrified but defiant. Ishikawa's jutting lower teeth gnawed his upper lip. Ejima held his stooped shoulders as high as he could. When they caught sight of Sano, their eyes wouldn't meet his. Sano and Hirata glanced at each other in alarmed confusion.

"Why are you arresting my men?" Sano asked.

"For the murder of Egen the tutor," General Isogai said.

Sano sensed a disastrous picture forming, but its details were as fragmented and unclear as a reflection in wind-rippled water. "How did you know about the murder? How do you know whether they had anything to do with it or not?"

"We got a tip."

"Don't tell me," Hirata said. "The tip was anonymous."

General Isogai shrugged.

"Anonymous tips are going around like a plague lately," Sano said as the picture came into focus. Someone had framed him for Egen's murder, then sent the police to the scene and pointed General Isogai to the men who'd supposedly acted on his behalf. Sano doubted it was Ishikawa and Ejima, two youths not bright enough to mastermind such a scheme. "You can't arrest my men on the basis of hearsay."

"I can arrest whomever I want," General Isogai said, backed by the shogun's authority. "Besides, your men have admitted they killed Egen on your orders. We didn't even have to torture them into confessing."

Sano was shocked: They'd committed the biggest violation of honor that a samurai could and given themselves up without a fight. He pushed past the troops that surrounded Ishikawa and Ejima and faced them angrily.

"You know I never ordered you to kill anyone. Why did you say I did? How could you betray me?" he said, even more hurt than enraged.

The men looked at the ground, too frightened or ashamed to answer.

At the sound of rapid hoofbeats in the passage, everyone turned to see Lord Matsudaira and his entourage ride up. Lord Matsudaira wore an air of predatory anticipation. "I received your message," he told General Isogai. "Why did you summon me?" He saw Sano, realized that something bad had happened to him, and smiled. "What have we here?"

"It's the result of your work," Sano retorted. "Why pretend you don't already know?"

"The tutor who testified against Chamberlain Sano's mother has been murdered," General Isogai said. "Chamberlain Sano's men did it for him. I've arrested them." He pointed at Ishikawa and Ejima. "They confessed."

Lord Matsudaira chuckled maliciously and said to Sano, "Well, that's like closing the stable door after the horse has escaped. Why kill the witness when he's already told his tale?"

"To punish him," General Isogai suggested.

Lord Arima was among the Matsudaira entourage, watching the drama with a pleasure that shone through the oil in his skin. He said, "That's understandable, but you've only made things worse for yourself, Chamberlain Sano."

"The shogun won't be pleased to hear that you assassinated the man who told the truth about his cousin's murder," said Lord Matsudaira.

"This is your doing, not mine," Sano said, trying to control his fury.

"You paid off the tutor," Hirata said. "He threw himself a last party on your money before he died."

"You subverted my men and ordered them to kill him," Sano said.

Lord Matsudaira and Lord Arima studied Sano with curiosity as well as scorn. Lord Arima said, "You seem to believe what you're saying. You're a better actor than I thought."

"Either that or you're deluded. I wouldn't waste my time stealing the dregs of your army." Lord Matsudaira's scorn included Ishikawa and Ejima as well as Sano. "I'm not responsible for the murder or for their actions."

"I'm going to prove you are," Sano declared.

"You won't have a chance," Lord Matsudaira said. "We're going to bring your men in front of the shogun to repeat their confession for him. That will be the end of you."

Events were moving too fast for Sano to think of anything to do except forestall what seemed inevitable. As General Isogai's troops began marching the two men off, Sano blocked their way. His troops and Hirata took up positions around him.

"You're not taking them anywhere," Sano told Isogai. "They're my retainers. I'll deal with them as I see fit."

"If you want to resist, by all means do." Lord Matsudaira's smile dared Sano to draw his sword inside Edo Castle, a violation of the law for which the penalty was death by seppuku. The troops from the army and the Matsudaira entourage advanced on Sano and his men. Sano had two choices: He could play into Lord Matsudaira's hands, or live to fight another day.

Sano, and his men, reluctantly stepped aside. Lord Matsudaira looked pleased because he'd won a round, yet disappointed because Sano hadn't given him the excuse to kill him on the spot.

General Isogai signaled his troops, who propelled Ishikawa and Ejima toward the palace. "Come along if you like, Honorable Chamberlain. Or are you too much of a coward to face the truth and the consequences?"

23

The dangerous fire season had put the shogun in fear for his life. Seated on the dais in the reception room, he wore a leather cape and helmet in case the palace started burning. Lord Matsudaira knelt at his right, Yoritomo on his left. Lord Arima and General Isogai sat below them, near Lord Matsudaira. Sano and Hirata were relegated to the lower level of the floor, with the two murderers. Sano's troops, Lord Matsudaira's, the Tokugawa army soldiers, and the shogun's personal guards stood ganged up in factions along the walls. The air was thick with antagonism and too warm from body heat.

"Who are those men, and why have you insisted that I grant them an audience?" the shogun peevishly asked Lord Matsudaira.

Lord Matsudaira introduced Ishikawa and Ejima. Their heads were bowed, their bodies trembling so hard that Sano could feel the floor shake. "Your cousin Tadatoshi's tutor was murdered last night. They did it. They confessed."

Sano's mind raced as he formulated and discarded plans. He felt his men's panic like a contagious disease in the air, but he drew upon his samurai training to calm his thoughts. He came from a long line of warriors who'd weathered crises and lived to tell. He watched for an opportunity to avert disaster.

"Well, ahh, that's unfortunate, but why should I care?" the shogun said.

"They're Chamberlain Sano's men. They assassinated the tutor. He ordered them to do it," Lord Matsudaira said.

Sano opened his mouth to contradict, but the shogun raised a hand for silence and said, "Why would Chamberlain Sano have done such a thing?" That he wasn't ready to take Lord Matsudaira's word for it gave Sano hope, but not much.

"He wanted to punish the tutor for incriminating his mother. And he hoped that once the tutor was gone, he could discredit the man's story and convince you that she's innocent." Lord Matsudaira hammered in his point in case the shogun had missed it: "He meant to trick you and save his own skin."

The shogun looked from Lord Matsudaira to Sano; his eyes narrowed with suspicion at them both. His face showed his fear that one or the other was playing him for a fool. While he chewed his lip and pondered what to do, everyone braced for his wrath, wondering on which side it would fall.

At last the shogun said, "I will have these men speak for themselves." He turned to Ishikawa and Ejima. "Well? Did you or did you not kill the tutor?"

"Yes, Your Excellency," they whispered. Sano could smell their rank odor of sweat and nerves.

"Was it on orders from Chamberlain Sano?" the shogun asked.

Sano fixed his gaze on his men. They wouldn't look at him. With all the ancient, bred-in-the-blood power that a master held over his retainers, he willed them to speak the truth.

Ishikawa hunched his shoulders up to his ears. Ejima clenched his teeth and swallowed hard, as if to prevent himself from vomiting. Neither said a word.

"Speak up!" Lord Matsudaira ordered.

The shogun hushed him with an irate glance and said, "Chamberlain Sano, instruct your men to answer my question."

Sano shifted position so that he faced them and spoke in a low, intense voice that projected the entire force of his will. "You know and I know that I never ordered you to kill that man. Now be honorable enough to admit you lied."

They burst into tears. "All right, we lied!" Ishikawa exclaimed. "It wasn't you that made us kill him."

"We're sorry, Honorable Chamberlain," cried Ejima. "Please forgive us!"

Relief washed through Sano. Lord Matsudaira, General Isogai, and Lord Arima exchanged appalled glances. But even though Sano felt vindicated and triumphant, he had a sense of something not right.

"What kind of, ahh, game are you playing?" the shogun indignantly asked Ishikawa and Ejima. "Either you killed that man on Chamberlain Sano's orders or you didn't. Which is it?"

"They did," Lord Matsudaira hastened to say. "They're only denying it because Chamberlain Sano put pressure on them."

He shot Sano a venomous look, then stalked off the dais toward the men. Fists clenched, thunderous with anger, he said, "Tell His Excellency that you killed the tutor because your master told you to!" He beckoned to his troops, who surged threateningly around Ishikawa and Ejima.

"Our master had nothing to do with it," Ishikawa said as he cowered and tears ran down his face.

Ejima gasped for breath; his chest heaved. "We swear on our ancestors' graves that Chamberlain Sano is innocent."

"Tell us who did send you to kill the tutor," Sano ordered.

His voice was drowned by the men's sobs, threats from Lord Matsudaira and General Isogai, and the shogun saying feebly, "Quiet, everyone quiet!"

"We must atone for betraying our master," Ishikawa cried. "We must restore our honor." He and Ejima reached under their sleeves and whipped out daggers.

Aghast, Sano lunged and grabbed for the weapons. So did Hirata, Lord Matsudaira, and a horde of troops. They and Sano collided while the shogun exclaimed, "What's going on?"

Amid the confusion, Ishikawa and Ejima plunged the daggers

into their bellies and ripped the blades through their innards. They screamed in agony.

Sano, Hirata, Lord Matsudaira, and the troops fell back from the two men, who collapsed onto the floor. Ishikawa and Ejima moaned and convulsed. Blood poured from their cut bellies.

"Merciful Buddha!" The shogun's complexion turned green. "I'm going to be sick!" He leaned over the edge of the dais and retched.

"You should have searched them for hidden weapons," Lord Matsudaira berated General Isogai.

"I didn't think there was any need," Isogai retorted. "Who knew they would commit seppuku right in the palace?"

"Someone fetch a doctor!" Sano shouted.

"It's too late," Hirata said. "Those wounds are fatal."

Ishikawa's and Ejima's faces turned white; the life rapidly drained from their eyes. Lord Matsudaira shouted, "Don't you dare die yet!" He grabbed the men by the front of their robes and shook them. "Not before you tell the shogun that Chamberlain Sano ordered you to assassinate the tutor!"

"Before you die, confess the truth," Sano urged, shoving Lord Matsudaira away. "It wasn't me. Who was it?"

Ishikawa raised a trembling hand and pointed toward the dais. A gout of blood erupted from Ejima's mouth as he spoke his last words: "It was Lord Arima."

In the shocked silence, everyone turned to stare at Lord Arima. He'd not spoken during the whole scene, and Sano had almost forgotten he was present. Lord Arima looked startled, but the expression vanished at once, absorbed by his oily skin.

"I had nothing to do with the murder," he said, unperturbed. "Those men falsely accused me."

"They incriminated you with their dying words," Sano said as he began to understand how and why the murder had transpired. Sano burned with anger at Lord Arima. "I believe them."

The shogun moaned as Yoritomo wiped his face. "Take them away," he ordered his guards. "I can't bear to look at them." As the guards carried the bodies out the door, he whined, "I don't understand. Why would Arima have wanted to assassinate the tutor? Why would he employ Chamberlain Sano's men?"

Sano heard breaths drawn by everyone in the room: The conversation had taken a dangerous turn. Lord Matsudaira said quickly, "He didn't, Cousin. This is all a misunderstanding. He's innocent. I'll vouch for him." His hard gaze told Sano that he'd better help gloss over the bad moment, or else.

But the suicides right before his very eyes had jolted the shogun out of his tendency to back down when Lord Matsudaira handled him. "I'm tired of your always, ahh, making excuses, always putting me off," he snapped. "I demand a better explanation."

And Sano was too furious at this latest attack on him by his enemies to collaborate with Lord Matsudaira in hoodwinking the shogun. Forsaking caution, he said, "Lord Arima acted on Lord Matsudaira's behalf."

"But why would Lord Matsudaira want the tutor killed and you incriminated?" the shogun said, confused and impatient.

Lord Matsudaira looked astonished by Sano's nerve. "Watch your mouth, Chamberlain Sano," he said in an ominous tone.

The troops stared at him and Sano. The atmosphere was noxious with their hunger for open, all-out conflict at last. Sano knew that things could go disastrously for him if he proceeded in this direction, but his anger goaded him on.

"Lord Matsudaira stands to benefit from everything bad that happens to me," he said.

"That's nonsense," Lord Arima said evenly. "Your Excellency, I don't know what the honorable chamberlain is talking about. If I were you, I wouldn't listen."

"Well, you're not me." The shogun stood up in a huff.

"Cousin, the honorable chamberlain is just upset and not thinking clearly," Lord Matsudaira said with a venomous glare at Sano. "In fact, we're all upset because of what his men just did. Let's postpone this discussion until we've had a chance to calm down."

"I'm calm enough!" the shogun said, shrill with hysteria. "Furthermore, I'm sick of everybody talking around me, arguing with one another, and acting as if they're hiding things behind my back. I want to know what's happening!"

"Nothing is," Lord Matsudaira said. "This meeting is adjourned." He beckoned his troops and began a hasty retreat. Lord Arima glided after them. "You're coming, too, Chamberlain Sano."

General Isogai and the army troops herded Sano toward the door, but the shogun cried, "Wait! I haven't given you permission to go. I order you to stay!" He told his guards, "Block the exit!"

They obeyed. Sano saw panic in Lord Matsudaira's eyes. He felt the same reckless excitement as when he'd embarked on what he'd thought to be a suicide mission in Ezogashima last winter.

"Nobody leaves until I get to the bottom of this." Standing on the dais, hands on his hips, the shogun swelled with righteousness. He'd even lost his stammer, Sano was amazed to note. "Now someone tell me: What is going on?"

Lord Matsudaira's and General Isogai's eyes shot warnings at Sano: If he replied, he was dead. Nobody spoke.

"Have you all lost your tongues?" the shogun said. "Well, then, I'll pick a volunteer." He pointed at Lord Arima. "You seem to be in the middle of everything. You answer me."

Unruffled as ever, Lord Arima looked to Lord Matsudaira for guidance. Lord Matsudaira mouthed, *Not a word.*

"Surround him," the shogun ordered his guards. "Draw your swords." Blades hissed out of sheaths. He said to Lord Arima, "Speak up or die!"

As Lord Arima stood in a circle of blades pointed at him, his calm manner didn't change, but Sano felt his thoughts spin as smoothly as greased wheels and then click to a stop.

"Lord Matsudaira wants to seize power over the regime," Lord Arima said. "He wants to destroy Chamberlain Sano and everyone else who stands in his way." In case the shogun didn't understand the implications for himself, Lord Arima added, "He wants to be dictator, Your Excellency. He's been preparing for years to overthrow you."

24

The secret was out.

The shogun beheld Lord Arima with openmouthed shock. Sano was suspended between disbelief, astonishment, and dread, the emotions he saw on the faces around him. Everyone was so still, and the room so quiet, that he could hear the wind gusting outside. Lord Matsudaira broke the silence.

"Lord Arima didn't mean it," he said. "He was just frightened into saying stupid things." Sano had never seen anyone look less frightened than Lord Arima. "It's not true. I'm not—"

"It is true." Ghastly enlightenment hushed the shogun's voice. He pressed a hand to his chest and swayed. "These past few years I thought I was imagining that you don't like me, that you think you're better than I, that you were envious. I told myself those were just my stupid fancies. But I was right. Now I understand. You're trying to steal my place!"

Sano was as surprised that the shogun had suspected it all along as he was shocked that any man could have ignored his truest instincts. He felt as though he were witnessing a miracle. The shogun had awakened at last.

"Traitor!" the shogun howled. "My own kin, plotting against me! Scoundrel!"

"My apologies," Lord Arima said to Lord Matsudaira with a rueful smile. "It was either you or me."

"I'll kill you!" Lord Matsudaira reached for his sword. His guards grabbed him, preventing him from committing the crime of drawing a weapon inside the castle. The shogun shouted at General Isogai, "Don't just stand there—arrest my cousin for treason!"

General Isogai and the army troops moved in on Lord Matsudaira, who yelled, "You wouldn't!" as he struggled with his own men. "You pledged your support to me!"

"Sorry," General Isogai said with scant regret. "The game's changed."

The army troops seized Lord Matsudaira. They wrestled him and his men toward the door. Lord Arima slithered out ahead of them. Sano ordered three of his troops, "Go after him. Watch him and don't let him leave town." After what he'd done, Arima had a lot to answer for, and he surely had flight on his mind.

"Honorable Cousin, I'm sorry if you were offended by anything I've done," Lord Matsudaira cried desperately. "But this is a mistake. I'm your own flesh and blood. Can we please discuss your concerns and work out a solution together?"

The shogun put up one hand to repel Lord Matsudaira's words, the other to screen his eyes. "I can't bear to look at you. General Isogai, put my cousin under house arrest until I decide what to do with him."

While he fought and the army hustled him out of the room, Lord Matsudaira called, "It's not me you should punish—it's Chamberlain Sano. He's the one who wants to seize control of the regime! He's been raising an army and fighting me because I'm trying to stop him and protect you. *He's* the traitor!"

The door shut. The sound of Lord Matsudaira's ranting faded down the corridor outside.

Standing in the depopulated, silent room, Sano found himself the center of attention, splattered with mud from Lord Matsudaira's parting shot. Hirata and his other men gazed at him in alarm. Yoritomo regarded Sano with a mixture of fright and sorrow. The shogun stared blankly, flabbergasted.

Sano opened his mouth to deny the accusation and defend himself, but too many shocks coming too fast suddenly paralyzed his mind. The diplomatic skills he'd gained during his more than ten years at court deserted him. He couldn't find words.

A moment that felt like an eon passed while the shogun's face expressed doubt, bewilderment, suspicion, and fear in alternating, rapid succession. At last he said, "I shall ignore what Lord Matsudaira said. He's already proved himself to be deceitful and untrustworthy. You, on the other hand, have never shown any hint of ambition or designs against me. I don't believe you would try to steal my place, Chamberlain Sano."

Relief coursed through Sano. He expelled the breath he hadn't realized he'd been holding. "Many thanks for your faith in me, Your Excellency."

Hirata and his other men relaxed. Yoritomo looked simultaneously glad and disappointed for some reason Sano had no time to figure out.

"Don't thank me yet. I am still very upset with you." The shogun spoke with more authority than Sano had ever seen in him: Dispatching Lord Matsudaira had built up his self-confidence. "Your mother stands accused of killing Tadatoshi, and I believe she's guilty. That reflects poorly on you. I gave you three days to prove her innocence, and if by the end of that time you haven't succeeded . . ."

That his voice trailed off on a weary sigh didn't diminish the threat he still held over Sano.

"Now go," the shogun said. "I feel quite ill, and I, ahh, presume you have much work to do."

As evening spread its veil of darkness across Edo, a fire burned like a flare in the cityscape. Alarm bells clanged. Smoke billowed, drifted on the wind, and cloaked Edo Jail in an acrid haze. The lanterns at the gates and in the turrets glowed through diffuse golden haloes. The noise and the smoke filtered through the window of the sickroom where Etsuko lay sleeping. The odor of burning wood penetrated her slumber and triggered memories long suppressed.

She and Egen ran hand in hand past buildings on fire, past fleeing crowds. She struggled to keep up with him as the smoke grew denser. They reached the canal where hundreds of people blocked the bridge. They were trapped in the mob. Egen's hand ripped loose from hers. He was lost in the crush. She was alone.

Someone called her name. It was Doi. He gripped her arm and pulled her along through the mob. Etsuko heard Egen shouting to them, saw his frantic face in the crowd, his hand waving. When she and Doi reached him, he grabbed her other arm. The men shoved, fought, and trampled their way out of the crush.

The scene suddenly shifted. Etsuko, Egen, and Doi fell to their knees, exhausted from running, inside the Koishikawa district. Edo Castle loomed above a neighborhood of walled samurai estates. Men on horseback and ladies in palanquins, accompanied by servants on foot who were loaded with baggage, moved toward the hills outside town. Brigades of leather-clad firemen wielded pickaxes, tearing down houses at the edge of the district, clearing bare space in an attempt to halt the fire's spread. They'd already leveled a swath littered with ruins.

"We'll be safe here," Egen said.

His face and Doi's were black with soot, their clothes charred. Etsuko coughed up phlegm that tasted like smoke. Then she saw a familiar figure among the crowd. Tadatoshi leaned against a wall, standing perfectly still, alone. His gaze was lifted toward the flames that rose from the burning city. His face wore the same sly, private smile as on that night in the garden. Etsuko saw in his eyes the reflections of the fire.

"There he is!" she cried, pointing.

Tadatoshi turned. His gaze met hers. The sudden anger in his eyes exploded their fires into a huge, red-hot blast. The fire engulfed Etsuko, clothing her in a kimono of fire.

Her own scream awakened her. She heaved up from her bed and found herself in a room that was not her own. She could still smell the smoke from the burning city. Through the barred window came a faint, menacing orange light.

Dazed from sleep and medicine, Etsuko heard the same shouts, wails, and hurrying footsteps as when she and Egen and Doi had run through the inferno in her nightmare. She stumbled to the door but found it locked.

"Help!" she cried, banging on the door. "Fire!"

Drafts faintly tinged with smoke penetrated the walls of the chamber where Reiko sat waiting for Sano to come home. The lantern flickered; twilight deepened outside the window. Reiko heard Masahiro and Akiko laughing and splashing in the bathtub down the corridor. She rose and went to look in on them. Masahiro was sailing a toy boat and chatting with the nurse, and he didn't notice Reiko, but Akiko did. As soon as her gaze met her mother's, she drew a deep breath that puffed out her cheeks, then ducked under the water.

Reiko knew from experience that Akiko would stay submerged until Reiko went away or pulled Akiko up half-drowned and hysterical. Tonight Reiko couldn't bear a scene. "I'm going, Akiko," she said. "You can come up now."

She took her hurt feelings back to her chamber. Soon she heard steps approaching, but it was Lieutenant Asukai, not her husband, who appeared at the door. The look in his eyes warned Reiko that he was bringing bad news.

"What is it?" Reiko cried in fright.

"The shogun has put Lord Matsudaira under house arrest." Asukai was jittery and breathless with excitement.

"Merciful gods! Why on earth?"

Lieutenant Asukai explained that the shogun had realized at last that Lord Matsudaira was plotting to seize power. "I don't know how the shogun found out. But my sources say that your husband was there when it happened. He'll be able to tell you the details."

Recovering from her shock, Reiko saw the ramifications of Lord Matsudaira's arrest. "But this is good. Lord Matsudaira is locked up. He'll have to stop fighting my husand. He won't be able to hurt anybody anymore."

With Lord Matsudaira out of the way, Sano could win back the shogun's favor, regardless of the murder case. Reiko felt a thrill of hope that the tide had indeed turned for Sano. What good luck!

Lieutenant Asukai said, "Unfortunately, that's not the only news I have. I just spoke with my friend who's one of Lord Matsudaira's personal bodyguards. He was there when Lord Matsudaira was brought home. He said Lord Matsudaira is desperate, and furious. He blames Chamberlain Sano. He swears he'll get revenge. He says Sano must die."

"That sounds like an empty threat," Reiko said, but a cold, nauseating horror gripped her. She'd long been aware of Lord Matsudaira's hostility toward Sano, but hearing it voiced, even thirdhand, made it more real for her. She felt as if she were breathing air laced with Lord Matsudaira's corrosive hatred.

"But surely he can't destroy my husband," she said. "His allies will be distancing themselves from him and his troubles. He can't fight a war."

"That's what he wanted to do at first. He wanted an honorable victory. But he's come up with a new plan." Lieutenant Asukai continued with breathless urgency, "The spy we caught wasn't the only one he had here. There are more."

Reiko's lips parted in shock. Just when she thought she'd dispensed with that particular threat! "How many?"

"Nine of them," Asukai said. "My friend doesn't know who they are. Lord Matsudaira didn't say. But here's the worst part: They're not just spies anymore. They're not looking for information, and setting traps for them won't work this time. Lord Matsudaira has sent them new orders. Their job is to assassinate Chamberlain Sano. If one man tries and fails and gets caught, the others are to keep trying until Sano is dead."

As Reiko's shock turned to horror, anguish showed on Lieutenant Asukai's face. He said, "I'm sorry to be the bearer of such bad news, Lady Reiko, and I'm sorry to say that's not all. I've come to warn you: Lord Matsudaira has ordered his assassins to kill you and the children, too. He doesn't want your son to grow up and come after him for revenge, so he's decided he'd better wipe out your whole clan."

25

"Solving Tadatoshi's murder should be easier with Lord Matsudaira under arrest," Hirata said.

"Thank the gods for that stroke of luck," Sano said, "and that the shogun doesn't know about my role in the power play, at least for now."

They sat in his office, where they'd taken refuge after the debacle at the palace. Hirata poured sake. "I propose a toast to Lord Matsudaira. With friends like Lord Arima, he doesn't need enemies."

Sano and Hirata drank. "We might as well enjoy this moment. It won't last long," Sano said, for the exposure of Lord Matsudaira's campaign to seize power would cause him new difficulties. "And we have a new crime to solve."

"The tutor's murder is a complication we didn't need," Hirata agreed.

"But every crisis creates opportunities," Sano said. "I can think of at least one new line of investigation to follow."

They discussed strategies. Sano said, "My wife will be anxious for news. I'd better go tell her what's happened." But he was interrupted by moans in the passage, accompanied by heavy footsteps that shook the floor. Something bumped the wall. Sano and Hirata hurried to the door. They saw Detectives Marume and Fukida carrying Sano's mother on a litter. She was swaddled in a blanket that held her body still, but her head tossed as she moaned.

"Mother!" Sano was glad to see her home, but disturbed by her condition. "What's happened?"

"There was a fire near the jail," Marume said. "The prisoners were let out."

The law stated that when fire threatened the jail, the prisoners must be freed, to save their lives. It was a rare instance of mercy toward criminals, due to the Great Fire, when the main neighborhood gate near Kodemmacho was closed to prevent the prisoners from escaping. All the prisoners, and many neighborhood residents—some twenty thousand people—had been trampled and killed in the crush at the gate. Now prisoners were released under strict orders to return when the fire was out. Usually they did, with a few notable exceptions.

"Mother, are you all right?" Sano asked anxiously.

Her eyes welled huge and black. They seemed to look through Sano at horrors visible to her alone. "The fire is coming," she cried. "We have to go across the river before it's too late."

She was reliving the Great Fire, Sano thought. As the detectives carried her down the passage and he accompanied them, he asked, "Was she hurt?"

"No," Fukida said. "Dr. Ito sent her to the castle with the men you left to guard her. We saw them waiting in the line to get inside. We brought her here."

"I'm grateful," Sano said, "but how did you get her past the sentries?"

"I talked them into letting her in," Marume said.

"Good work." Sano could imagine the fast talking and intimidation that Marume must have employed.

"It helped that there's a lot of confusion in the castle," Fukida said as he and Marume maneuvered the litter around a corner. "Everyone is running around like ants whose hill has been stepped on. What's the matter?"

"The shogun found out that Lord Matsudaira has been trying to take over," Hirata said. "Lord Matsudaira is under house arrest."

The detectives set down the litter in the guest chamber and stared in disbelief. "Well, well, I guess we've been away too long," Fukida said to Marume.

"We didn't find any witnesses, and we missed all the fun," Marume lamented. "How did it happen?"

"I'll fill you in." Hirata led the men out of the room, leaving Sano to tend to his mother.

The door between the room and the adjacent one slid open. Sano saw Reiko standing on the other side. Behind her, the children sat with Lieutenant Asukai and their old nurse, O-sugi. Everyone beheld Sano and his mother with surprise.

"Grandma's back," Masahiro said, rising from the table where he'd been playing chess with Lieutenant Asukai.

He ran over to her, and Akiko followed, leaving her dolls with O-sugi. When Sano's mother muttered and wailed, the children backed away, puzzled and curious.

Reiko was relieved to see her mother-in-law out of jail, but the old woman's condition and Sano's expression made it obvious that all was not exactly well. "What happened?"

Sano explained about the fire, then told her how and why Lord Matsudaira had been arrested.

"I know about Lord Matsudaira," Reiko said. "Lieutenant Asukai heard and told me."

Since then, Reiko had not let the children out of her sight. She'd kept Lieutenant Asukai and O-sugi with them for additional protection. They were the only people in the household that she could completely trust.

So far nothing had happened, but of course not enough time had passed for Lord Matsudaira's plan to be set in action.

"Do you think Lord Matsudaira will fall?" she asked, hopeful that he would before his assassins could strike.

"I'm not going to count on it," Sano said, "and I'm not off the hook yet." He told Reiko about how he and Hirata had found the tutor dead. "Not only do I now have two murders to solve, I'm a suspect in this one, even though Lord Arima has been implicated. As long as it's his word against mine and that of two men who are dead, my name will never be clear."

The fear that had plagued Reiko since she'd heard of Lord Matsudaira's plan resurged in the wake of her disappointed hope.

"In the meantime, we'd better make my mother comfortable," Sano said.

"I'll fetch a maid to fix her bed," Masahiro volunteered.

"No!" Reiko said. "Stay here!"

Sano's and Masahiro's eyebrows flew up in surprise at her sharp tone. Reiko said, "I'll make the bed. Masahiro, you can help."

"All right," Masahiro said.

While Akiko returned to her nurse and her dolls, he and Reiko hauled the futon out of the cabinet and laid down quilts. Sano loosened the blanket around his mother, lifted her from the litter, and eased her into bed. Reiko drew the quilt over her, noticing how much weight she'd lost in the past few days.

"Can I go now?" Masahiro said. "My friends from Papa's army are coming to say good night to me, and I want to talk to them before I go to bed."

He'd made friends among Sano's younger troops, whose company he preferred to boys his own age. Reiko had never minded before; she and Sano had thought they were good examples for him. Now she feared that Lord Matsudaira's assassins numbered among them.

"No," she said.

"Why not?" Masahiro was disappointed.

"Yes," Sano said.

His word overruled Reiko's. As Masahiro ran off, Reiko told Lieutenant Asukai, "Go with him. Don't let him out of your sight."

When she and Sano were alone with his mother, Sano said, "Why are you keeping Masahiro on such a tight rein?"

Now was the time for Reiko to tell Sano what she'd heard. "He's in danger."

"That's nothing new. I seem to remember that Lord Matsudaira did have him kidnapped."

"But Lord Matsudaira doesn't just want to kidnap Masahiro," Reiko said. "He wants to kill him, and you and me and Akiko."

"Well, I wouldn't be surprised," Sano said. "As far as he's concerned, we're all fair game, and with what happened to him today, he must really want our blood." Sano's gaze wandered, and Reiko could tell he was thinking of the other problems he needed to solve. "But don't you think the children are as safe as possible? Why start being extra vigilant?"

"Because Lord Matsudaira has nine assassins planted among your men. They're under orders to kill us all!"

Sano refocused his gaze sharply on her. "How do you know?"

"Lieutenant Asukai has a friend among Lord Matsudaira's bodyguards, who overheard Lord Matsudaira talking about his plans."

Shock opened Sano's mouth. Then he blew out his breath. "Well, thank the gods for friends in the right places. And thank Lieutenant Asukai for this valuable bit of intelligence." Then he shook his head, and Reiko saw anguish in his eyes. "So the enemy has spread farther into our midst. Nine more of my men are traitors and assassins."

Reiko hated to be the messenger of such upsetting news, but at least she'd made Sano aware of the threat. "Now you understand why Masahiro and Akiko are in danger at home. What are we going to do?"

"I'll find out who those nine traitors are," Sano said, harsh with determination. "In the meantime, I'll have Detectives Marume and Fukida guard the children."

"How do you know you can trust them?"

"How do you know you can trust Lieutenant Asukai?" Sano countered.

"He's been my bodyguard for years," Reiko said. "I have no doubt of his loyalty."

"Marume and Fukida have served me for years," Sano said. "I've never doubted their loyalty, either."

He and Reiko gazed at each other in dismay that they dared not trust anyone in their household. Sano's vast army offered no security;

it harbored nine assassins, hiding like snakes in a forest. The walls that repelled attacks from outside couldn't protect Sano and his family from treachery within. Until the traitors were caught, none of them was safe.

"I can't stay home and watch over the children. I still have to clear my mother's name, not to mention my own." Sano sounded torn between conflicting responsibilities. "Or else we're dead even if Lord Matsudaira's assassins don't get us." He rose. "You'll have to guard Masahiro and Akiko."

"With my life," Reiko vowed. "Where are you going?"

"To take care of some business. Will you be all right?"

Even though consumed by fear for her children and hating to see Sano leave, Reiko nodded. At least their shared trouble had put their quarrel behind them, and they were reunited.

Reiko looked at her mother-in-law, who lay curled in bed, whimpering in a fitful slumber. Even though Reiko foresaw a new opportunity to get the truth out of Etsuko, she resisted the temptation to try. She'd made that mistake once, and whatever Etsuko might be hiding was Sano's task to uncover, not Reiko's.

Sentries guarding the portals of the estates in the *daimyo* district looked up and down the broad, empty streets. The evening sky glowed with a smoky orange haze from fires burning in the city. High above the roofs, in the fire-watch towers, the watchers stood alert. They suddenly aimed their spyglasses downward, at a group of mounted samurai that galloped into view.

Sano and his troops reined in their horses outside Lord Arima's estate. Two of the soldiers he'd assigned to watch Arima stepped from the shadows between the lanterns at the gates. One said, "He hasn't moved since he left the palace."

"Good. It's time he and I had a talk." Sano told the sentries, "I want to see your master. Bring him out."

The man they fetched wasn't Lord Arima. He was a samurai in his forties, with features that looked as if they'd been squashed vertically, the brow and chin converging toward his nose. "I'm Inaba Naomori, chief retainer to Lord Arima," he said. "I regret to inform you that my master isn't here." His compressed mouth widened into a smug smile when he saw the look of dismay that passed between Sano and his men. "He left the house hours ago."

"He couldn't have," protested Sano's soldier. "We would have seen."

"You're welcome to search the premises," Inaba said, "but you won't find him, Honorable Chamberlain."

The rat had slipped the trap. Either Lord Arima's men had smuggled him out in disguise or the estate had secret exits, tunnels underground. "Where did he go?" Sano asked angrily.

"Sorry, I don't know," said Inaba. "Neither does anyone else here. He didn't tell us his destination."

"I'm sure," Sano said. Lord Arima clearly didn't want to be traced and held accountable for ordering the death of a witness in the murder case or for betraying Lord Matsudaira. But Sano could smell that Inaba wasn't telling the truth.

"Whatever business you have with my master, you'll have to conduct with me," Inaba said pompously. "I'm in charge."

"I'm delighted to hear that," Sano said. "Now is your chance to stand in for Lord Arima. I regret that I missed him, but you'll do. You're coming with me."

He gestured to his troops. They leaped from their horses and seized Inaba, who protested, "Hey! You can't do that!"

"Just watch me," Sano said.

As the troops marched him down the street, Inaba called, "Help!" But Sano's other troops pointed swords at the sentries, who stood idle rather than risk their own lives.

"I don't deserve this kind of trouble," Inaba fumed. "I haven't done anything wrong!"

Sano laughed with sardonic amusement. "Since when did that matter in this world?"

* * *

Before Hirata went out to pursue his inquiries, he stopped at home to check with his staff on the progress of work ordered by the shogun. The noise of laughter drew him to his children's room. From the doorway he saw Taeko and Tatsuo romping on the bed, swatting each other with pillows. Midori scolded them good-naturedly. A hollow sensation ached in Hirata's stomach. He felt like a starving man watching a banquet to which he wasn't invited.

Midori's gaze met his and turned somber. The children saw Hirata, stopped playing, and fell silent. Midori folded her hands and waited for Hirata to say what he wanted or leave. Now Hirata felt ashamed of his wish to be part of his family, and angry at Midori for excluding him. He gave up his plan to bide his time and wait for her to make a move toward him so they could have a showdown.

"I want to talk to you," he said.

"Very well," she said meekly, and followed him down the passage to their chamber.

"What do you think you're doing?" Hirata said.

Midori didn't flinch from the belligerence in his voice. "Nothing, Husband."

Angrier than ever, he said, "You're treating me as coldly as if I were a stranger. And your attitude has rubbed off on the children. You've turned them against me. Are you still trying to punish me for leaving you?"

"That isn't it."

Hirata didn't believe her, although there was a steadiness about her that told him she wasn't lying. Her feelings about his abandonment of her and the children had shifted in some way that he couldn't define. That his mystic martial arts powers were so useless with his wife!

"Well, if you have some other grievance against me, just say it," he ordered. "Don't play games! Stand up and fight!"

Annoyance twitched Midori's mouth. "I'm not some enemy warrior. I'm your wife."

"Then act like it!" Hirata exclaimed in frustration. "I said I was sorry for leaving. Now that I'm home, can't we just go back to the way we were before?"

"Maybe you can. But I can't." Midori's manner was sad but calm. "I can't forget that you were gone for three years."

Those three years had been some of the most challenging and fulfilling in Hirata's life. But he suddenly realized how they must have seemed to Midori—an eternity of waiting, loneliness, and wondering if he would ever return. He felt guiltier than ever, and impatient with her for not seeing his side.

"I had no choice but to go," he said. "It was my destiny."

"I understand," Midori said, devoid of the anger that she'd expressed when he'd previously spoken those words. "I also understand that if your destiny calls you to go away again, you will. You must do what you must. And I must do what I must."

For the first time since his return from Ezogashima, he really looked at Midori. He was shocked at how much she'd matured since he left. Their separations had aged her far beyond her twenty-four years. She wasn't the innocent girl she'd been when they'd married for love, over the strenuous objections of their families. She was a woman he didn't know.

"If you want me to be your wife, I will," Midori said. "Whatever you ask me to do, I'll obey. I'll live with you, share your bed, make our children be nice to you, and bear you others if you want. I'll speak or not speak at your command. But nothing more."

The life she proposed, which described that of most other married couples, wasn't what Hirata had ever wanted. As he gazed at her in alarm, he couldn't think of anything to say except, "You are trying to punish me. You're still angry."

Midori shook her head; her expression was bleak, resigned. "I've buried my anger. Those are the terms on which I can continue our marriage." She spoke with an uncharacteristic formality. "By accepting them, I won't care when you leave the next time."

Hirata was speechless, and appalled.

Until this moment he'd never truly regretted choosing his martial arts studies over Midori. Their quarrels had vexed him so much that he'd thought she deserved to be abandoned any time he felt like leaving again. Now he realized that her behavior wasn't an act, wasn't a ploy to nettle him or force him to prove his love for her. Along with her anger she'd buried her love for him. And Hirata had lost not just his wife but his entire family. They were his by law, to command as he wished; yet he couldn't force their affection.

"Now if you will please excuse me, Husband," Midori said, "I must put the children to bed."

She stepped past Hirata and exited the room. Hirata stood alone, more helpless than ever in his life. He'd never met a problem that he couldn't confront head-on, with physical strength and mental agility, as a samurai should. But this one was different. How was he going to solve it?

26

The Sumida River flowed past the sleeping city. The glow in the sky stained the rippling water orange, as if fires burned beneath its surface. The rhythmic, clacking noise of watchmen's clappers echoed over barges and boats moored at the docks. Warehouses on the banks raised solid walls and closed doors against intruders. By day a place alive with people and commerce, the riverfront was deserted at night, a private place for business best conducted in the dark.

Sano owned a warehouse that stored the huge quantities of rice with which he paid his retainers. Inside, he and his troops surrounded Inaba, who knelt on the floor. The cavernous room was dimly lit by one lantern. Straw rice bales, stacked against the walls up to the roofline, ensured that sounds made within wouldn't reach passersby outside. Sano could have questioned his captive in the comfort of his estate, but that wouldn't have had the same intimidation value.

"I'll ask you one more time," Sano said. "Where is Lord Arima?"

Inaba's squashed features glistened with sweat and his eyes with terror, but he said insolently, "I already told you: I don't know. You're wasting your time."

But Sano was determined to find out more than Lord Arima's whereabouts. He believed Lord Arima was the key to figuring out more than the two murders. "I bet I can persuade you to change your mind."

"How? By torturing me?" Inaba forced a laugh. "You won't. You're too squeamish. Everybody knows your reputation."

Everybody did know that Sano was opposed to torture even though it was a legal means for forcing people to talk. Many thought him a coward about inflicting pain. But although he was capable of it, he'd always found other means worth trying first.

"I can make an exception for you," he said, "but instead I'm going to offer you a deal. You have two choices: Either you talk to me, or you talk to Lord Matsudaira."

"What do you mean?" Inaba said, disconcerted.

"Answer my questions, or I'll drop you off at Lord Matsudaira's estate. He would be interested to know that your master has skipped town and where he is."

Panic tensed Inaba. Everybody knew Lord Matsudaira didn't share Sano's qualms about torture. Inaba's gaze lifted to the ceiling, in the futile hope of climbing out the skylights or in prayer to the gods. "All right, I'll tell you. Lord Arima is on his way to his province, disguised as one of his own soldiers."

Sano said, "I don't like that answer." He could track down Lord Arima eventually, but not soon enough, and he sensed Inaba was hiding something. He started toward the door and beckoned his troops. "Let's go."

Inaba cried, "No! Wait!"

"You're the one who objected to wasting time," Sano said. "Be glad that Lord Matsudaira will make quick work of you."

Inaba fell forward onto his hands. They clawed the earthen floor as if trying to root himself in it. Gasping and frantic, he said, "I know things you'll want to hear. Spare me, and I'll tell you."

Sano knew that if he was too eager for information, the man would feed him a pack of lies. "Spare me the bluffing." His troops closed in on Inaba. Sano kept moving. "We're finished."

The troops dragged Inaba toward the door. He cried, "Lord Arima was responsible for ambushing your wife!"

Surprise halted Sano. He turned to face Inaba and signaled his troops to pause.

"It's true! Lord Arima had spies watching your house." Straining against the troops while they held his arms and legs, Inaba said, "When Lady Reiko went out in her palanquin, they alerted him. He sent the assassins after her. He had them wear Lord Matsudaira's crest. He wanted you to think they were sent by Lord Matsudaira."

Sano remembered how strenuously Lord Matsudaira had denied attacking Reiko. "Weren't they?"

"No. Lord Matsudaira didn't even know. It was all Lord Arima's idea."

Lord Matsudaira had been telling the truth: He hadn't given the order to kill Reiko; he hadn't employed his own troops. But he was just as responsible as if he had. "So Lord Arima does Lord Matsudaira's dirty work and Lord Matsudaira keeps his hands clean," Sano said. "That's what lackeys are for. So what?"

"So I thought you'd be interested," Inaba said, anxious to please, yet put out by Sano's indifference.

"Oh, I am. And when I catch Lord Arima, he'll pay. But why should I let you go just for telling me that?" Sano eyed Inaba with scorn. "Why shouldn't I just hand you over to Lord Matsudaira and let him save me the trouble of killing you for everything your master has done?"

Slyness gleamed through the panic in Inaba's eyes. "Because that's not all there is to the story. Lord Arima hasn't only done Lord Matsudaira's dirty work—he's done yours."

"What are you talking about?" Sano was tired of Inaba's efforts to manipulate him, but at last the man had truly snared his attention.

"The bomb at Lord Matsudaira's estate. That was Lord Arima's doing, too. He was there that day. So was I. My job was to distract the Matsudaira guards while our men sneaked up to the women's quarters and threw the bomb."

Sano stared in outrage as well as astonishment. "I never asked Lord Arima to do any such thing."

Inaba smirked despite his terror. "Just as Lord Matsudaira never asked Lord Arima to assassinate your wife. Just as neither you nor

Lord Matsudaira asked him to ambush each other's troops or destroy each other's property on all those past occasions. He did it entirely on his own. He had each of you blaming the other, as he intended."

Sano realized that his suspicions were well founded: The series of attacks that had escalated their conflict weren't Lord Matsudaira's fault any more than they were his own. Even as Sano felt awash in confusion, a thought occurred to him. "When Lord Arima betrayed Lord Matsudaira, it wasn't only because the shogun threatened him, was it?"

"Call off your dogs, and I'll tell you," Inaba said.

"Release him," Sano ordered.

The troops flung Inaba on the floor. He landed with a thud, winced, and said, "No. Lord Arima wanted to deal a blow to Lord Matsudaira. When the shogun put the question to him, that was his once-in-a-lifetime chance."

Sano shook his head. "If what you're saying is true, then why would he tip the balance in my favor when he's clearly no friend of mine?"

Inaba smiled, relishing Sano's confusion. "He would have told the shogun that you're Lord Matsudaira's rival for power, but he didn't have time before all hell broke loose."

"So Lord Arima was playing against both sides," Sano concluded. "Why?"

"He kept it to himself." Inaba's voice was thick with rancor toward his master for leaving him in the dark, leaving him to suffer the consequences. "He told his people only as much as he thought they needed to know. I have no idea."

Hirata rode across the Nihonbashi Bridge, alone in the scant traffic moving along its high wooden arch. He felt like a nobody even as peasants made way for him and samurai bowed polite greetings. Rigid with unhappiness, he inhaled deeply. Through the acrid smoke that obscured the night sky, he smelled the distant ocean, mountains, and forests. He longed for the faraway places where he'd traveled. How he missed his nomadic life, the blessed freedom from personal complications!

He recalled how ambitious he'd once been, how eager to climb the ranks of the *bakufu*. Now the high position he'd achieved didn't matter. Without Midori's love, there seemed nothing left in Edo for him. Hirata looked over the railing of the bridge at a boat floating down the canal to the river to the sea, and he wished he were on it. But he had his duty to Sano to fulfill.

That, at least, he could manage.

At the foot of the bridge was the first station of the Tōkaidō, the highway that led from Edo to points west. On one side of the road lined with inns and shops stood the post house. The white plaster building was the checkpoint through which everyone entering town must pass. Its courtyard contained stables for packhorses and an area where the men who carried *kago*—basket chairs suspended from poles—waited for fares. At this late hour, few people straggled into town.

A merchant in a *kago,* his servants carrying iron money chests, and his *rōnin* security guards lined up outside the window of the post house. Inside by the window sat two clerks, examining the travelers' documents by the light of a lantern. Hirata dismounted, marched up to the window, and cut in front of the merchant. The merchant looked annoyed, but noticed the Tokugawa crests on Hirata's garments and didn't object.

Hirata stated his name and title to the clerks. One was a gray-haired samurai who'd probably worked as an inspector for so long that no faked travel passes could ever fool him. "How may we serve you, master?"

"I'm trying to trace a man who recently arrived in town," Hirata said. "Could you look him up in your records?"

The second clerk had a stout body and an expression that brooked no nonsense. "What's his name?" He hefted a stack of ledgers onto the counter.

"He's dead now. His name was Egen."

Something about the tutor had never smelled right to Hirata. Although he couldn't define exactly what, his senses had perceived a wrongness in the energy field that Egen had emitted.

The stout clerk paged through listings of people who'd entered Edo. "When did he come?"

Hirata didn't know exactly. "Start three days ago and work backward."

The gray-haired clerk helped, reading over his colleague's shoulder, to the displeasure of the people waiting in the line. Finally the stout clerk said, "We've gone back five months and still haven't found your man."

Egen had lied to the shogun. Had he also lied when he'd told the people at the inn that he'd arrived recently? Hirata said, "Maybe you remember him. He was over sixty years old, and he was covered with terrible pockmarks."

"As a matter of fact I do," the gray-haired clerk said, his sharp eyes brightening.

"So do I. That face of his wasn't something you'd forget," said the other clerk. "He came through here not a month ago."

"He was a good singer," said his colleague. "He entertained everybody in line while he waited his turn."

Hirata remembered Egen addressing the shogun in his dramatic, resonant voice. "He must be the same man. Why isn't his name in the ledger?"

"Because his name wasn't Egen," said the gray-haired clerk. "I remember now—it was Arashi." He leafed through the ledger, turned it around for Hirata to see, and pointed at a column of written characters. "Here he is."

Hirata read the full name, *Arashi Kodenji*. In the space provided for recording the traveler's place of residence was written *Shinagawa,* the highway post town nearest Edo. Hirata frowned in surprise as he saw what was listed as Arashi Kodenji's occupation.

Actor.

Sano met up with Hirata on the main street that ran through the Nihonbashi merchant district. The moon ascended the smoky sky above the rooftops, pale as a dead carp floating in a polluted pond. Hirata maneuvered his horse into step beside Sano's. They rode at the head of Sano's entourage, past shops closed for the night. A brigade of firemen carrying ladders trudged across a side street. Their faces were black with soot. They trailed the odor of smoke.

"I have news," Hirata said.

"So do I," Sano said. "You go first."

"The man we thought was Egen the tutor actually wasn't." Hirata described his visit to the post house. "His real name was Arashi Kodenji. He was an actor from Shinagawa."

"Today is certainly a day for revelations." As Sano recovered from his surprise, he absorbed the implications of Hirata's news. "So this Arashi Kodenji impersonated the tutor."

"He acted the part of Egen as if it were a role in a Kabuki play," Hirata said. "His scars probably kept him from getting lead roles on the stage, but they were an advantage in this case."

"If he happened to run into people who'd known Egen, they would think his face had been disfigured by the pox and that was why he didn't look like the man they remembered. That's what happened with my mother." Sano recalled how shocked she'd been at seeing how much her onetime lover had changed.

"That was quite a show he put on at the palace," Hirata said, his disgust tinged with admiration.

Sano smiled ruefully. "It must have been the biggest performance of his life. I recall thinking it seemed theatrical."

"But why would he tell lies about a woman he didn't even know? Certainly not just for the attention."

"More likely for money," Sano said. "We can assume that's how he got rich."

"And we can guess where the money came from." But Hirata sounded uncertain. "Maybe I've underestimated Lord Matsudaira, but I never thought him devious enough to do something as original as hiring an actor to impersonate your key witness."

Suspicions that had arisen in Sano's mind since he'd begun investigating the first murder now revolved around the new facts about the second victim. "I don't think he is. This situation smells more rotten than Lord Matsudaira."

"You're right. But then who——?"

Sano was beginning to get the idea. "Before I tell you, listen to my news." He described how he'd learned that Lord Arima was behind the ambush of Reiko, the bombing of Lord Matsudaira's estate, and the many other attacks that Sano and Lord Matsudaira had mistakenly attributed to each other. "Lord Arima wasn't Lord Matsudaira's ally as he pretended to be. But he wasn't mine, either."

Hirata shook his head, astonished. "Lord Arima played you off against each other, then betrayed Lord Matsudaira to the shogun. Why? Did he think he could make a bid for power himself?"

Sano's ideas shifted in the new light cast by the revelation about the fake tutor. "At first I thought so. His chief retainer couldn't supply any other explanation." He'd interrogated Inaba about Lord Arima's motives, in vain. Even the threat of being handed over to Lord Matsudaira had failed. Finally, realizing he'd exhausted the man's knowledge, Sano had sent Inaba home. "But now I doubt Lord Arima wanted to make a power play. He's not that reckless."

"His army isn't big enough, and he's not popular enough to attract support," Hirata agreed. "Besides, he skipped town instead of taking advantage of the upheaval he caused and moving into Lord Matsudaira's position."

They left the merchant quarter and entered the *daimyo* district. A procession of samurai on horseback rode toward them. "Aren't those friends of yours?" Hirata asked.

Sano noted the banners that bore the crests of three feudal lords who'd sworn allegiance to him. As the men passed, they didn't so much as look in Sano's direction. He saw the other banners that their troops wore on poles attached to their backs. These sported the triple-hollyhock-leaf Tokugawa crests.

"It was inevitable," Sano said. "My allies are deserting me and rallying around the shogun."

They'd clearly decided to join forces with the shogun, who had the hereditary right to rule, the sanction of the emperor, and a strong following of old-time loyalists who'd never approved of Sano. Which meant that Sano had fewer allies to defend him in the event of war.

"Lord Matsudaira's allies are probably doing the same thing," Hirata said.

"True, but that won't help me if I don't solve the murders." Sano turned the conversation back to the subject they'd been discussing. "We have the same situation with Lord Arima as with the fake tutor. Both of them acting strangely, neither on his own."

"They were both working for somebody else," Hirata concluded.

"We didn't run across any evidence that they knew each other, but there's a connection between them."

"The murder of the actor."

"Yes. Ishikawa and Ejima said that Lord Arima sent them to kill the man we thought was the tutor. At first I didn't know whether to believe them, but now . . ." Sano accepted their dying confession as the truth. "And I don't believe Lord Arima did the murder for Lord Matsudaira."

Puzzlement creased Hirata's brow. "Then who could it be that they and the actor were working for?"

"Don't laugh when you hear," Sano warned. They were nearing Edo Castle. Although the boulevard was deserted, Sano knew that spies lurked in shadows, and he refrained from naming a name. "I think it's an old friend we thought was safely out of the picture."

As Hirata comprehended Sano's meaning, his expression rearranged into shock. "That can't be. If he were back, how could he have kept it a secret?"

"He's clever, and he has supporters to hide him. Besides, this situation stinks of him."

"The reports from Hachijo don't say a word about any escaped prisoners," Hirata pointed out.

"You and I both know that reports don't always tell the truth."

"But how can you be so sure?" Hirata eyed Sano as if questioning his sanity.

"I just am."

Sano's certainty was more than a hunch built from odd incidents and facts and glued together with logic. For eleven years he and the man had lived through rivalry and truce, through violence, bloodshed, and the threat of death, through clashes and collaboration. Sano had come to know the man as well as himself. He knew the pattern of the man's thoughts, the distinct texture of his vision. The two of them had developed a preternatural awareness of each other, as if the space between them were charged with energy like the air before a thunderstorm. When one moved, the other felt the sensation in his nerves.

Sano had felt that sensation for some time now. One thing happening after another had made it grow stronger, impossible to let common sense push to the back of his mind anymore. "If I'm right, it would explain a lot of things."

"Such as the increase in activity by his underground partisans," Hirata said, not convinced but willing to test the theory. "Add to that the attacks on Lord Matsudaira—who's his biggest enemy—and on you, the man who took his post."

"Those attacks include the one in Ezogashima last winter," Sano said.

"We were never able to determine who threw that knife at you," Hirata recalled.

"I suspected then, and I do now, that our friend sent an assassin to kill me in Ezogashima," Sano said.

"If he knew you were going there, and if he knows enough about the murder investigation to meddle in it, then he must be close by."

Sano could almost see the shadow of a tall, familiar figure move across their path. Hirata lifted his head, and his nostrils flared as if smelling their old adversary's scent.

"He must have friends at court who keep him well informed." Sano could guess whom they included. He thought of Yoritomo's strange behavior. More mysteries became less perplexing.

"Suppose you are right," Hirata said. "We can't let him keep pulling strings and wreaking havoc from behind the scenes. But we can't hit an invisible target, either. What are we going to do?"

"I'll think of something. But there's no time now. I have to exonerate my mother by the end of the day tomorrow." Amid the dark, tangled wilderness of his troubles, Sano saw a faint glow of hope. "And I know one more place to look for proof that she's innocent."

27

The next morning found Sano and Hirata in the forest where Tokugawa Tadatoshi's skeleton had been discovered. They stood gazing down at the closest thing they had to a crime scene.

The grave had been filled in. All Sano could see of it was bare dirt with white salt crystals sprinkled on top to purify it. The tree knocked over by the wind had been removed. The forest was peaceful, enlivened by birdsong. A gentle breeze swayed boughs green with new foliage. Patches of sunlight and shadow formed a moving tapestry on the leaf-covered earth. Sano breathed air that was fresh and clean in these hills far above the city and the fires.

"There's nothing here related to Tadatoshi, his death, or whoever killed him," Hirata said.

Sano knew that Hirata had trained his senses to perceive the energy that every living thing gave off and any disturbance to the world of nature. Hirata had employed this unique talent to help solve the murder case they'd investigated in Ezogashima, and if he said there was no evidence here, Sano believed him. But Sano wasn't discouraged.

"Fortunately, there are other kinds of evidence besides physical clues." Sano turned to the man waiting on the path, who'd shown Sano and Hirata to the graveside. It was the priest who'd discovered Tadatoshi's skeleton. "Were you here during the Great Fire?"

"No," said the priest. He wore a dark blue kimono over gray trousers instead of his ceremonial white robe and black cap. His placid face, oval in shape and speckled with age, reminded Sano of a quail's egg. "I came here three years after."

"Are there any people around who were?" Sano said.

"Many, all over Edo, I suppose," the priest said. "These hills were a refuge for people escaping from the fire. The shrine gave shelter to hundreds."

"Too many witnesses are better than too few," Hirata said.

"But searching the whole city for them will take more time than I have left to solve the murder," Sano said.

"Perhaps I can save you some trouble," said the priest. "If you will please come with me?"

He led Sano and Hirata out of the forest to the shrine, which embodied Shinto religious architecture in its simplest form. They walked through a torii gate to a small, plain wooden building that waited ready for the spirits to occupy. Outside stood a gong for summoning the spirits and a basin of water for visitors to wash their hands. The shrine was off the main routes, visited mostly in the summer by people who flocked to the hillside villas to escape the city heat. Today the shrine was deserted except for an old man who sat on a stone bench, his hands propped on a cane, eyes closed, face lifted to the sun.

The man turned as Sano and his companions approached. The priest said, "This is Rintayu. He was the priest here before me. Now he's a pilgrim who travels from shrine to shrine. He returns here every year. He just arrived yesterday."

Rintayu nodded and smiled. He was over eighty, his face tanned and wrinkled, his mouth toothless, his hands gnarled. His expression was benign and sunny. The priest introduced Sano and Hirata to him, and Rintayu bowed. He said in a quavering but clear voice, "It's an honor to meet you."

"They need your assistance," the priest told him.

"Whatever I can do for you, just ask," Rintayu said, without opening his eyes.

"He's blind," the priest explained.

Sano regarded the old man with concern. "How long have you been blind?"

"Since I was five years old," Rintayu said.

"It's amazing how well he manages," the priest said. "He can do almost everything a normal person can."

"But you won't be able to help me," Sano said, disappointed.

"We're looking for a witness to something that happened here when you were the priest," Hirata said. "You couldn't have seen it."

"Begging your pardon, but a man can see without eyesight," Rintayu said in a tone of gentle rebuke. "When he's blind, the other senses take over."

He trained his attention on Sano. "You're about forty years old, and you just came from the city—there's smoke on your clothes. You're taller than your retainer, who's about ten years younger." Rintayu turned to Hirata. "You limp on your left leg, and you ate fleece flower stems in your morning meal."

Sano and Hirata exchanged glances. The priest smiled at their surprise. "He's good, isn't he?"

Rintayu cocked his head, listened, and said, "There's a squirrel in the tree about twenty paces behind you."

Sano turned, looked up, and saw a bushy tail twitch on a branch and heard the squirrel's faint scolds. Hirata said, "Let's try a test." He reached for his sword.

Rintayu flicked out his cane, swatted Hirata's hand, and cackled while Hirata and Sano gaped. "I've surprised quite a few louts who think a blind man is an easy target."

"All right. I stand corrected," Sano said. "How's your memory?"

"Don't ask me what I did yesterday, but I can remember everything that happened thirty or forty years ago. That's a blessing or a curse of old age, depending on how you look at it."

"It may be a blessing in this case," Sano said. "I'm investigating a murder that took place in these woods around the time of the Great Fire. I need a witness, and you're my best hope."

"A murder?" Rintayu apparently hadn't heard of the discovery of the skeleton. His face underwent a sudden change, as if a cloud had passed across his features, eclipsing their sunshine. "Who was killed?"

"The shogun's cousin," Sano said. "His name was Tokugawa Tadatoshi. He was fourteen years old."

"So that's who the boy was." Rintayu's voice was hushed with impressed enlightenment. "I've thought of him many times. I've always wondered."

An accelerating current of excitement coursed through Sano. This seemed too good to be true. "You mean you know something about his death?"

Rintayu nodded. "I was there."

Sano caught Hirata's eye, and they shared the elation born of running across unexpected treasure. Sano said, "Tell me what happened."

"It was two nights after the fire had burned out," Rintayu said. "The smell of the smoke had faded and the alarm bells had stopped ringing. The hills were full of people who'd run away from the city. Dogs, too—hundreds of them that had escaped. All day I could hear movement through the woods. At night I could hear the dogs howling and the people crying."

Sano imagined the aftermath of the fire as perceived by a blind man. It must have seemed a black netherworld that echoed with the sounds of suffering.

"They came to the shrine for help," Rintayu continued. "I gave them the food I'd stored for the winter. I sheltered as many as I could in my cottage. When the food ran out, when I had nothing to offer them except prayers, they grew desperate. Some tried to break into the shrine to look for a warm place to sleep. I had to guard it. That night, I was standing outside the shrine when someone ran past me into the woods. He was panting and crying. It was the boy."

Rintayu lifted his head as if at a sudden disturbance, as he must have done that night. His ears pricked backward like an animal's; his nostrils flared. "More footsteps came after him, running. It was two young men. One of them shouted, 'Don't lose him!' The other one shouted, 'Where did he go?'"

Two young men. Sano felt a tentative relief. Whoever they were, it didn't matter. What mattered was that they, not his mother, had apparently chased Tadatoshi with intent to harm, into the forest where his grave had been found.

"I knew he was in danger," Rintayu said, "and I wanted to help, so I followed the men. It was dark, so they didn't see me. I could hear them crashing through the woods, tripping and falling and yelling. But the sounds were echoing off the trees, and I couldn't tell where they were. Then I heard a thud. The boy screamed. One of the men shouted, 'I've got him!' "

Sano pictured a figure hurtling out of the dark woods, tackling Tadatoshi, bringing him down. Rintayu said, "There were more screams, and sounds of struggling and hitting. The man said, 'Hold him still.' The other said, 'What are we going to do?' The first said, 'We have to kill him. What choice do we have?'

"The boy was crying. There were more fighting noises. Then I heard a thump, and the first man swore. I could tell by the sound, and his voice, that the boy had hit or kicked him in a bad spot. He shouted, 'Come back here!'

"There was more running, more struggling. And more blows, and the boy screaming louder and crying. They were killing him." Rintayu's face showed the memory of his horror. "I hurried toward the noises." He pantomimed running, the cane raised, his free hand groping his way. "But the boy stopped screaming. I was too late."

Sano felt his heart beating as fast and hard as if he'd been at the scene himself. Elation swept through him. "Those two men killed Tadatoshi. No one else was there." Sano finally had the witness to prove that his mother was innocent.

"But there was," Rintayu said. "A woman. Didn't I say?" He looked sheepish. "I guess I forgot to mention her. She was shouting and running with the men. She screamed while they were beating the boy. Afterward, she started to cry, and the men said, " 'Don't be upset. It's over. We did what we had to. It's all right, Etsuko.' "

* * *

When Sano got home, he ignored the officials in the antechamber and the clerks who besieged him with urgent messages. His secretary ran alongside him, saying, "Honorable Chamberlain, the shogun wants to see you!"

"That's too bad." Sano kept going. He didn't care if he offended the shogun; he didn't care that this was a time when he could least afford to tax his lord's goodwill.

"But he's sent four messengers since you've been gone," the secretary protested. "He's been waiting for you all day. You must go to him immediately."

"Let him wait." Sano had business more important than catering to the shogun. He had to talk to his mother.

As he stormed down the corridor to the private quarters, he relived the moment when he'd heard Rintayu reveal that his mother had been present during the murder. "That can't be," he'd said in a turmoil of horror and astonishment. "Are you sure about her name?"

"As sure as I am that you want me not to be," Rintayu had replied.

"Who were those men?"

"I don't know. The woman heard me coming, and they all ran away."

Sano's belief in his mother's innocence had died along with his hope of proving it. Rintayu's story was the evidence he'd dreaded discovering, even as he'd pursued the truth about Tadatoshi's murder. Shattered, he'd listened as Hirata had continued interrogating their witness.

"What happened then?" Hirata asked.

"I looked for the boy," Rintayu said. "I hoped I could save him. But when I found him, he was dead. There was blood all over his body where they'd beaten him and cut him."

"And you didn't do anything?" Censure crept into Hirata's voice.

"I did," the old man insisted. "I couldn't leave the poor boy out in the open, where the dogs would get him. They were starving; they'd have eaten him in no time. I got a shovel, dug a hole under an oak tree, and buried his body."

Sano was stunned to learn that Tadatoshi's killers hadn't put him in his grave. He'd been buried by an innocent bystander who hadn't seen, or had reason to fear, that he could be identified by the characters on his swords.

"No, I mean, didn't you report the murder?" Hirata said.

"Not right away. There was no one to report a murder to. The police who hadn't died in the fire had their hands full keeping order in the city. Later, when things settled down, I told them what had happened. But they weren't interested. So many people had died; who cared about one boy? They figured he'd been killed in a fight over food. That happened a lot during those days."

The police hadn't known he was a member of the Tokugawa clan, or they would have investigated his murder, Sano thought. But his mother had known Tadatoshi. She'd known very well who he was. And she'd known that she had taken part in his murder all the while she'd told Sano she was innocent.

Now fury quickened Sano's pace along the corridor. He remembered that Hirata had said, on their way back to the castle, "You shouldn't be too quick to believe Rintayu. He's a total stranger. Why take his word over your mother's?"

"Because he has no reason to lie," Sano answered, "whereas she obviously does." And he'd felt certain all along that she had withheld the facts.

Reiko had been right about his mother's guilt.

He arrived, winded and panting, in the guest room. His mother knelt at the dressing table, her profile toward him. She wore a silk kimono, patterned in lavender and forest green, that Reiko must have loaned her. She was brushing her hair. The kimono's subdued yet rich colors and her long, loose hair gave her a semblance of youth and Sano a glimpse of how beautiful she'd been when she was young—when she'd murdered a boy. His rage at her burned hotter.

She turned to him and reverted to the old woman she was. Her wrinkled face brightened with the same fond affection as always when she saw Sano. Then she noticed his expression. "What is it?" she asked, her smile fading.

228

Sano said, "Tell me what happened to Tadatoshi. This time I want the truth."

"I already told you everything. Stop hounding me!"

Her command momentarily silenced Sano. He flashed back to the time when his mother had been the boss, so long ago he'd almost forgotten. Recovering, he said, "You told me that you and Egen the tutor were lovers, that the two of you spied on Tadatoshi after you caught him setting a fire. But you didn't tell me everything."

Alarm opened her eyes and mouth wide. "When did I tell you that?"

"When you were in jail," Sano said. "Dr. Ito gave you a potion that loosened your tongue."

"Oh, no." An ugly blush stained her face, which she covered with her hands. "I never wanted you to know about me and Egen. I'm so ashamed!"

"What else didn't you want me to know?" Sano grabbed her wrists and yanked her hands away from her face. "What did you do to Tadatoshi?"

Her gaze was woeful yet vexed. "I didn't—"

"There's no use denying it." Sano held her wrists while she strained to pull free. "I went to the shrine today. I met the man who was its priest at the time of the Great Fire. He overheard Tadatoshi's murder. You were there, with two men. He heard them speak your name."

She stiffened, her face a mask of shock. Sano heard her draw in a long, hissing breath. Then she went limp in his grasp as the breath drained out of her. "I remember hearing someone in the woods that night," she whispered.

"You might as well tell me what happened," Sano said, releasing her hands. "Based on what the witness said, it sounds as if you and those men killed Tadatoshi. I want your side of the story."

Despite his anger at her, despite the evidence against her that included the blood Hana had seen on her clothes, Sano still hoped that his mother was innocent, that the witness hadn't heard what he'd thought. Despite his effort to be objective, a part of him believed her incapable of murder.

"I can't tell you." Her voice quavered.

"You must," Sano said, "so that I can help you." He couldn't help wanting to despite his fury at her deception, her past behavior. "I have to know the truth and minimize the damage before anyone else learns you were at the shrine when Tadatoshi died."

He doubted he could keep it quiet even though he'd sworn the old man and the current priest to secrecy. People talked; it was human nature. And Sano's enemies were good at digging up the most carefully buried information.

"You told me most of the story. Now tell me the rest," Sano said.

An internal struggle beset his mother; her habit of obedience vied with the resolve that had kept her past a secret. She bit her lips as though to prevent them from speaking; she sat still, her head cocked and gaze directed inward, as if listening to an argument in her head. Then she let out a sad, defeated sigh.

"All right," she said. "But if you don't like what you hear, please don't be angry."

28

MEIREKI YEAR THREE (1657)

They searched all day for Tadatoshi.

All day the fire burned and spread, flames leaping roofs and canals, consuming the city. Etsuko and Egen roamed deep into the Nihonbashi merchant quarter. When night came, the fires lit the sky more brilliantly red than any sunset. Etsuko and Egen stopped to rest in a doorway in an abandoned neighborhood.

"We'll never find him. We might as well give up," Egen said, wiping sweat off his face. The fire had heated the winter night; the air was as warm as in summer.

"His father said not to come back without him." Etsuko opened her cape and fanned herself with her leather helmet.

They gazed at the terrible red sky. They could hear the fire crackling in the distance, smell the black smoke that billowed to the heavens like gigantic, shape-changing demons.

"It's too dangerous to stay out here," Egen said. "We tried our best. Let's go home."

Tired, hungry, and defeated, Etsuko agreed. She and Egen ran hand in hand past buildings on fire, past fleeing crowds. She struggled to keep up with him as the smoke grew denser. They reached a canal, where hundreds of people blocked the bridge. They were trapped in the mob. Egen's hand ripped loose from hers. He was lost in the crush. She was alone.

Then Doi miraculously appeared beside her. He pulled her along through the mob. Etsuko sobbed with gratitude that he cared enough about her to save her, even after she'd betrayed him. She heard Egen shouting her name, saw his frantic face in the crowd, his hand waving.

"Egen's over there!" she said.

Doi plowed past the people who separated him and Etsuko from Egen. The men shoved and fought everyone in their way. When they broke free of the crush, Doi said, "We can't go home. The fire has already burned down the estate. I saw."

Etsuko was horrified. "What's become of everyone?"

"I don't know," Doi said.

"The fire's coming. Where do we go?" Egen said urgently.

Doi led Etsuko and Egen on a mad dash through the inferno. They raced holding hands, their quarrel forgotten, united by the desire to survive. Every neighborhood they traversed was on fire. Tongues of flame shot into masses of people who pushed wheeled chests filled with their possessions. Etsuko, Egen, and Doi climbed over abandoned chests that blocked the gates and intersections. Not until morning did they find refuge.

They fell to their knees, exhausted, inside the Koishikawa district. Edo Castle loomed above a neighborhood of walled samurai estates. The fire had so far spared the district, but men on horseback and ladies in palanquins, accompanied by servants loaded with baggage, moved in processions toward the hills. Firemen wielded pickaxes, tearing down houses at the edge of the district, clearing bare space that the fire couldn't cross. They'd already leveled a swath littered with ruins.

"We'll be safe here," Egen said. His face and Doi's were black with soot, their clothes charred.

Etsuko coughed up phlegm that tasted like smoke. She felt dizzy and sick from breathing it all night. Doi said, "I'll climb up that firewatch tower and see what's happening."

When he came back, he said, "Half the city is gone. Yushima, Hongo, Hatchobori, Ishikawajima, Kyobashi, Reiganjima—" His voice broke during his recitation of the districts destroyed. "And the fire is still burning."

He and Etsuko and Egen wept for Edo and all the people who must have died. But Etsuko hadn't forgotten the mission that had sent them into hell.

"What about Tadatoshi?" she asked.

"Never mind him," Doi said, angrily wiping off his tears with his fists. "He's probably dead."

Some instinct made Etsuko look into the crowds. She saw, not thirty paces away, Tadatoshi standing against a wall. He wore his swords at his waist. His gaze was lifted toward the flames that rose from the burning city. His face had the same sly, private smile as on that night in the garden. At first Etsuko was astonished to have found him, but then she realized that many people who'd survived the fire had flocked to this small, unburned oasis.

"There he is!" she cried, pointing.

Tadatoshi's gaze met hers. The sudden anger in his eyes flashed across the space between them, hot as the fires, in the moment before he turned and ran.

Etsuko staggered to her feet. "Let's catch him! Hurry!"

Egen and Doi followed her. Perhaps they couldn't think of anything better to do. Tadatoshi raced in and out of the crowds, around corners. The Koishikawa district was home to the officials who tended the shogun's falcons. The processions included oxcarts laden with cages that contained hawks and eagles. Other birds had escaped. They winged over Etsuko, bound for the hills. She lost sight of Tadatoshi, but Egen called, "He went in there!"

He and Etsuko and Doi burst through a gate into a courtyard outside a mansion. The sudden quiet rang in Etsuko's ears. Doi put a finger to his lips. The three tiptoed around the mansion. At the rear were outbuildings. Etsuko heard a scrabbling noise from one. She and the men peered through its open door into a kitchen. Tadatoshi crouched, blowing into a brazier. Flames licked the coals.

That he would set a fire after so much of Edo had already burned!

Doi shouted Tadatoshi's name. Tadatoshi leaped up and backed away as Doi and Egen moved toward him. His eyes danced with manic light. He grinned and Etsuko saw, in his hands, a ceramic jar.

"No!" she cried. "Look out!"

Tadatoshi flung kerosene from the jar onto the brazier. The flames exploded into a huge, red-hot blast. Etsuko, Doi, and Egen screamed and reeled backward from the fire. Tadatoshi giggled wildly. He kicked the brazier, scattering the coals, and dashed kerosene around the room. More fires ignited.

"Help!" Doi cried.

He writhed on the floor, his cape on fire. Etsuko beat the flames out with her gloved hands. Egen pulled Doi to his feet, yelling, "We have to get out of here!"

They and Etsuko ran from the kitchen. It burst into flames that the wind blew high and far. Before they were out the gate, the mansion had caught fire. Sparks leaped to the other houses. In a mere instant the whole district was ablaze.

"We'll go to the castle," Doi said. "It's the most protected place in town."

But as they and the crowds hastened uphill, the fire overtook them. The streets became tunnels with walls of flames that spewed in every direction. Women shrieked as their clothes and hair caught fire. They flailed their arms, whirled, and dropped. The flames stripped them naked and bald, blackened their skin. Etsuko retched at the sight and smell of flesh burning, of blood boiling.

"Turn back!" Doi shouted.

He and Egen hauled Etsuko in the opposite direction. Coughing and gasping, they trampled people who'd succumbed to the smoke, over bodies burned to the bone. They ran past an intersection where hundreds of men stood massed together, arms raised, forming a human wall against the fire in a desperate attempt to hold it back and let their families escape. The fire washed over them like a brilliant orange tidal wave.

Doi spied some abandoned water buckets. He snatched them up

and flung water over Etsuko, Egen, and himself. As they ran on-
ward, the water steamed off them, protecting them while other
people burned and died.

"We have to get to the river," Egen panted. "It's our only hope."

When they reached the waterfront, the lone bridge across the
Sumida River was already packed with crowds, the warehouses already burning. People swarmed the wharves and docks. Men and
children, and mothers with babies in arms, samurai and commoners,
jumped into the river. The crowd swept Etsuko, Egen, and Doi off
the dock. Etsuko cried out as they plunged into freezing water where
thousands of heads bobbed. The river was so thick with humanity
that she could barely move. Arms struck and legs kicked her. People
sank and drowned. Somehow Doi, Etsuko, and Egen broke through
the jam, into the deep middle of the river, in the fast-moving current.

Doi submerged, crying, "I don't know how to swim."

Neither did Etsuko. Egen grabbed her and Doi, locking his arms
around their necks. Holding their heads above the water, he lay on
his back and kicked. Etsuko and Doi floated with him. As the current
carried them along, Doi pointed up at the city and cried, "Edo Castle
is burning."

Etsuko was aghast to see that its roofs were sheets of flame, the
tall, square tower of the keep burning like a giant torch. "That's
from the fire Tadatoshi set. If only we'd found him sooner!"

An eternity later, Etsuko and her companions crawled,
half dead from cold and fatigue, onto the riverbank near a fishing village. The villagers gave them food, shelter, and warm clothes. Two
days afterward, they made their way back to Edo.

The city lay in ruins. Most of it had burned to the ground. Etsuko,
Egen, and Doi walked in horrified awe through streets littered with
smoking debris. Charred skeletons lay amid the wreckage. Survivors
wandered, searching for the remains of their homes, mourning the
dead. Orphaned children cried and called for their mothers. The air was
frigid. All over the city, people huddled in miserable, shivering groups.

Etsuko felt an overwhelming sorrow, helplessness, and anger. "How many deaths must be Tadatoshi's fault?"

"Too many," Egen said grimly.

Doi said, "If the little demon is still alive, I swear I'll teach him a lesson. That is, if I ever find him again."

Snow began to fall, white as ashes. Etsuko craved action as well as revenge. "I think I know where to look."

The city was unrecognizable, but Etsuko had a good sense of direction. She led the men to the place that had once been Koishikawa. Soldiers were unloading bundles from handcarts and passing out food to the starved crowds. Among these Etsuko saw Tadatoshi. He was gazing upon the black timbers and scattered roof tiles of the house he'd set on fire. He'd come through the disaster completely unscathed.

Finding him again was no miracle. Etsuko's suspicion that Tadatoshi would return to the scene of his crime had proved correct.

"Hey!" Doi stalked over to Tadatoshi. "Come to look at what you did?"

Tadatoshi smiled his strange smile. "Wasn't the fire the most exciting thing you've ever seen? Especially when the castle burned?"

Not only did he have no remorse; he wanted credit!

" 'Exciting'?" Egen stared at Tadatoshi. "You killed thousands of people, and you enjoyed it. You're mad!"

Tadatoshi shrugged. "What are you going to do about it?"

"We're going to report you to the authorities," Egen said.

"Go ahead." Tadatoshi sniggered. "I'm a Tokugawa. You people are nobodies. They'll never believe you."

He was right, Etsuko realized.

"Then we'll make you pay!" exclaimed Doi.

"You'll have to catch me first." Tadatoshi turned and ran.

"Don't let him get away this time!" Etsuko cried.

As she and Doi and Egen pursued him, she shouted, "That boy set the fire that burned down the castle! Stop him!"

Soldiers and crowds only stared, too numb to react or thinking she was crazy. Tadatoshi led Etsuko and her companions on a chase across intact neighborhoods where people broke into shops and fought over the loot. He dashed up a road to the hills. Etsuko strained to keep him in sight among the thousands trudging away from what they'd lost. Night fell. Etsuko, Egen, and Doi were exhausted. Tadatoshi looked over his shoulder, then split from the crowd.

"He's going into the woods," Egen panted.

"Hurry!" Etsuko cried.

They forged up the trail he'd taken, between cedar trees. It was so dark they could hardly see his loping figure. High in the hills, they stopped near a torii gate, the entrance to a shrine. Here, above the smoky haze that still shrouded the city, the cold air was clear, the moon bright. Etsuko saw Tadatoshi flopped on the ground. She and her comrades staggered over to him. His chest heaved as he stared at them. His eyes shone with fear and defiance.

"We've got you now," Doi said.

"What should we do with him?" Egen asked.

The answer came from some deep, steady, unforgiving place inside Etsuko. "We're going to kill him."

Doi gaped. "I can't. He's my master."

"He's an arsonist and a murderer," Etsuko said. "He deserves to die."

"Whatever he's done, killing him would be a disgrace to my honor," Doi protested.

"We must kill him," Etsuko said, "or he'll keep setting fires wherever he goes."

"I can't do it, either," Egen said. "When I took my religious vows, I swore never to take a life."

"How many more lives will he take when he sets his next fire? Who but us can protect innocent people from him?" Angry at her comrades, Etsuko said, "If you won't do it, I will."

She reached over to Doi, yanked the long sword at his waist from its sheath, and swung it at Tadatoshi.

The boy screamed. A natural coward, he cringed instead of drawing his own weapon and defending himself. Doi shouted, "No!" and grabbed her wrist. Tadatoshi jumped up and fled.

Etsuko wrenched free of Doi, the sword in her possession, and chased Tadatoshi. Doi and Egen ran after them into the woods. Et-suko bumped into trees and tripped over fallen branches. She followed the sound of Tadatoshi's panting and sobbing. In the moonlight that penetrated the foliage she saw glimpses of him, flickering in and out of view.

"Don't lose him!" Doi shouted.

"Where did he go?" came Egen's voice.

The men crashed through the woods, cursing as they tripped and fell. Tadatoshi sped past Etsuko. She grabbed at him but missed. Doi hurtled out of the darkness and shouted, "I've got him!" He and Tadatoshi fell together with a thud that shook the earth. Tadatoshi screamed and struggled. He began hitting Doi, who punched him and ordered, "Hold him still."

Egen came panting up beside Etsuko and said, "What are we going to do?"

"We have to kill him," Doi said with sorrowful reluctance. "What choice do we have?"

Tadatoshi fought and sobbed. Doi grunted, swore, and tumbled off the boy. He curled up, holding his groin. He shouted, "You devil! Come back here!"

Etsuko and Egen charged after Tadatoshi. She heard him fall but didn't see him until she and Egen tripped over his body. A murderous temper possessed Etsuko. She hacked at Tadatoshi with the sword. She wanted to strike him as many blows as the number of people he'd killed. She screamed while he screamed. Egen joined in, consumed by the same urge. He punched and kicked Tadatoshi. Doi grabbed the sword from Etsuko and slashed at Tadatoshi until his screams stopped.

Etsuko, Doi, and Egen stood over his body. The forest was silent except for their rapid, fevered breathing. As her temper cooled, Et-suko realized what they'd done. She began to cry.

The men embraced her. Doi said, "Don't be upset. It's over." His cheek against hers was wet with his own tears. Egen said, "We did what we had to. It's all right, Etsuko."

The sound of footsteps crunching through dried leaves silenced her sobs. "Someone's coming. We have to get out of here. Hurry!"

They ran far from the scene of their crime before they stopped in a clearing. "Swear that you'll never tell what we did," Doi said, extending his hand palm-down to Egen and Etsuko.

Etsuko laid her hand atop Doi's. Egen pressed his hand onto hers. "I swear," they all said.

They returned to the city and joined the thousands of homeless people who drifted around, searching for family, friends, and places they'd known. They ate stew cooked in camps set up by the government, but relief was inadequate. Every day they saw more dead bodies, of people who'd frozen or starved. At night they slept bundled together in quilts they'd stolen from an abandoned house. They hardly spoke; they couldn't look at one another. They were too ridden by their shared guilt.

Days later, Etsuko learned from a stranger that Hana was looking for her. She and her friends rushed to the tent city. When she found Hana, Egen and Doi walked away: They were too ashamed to face anyone they knew. Etsuko broke into shuddering, uncontrollable sobs.

Hana exclaimed, "There's blood all over you!"

Etsuko and her friends hadn't washed Tadatoshi's blood off their clothes; there'd been no place to wash. When Hana asked what had happened, Etsuko refused to tell and became violently ill. For days she lay in the tent, so nauseated she couldn't keep food down. She thought her sickness was a punishment from the gods.

Not until a month later did she learn its real cause.

By then she and Hana were reunited with her parents, at her family home that had survived the fire. Etsuko hadn't seen Egen. Maybe he didn't know where she was, and she couldn't go looking for him. Her parents wouldn't let her outside because Edo was a chaotic, dangerous place. She sat in her room and prayed, *Please let him come!*

One day her mother called, "Etsuko! We have visitors!"

Her heart rejoiced; it must be Egen and Doi. When she went to the parlor she found Doi—sitting with his parents and hers. Doi's father said, "Now that the fire is over, we'd like to set a date for our children's wedding."

"That would be fine with us," said Etsuko's father.

Etsuko was horrified. She saw in Doi's eyes that he still wanted her and was willing to forget the past. If only Egen would appear and save her from this loveless union!

Doi's mother regarded Etsuko with a suspicious, penetrating gaze. "Come closer. Give me a look at you."

Etsuko obeyed. The woman studied her swollen figure, then announced what Etsuko had been hiding. "You're with child."

Her parents exclaimed in appalled shock. Doi looked stunned. His father said, "Since Etsuko is no longer a virgin, we must break the engagement."

Etsuko was so ashamed that she ran sobbing from the house. Doi followed her into the alley. "Is it Egen's?" he demanded.

She couldn't answer; she didn't have to. Doi looked ready to cry himself. "Does he know?"

"No. I didn't have a chance to tell him."

"Well, you won't ever have one." Anger darkened Doi's face. "He's left town. He said he's not coming back. Because he can't stand to see me, or you, ever again."

As Etsuko wept, heartbroken because Egen had deserted her and would never marry her as she'd prayed he would, Doi shouted, "It serves you right! You're nothing but a whore!"

He slapped her face so hard that she fell. Then he walked out of her life.

That night Etsuko miscarried the child. She grieved, for it was all she'd had of her beloved. Her parents were upset because she was still damaged goods. What man would marry her now?

Six months later, her parents heard of a man who might be willing. They took her to meet him, and Etsuko's heart sank. He was at least ten years older than she, and so severe! Even worse, from her parents' standpoint, he was a *rōnin* who operated a martial arts school. What a grievous comedown from the match they'd planned for her with Doi! But he made a proposal of marriage, and her parents accepted, eager for him to take their wayward daughter off their hands.

Etsuko had no choice but to marry the *rōnin*. Her parents disowned her, and she lost contact with everyone and everything familiar. She swallowed her grief and pride, accustomed herself to living in near poverty, and worked hard at keeping house for her husband. She never told him about the murder. She bore him a son, who eventually became the shogun's second-in-command.

29

"Now you know why I couldn't tell you the truth," Sano's mother said.

Shocked beyond words by her tale, Sano turned away from her, rubbed his hand down his mouth, and gazed into space.

"Egen and Doi and I killed Tadatoshi," she said. "We were all responsible, but I was the most."

Reiko had known the gist of the story, albeit not the details, Sano thought. He should have listened to his wife.

Now he knew why the real tutor had skipped town, and why Colonel Doi was bitter toward Etsuko after all these years. Sano had been right about Doi having a hand in the murder. Perhaps Doi's guilt had motivated his heroism during the relief efforts after the fire. Sano also knew he could never prove his mother's innocence, for she was as guilty as he'd ever feared. Her hands that had nursed him during his childhood had once taken a life in cold blood. But he felt sick and shaken for a reason even more personal.

His earlier discoveries had contradicted facts he'd taken for granted about his family background, but his mother had just demolished the foundations of his self. He wasn't only the son of a poor but upstanding *rōnin*; he was the son of a fallen woman, a murderess. His emotions in turmoil, he couldn't separate what he thought about the fact that she was guilty of the murder from what he felt about the rest of her confession.

"How could you?" he said, turning on his mother, venting his emotions in fury.

She extended her hands, palms up. "It was right."

Her fear and weakness had vanished. Telling her story had given her a calm, dignified strength. But it had undone Sano.

"You not only had an affair with the tutor, you bore his child," he said. Hana knew that part of the story, if not the rest; that explained her reluctance to talk. "Then you married my father and pretended it never happened. You hid your crime from him. Our whole life was a lie."

Her secret was a skeleton that had been buried beneath the surface of their existence while Tadatoshi's bones lay in his hidden grave. Those bones had conveyed messages from the past, and repercussions for the future, to Sano. They were indeed oracle bones.

"How can I not be angry?" Sano demanded.

His mother rose, undaunted by his outburst. "It wasn't a lie. Your father and I were as happy together as most married couples. He was a decent man, and I served him faithfully until he died."

That sounded meager compared with her passionate love for Egen—and Sano's own for Reiko. Even in the heat of his rage Sano could pity his mother. He could begin to see her life from her point of view.

"You gave up everything," he said, shaking his head in wonder. "Your life of luxury, your samurai status, your honor." He was appalled by her disgrace and knew she must have felt the same. "How could you bear it?"

"There were compensations." She laid her hand against his cheek and smiled. Her eyes brimmed with love. "I had you."

Sano resisted her affection. He was even more upset by the truth about his origins. He was as much a result of his mother's illicit affair as if he'd been the fruit of it. If not for her illegitimate, miscarried child, she would never have married his father, and Sano would never have been born. He owed his existence to the affair—and to the crime that had divided her from the man she'd loved. And he began to see what else he owed to his mother the murderess.

He'd always wondered where he'd gotten his inclination to put himself in jeopardy for the sake of a cause, his belief that justice was all-important, even if it required actions that society disapproved of or the law forbade. His nature didn't come from his father, who'd adhered strictly to Bushido's code of conformity to social mores and discouraged individual initiative in his son. Sano had long ago decided that his rogue tendencies were entirely his own creation. But now, as his mother dropped her hand from his face and he looked into her eyes, he saw their source.

She said, "When you were a boy, I watched you growing into the same sort of person I was when I was young. I feared you would get in trouble and ruin your life the way I did mine. Well, I was wrong." She beamed at Sano. "My son the chamberlain!" Her smile turned rueful. "But I was right, too."

Sano couldn't quite smile at the memory of the times he'd stubbornly pursued murderers and delivered them to justice, risking his position and his life to uphold his personal definition of honor.

"Perhaps I'm lucky that you take after me," his mother said. "Because you can understand why I had to kill Tadatoshi and why I convinced Doi and Egen to help me."

To his credit and discredit, Sano did. Tadatoshi the arsonist had been the greatest criminal of all time, his death toll thousands of times greater than any killer Sano had ever faced. "Yes," Sano admitted. "If I'd been in your position, I would have done the same as you did. I'd have taken the law into my own hands, the consequences be damned."

More revelations astounded Sano. Was his mother's partnership with Doi and Egen not a precedent for Sano's partnership with Reiko and their missions into shady territory outside the law? Many people wondered why Sano put up with a wife as strong-willed and venturesome as Reiko; he'd often wondered himself. Now he saw that his acceptance of her had to do with more than love.

He must have unconsciously perceived his mother's true nature,

244

and she was his standard for what he wanted in a mate. His affinity for an unconventional woman had been bred in the womb. There was no part of his life that his mother and her actions hadn't influenced.

But it didn't matter that he understood what she'd done. His wasn't the opinion that counted.

"Can you forgive me?" she asked anxiously.

Sano couldn't find in himself the capacity to forgive. Emotion choked him; he didn't trust himself to speak. And his finally learning the story didn't help his mother. This was his last day to exonerate her, and he couldn't. He'd always believed the truth would save the innocent, but this time it would damn the guilty.

He cleared his throat and said, "It's not my forgiveness you need. The shogun will be expecting the final results of my investigation." So would his enemies, who would pressure the shogun to condemn Sano and his mother. "I don't know what to say to him." If the shogun were to hear that she'd killed Tadatoshi because he was an arsonist and a mass murderer, he would think she was trying to justify her crime by slandering his poor dead cousin. "I can hardly tell him your story."

"You don't have to tell me," a voice said behind them. "I, ahh, heard the whole thing."

Sano and his mother started, turned, and saw the shogun in the doorway. "Your Excellency," Sano exclaimed, unable to hide his horror that the shogun had come for another visit at the worst possible time. "What a pleasure to see you. I didn't know you were coming."

"Obviously not," the shogun said tartly, "or you and your mother wouldn't have been having such a, ahh, fascinating conversation."

"Please come in and sit down," Sano said. "Have you eaten yet? May I offer you some refreshments?"

Ignoring Sano's attempt to divert him, the shogun crept into the room. His expression wavered between confusion, shock, and outrage. "She said my cousin set the fire in Koishikawa," he said, pointing at Sano's mother. "Is it true?"

She looked from him to Sano, stunned wordless. Sano hurried to reply, "That's not what she said. You misheard. Now how may I be of service?"

The shogun waved Sano away. "Your mother shall answer my question. Perhaps she is the one person in this entire country who will tell me the straight facts instead of talking in circles." He turned to her. "Did you really say that my cousin set that fire?"

This time Sano's mother showed no fear, didn't cringe. "Yes," she said with quiet conviction. "I saw him with my own eyes— exactly as you heard me tell my son."

Sano suppressed a groan. That she'd accused a member of the Tokugawa clan of a capital crime! That she'd committed this act of treason to the shogun's face! She seemed intent on using the truth to seal her doom.

"You saw him set the fire that burned the castle?" The shogun's voice rose shrill and loud with appalled incredulity.

"Mother," Sano said, "let me handle this."

"Quiet!" the shogun ordered.

"Yes," Sano's mother said.

Sano despaired of trying to rescue her from herself. The shogun would call his guards to arrest her, Sano, and their whole family. Sano drew a breath to call his own guards. He braced himself for a fight.

The shogun sank to his knees. His assertiveness crumbled; his complexion turned pale, sickly. Sano was so disconcerted by his lord's sudden change of mood that he exhaled and hesitated.

"I was in the castle during the Great Fire," the shogun said in a tremulous, broken voice. "With my mother. We thought we would be safe, until the second day, when the fire started in Koishikawa. It came blazing up the hill." He shrank into himself; his voice grew thinner and higher as he reverted to the scared little boy he'd been during the disaster.

"The wind blew the fire to the castle. We were in the middle of a sea of flames. They leaped the walls and burned the corridors on top. Then they were raging inside the castle. We hurried to the West Quarter, which was farthest away from the fire. We hid there while the rest of the castle burned."

His gaze was clouded by the memory of that awful day, by his un-forgotten terror. "If our soldiers hadn't managed to put out the fire before it could reach the West Quarter, my mother and I would have perished." Outrage cleared his eyes. "The fire that Tadatoshi set virtually destroyed my castle." Thumping his palm against his chest, the shogun said, "He almost killed *me!*"

Astonishment struck Sano. The shogun had accepted his mother's story as the truth. And he cared only about the part of the story that directly concerned himself. Recovering from his first shock, Sano realized that the shogun was behaving completely in character.

"Tadatoshi killed thousands of people," Sano's mother said.

The shogun made an impatient, dismissive gesture. "Because of him, *I* almost died! Even though I didn't, I was frightened out of my wits!"

Sano's mother frowned at his self-centeredness. Her lips parted, but Sano silenced her with a glance before she could rebuke the shogun as she had Sano when he'd behaved callously toward other people during his childhood. He floated a question as cautiously as if releasing a butterfly to test the wind.

"Do you understand why my mother and her friends had to kill Tadatoshi?"

"Yes, yes." The shogun's head bobbed. "He deserved to die for what he did to me."

"And you understand that if they hadn't killed him, he would have continued setting fires?" Sano drove his point into what the shogun would deem the heart of the matter. "His next one might have killed you."

The shogun pursed his mouth. "Ahh, I hadn't thought of that." He sounded awed by his narrow escape. "But yes, you're right."

"So you might say that my mother not only punished an arsonist, but she saved your life," Sano said.

"Yes, indeed!" the shogun exclaimed. Then he said, "What I don't understand is Colonel Doi. Why did he say she, ahh, kidnapped Tadatoshi and murdered him for money? He knew what really happened to Tadatoshi because he was in on it. Why didn't he, ahh, just tell me the truth?"

For the same reasons his mother hadn't wanted to, Sano thought.

Their pledge, and their fear of punishment, had kept them both silent for forty-three years. Doi had counted on her to honor the pledge even after he'd accused her of murder. But that explanation didn't best suit Sano's purposes.

"Doi didn't want anyone to know he was a coward who hesitated to kill an arsonist," Sano said. "He didn't want to admit that my mother, a mere girl, was the one brave and virtuous enough to do what needed to be done."

Nodding, the shogun turned to her. "Yes, you were brave." Admiration filled his voice. "In fact, you are a heroine!"

Sano's mother looked mortified by the praise. She gave Sano a glance that said she disapproved of his manipulating the shogun but knew she was in no position to object. She knelt, bowed, and said humbly, "You're too kind, Your Excellency."

Sano pressed his advantage. "Will you pardon my mother?"

"Yes, of course." The shogun declared, "I pronounce her innocent of all evildoing and set her free."

The turn of events left Sano breathless. Just like that, his fortunes had changed. What part did it owe to the divine power of the truth, and what to the force of human selfishness?

But the shogun's mood turned peevish. "Don't be too relieved, Chamberlain Sano. Your mother is out of trouble, but *you* are still under suspicion in the, ahh, killing of the witness in my cousin's murder case. Or had you forgotten?"

Sano hadn't, although he'd hoped the shogun had. "I have news about that. The man who was murdered wasn't Egen the tutor. He was an impostor."

As Sano explained how the discovery had been made, his mother's features went slack with astonishment. This was the first she'd heard of it; Sano hadn't had a chance to tell her sooner. "He wasn't Egen," she whispered. "I should have known."

"An actor, fancy that," the shogun said. "But you still could have killed him." He rose and pointed his finger at Sano. "And don't try to wiggle out of trouble! I'm tired of people playing me for a fool!"

Sano eased out of the room, drawing the shogun with him. He saw that his mother was offended by the shogun's treatment of him, and he didn't want her to say something that would change the shogun's mind about pardoning her. He ushered the shogun to the reception room.

"I beg you to let me prove my innocence," Sano said. "With your permission, I'll go and work on that now."

"Permission denied!" The shogun clutched Sano's sleeve. "I came to talk to you because I am, ahh, faced with a terrible crisis. You're not going anywhere until you help me!"

"I'll be glad to help," Sano said. "What is this crisis?"

The shogun paced the room, frantic with worry. "Ever since I found out that Lord Matsudaira wants to take my place, people have been urging me to declare war on his whole branch of our clan. They think I should lead a battle not only to crush him for good, but to subjugate his sons, his other kin, and his thousands of retainers. They talk and argue and pressure me." He clasped his hands over his ears. "They won't stop!"

Sano wasn't surprised. The samurai class had grown restless since the war between Lord Matsudaira and the former chamberlain Yanagisawa, a minor skirmish during a peace that had lasted almost a century. Civil war was the logical outcome of escalating political strife, and a ruler under threat must launch a defense. Although Sano dreaded what a war would do to Japan, battle-lust enflamed his samurai blood. He welcomed the chance for a showdown with his enemy. And he knew his duty.

"If you want to go to war with Lord Matsudaira's people, you can count on my support," Sano said.

"But I don't want to! I don't like fighting. All I want is to live in peace!" The shogun faced Sano with shoulders hunched and clasped hands extended. "What shall I do?"

"You could put Lord Matsudaira to death," Sano said. "He's a traitor; he's already under arrest. Executing him is a logical next step. It would spare you the trouble of a war." And spare Sano and his family more attacks from Lord Matsudaira.

"I can't do that!" The shogun was horrified at the idea of taking responsibility for such drastic action.

"Then tell everyone that you forbid a war," Sano said, honor-bound to serve his lord's wishes and put aside his own agenda. "You're their master. They have to obey."

Although the shogun looked tempted, he said, "But if I do that, they'll know what a coward I am. They'll think I don't deserve to be shogun."

They would, and they would be right, but Sano said, "It doesn't matter what they think. The emperor grants the title of shogun. By divine law, nobody else can take it away from you."

"The emperor is in his palace in Miyako. He doesn't care who is shogun. Nor does he want to, ahh, get involved in any trouble. Rather than stand up for me, he would just as soon grant the title to an ox!"

Having met the emperor nine years ago, Sano had to admit that this assessment of him was correct. Japan's emperors hadn't had any political or military power in centuries, and this one wouldn't likely change the status quo.

"If I refuse to fight Lord Matsudaira, everyone will switch their allegiance to him," the shogun wailed. "They'll band together and destroy *me*!"

They must have used that threat to coerce the shogun. Sano said reluctantly, "Then your only alternative is to make peace with Lord Matsudaira. Invite him to talk. Negotiate a truce."

"I can't." The shogun wrung his hands. "It's too late. Lord Matsudaira has already made the first strike."

"What?" Surprised and alarmed, Sano said, "When?"

"Not two hours ago. His troops ambushed and killed ten of mine on the Ryōgoku Bridge."

Sano supposed that Lord Matsudaira might have ordered the ambush . . . but he saw a familiar pattern, smelled a familiar scent. He was sure about who had attacked the shogun and implicated Lord Matsudaira in order to force the shogun's hand.

"If I don't retaliate, I'm not just a coward, I'm a fool." The shogun moaned. "Chamberlain Sano, I can't bear all this trouble. Make it go away!"

Sano had a sudden memory of the last time he'd heard those words, three or four years ago. Masahiro had had a nightmare and awakened screaming. When Sano and Reiko had hurried to his bedside, he'd told them there was a ghost in the house. *Make it go away!* he'd begged.

The shogun was looking at Sano with the same fright Sano had seen in Masahiro's eyes.

That night Sano had roved the house, slashing his sword at the ghost while Masahiro had trailed him anxiously. When Sano had exorcised every room, he'd said, *It's gone.*

But he couldn't banish the shogun's troubles by playing games . . . Or could he?

Sano experienced one of those rare moments of clarity, when he saw his path charted like torches lighting his way through a dark labyrinth. The clarity sprang from all his experience, wisdom, cunning, and more. The steps he must take came to him as fully realized as in a divine vision.

"All right," Sano said, "I'll fix everything."

"How?" The shogun regarded Sano with eagerness to believe and fear of disappointment.

Sano couldn't yet articulate his plans in words; they were akin to a message communicated to him by a mute stone Buddha. "For your sake it's best that you don't know in advance."

"Very well," the shogun said uncertainly. "What happens first?"

"You'll see soon enough." Sano knew in his deepest spirit that at the end of his path was the solution not only to the shogun's problems but to his own.

"What should I do?"

"One simple thing," Sano said. "Whatever I do, just play along and trust me."

30

Sano and Hirata strode into the wing of the palace where the shogun's male concubines lived. They found the youths rehearsing a play. A dais in a reception room served as a stage. Sano and Hirata stood behind the audience of boys. These ranged from children to adolescents, who lounged on the floor, joking and making so much noise that they didn't notice Sano's and Hirata's presence. Two actors occupied the stage.

One was costumed in a long black wig, a white silk kimono, and a mask with the face of a beautiful girl. The other wore a mask of a handsome young man and a priest's saffron robe. The girl pursued the priest back and forth across the stage in slow, ritual motion. They circled a wooden model of a temple bell while a chorus of eight boys sang and chanted their lines, and musicians at the rear of the stage played a flute and drums. Sano recognized the drama as *Dojoji,* a play about a demon woman who falls in love with a priest. He has taken a vow of celibacy and tries to escape her seduction.

As her pursuit grew more desperate, the priest pantomimed fright. The chorus sang louder and faster; the drums' rhythm accelerated. Sano spotted Yoritomo among the musicians, playing the flute. The priest hid under the temple bell. The woman flung off her robe, revealing another patterned with green, reptilian scales. Her mask, which had moving parts, changed into the snarling face of a serpent. She hissed and coiled around the bell. Sano was wondering how she would manage the part where flames came out of her fangs and killed her and the priest, when the stage exploded with a loud bang.

Red light flared behind the bell. The music stopped. Pungent smoke engulfed the bell, the serpent, chorus, and musicians. The audience cheered.

"Gunpowder," Sano said to Hirata.

They clapped. The audience turned, saw them, and quieted. As the smoke cleared, the priest crawled out from under the bell. Everyone regarded Sano and Hirata with surprise.

"Chamberlain Sano," Yoritomo said. His smile faded as he noticed Sano's somber expression. "What is it?"

"Come with us," Sano said.

Yoritomo rose uncertainly and stepped off the stage. "May I ask why?"

Sano hated what he had to do to Yoritomo. He was truly fond of the youth, but this was the necessary first step in his plan. "You're under arrest."

"Arrest?" Shock froze Yoritomo's face. He looked at the troops who entered the room. "For what?"

"For treason," Sano said.

Excited whispers swept through the assembly. Yoritomo beheld Sano with disbelief, fear, and guilt. As Sano, Hirata, and the troops advanced up the room toward him, he stammered, "But I haven't— You can't—"

The troops escorted him out the door. The other young men watched, some with pity, others with glee, all with astonishment. Yoritomo called frantically to Sano, "Where are you taking me?"

"To your trial," Sano said.

During the next few hours, Sano's troops distributed announcements of Yoritomo's trial. By nightfall, the notices had circulated throughout Edo Castle, the *daimyo* estates, the districts where the Tokugawa vassals lived, and all around town. They covered every public information board and passed from hand to hand among the townspeople. News sellers wandering the streets took up the cry: "The shogun's boy lover will be tried for treason in the palace at the hour of the dog!"

Inside her chamber, Reiko knelt on the futon. "Come sleep with Mama tonight," she called to Akiko. She patted the quilt and smiled.

Akiko stood at the threshold with Midori. "No," she said obstinately, clutching Midori's skirts.

Reiko felt her smile strain the muscles of her face. "Why not? Masahiro is going to sleep here, too." He sat in the bed, the quilt drawn over his knees. "It will be fun."

"Don't want to," Akiko said.

All day Reiko had watched over her children, never letting them out of her sight. All day she'd waited for Lord Matsudaira's assassins to attack. Nothing had happened yet; perhaps her vigilance had thwarted them. Reiko was exhausted from following the children around, her nerves on edge. And she was hurt because all day her daughter had made it clear that her presence was unwelcome.

"Well, I don't care what you want," Reiko snapped. "You're sleeping here, and I'm not going to argue."

She had to protect her daughter, no matter how her daughter felt about her. Reiko rose, marched up to Akiko, and grabbed her hand. "Midori-*san,* you'd better go," Reiko said as she pulled the little girl toward the bed. "She has to get used to me sooner or later. It might as well be now."

Akiko screamed and dragged her feet. Midori pressed her hands together below her lips, her eyes filled with concern. She knew about the assassins; Reiko had told her. "Maybe Akiko would be just as safe in the next room. If anybody comes near her, you'll hear, and I can stay with her if you want."

"So can I," Masahiro said. He removed his sword from under the bed. Reiko had also told him about the assassination plot. "I'll protect her."

"No! You stay where you are!" Reiko ordered.

"I can guard her just as well if she's in the next room," Lieutenant Asukai said from the corridor.

"You stay out of this!" Reiko hardly knew which made her angrier—that Lord Matsudaira meant to kill her children, or that nobody would do what she said. She wrestled Akiko into the bed. Akiko flailed, shrieked, and kicked Reiko.

"Ouch!" Reiko shouted. "Hold still and be quiet, or I'm going to spank you!"

Akiko obeyed, but Reiko saw in Akiko's eyes a fury that matched her own. That her child could feel such enmity toward her took her breath away. Then Akiko began to cry.

Reiko was so ashamed of threatening her child that tears filled her own eyes. But now that she had Akiko where she wanted, she wouldn't give in. She lay down on the side of the bed and pulled the quilt over Akiko and herself. She set her jaw and endured Akiko's sobs.

"The bed is big enough for one more. Can I stay?" Midori asked. "Maybe that will help her settle down."

"All right." Reiko didn't know when Sano would be back, she could use help guarding the children, and Midori was the only person besides Lieutenant Asukai that Reiko could trust.

Midori blew out the flame in the lantern, then got in bed between Reiko and Akiko, a buffer separating them. They and Masahiro lay awake in the darkness.

Yoritomo's trial took place in a makeshift courtroom in the palace. The doors between several chambers had been opened to create a space large enough for the horde of spectators. Men knelt on the floor, smoking pipes, facing the dais. There Sano sat, dressed in black ceremonial robes stamped with his flying-crane crest in gold. Surveying the crowd, he spotted prominent officials and *daimyo*. The announcements had done their work. Nobody who mattered was absent.

Below him, white sand had been spread on the floor to form a *shirasu,* symbol of truth. On a straw mat on the sand knelt Yoritomo, his wrists and ankles bound, his face dripping sweat. His head turned from side to side; his eyes pleaded for help.

None came from Sano's troops stationed along the walls. None came from the audience, which included Yoritomo's father's enemies; they were eager to see the youth they considered an unhealthy influence on the shogun take a fall. If any man had objections to the trial, he didn't voice them, for none came from the shogun. He knelt beside Hirata, on the far right side of the dais, lending his tacit approval to the proceedings. He looked frightened and bewildered yet resigned, like a child who'd been forced to swallow bad-tasting medicine.

"The first witness will come forward," Sano said.

A man entered the room through a door near the dais. He knelt and bowed to Sano and the shogun. The audience leaned forward to see; men in the back craned their necks. He was a strapping young man in worn, faded clothes, a kerchief tied around his shaved head.

"State your name and position," Sano ordered.

"Itami Senjuro," the man said. "I'm a *rōnin.*"

He wasn't a *rōnin,* and that wasn't his real name. He was a gardener at Sano's estate.

"Do you know the defendant?" Sano asked.

"Yes, Honorable Chamberlain," Itami said.

Yoritomo regarded Itami, and Sano, with incredulous dismay.

"How do you know him?" Sano asked.

"He hired me and some other *rōnin* to attack your soldiers."

The audience stirred, excited by the news. Yoritomo cried, "I didn't! That's a lie!"

"Be quiet," Sano ordered sternly. "You'll have your turn to talk later." He said to Itami, "When was this attack?"

"Last autumn."

"Tell me what happened."

Itami repeated the story Sano had instructed him to tell: "Yoritomo gave us guns. We hid in the woods along the highway. When your soldiers rode by, we shot them."

Yoritomo was shaking his head, horrified because he realized the trial was rigged. Sano asked, "What else did Yoritomo give you besides guns?"

"He gave us clothes decorated with Lord Matsudaira's crest," Itami replied. "We wore them to the ambush."

Whispers broke out among the audience. Sano saw heads leaning together, speculative glances exchanged. The atmosphere was thick with tobacco smoke, warm from body heat. "Why did he want you to wear Lord Matsudaira's crest?" Sano asked.

"So that people who saw us would think Lord Matsudaira sent us," Itami said.

"That will be all," Sano said. "You're dismissed."

Itami bowed and left the room. Sano said, "I call the next witness."

Through the door came another, older man, his nose misshapen and cheeks scarred from many fights. The tattoos on his thick, muscular arms provoked rumbling and hostile stares from the audience.

After the witness knelt and bowed, Sano said, "State your name and occupation."

"Uhei," the witness said in a coarse, sullen voice. "I'm a gangster."

That actually was his name, and he actually was a gangster, whom Hirata had met and often arrested during his career as a police officer. Hirata had thought Uhei would add authenticity to the trial and threatened him with jail if he didn't cooperate. Questioning by Sano revealed that Uhei, like the *rōnin,* had been hired last autumn by Yoritomo.

"To do what?" Sano asked.

"To bomb Lord Matsudaira's villa by the river," Uhei replied.

His words set off low exclamations among the assembly. The shogun was as stiff and mute as a wooden puppet. Yoritomo gazed at Sano with eyes full of pain, devastated by Sano's betrayal.

"What happened?" Sano steeled his heart against his onetime friend. Yoritomo was guilty by association if not deed. He knew it as well as Sano did. And the attacks on Sano and Lord Matsudaira weren't his only crimes.

"I went to the villa with another man Yoritomo hired," the gangster said. "He lit the bomb and threw it. I was the lookout. He was caught by Lord Matsudaira's guards. I got away." He sounded pleased by his fictional exploit.

"Whose crest did you wear on your clothes?" Sano asked.

"Yours."

Confusion rippled through the audience. That Yoritomo, the shogun's plaything, had apparently mounted attacks on two such powerful men was a shock to everyone. Sano was certain they would be more shocked if they knew what Yoritomo was really up to. Yanagisawa was undoubtedly calling the shots from behind the scenes, but he needed help from someone who could come and go freely, who had access to information. Yoritomo was his henchman and spy at court.

"Yoritomo wanted Lord Matsudaira to think I ordered the bombing?" Sano said.

"Yes."

"Why?"

"I don't know," the gangster said. "He didn't tell me."

"Perhaps the next witness can shed some light on the matter," Sano said.

The next witness was a young woman who minced into the courtroom on high-soled sandals. She caused exclamations and mutters from the audience. Her long hair draped her pink and orange floral kimono. Her pretty face was plastered with thick white rice powder and bright red rouge. She dimpled at the men, and Sano felt the heat in the room rise.

When he asked her to identify herself, she said, "My name is Kiku. I'm a maid at the Plum Blossom Teahouse."

She was really a maid at Sano's estate. His large household could supply actors to fill any sort of roles. Sano asked, "What is your relationship with Yoritomo?"

Kiku preened and giggled. "We're lovers."

The shogun gasped, hurt because his favorite had apparently cheated on him with this female. Every gaze in the room flew to him as he leaned forward to protest. Hirata whispered in his ear. He settled back on his heels, miserable and docile as a whipped dog.

"No!" Aghast, Yoritomo said, "I've never even met her! She's lying!"

"One more outburst from you, and you'll be beaten," Sano said, then asked the girl, "How long have you and the defendant been lovers?"

"Oh, three years now," Kiku said, giggling. "He came into the teahouse, and when we saw each other, it was love at first sight—"

"Did Yoritomo tell you why he staged the attacks on Lord Matsudaira and myself?" Sano cut her off because she was embellishing the story he'd ordered her to tell.

"Oh, yes." Kiku clearly enjoyed the audience's attention; she smoothed her kimono that Sano had borrowed from Reiko's chest of old clothes. "We told each other everything that was on our minds. We had no secrets—"

"Why did he do it?"

Kiku sighed, reluctant to deliver her last lines and end her performance. "He wanted you and Lord Matsudaira to blame the attacks on each other," she recited. "He wanted to start a war between you. After you destroyed each other, he could step in and take power over the regime."

The murmuring in the audience rose to a roar. Sano could tell from its tone that many of the *daimyo* and officials had believed Yoritomo wanted the power his father had craved, and now they thought their suspicions were confirmed. The shogun dropped his head into his hands, rocking back and forth. Yoritomo sat motionless and stunned. To Sano he resembled a stone statue that had been struck a mortal blow, cracks spreading through it, ready to crumble.

"That's enough," Sano said to the girl.

She bowed, rose, and flounced out of the room, all smiles. Sano said, "The evidence proves that Yoritomo is guilty of subversive actions that amount to treason. But the law gives him the opportunity to speak in his own defense." He turned to Yoritomo. "Speak now if you will."

Yoritomo addressed the man whose opinion was the one that really mattered. "Your Excellency, I've never seen any of those people before in my life. I didn't do what they said I did. They're all liars. I'm being framed. I swear I'm innocent!"

His voice rose on a high, unnatural note and broke. He was a terrible liar. Sano felt the sentiment in the audience weighing further against Yoritomo. But the shogun leaned toward his lover, his eyes filled with pain, pity, and yearning.

Hirata slipped his hand under the shogun's sleeve and closed his fingers around the shogun's wrist. No one noticed except Sano. The shogun stiffened, coerced into playing along with this game Sano had staged.

"I swear that girl isn't my lover," Yoritomo declared. "I've never spoken to her, never touched her. I've never looked at anyone else since I met you, Your Excellency. I've never been unfaithful or disloyal. After everything you've given me, I would never plot behind your back to seize power from you!" His voice wavered with a blend of truth and falsehood. "Please have mercy!"

As the assembly watched in suspense, the shogun looked miserable. He chewed his lip, then said, "Chamberlain Sano——"

Hirata squeezed the shogun's wrist. The shogun jerked and grimaced. The resistance leaked out of him, drained by the pressure Hirata had applied to a nerve junction. "Proceed," he said dully.

"Your word isn't enough to prove your innocence," Sano told Yoritomo. "Can you offer any evidence or witnesses?"

"How could I?" Yoritomo demanded, angry as well as terrified. "You've given me no time to gather any!"

That had been one point of rushing him to trial: Sano wanted no challenge to the verdict. The other point was that Sano wanted to set events in motion as quickly as possible.

"Then I must pronounce you guilty of treason," Sano said.

Yoritomo lifted his face skyward, his eyes and mouth wide open, as if asking the gods to explain how this fate could befall him and praying for rescue. The audience's faces and murmurs expressed satisfaction. The shogun buried his face in his hands and wept.

"I sentence you to death by decapitation," Sano said.

The audience buzzed with surprise. Samurai weren't usually executed for crimes, not even for treason, the worst. They had the right to commit ritual suicide and redeem their honor. But that wouldn't serve Sano's purposes.

Yoritomo didn't object or weep. His eyes flashed Sano one last hurt look, then went opaque as he withdrew into himself. He sat upright, head high, shoulders squared, courageously accepting his fate. Sano had to admire him. The young man had dignity despite his life as a political pawn. Sano tasted guilt, sour as bile, for tormenting this young man who was as much a victim as a genuine traitor.

"You shall be executed at Kotsukappara tomorrow at noon," Sano announced.

That should give his publicity campaign enough time to work.

31

Reiko lay on her back, eyes half open, floating on the surface of sleep. Her body relaxed, but her mind was alert to the world around her. As a mother she excelled at napping while awake. When Masahiro had been a baby and gotten sick, she'd rested beside him at night, ready to spring to action at his faintest cry. Now she applied her talent to the purpose of guarding her children's lives.

She could hear their breathing as they slept in the bed with her. She heard the wind rustling the trees outside, the voices and footsteps of the patrol guards, and a dog howling in the distance. The house was quiet. All was well . . . for now.

In the distance, beyond the range of Reiko's hearing, the floor in the passage creaked softly under stealthy footsteps.

Night thinned the crowds in the Ginza district. The theaters closed their doors; the actors, musicians, and patrons headed home. The wind swept paper flowers from costumes, crumpled handbills, and sunflower-seed shells along the streets. People in search of more entertainment repaired to the teahouses.

In the room behind the teahouse with the red lanterns hanging from its eaves, Yanagisawa hunched over the charcoal brazier. The wind whistled through cracks in the walls, and the room was freezing. He listened to the customers making bets, arguing, cursing, and slapping down cards, the rattle of dice, the wine splashing into cups, the discordant samisen music. He fretted with impatience.

Yesterday Lord Arima had followed his orders and told the shogun that Lord Matsudaira was trying to seize power. The results had delighted Yanagisawa. He'd gloated over Yoritomo's descriptions of Lord Matsudaira stunned, frantic, and put under house arrest. He'd savored his own cleverness.

But that was the last news he'd heard. Today his troops should have attacked the shogun's army while wearing the Matsudaira crest. The shogun's allies should have interpreted the attack as a strike by Lord Matsudaira and pressured the shogun to declare war. Had it happened yet? Yanagisawa fumed. Why hadn't Yoritomo come with good tidings?

The maid sauntered into the room. She carried a tray, which she plunked down beside Yanagisawa. The tray held his dinner of soup, rice balls, pickles, and grilled fish. By the food lay a folded paper.

"The boss thought you should see this." The maid pointed at the paper, then left.

Yanagisawa read the paper, an announcement torn off a public notice board. *The shogun's companion, Yanagisawa Yoritomo, has been arrested for treason. His trial will take place tonight at the hour of the dog. If he is pronounced guilty, he will be put to death at the Kotsukappara execution ground at noon tomorrow.*

"No!" Disbelief and shock punched the breath out of Yanagisawa. Here was the reason Yoritomo hadn't come. Yanagisawa reread the notice, seeking an explanation of why his son was suspected of treason and who had arrested Yoritomo. But the space between the lines remained maddeningly blank.

Yanagisawa's heart drummed in his ears, pumping currents of panic through his body. Had someone found out that he'd returned from exile? If so, who? Had whoever it was also discovered that Yoritomo was conspiring to put his father back in power?

Whatever the answers the trial would have been finished hours ago.

It would surely have ended in a guilty verdict, as most trials did. The thought of his son imprisoned, alone, and terrified, helplessly awaiting death, made Yanagisawa shout in rage. He crumpled the notice, flung it across the room, and jumped to his feet. He must take action.

A premonition of danger startled Reiko. She bolted upright, fully awake, her heart racing. A strangled cry sounded in the darkness. The door slid open, and she saw the figure of a man enter the room. The faint light that shone through the paper-paned lattice wall glittered on the blade in his hand. Reiko instinctively snatched up her own sword. As the man loomed over her, she thrust the weapon at him with all her might.

A grunt like that of a wounded animal erupted from him. He thudded across her legs. Masahiro woke up and cried, "Mama!"

The man writhed on the bed, atop Reiko and Midori and Akiko. She smelled his leather armor, sour breath, and sweat. Midori said, "What?" in a sleepy voice. Akiko began to keen. Reiko saw the man thrashing. Her sword protruded from his belly.

"Mama, you got him!" Masahiro shouted.

But the man raised himself. His hand still held his dagger. He lunged at Masahiro, weapon raised. Masahiro yelled. Reiko sprang up and grabbed the assassin's wrist. They fell onto Akiko and Midori.

"What's going on?" Midori said as Reiko fought with the assassin. Akiko began to cry. "Who is that?"

The man was too big and muscular for Reiko to overcome. He threw her off him as if she weighed nothing. When she leaped at him again, he backhanded her jaw.

Reiko's head rang. As she fell backward, she heard Akiko crying and Midori calling, "Help! Help!" The floor shook. Reiko pushed herself up on her elbows. Human shapes moved across her blurred vision. She blinked and saw the assassin chasing Masahiro. The boy sped past Reiko. The assassin followed, staggering. Reiko focused on her sword that still stuck out of the assassin's belly. She grabbed its hilt with both hands and pulled.

The man roared in agony as the blade ripped free of his flesh. He dropped to his knees. Reiko lashed the sword at him. The blade cut into his throat. He made an awful, gurgling noise. A hot, wet spew of blood drenched Reiko. The assassin collapsed with a crash.

"Mama! Good work!" Masahiro exclaimed.

He was unhurt, jumping up and down in triumph. Reiko tasted the blood that ran down her face. She gagged and retched. Midori lit a lantern. The whole, horrific tableau sprang into bright view.

The assassin lay dead on the floor, Reiko's sword cleaved halfway through his neck, in a spreading puddle of blood. He wore the plain kimono, trousers, and armor tunic of Sano's foot soldiers. His dagger had fallen beside his hand. His eyes were open and his mouth flaccid. Midori and Akiko huddled together in bed, staring at him in shock. They turned to Reiko, their eyes filled with horror.

"Put out the light!" Reiko cried.

It was too late. Her daughter had already seen her covered with blood, a monster from a child's worst nightmare. Akiko screamed and screamed and screamed.

Her screams brought troops rushing into the bedchamber. Sano followed on his men's heels. Dressed in formal clothes, he'd apparently just arrived home. Reiko saw him take one look at her and the corpse and realize what had happened.

"Take the children away," he ordered Midori.

Midori's complexion was white, and she appeared ready to be sick, but she scooped the hysterical Akiko into her arms and hustled Masahiro out the door. As Sano studied the corpse, anger and hurt suffused his features. "That's Nabeshima. He's served me for ten years." He told his troops, "Get him out of here."

The men wrapped the corpse in the bloodstained quilt from the bed and carried it off. Sano said to Reiko, "Are you all right?"

Reiko gulped and nodded even though her jaw was swelling painfully, her stomach nauseated. The children were safe; nothing else mattered. She wiped her face on her sleeve and ran her hands through her hair, which was wet and clotted with blood. She reeked of its salty, metallic stench.

"Thank the gods," Sano said in relief. "Let's go to the bathchamber so you can wash."

A frightening thought occurred to Reiko. She remembered the cry she'd heard right before the attack. "How did that man get into the room? Where's Lieutenant Asukai?"

Sano's somber expression was reply enough.

A cry burst from Reiko. "No!"

Sano nodded unhappily. "We found him in the corridor. He'd been stabbed. Either he didn't hear Nabeshima coming or didn't realize Nabeshima meant any harm until it was too late."

As sobs shuddered through her, Reiko said, "I want to see him. I want to say good-bye."

She rose and would have hurried from the room, but Sano gently held her back. "Later. He's already been taken away."

"How could it happen?" Reiko wept in Sano's embrace.

Sano told her that he'd also found two patrol guards dead outside the private quarters. "The other assassins must have done it. They and Nabeshima worked as a team. They cleared his way to you and the children."

Reiko couldn't spare any grief for the other casualties. Her loyal bodyguard had died in her service, and she couldn't even thank him. Now her knees buckled under the heavy, terrible weight of grief and gratitude.

"He put himself between me and danger. His presence delayed the assassin long enough for me to realize we were under attack. If not for him, we would be dead now." Asukai had kept his promise. "He protected us, at the cost of his own life!"

"It's over," Sano said, trying to comfort her. "You killed Nabeshima. He can't hurt anybody now."

"Yes," Reiko said, "but it was too close a call. And I only killed one assassin. There are eight more inside the house and who knows how many outside! What's going to happen when the next one strikes? How will we protect the children?"

* * *

In the morning, a large procession left Sano's estate. Troops bristling with spears surrounded Sano, Hirata, Reiko, and the children. Akiko and Masahiro walked between Sano and Hirata. Sano and Masahiro held Akiko's hands. Midori and Reiko followed. Detective Marume led and Detective Fukida brought up the rear of their little band. Reiko couldn't see a thing ahead of or above her because the troops raised their shields to protect her family from arrows and gunshots. But she was more afraid of treachery from within the escort that Sano had organized than from dangers outside. Among his troops might be the eight assassins.

She and Sano had decided that the children would be safer away from home. They'd agreed to place the children in Hirata's house, under Hirata's guard. "The children will be fine along the way if they're protected by so many troops that any assassins within the ranks are outnumbered by men loyal to me," Sano had said.

His mother hadn't wanted to go. She'd insisted that she would be safe enough at his house and his family would be safer away from her. Sano hadn't argued.

As the procession wound slowly through the passages, like a caterpillar with a thousand legs, Reiko had second thoughts. The press and movement of the soldiers' bodies too near her generated heat. Their breath soured and moistened the air. Her skin prickled. One or more of those men could attack before the others could stop them. Reiko felt as if she and her children were in the belly of a monster.

She wished she could walk between Masahiro and Akiko, hold them close, shield them with her own body. But Masahiro didn't want her fussing over him, and Akiko screamed every time she looked at Reiko. Even though Reiko had bathed and put on clean clothes, her daughter wouldn't forget the sight of her drenched in the blood of the man she'd killed.

At last they reached Hirata's mansion. The troops arranged themselves in a blockade that extended far down the passage on either side of the portals. Hirata and Sano hurried Reiko, the children, and

Midori inside. When the gate closed behind them, Reiko sighed with fleeting relief. They were surrounded by Hirata's troops; Hirata had vouched for them, and he claimed that if any harbored evil designs, he would sense it. Reiko only hoped his instincts were right.

Sano hesitated before leaving his family. "You should be safer here than anywhere else," he told Reiko.

"I'll protect Mama and Akiko," Masahiro declared.

He was child enough to view this as a game, Reiko observed. He thought that when she'd killed the assassin she had won the first round. Akiko hid her face in Midori's skirts. Reiko wished Sano could stay with them, but she knew he must go.

"Will you let me know what happens?" Reiko asked.

"As soon as I can," Sano promised.

Earlier, he'd told her his plan and what had led up to it. Reiko thought it very clever, but she had doubts about whether it would solve all their problems. "May you have good luck," she said.

Sano smiled. "May I not need to depend too much on luck."

Then he was gone.

Hirata and Midori ushered Reiko and the children into the house. Hirata's children happily greeted their playmates. They towed Masahiro and Akiko by the hands into a warm, bright room filled with toys. The adults followed.

"We'll stay together in here," Hirata said. "My guards will be outside."

Reiko felt trapped rather than protected. She knelt in a corner while the children played, while she dwelled on last night's attack. Her mind picked out instants where things could have turned out differently, for the worse.

What if she hadn't managed to stab the assassin? What if she'd been unable to pull her sword out of him and cut his throat? All Reiko's alternative, imagined scenarios ended with her children murdered.

Servants brought food for the hosts and guests. When Reiko joined the others to eat, Akiko screamed. She wouldn't stop no matter how hard Midori and Masahiro tried to soothe her. Blinking, Reiko said, "I'd better leave."

"No, don't," Hirata said, and Reiko saw pity in his eyes. "I have an idea." He positioned a lattice screen. "Maybe if you sit behind this— just for a while, until she gets over what happened . . . ?"

Reiko took her place behind the screen and ate her meal. The screen hid her from Akiko, who quieted at once, but Reiko could see and hear everyone through the lattice. She watched Akiko eat and Midori wipe her face; she listened to Masahiro and Hirata talk about archery. She noticed the tension between Hirata and Midori. Her children and friends seemed so far away. She felt like a lonely wild beast in a cage.

And all she could do was wait for the news that Sano's plan had succeeded—or failed.

32

A long procession straggled up the Ōshū Kaidō, the highway that led north out of Edo. At its front Sano rode with Detectives Marume and Fukida, leading the shogun in a palanquin and his personal bodyguards on horseback. Behind them, a cart drawn by an ox and driven by a peasant man carried Yoritomo. The movement jolted his kneeling figure, which was tied to a post mounted on the cart. His wrists and ankles were bound, his face covered by a black hood with a breathing hole cut over his nostrils. Next followed a horde of Sano's foot soldiers and mounted troops. At the rear, *daimyo* and Tokugawa officials in palanquins and on horseback, accompanied by attendants, formed a tail that snaked back to town.

As noon approached, the sun ascended above the cedar trees that lined the road. Its rays glinted through drifting clouds, through the funereal leaf canopy, off metal helmets. No one spoke. The only sounds were the wind, the horses' hoofbeats, the marchers' footfalls, the cart's wheels rattling.

The head of the procession reached Kotsukappara Keijo, one of Edo's two execution grounds. It was a huge open field, the ground trampled flat, bordered by tangled shrubbery and skeletal pine trees. Hundreds of townsfolk were gathered around the perimeter.

"Your notices have brought out a crowd," Fukida remarked.

Riding across the field, Sano scanned the spectators. Men, women, and children sat on mats, eating and drinking refreshments they'd brought in baskets. They reminded Sano of the audiences in theaters. They had the same cheerful, anticipatory air as people waiting for a play to begin. When they saw the procession, they buzzed with the same excitement as when actors take the stage. Around the field stood advertisements for what they'd come to see today.

Four gibbets held the heads of recently executed criminals, impaled on nails and propped up with clay so they wouldn't fall off. Flies swarmed on the heads and in the drippings under them. Ravens pecked at their eyes. On a cross built of rough boards hung a man's naked corpse. Red gashes on his torso had spilled blood down his legs; he'd been stabbed to death while crucified. The crowd didn't seem to mind the grisly relics, or the stench of dead, decaying flesh.

"I don't see the guest of honor," Sano said.

"There's still time," Marume said.

Sano directed the oxcart driver to the center of the field. Troops untied Yoritomo and dumped him on the ground; he lay inert. The oxcart rolled off to the sidelines. The procession gathered in a wide circle around Yoritomo. Mounted samurai remained on their horses. Sano and the detectives grouped by the shogun's palanquin. The shogun climbed out, and his bodyguards seated him on its roof, for a good view of his lover's execution. The audience stood; necks craned. The executioner and his assistants approached Yoritomo. Their clothes were stained with old blood. Fukida conferred with the executioner, who nodded, then led his assistants to a shed at the edge of the field. They returned carrying shovels and saws.

Exclamations burst from the townsfolk. *Daimyo,* officials, and soldiers muttered among themselves as the assistants began digging a hole. No one had expected to witness the most extreme form of capital punishment—*nokogiri-biki,* in which the criminal is immobilized in a pit and his head sawn off while he is alive.

"This is a good touch," Marume complimented Sano.

"I wanted the maximum drama," Sano said.

The assistants finished digging the pit and lowered Yoritomo into it. He neither resisted nor cooperated. He was limp, a dead weight. The assembly watched in silence. Yoritomo knelt at the pit's bottom, supported by its sides, his head protruding above the surface. The assistants shoveled dirt into the pit until he was buried up to his neck. The executioner hefted his saw.

Sano looked at the sky. The sun was poised at the top of its trajectory. Bells from distant temples tolled the noon hour. Sano raised his hand, signaling the executioner to wait, despite groans from the townsfolk and impatient glances from his fellow samurai. He looked past the trees, where vultures waited for a fresh kill. Straining his ears, he listened.

Imprisoned within his estate, Lord Matsudaira paced the floor of his chamber. He'd been drinking since the shogun had put him under house arrest, and the room was fumey with liquor and stale perspiration. The shutters were closed to protect his sore, bleary eyes from the daylight. Three bodyguards stood by the door. They watched him nervously, as if he were a bear who'd just awakened from hibernation, clumsy but ravenous.

He lifted a jar from a table. His hand shook as he poured sake, rattling the jar against the cup. He wore nothing but a dressing robe. His hair hung in shaggy locks around his shaved crown. His face was puffy, his speech slurred. "This can't be happening to me. What am I going to do?"

At first he'd raged against the injustice that had been done to him. He'd called the shogun a mean, stupid fool. He'd cursed Sano for landing him in this predicament and set assassins on Sano and his family. He'd vowed to triumph in the end. But as the hours had passed and ranting accomplished nothing, Lord Matsudaira's anger had given way to helplessness.

Lord Matsudaira gulped his sake and said, "That I could fall into such a wretched state, a prisoner in my own home, with the threat of death hanging over me!" His voice quavered and broke. "When all my life I believed I was destined for greatness!"

His men eyed him with awe and dismay: He wasn't the man they knew, but his shrunken, enfeebled shadow. They clearly hated to witness his deterioration.

"All my life I tried to live up to my destiny," Lord Matsudaira said. "I excelled at everything I did." A weak pride inflated his spirit. He heard in his own voice an echo of his despised cousin the shogun. "Even when I was young, other men lined up behind me and followed me wherever I led them. I ruled my province with wisdom and benevolence. Everyone admired me as well as obeyed me. I knew myself to be a good samurai, a decent man. But somewhere I went wrong.

"I began to think I should rule Japan. And why not? I had far more wits and courage than my cousin." He tasted his scorn, bitter and vile. "My cousin would wipe his rear end on Japan and throw it away! I only wanted to save it from his foolishness!"

He'd never confided these treasonous thoughts to anyone, but the drink and his need to justify himself had loosened his tongue. "But I was forced to bow down to my cousin while he rubbed my face in the fact that he was shogun and I could never be. The time came when I could no longer bear it. I recruited allies who were also eager to be out from under his weak thumb. I began my campaign to seize power."

Lord Matsudaira swelled with the memory of those glorious days. "I eliminated my first obstacle. I sent that scoundrel Yanagisawa into exile." Then his shoulders sagged. "How was I to know that his partisans would keep fighting me?" His voice rose in a whine. "How could I have known that Sano Ichirō would challenge me for control over Japan? Now everything I've worked so hard for has crumbled into dust. My allies have deserted me in favor of my cousin." He shook with impotent anger, swayed with drunkenness. "What will become of me?"

The bodyguards exchanged glances, each loath to answer. One said cautiously, "Bear up, master. The trouble will pass. Things will be all right."

"Yes, yes, of course." Even as a sob wracked Lord Matsudaira, he tried to recover his confidence. "I'll get through this, I swear."

He heard footsteps in the corridor and looked up as his chief retainer entered the room, looking dire.

"What is it?" Lord Matsudaira demanded.

"I'm sorry to say that your assassins attempted to kill Chamberlain Sano's wife and children last night and failed. One of the assassins is dead."

"Well, the others will just have to keep trying," Lord Matsudaira said impatiently.

"I'm afraid that's not all that's happened," the chief retainer said. "Chamberlain Sano has taken Yoritomo to the execution ground."

"Then he really intends to go through with his farce of putting the boy to death for treason. Good riddance. So what?" Lord Matsudaira retorted.

"Maybe he doesn't. Have you thought of what else Sano might be up to?"

Lord Matsudaira hadn't, but now he did. Suddenly, in one of those moments of pure, astounding clarity that sometimes strike drunken men, he understood what was going on, what Sano meant to accomplish. The breath gushed out of him as he also understood the ramifications for himself. The hardest blow had fallen at the wrong time. He sank to his knees and groaned.

"I could take down one or the other," he said, "but not both at once." His bodyguards stared; they didn't know that he'd just figured out who was really behind his troubles, that he'd made a critical error in concentrating his animosity on Sano. But he saw that they sensed the defeat that hissed under his skin.

"There'll be no coming back, it's over for me," he lamented. "All is truly lost."

The men regarded him with fear for their own fate as well as his. His chief retainer said, "What shall you do?"

Lord Matsudaira gazed inward at scenes of his life that flickered through his mind. He remembered its challenges and satisfactions and woes. The scenes halted at the black impasse that was now. He laughed, a bleak, mournful chuckle.

"There's only one thing I can do. If I'm going down, I'll go on my own terms."

Sano felt the fast rhythm of hooves before he heard the sound. It grew louder. The horsemen galloped onto the field, more than a hundred strong. Some wore armor, some tattered cotton clothes; some were armed with spears or with bows and arrows; all wore swords. The audience cheered the ragtag army's arrival. The lead rider shouted at Sano, "Free your prisoner!"

His tall figure was regal despite his mismatched armor. The visor of his battered metal helmet covered his face, but Sano recognized him instantly. He expelled his breath in satisfaction.

The newcomers ranged themselves against Sano and his troops, on the opposite side of Yoritomo. Sano said, "Greetings, Yanagisawa-*san*. We meet again."

Gasps rose from the *daimyo* and officials, none of whom had expected Yanagisawa to reappear now, or ever. The shogun squinted and said, "Yanagisawa-*san*? Is that really you?"

Yanagisawa removed his helmet. Everyone who knew him, including Sano, stared in astonishment: His head was shaved bald. But his face was as handsome as ever, his expression as malevolent and cunning.

"How did you get here?" the shogun cried, so excited that he jumped off the roof of his palanquin. Sano saw that he was overjoyed to see his old friend; he must have been hoping all along that Yanagisawa would come back to him someday.

"By ship, by foot, and by horseback," Yanagisawa answered the shogun, but watched Sano. "It's a long story. Perhaps we could discuss it later." He looked down at Yoritomo, and his expression turned anxious. "Son? Are you all right?"

Yoritomo didn't speak. Yanagisawa demanded, "What's wrong with him?"

"He's been drugged so he won't suffer any pain," Sano said. "You should thank me for my mercy."

Yanagisawa's glare said he would rather kill Sano.

"Why didn't you return to me earlier?" the shogun said plaintively. "Why come as such a, ahh, surprise now?"

"I've come to rescue my son."

"That's no surprise," Sano said, "but I was beginning to wonder if you would show up in time."

Disgust tinged Yanagisawa's smile. "So this is a trap. I suspected as much. Yoritomo's trial was a farce, and so is this execution. Don't think you tricked me."

Sano was glad that his measure of the bond between father and son had proved correct. Danger to Yoritomo was the only bait that could have lured Yanagisawa out of hiding. "Don't think I wouldn't have killed Yoritomo if you hadn't come. Don't think I still won't."

"Why should you?" Yanagisawa said. "It's me that you want. Leave my son alone."

"He's a traitor," Sano said, "and he deserves to die even though he's just your accomplice in your conspiracy to regain power."

Shock appeared on the faces of the men around Sano as they realized the true nature of Yoritomo's crimes and the fact that Yanagisawa had been busy mounting his comeback.

"You won't kill him." Yanagisawa's controlled manner didn't hide his anxiety. He said to the executioner's assistants, "Dig him up."

"Proceed with the *nokogiri-biki*," Sano countermanded.

The executioner stepped forward. While the assistants held Yoritomo's head and the executioner brandished the saw, the townspeople whispered excitedly. Sano saw spines stiffen and throat muscles clench among his samurai companions, and naked horror on Yanagisawa's face.

"Don't!"

Yanagisawa spurred his horse forward, between Yoritomo and the executioner. His men moved after him. Sano, Marume, and Fukida advanced with their troops. Sano said, "Back off. You're outnumbered. If you try to take Yoritomo, you'll both be killed in the battle."

Yanagisawa stared at Sano with fury and hatred. "You don't need my son. You've exposed me. Isn't that enough?"

"Not nearly," Sano said.

"Then what in hell do you want?"

"I want you to answer a few questions."

Suspicion narrowed Yanagisawa's eyes. "About what?"

"That's for me to decide," Sano said. "Agree now, or I proceed with the execution."

The Tokugawa officials and the *daimyo* whispered in speculation. The townsfolk moved closer to hear what was going on. Yanagisawa hesitated, sensing a trap within the trap.

"Dear me, Sano-*san,* you're not really going to kill him?" the shogun piped up fretfully. "When I agreed to go along with whatever you did, I didn't, ahh, realize you would go so far."

"All right," Yanagisawa said in a voice that promised Sano retribution. "What do you want to know?"

"Were you responsible for the bombing of Lord Matsudaira's estate?" Sano asked.

Yanagisawa gleamed with sardonic satisfaction. "Oh, you finally figured that out? Congratulations."

"So you have agents who followed your orders to throw the firebomb?" Sano said, hammering in the point in case anyone had missed it.

"Well, yes," Yanagisawa said. "I couldn't exactly stroll up to the castle gate, give my name, and say, 'I'm here to bomb Lord Matsudaira's estate. Let me in.'"

On the periphery of the execution ground, two mounted samurai edged toward the road. Sano called, "If you're planning to run to Lord Matsudaira and break the news, don't leave yet. He'll want to hear the rest."

The horsemen halted. Sano said to Yanagisawa, "Were you also responsible for ambushing my wife?"

"Guilty as charged." Yanagisawa glanced at Yoritomo. His flippant manner didn't hide his growing panic.

"What about the previous attacks, on Lord Matsudaira's troops and mine?" Sano asked. "Were they your doing, too?"

"You should thank me," Yanagisawa retorted. "I did for you and

Lord Matsudaira what you both wanted to do to each other but were too cowardly to risk."

"So you sent your underground rebels in disguise to attack us and goad us into a war. Neither of us is to blame."

"It's about time you gave credit where credit is due."

Sano addressed the two waiting horsemen: "You can go now." As they galloped away, Sano hoped they would reach Lord Matsudaira before his assassins struck again.

"Are we finished with these questions?" Yanagisawa said.

Whether Lord Matsudaira would believe Yanagisawa's confession, let go of his hostility toward Sano, and call off his dogs was beyond Sano's control. Sano concentrated on wringing the maximum value out of Yanagisawa. "Far from it. Let's talk about an actor by the name of Arashi Kodenji. Do you know him?"

Yanagisawa's expression turned wary: He knew the conversation was headed into dangerous territory. He looked at Yoritomo, buried up to the neck in the dirt, his head covered, as vulnerable as a swaddled baby. "Yes."

"For everyone's information, Arashi is the man we knew as Egen, tutor to the shogun's murdered cousin," Sano announced. "But he was only acting the role."

Confusion rumbled among both audiences. Sano's colleagues hadn't heard the news, and the townsfolk weren't familiar with the story behind this drama. Sano said, "Did you hire Arashi to impersonate the tutor and slander my mother?"

"Yes, and you fell for it." Yanagisawa couldn't resist enjoying his own cleverness and Sano's gullibility. "I'd have given a lot to be there."

"You didn't need to be there. You had eyes and ears inside the castle," Sano said, pointing at Yoritomo. "Did you kill Arashi after you paid him off?"

The audience stirred with consternation and excitement as Sano's colleagues realized that Yanagisawa had interfered with matters besides the conflict between Sano and Lord Matsudaira. Even the townsfolk realized that Sano was forcing Yanagisawa to put himself in jeopardy.

"Arashi was supposed to leave town as soon as he'd testified against your mother." A tremor in his voice betrayed how frantic Yanagisawa was to save Yoritomo. "Instead, he hung around, and he couldn't keep his big mouth shut. Sooner or later he'd have told someone I'd hired him. He'd have spread the word that I was back from exile. He had to go."

"I take it that means yes, you ordered his death," Sano said.

Yanagisawa hastily added, "He was a peasant, a nobody. What does it matter?"

A samurai had the legal right to kill a peasant. "It matters that you interfered with a murder investigation ordered by His Excellency, and this particular peasant was a key witness." Sano turned to the shogun. "Yanagisawa told Lord Arima to arrange the murder. Lord Arima recruited two of my soldiers and sent them to do Yanagisawa's dirty work. They killed Arashi, but on his orders, not mine. His confession is the proof of my innocence."

"Yes, I see," the shogun said, trying to sound as if he did. "Chamberlain Sano, excuse me for suspecting you. Consider the accusation against you, ahh, dropped."

"How nice for you," Yanagisawa said spitefully to Sano. "Enough already! Free my son!"

"One more question," Sano said. "Was it your troops, and not Lord Matsudaira's, who attacked His Excellency's yesterday?"

Yanagisawa's face went livid with anger and fright because Sano had named the final price for his son's freedom: He must admit to the attack, which constituted treason. He said, "I most certainly did not."

"Tell the truth, or your son dies," Sano said. "You ordered Lord Arima to tell His Excellency that his cousin wanted to overthrow him. You sent your troops after his, wearing Lord Matsudaira's crest. You wanted His Excellency to go to war with Lord Matsudaira and crush him. It was all part of your plan."

"You're dreaming," Yanagisawa said contemptuously.

Sano shrugged. "Suit yourself." He nodded to the executioner, who applied the saw to Yoritomo's neck. "Here we go."

33

"No!" squealed the shogun.

"Stop!" Yanagisawa charged at the executioner.

The executioner dodged. Yanagisawa's troops galloped around the pit, scattering the assistants. Sano, the detectives, and their troops rushed Yanagisawa, swords drawn. The fray swirled around Yoritomo's head like a storm circling its eye. Sano and his forces drove Yanagisawa away from Yoritomo. With an outraged cry, Yanagisawa rode at the townsfolk. He jumped off his horse and caught a little girl. He drew his sword, held it against her throat, and shouted, "Let Yoritomo go, or she's dead!"

Sano stared in horror. The girl was perhaps six years old, with round cheeks, hair tied in two ponytails, chubby in her padded blue kimono. Helpless in Yanagisawa's grasp, she cried, "Mama, Mama!"

Her parents begged Yanagisawa to let her go. The crowd around them agitated because the drama had suddenly turned too real. Sano couldn't sacrifice an innocent child, and Yanagisawa knew it, just as Sano had known Yanagisawa would come to rescue his son. They were aware of each other's weaknesses after their many years as sometimes rivals, sometimes comrades.

Yanagisawa bared his teeth in a fierce smile. "Her life in exchange for Yoritomo's."

"All right." Sano dismounted beside Yoritomo's head, beckoned to Yanagisawa, and said, "Put her down, and I'll call off the execution."

Gripping his terrified little hostage, Yanagisawa walked toward Sano. Their troops and the spectators moved back in a wide circle around them. "That's not all I want," Yanagisawa said. "I want a safe passage out of here for Yoritomo and me. I want your promise that you won't touch us."

"I promise," Sano said.

Grumbles from the samurai in the audience said they deplored Sano's caving in. Sano nodded to the executioner's assistants. They took up their shovels.

Yanagisawa's lip curled with contempt. "If you were any other man, I wouldn't trust your promise, Sano-*san*. But your honor has always been your downfall and my blessing."

He flung the girl away from him. As her parents rushed up and carried her to safety, he hastened toward Yoritomo.

"Not this time," Sano said.

He gripped his sword in both hands, swung it up, and brought it down in a vicious arc. The blade struck Yoritomo's neck, slicing through flesh and bone. Yoritomo's head fell on the ground with a thud that drowned in the cries of astonishment that rose from the crowd.

"*No!*" Yanagisawa screamed.

His face was so twisted by rage and grief that he barely looked human. He fell on his knees beside Yoritomo's head. Sano saw everyone including his own troops, except for his detectives, gazing at him in shock: They hadn't thought him capable of what he'd done. Vengeful satisfaction filled Sano. Let Yanagisawa suffer the worst agony that a father who loved his son could. Let him pay the price for all the trouble he'd ever caused Sano, the political strife he'd fomented, the violence his actions had provoked.

As Yanagisawa cradled the head in his lap, sobbed, and tugged off the hood, the spectators' expressions changed from shock to puzzlement. "There's no blood," someone said.

Blood hadn't gushed from Yoritomo's neck as it should have;

none stained the ground. Sano's sword was clean except for a dark smudge on the blade. Another cry rang from Yanagisawa as he beheld the head he'd uncovered.

"This isn't my son!"

The head belonged to a man with cropped, bushy hair and missing teeth. His eyeballs were purplish and deflated like rotten berries, swarming with maggots. The neck of the body buried in the ground resembled a cut of old meat, shriveled and juiceless. The wind blew up a powerful stench of decayed flesh. The shogun turned away, doubled over, and retched.

Marume and Fukida grinned at Sano. They alone in the audience had known Sano's whole plan. Sano had decided not to bring Yoritomo to the execution ground. He'd wanted to hold Yoritomo in reserve in case he needed further leverage against Yanagisawa. He and his detectives had obtained a body from Edo Morgue, dressed it in Yoritomo's clothes, and covered its face with the hood. Sano had decapitated a corpse.

The assembly gasped, murmured, and exclaimed like a crowd awed by a magician. Yanagisawa hurled the head at Sano and leaped to his feet, his grief transformed into rage. "A curse on you for your blasted trickery!"

He lunged at Sano, drawing his sword. Sano's troops rode into the circle to stop him, but Yanagisawa's headed them off. Sano raised his blade and deflected Yanagisawa's cut. The field erupted in riotous action. The commoners ran for their lives while Yanagisawa's troops assailed Sano's. The shogun staggered around, crying, "Help! Somebody save me!"

As he and Yanagisawa lashed at each other, Sano felt a bloodlust hotter than any he'd known in previous battles. It stemmed from their turbulent history together. And he felt the same heat, the same murderous intent, flaming from Yanagisawa.

"Where's my son?" Yanagisawa demanded as he dodged Sano's cuts. He pivoted, then struck and struck again, driving Sano backward into the battle that raged between their armies. "What have you done with him?"

"Yoritomo is alive," Sano said as he parried, sliced, and forced Yanagisawa to retreat across the execution ground. He'd hidden the young man in his rice warehouse. "Surrender, and I'll let you see him."

But Sano hoped Yanagisawa wouldn't surrender. He wanted to fight to the finish even though he'd intended to take Yanagisawa alive. His samurai heritage compelled him to conquer and kill.

Yanagisawa laughed with bitter scorn. "I won't. Not after you've shown me what your promises are worth."

As they fought, Sano experienced a strange sensation that the boundary between himself and Yanagisawa had dissolved. He knew every move that Yanagisawa was going to make. He parried by instinct; he effortlessly evaded strikes. This was what the martial arts masters called "oneness with the opponent," the concept that a samurai and his adversary are partners in battle. Sano had always been skeptical about it, for how could he be partners with someone who was trying to kill him? But now Sano and Yanagisawa merged into one person. Their history fused with the mystical energy of warfare.

He was his enemy; his enemy was him.

Although their union improved his defenses, it played havoc with his offensive. Every slash that Sano launched, Yanagisawa avoided. Sano knew he was the superior fighter, but he couldn't score a single cut. They grew breathless from attacking each other and missing. Sano saw, from the corner of his eye, that many of the *daimyo,* the officials, and their men had joined the battle. Most were fighting Yanagisawa's troops, but others fought Sano's. Yanagisawa had won many allies. Taking count would have given Sano a clear lie of the political land, but he was too caught up in his and Yanagisawa's battle.

They circled each other around a gibbet, their blades whistling around the posts. They were both panting and sweating. If one or the other didn't win soon, they would both die of exhaustion. Faster and faster Sano wielded his sword. Faster and faster Yanagisawa parried. Their blades were a metallic whir between them. Yanagisawa's face tightened into a snarl, a mirror of Sano's own face. Sano felt their blows ring through his bones. His wrists, elbows, and shoulders grew sore from twisting and flexing. He could feel the same pain echo from

Yanagisawa's joints. His sense of himself as a separate individual blurred.

Sano mustered his fading energy, put all his strength into each cut. He felt the spasm of a strained tendon in Yanagisawa's arm, felt it in his own, heard the pained cry from both their mouths. Yanagisawa let go of his sword, which spun away through the air. Sano's foot slipped in a patch of slime. Before he could regain his balance, Yanagisawa hurled himself at Sano. Together they fell.

They crashed to the ground. Yanagisawa landed on top of Sano and grabbed for Sano's sword. His hands clawed Sano's, trying to pry them off the hilt. As Sano fought Yanagisawa for control of the weapon, they rolled across the fetid dirt while horses stomped and riders battled around them. Their faces were so close that Sano could see his reflection in Yanagisawa's eyeballs. They gasped each other's breath. Locked with Yanagisawa in an embrace more intimate than sex with a woman, Sano felt their muscles straining, their pulses pounding with the same fast, furious rhythm, the heat in their blood rising.

It no longer mattered who killed whom. Sano gave up the notion that he deserved to win because he was good and Yanagisawa evil.

They were two incarnations of the same being.

Still, Sano and Yanagisawa grappled, struggled, fought with all their savage might. Stripped of individuality, reduced to the most basic principle of combat, they must kill or be killed.

A high-pitched cry rang out above the noise: "I order you all to cease fighting!"

Sano barely recognized the shogun's voice. He threw himself onto Yanagisawa, who writhed and bucked under his weight. A tiny part of Sano's awareness registered that the shogun stood on his palanquin, waving his arms and shouting, "I don't like fights. Stop at once!"

Across the field, combatants retreated. The shogun's word was law. Only Sano and Yanagisawa ignored his command. The sword was between them, their hands clenched around the hilt under their chins, the blade all that separated their faces. Sano forced the blade down toward Yanagisawa, who pushed it up at him. They clenched their teeth, grunted, and strained. They both knew the end was near for somebody.

Men crowded around them. Sano was seized and pulled off Yanagisawa. The sword ripped out of Yanagisawa's hands and came away in Sano's. Their mystical union snapped like a rope stretched too tight. Detectives Marume and Fukida wrested the sword away from Sano. Other men restrained Yanagisawa, who struggled to attack Sano. As they gasped for breath and glared at each other through the sweat dripping into their eyes, the shogun minced into the space between them. Placing one hand on Yanagisawa's heaving chest and the other on Sano's, he said, "Whatever your, ahh, quarrel is, you can settle it later."

He laughed with joy as he announced to the crowd, "My beloved Yoritomo-*san* is alive. Chamberlain Sano is innocent, and my dear old friend Yanagisawa-*san* is home! Let's all go back to the castle and celebrate!"

34

The celebration lasted five days.

Spring came. Gentle rains put out the fires that had plagued Edo and washed the air clean of smoke. Cherry trees all over town burst into dazzling pink bloom.

Inside the castle, the shogun and his guests feasted at a continuous banquet. Musicians, dancing girls, acrobats, jugglers, and magicians entertained. Theater troupes performed plays. The revelry spilled into the garden, where lanterns hung from the blossoming cherry trees. Men sneaked off for a few hours of sleep here and there, but nobody dared stay away for long. The shogun was in his finest, silliest form as he led singing, poetry-reciting, and drinking contests, Yoritomo at his side.

He didn't care that Lord Matsudaira, the traitor, was dead.

After the battle at the execution ground, Sano had taken his detectives and a squadron of troops to confront Lord Matsudaira. Sano had intended to force his enemy to remove the assassins from his house. Later, he would persuade the shogun to execute Lord Matsudaira. He was sure Yanagisawa would help him with that, even though they were bitter foes once again. But when Sano arrived at Lord Matsudaira's estate, he discovered that those efforts would be unnecessary.

The gates stood open; Matsudaira troops from all over the castle poured inside. Leaping from his horse, Sano asked the sentries, "What's going on here?"

"Our master has committed seppuku," one of the men said. Tears ran down his face.

Sano was disconcerted, yet not really surprised. "Why?"

"His spirits were broken by his arrest. He saw himself going down. And when he learned that Yanagisawa is back, that was too much for him." The sentry gazed at Sano with sorrowful resentment. "He could have beaten you or Yanagisawa separately, but not both of you at once. He decided to end his life rather than face defeat and disgrace."

Sano believed the sentry was telling the truth. The story must have already circulated through the castle, and the Matsudaira troops were rushing home to pay their last respects to their dead master. But Sano couldn't quite believe that after all these years of escalating strife, his enemy was suddenly gone.

"Come on," he told his men. "This I have to see for myself."

They joined the rush into the estate, to Lord Matsudaira's quarters. Sano and Detectives Marume and Fukida shoved their way past the horde of soldiers blocking the door. Outside the building, and in the hall, the soldiers talked among themselves, exclaiming in shock and grief. Inside Lord Matsudaira's private chamber, all was eerily quiet. Sano and the detectives squeezed through the crowd of top Matsudaira retainers who stood in a circle around the death scene.

Lord Matsudaira lay fallen on his side, legs curled. His white silk robe was open, showing the zigzag slash he'd cut into his belly. The short sword still protruded from the cut, which had leaked crimson blood onto his skin, his robe, and the *tatami* floor. His hands still gripped the weapon. His eyes were open, but no spirit animated them. Sano saw on Lord Matsudaira's face an expression of resignation, of peace at last.

"Wouldn't you know," Marume said with disgusted rancor, "he did himself in before we could."

"Chamberlain Sano dealt him the final blow," Fukida said, "by flushing Yanagisawa into the open."

That Yanagisawa had turned out to be the secret weapon Sano had used to defeat Lord Matsudaira!

No one else spoke. Lord Matsudaira's men were apparently too numb with shock to take issue with the detectives' words about their master. Sano, gazing down at his fallen enemy, felt his anger and hatred wane. Even after all the evils Lord Matsudaira had perpetrated against him, he could sympathize with and even admire the man. Lord Matsudaira had taken the hardest rather than the easy way out. He'd reclaimed his honor. Sano only hoped that were he ever in a similar predicament, he would have as much courage.

Now, at the palace, Sano looked around the party. The shogun was singing out of key; he slurped wine between verses. He didn't realize that his party was a staging ground for a reorganization of the political arena. Nor did he notice that the party revolved around Sano and Yanagisawa.

Daimyo and officials flocked to them like iron fragments to the poles of a magnet. New alliances formed in the vacuum created by Lord Matsudaira's death. Sano and Yanagisawa never spoke to or stood too close to each other, but Sano was keenly aware of Yanagisawa's presence, as he knew Yanagisawa was of his. Whenever their eyes met, their hostility flared, but each bided his time. Crucial matters had yet to be settled. Neither man could afford a wrong move.

On the morning of the fifth day, the shogun yawned at the banquet table. His eyes were so bloodshot, the skin under them so purple, his face so puffy, that he looked as though he'd been beaten up. He announced, "I, ahh, believe I've had enough celebration." He rose unsteadily. "Sano-*san,* Yanagisawa-*san,* escort me to my chamber."

Sano and Yanagisawa walked on either side of the shogun. He leaned heavily on them both. As they strolled along the corridor, they glared at each other across him. The game was between the two of them; it had been since the day of their first clash more than a decade ago. Lord Matsudaira had been a fleeting distraction. And Sano knew his showdown with Yanagisawa was yet to come.

The shogun didn't notice their antagonism. Even though he'd seen them fighting at the execution ground, he seemed oblivious to the fact that they were enemies. After his fiasco with Lord Matsudaira, he'd decided that life with blinders on was more comfortable, Sano thought.

Yanagisawa said, "Now that I'm back, Your Excellency, I would be glad to resume my duties as chamberlain."

"I would be just as glad to continue them," Sano said.

"Must we talk about business now?" The shogun sighed wearily. "Ahh, I suppose so. I need to decide which of you will be my second-in-command. But it's such a, ahh, difficult decision. You've both served me so well and so loyally."

He didn't know that Sano and Yanagisawa had both fought Lord Matsudaira for control of Japan. A conspiracy of silence still reigned. Only the conspirators had changed. This was the first round of their game: a competition for the highest position in the regime.

As Sano and Yanagisawa spoke simultaneously, each quick to put forth his best argument in his own favor, the shogun said, "Wait! I have a brilliant idea!" He smiled proudly. "You can both be chamberlain. You can share the post!"

Sano and Yanagisawa stared at him, then at each other, appalled. Two dogs plus one bone equaled certain disaster.

In her room at Sano's estate, Etsuko packed her belongings. Hana said, "The palanquin is waiting. Are you ready?"

Etsuko tied the corners of the cloth she'd wrapped around her things. "Almost."

"It'll be good to get home," Hana said.

"Yes." When she'd been arrested, all Etsuko had wanted was to return to her own house, her peaceful life. But now the prospect seemed less inviting. She felt as if she'd taken on a new shape that her former existence couldn't accommodate.

"I'm glad this awful business is over," Hana said.

Etsuko donned her cloak. "So am I." She was free of more than a murder charge and the threat of execution; she was rid of the burdensome secret she'd carried for forty-three years. The nightmares had stopped. But her journey into the past, and the glorious spring-time outside, had revived vague, restless yearnings.

Sano's chief retainer appeared in the door. "Excuse me, Etsuko-*san*. You have a visitor."

"A visitor? For me?" Etsuko was puzzled. "Who is it?"

"Come with me and see," Hirata said.

He led her to the reception room. Its doors were open to the garden of blossoming cherry trees. Inside, an elderly man stood alone. He was slight, with silver hair, dressed in modest cotton garments. His face was tanned but well preserved. At first Etsuko had no idea who he was. Then, as they walked toward each other, she looked into eyes that she had never thought she'd see again except in dreams.

"Etsuko-*san*?" he said in a familiar voice roughened by age.

Her heart began an uproarious thudding. Her knees buckled. She almost fainted. "Egen," she whispered.

She heard Hirata say, "He saw the notices posted along the highway," as he quietly left the room. Then she was aware of nothing except Egen. Time flew backward, and she saw the handsome monk she'd loved. He smiled as if he saw the beautiful girl she'd been. The illusion shimmered in the tears of joy that welled in her eyes, then vanished. They were two old people, their youthful love long past.

"Where have you been all this time?" Etsuko asked, still in shock.

"When I left Edo, I left my religious order. I wandered around Japan. I supported myself by digging canals, working on farms, loading boats—any work I could get. After ten years, I settled in Yamato." That village was within a few days' journey from Edo. "I've made a humble living as a scribe, a teacher, and a poet."

Etsuko exclaimed in delight, "You became a poet! Didn't I say you could?"

His eyebrows rose in surprise. "Ah, you remember."

"I haven't forgotten anything," Etsuko said solemnly.

The memory of their ill-fated romance and their other troubles cast a pall over Egen's features. "I heard about what happened to you.

I came as soon as I could. I wanted to take the blame for Tadatoshi's murder myself. Hirata-*san* told me that everything turned out all right for you, but I'm sorry I was too late."

He'd cared enough about her to rush to her rescue! Etsuko was thrilled, but also dismayed. "How much did Hirata-*san* tell you?"

"Everything you confessed to your son."

Etsuko averted her face as she relived the shame, humiliation, and pain she'd suffered in Egen's absence.

"I was a selfish coward to leave you," he said. "But if I'd known about our child then, I would have come back to Edo right away instead of waiting three years."

Etsuko stared in shock. "You knew? You came back?"

Egen nodded. "I couldn't forget you no matter how hard I tried. I went to Doi, because I thought you'd married him. He told me you'd lost my child and married someone else. He said you had a son, and you were happy, and I shouldn't bother you because you never wanted to see me again. So I went away."

Etsuko was aghast at what Doi had done. Bitter because she and Egen had betrayed him and drawn him into a murder conspiracy, he'd taken revenge even before he'd accused her of the crime. The shogun had pardoned Doi for his role in it, but Sano hadn't forgiven him for accusing her. Doi had fled Edo. Nobody knew where he was.

"I did want to see you!" she cried. "It was all I wanted! I would have given up everything for you!"

"If you had left your husband for me, you'd have been the wife of a pauper," Egen said sadly. "You'd have lost your son. Perhaps things turned out for the best."

Etsuko saw that good things had come of their separation. She'd grown to love and respect her husband. She had Sano, a son to be proud of, who had saved her from her past, whose investigation had reunited her with Egen. But she wept for their lost love. She wept because of guilt.

"It was my fault. I was the one who wanted to chase Tadatoshi. If not for me, you and Doi wouldn't have killed him." She fell on her knees before Egen. "I'm sorry. I ruined your life. Will you forgive me?"

He knelt, too, and she saw tears in his eyes. "Yes, if you can forgive me for abandoning you. But you didn't ruin my life. I am responsible for what I did. And things haven't turned out too badly for me, either."

Although she couldn't bear to ask, she had to know. "Did you ever marry?"

Egen shook his head. "I couldn't. Not when my heart belonged to you." He took her hand in his, pressed it to his chest, and said, "It still does."

Now Etsuko wept with relief and joy. The spring was a time of youth and hopes restored, of a new beginning. But she still harbored painful regrets. "I wish I could have waited for you!"

Egen's tanned face crinkled, all smiles. "It looks as if you did."

Outside the reception room Hirata loitered under the cherry trees in the garden, watching Etsuko and Egen. He smiled, glad that he'd brought them together, moved by their emotions. His children and Sano's ran and frolicked under the pink petals that fell like snow.

Midori came up to him. His senses tingled alive. He held himself as still as if she were a wild deer in a forest and any move from him would scare her off. They stood side by side, watched Egen place Etsuko's hand over his heart. As the old woman wept joyfully, Midori said in awe, "They're still in love. After such a long separation."

Hirata fought the impulse to respond instinctively, as he would in combat, with a move that would defeat his opponent. He chose his words carefully, for much more was at stake than his life. "Yes. They've been apart since before we were born." He paused, then said, "It makes our separation seem short."

He felt Midori tense. "Perhaps." Her tone was grudging yet thoughtful. They watched Etsuko and Egen happily conversing, catching up on each other's lives, making plans. "They look so happy," Midori said. "But they're so old. How much time can they possibly have together?"

Hirata pondered, took a deep breath, and said, "Not as much as we can."

He turned to Midori. She folded her arms, suspicious and defensive.

Hirata spoke urgently, from his heart instead of his intellect. "I don't want us to be like them in forty-three years, looking back on the time we wasted apart when we should have been together, regretting the past. Because I love you. And I hope you still love me."

His voice went gruff. It was harder to express his feelings to his wife than to conquer the most powerful enemy. "If she can forgive him for leaving her, can't you forgive me? If they can make a new start, can't we?"

Midori's eyes shone with tears. Hirata saw in them her pain, her anger at him, and her fear that he would leave her again. The mystic martial arts still exercised a powerful hold over him. He must pursue his destiny wherever it led him, whenever it called. And Midori knew that if they were to go on, she must learn to cope in his absences. He also saw love for him in her eyes. He held his breath. Was her love strong enough that she thought brief periods of time together were better than nothing?

Was he strong and wise enough to deserve her love, to preserve their marriage, against all odds?

Midori said, "I suppose we can try."

Reiko sat in the pavilion in the garden, amid the pink blaze of cherry blossoms. She was glad to be home. She was glad she'd lived to see this day.

Lord Matsudaira was gone, her family safe from him. After his death, his retainers had flocked to pledge their service to Sano. Joining their lord's enemy's camp was preferable to a disgraceful existence as masterless samurai. One had offered a gift to convince Sano to take him in: He'd identified the assassins sent to kill Sano's children. Those men had been executed.

Reiko watched Masahiro run about the garden with Akiko. They rolled in the pink blanket of petals that covered the grass. Masahiro laughed, carefree for once, his obsession with martial arts practice temporarily forgotten. He'd regained his childhood, at least for today. Reiko was glad of that. But she felt no peace.

She grieved for Lieutenant Asukai. She'd left the estate for the first time since the ambush during which he'd saved her life, in order to attend his funeral. She would miss him forever. And she was concerned about Sano.

He'd returned to her five days ago, weary but elated. He'd told her that he'd forced Yanagisawa to surface, and Lord Matsudaira was dead. He'd also told her the details about how his mother had confessed to the murder and the shogun had overheard. After summarizing the consequences, he'd said, "The shogun is hosting a banquet to celebrate Yanagisawa's homecoming. He expects me to be there. I have to go."

Reiko hadn't seen him since, except from a distance, when he came home once in a while to sleep or tend to official business. They hadn't discussed his mother. Reiko had used the time while he was gone to woo her daughter, employing treats and gentle talk, as one might a wild rabbit. Even though Akiko was still shy, she no longer screamed whenever she saw Reiko.

Now Akiko came running up to the pavilion. She held a sprig of cherry blossoms. She stopped and regarded Reiko with somber black eyes. Reiko smiled and said, "Come here, Akiko. Show me your flowers."

For a long moment Akiko didn't move. Then she slowly, hesitantly, climbed the steps of the pavilion. She extended the flowers to Reiko, who accepted them. Then Akiko ran off to play. Reiko's eyes stung. She felt new hope for a reconciliation.

Then she saw Sano walking across the garden toward her, his face closed and stoic. Her heart began to pound with anxiety for him. He entered the pavilion and crouched beside her. He didn't look at her, and she kept her eyes averted from him because she perceived that he was trying to contain his emotions and wouldn't welcome her scrutiny. She waited until the silence grew unbearable.

"Has anything happened?" she said, hesitant to speak but eager for news, political and personal.

"The shogun has given the post of chamberlain to both Yanagisawa and me." Sano's voice was calm, controlled. "It looks as if we'll be fighting our battle to the finish while running the government together."

Reiko was astounded. "That's another in the recent series of shocks."

"But not the biggest." Sano turned to her, and Reiko saw disbelief, astonishment, hurt, and anger on his face. "You were right about my mother."

Reiko felt no triumph. She couldn't throw in his face the fact that he'd been wrong. "I'm sorry," she said, feeling his pain as her own.

"Even though I saved her, even though I'm glad, I can't accept what she did," Sano said. "She has the blood of my lord's kin on her hands."

This was a sin that any honorable samurai would find difficult to overlook, no matter the circumstances, Reiko knew. She herself hadn't known how to treat her mother-in-law. When she'd returned home, she hadn't known what to say to Etsuko.

Etsuko had spoken first. "Honorable Daughter-in-law, I killed the shogun's cousin—just as you thought. I'll explain why, if you like." Her quiet manner had a new confidence and dignity. "But I'm a murderess, and if you want me out of your house, I'll leave at once."

Reiko was too surprised to say anything but no, Etsuko must stay until Sano returned; he would want to see her. Since then, Reiko had been cautious with Etsuko, aware that they were on new, equal terms. Reiko saw that there would be no more condescending to her mother-in-law, who would no longer shrink before her. The truth had turned Etsuko into a force worthy of esteem. Reiko realized that they weren't so different after all. Both of them were women with strong principles, who would risk their lives and flout convention for a good cause. Reiko began to like her mother-in-law better than she'd ever thought possible. Perhaps they could be friends someday. Now she rose to Etsuko's defense.

"Tadatoshi deserved to be killed," Reiko said. "Your mother did the world a service."

"I know. She probably saved thousands of lives." Wanting to believe, yet unrelenting, Sano shook his head.

"She was a young girl who'd just been through hell on earth during the Great Fire," Reiko said. "When she came across Tadatoshi afterward, it would have been easier and better for her to let him go. But she was selfless enough to think of the people he'd killed, the people he would kill in the future. And so she took justice into her own hands. She had courage."

Although Sano nodded, the unhappiness in his expression deepened. "She also had the nerve to lie about what she did, not only to the shogun, but to me."

That bothered him almost as much as did the fact that his mother was a murderess, Reiko saw. "But she finally told you the truth. If she'd done so sooner, you might not have had the spirit to work as hard as you did to save us all. Things might have turned out for the worse."

Sano was silent, frowning, resistant. Reiko could guess at part of what troubled him, even if he wasn't conscious of it. Throughout their marriage she'd constantly ventured beyond the limits of what society deemed acceptable behavior for a wife, a woman. Sano had continually stretched his own limits because he loved her, he wanted her to be happy, and he'd often benefited from her actions. But it was harder for Sano to live with the fact that his mother—the woman sacred to him because she'd borne and raised him—had also defied convention, broken the law.

"She begged me to forgive her," Sano said at last. "I want to, but how can I?"

"You'll find a way," Reiko promised. "Because you love her, and she loves you, and she'll do everything in her power to make it up to you." Reiko thought of herself and Akiko, of her and Sano's past quarrels. She believed that forgiveness was always possible where there was love.

Sano glanced at her. "I forgive you for being right," he said with a wry smile.

Reiko smiled back, glad to see his sense of humor returning. "That's a good start."

He rose, gazed off into space, and Reiko saw his thoughts take a new direction. He said, "Not all my mother's family can be dead. I vaguely recall hearing of the Kumazawa clan. Somewhere out there is a whole set of relatives I don't know."

"They know of you. Everybody does," Reiko said. "And I'm sure they know that you're from their clan. My intuition tells me that somebody among them has kept track of your mother all these years. And since you became the shogun's investigator, then the chamberlain, they've been watching you with much interest."

Amusement crinkled Sano's eyes as he turned to her. "If your intuition says so, then I'd better believe it."

"Why don't you look them up and meet them?" Reiko said. She thought of the blood that joined her children and husband to their yet unknown family, the tie buried forty-three years ago and exposed by the murder investigation. She saw much uncharted territory yet to explore.

Sano's expression showed reluctance, and perhaps qualms about how he would be received by the people who'd disowned his mother. "Not now. I have too many other things to do," he said with an air of gladly dispensing with personal matters and moving on to business. "Yanagisawa isn't going to cooperate with me for the good of the country. He'll oppose everything I do. And the political scene is still in flux. Who knows how many allies will fall on his side and how many on mine? People are already taking bets on which of us will win."

Reiko sensed his excitement and eagerness for the challenge. "There's bound to be more crises, more treachery," she predicted. She rose and stood close beside Sano. Together they looked at the blossoming cherry trees, at Masahiro and Akiko running under the snowfall of pink petals. Their gazes focused on the future.

Sano said with relish, "This should be the dirtiest fight ever."

Laura Joh
Rowland

A SANO ICHIRO
NOVEL

SANO ICHIRŌ is suspicious
of his old rival, Yanagisawa,
who has been oddly cooperative
since returning from exile.
But just as Yanagisawa's true
motives begin to emerge,
Sano's estranged uncle comes
to him for help: His daughter
has disappeared, and he begs
Sano to find her before it
is too late.

THE Cloud
Pavilion

MINOTAUR
BOOKS

*Visit Minotaurbooks.com for a chance to win free books
and connect with your favorite authors.*